THE RACE

RICHARD NORTH PATTERSON is the author of fourteen previous bestselling and critically acclaimed novels. Formerly a trial lawyer, Patterson was the SEC's liaison to the Watergate special prosecutor and has served on the boards of several Washington advocacy groups dealing with gun violence, political reform and women's rights. He lives in San Francisco and on Martha's Vineyard.

Praise for Richard North Patterson's fiction

'An astonishing book, a hugely entertaining human drama'
Bill Clinton

'Every now and then – but a lot more rarely than that implies – you come across a thriller so important that it absolutely demands to be read. This is one'   *The Times*

'A stunningly ambitious novel [that shows] how much a thriller can encompass'   *Sunday Times*

'A fine example of the genre: a strong story about a real dilemma with colourful characters'   *Daily Mail*

'Richard North Patterson has combined the legal and political thriller genres with this gripping tale'
Daily Telegraph

KT-473-340

THE
RACE

A Novel

RICHARD NORTH
PATTERSON

PAN

First published 2007 by Henry Holt and Company, New York

First published in Great Britain 2007 by Macmillan

This edition published 2008 by Pan Books
an imprint of Pan Macmillan Ltd
Pan Macmillan, 20 New Wharf Road, London N1 9RR
Basingstoke and Oxford
Associated companies throughout the world
www.panmacmillan.com

ISBN 978-0-330-44015-8

3 5 7 9 8 6 4 2

A CIP catalogue record for this book is available from
the British Library.

Printed and bound in the UK by
CPI Mackays, Chatham ME5 8TD

For John Sterling

PROLOGUE
THE HERO

IN THE TIMELESS DARK OF HIS CAPTIVITY, BEFORE the president made him a hero for the careless act that had cost a friend his life, Captain Corey Grace distracted himself from guilt and the pain of torture by recalling why he had wished to fly: to escape from darkness to light.

His earliest memories were of the metaphoric prison of his parents' joyless house: the way his father's mute and drunken rage turned inward on itself; his mother's tight-lipped repression of her own misery, as clenched as her coiled hair. Even the Ohio town they lived in, Lake City, felt cramped—not just the near-identical shotgun houses and postage-stamp lawns, but the monochromatic lives of those who never seemed to leave, the gossip one could never erase, the pointless bigotry against minorities no one had ever met. Only in captivity, when shame and belated charity eroded his contempt for his family and his past, did Corey see this pitiless lens as yet another reflection of his vanity.

You're special, they had always told him: teachers, coaches, ministers—even, in their crabbed ways, Corey's own mother and father. From his early youth, good looks had been among his many gifts: the ready smile and dark brown eyes—perceptive, alert, and faintly amused—strong but regular features, arrayed in pleasing proportion to one another. He excelled in school; became captain of three sports teams; grew articulate and quick-witted in a way he could not trace to either parent; learned to conceal his alienation with an easy charm that made girls want him and other boys want to be like him. His parents were strangers—not just to Corey, but to each other.

"I wonder who you'll marry," his mother had mused aloud on the night of his senior prom.

Needlessly fussing over his tuxedo tie—as open a gesture of maternal fondness as she could muster—Nettie Grace looked up into his face. With an instinctive fear that, somehow, this life would ensnare him, Corey realized that his mother still wished to imagine him marrying someone from Lake City—maybe Kathy Wilkes, the bubbly cheerleader who was his prom date. Perhaps his mother spoke from sentiment, Corey thought; perhaps it was only fear that he would leave their life behind. Even his parents' pride in him seemed sullied by their own resentments.

Gazing into his mother's eyes, he answered softly, "No one from here."

Nettie Grace let go of his bow tie.

Slowly, Corey looked around the tiny living room, as if at a place he would never see again. His father stared at the television, a beer bottle clutched in hands knotted from his work as a plumber. In the corner, Corey's five-year-old brother, Clay—whose very existence conjured images Corey could scarcely entertain—gazed up at Corey with a child's admiration. Looking at this slight boy's tousled brown hair and innocent blue eyes, Corey felt the empathy he wished he could summon for his parents. He already sensed that Clay—who, to his father's evident satisfaction, did not seem all that special—would never escape their family.

Impulsively, Corey scooped Clay up in his arms, tossing him in the air before bringing the boy's face close to his. Clay wrapped his arms around Corey's neck.

"I love you, Corey," he heard his little brother declare.

For a moment, Corey held Clay tight; then he lifted him aloft again, wondering why his own smile did not come quite so easily. "Yeah," he told his brother. "I love you, too. Even though you're short."

Putting Clay down, Corey kissed him on the forehead, and left without another word to anyone.

He was leaving them all behind—his mother and father; the friends who thought they knew him; the prom date who would offer to sleep with him in hope that this moment, the apex of her youthful imaginings, was a beginning and not the end; even his kid brother. And he had known this ever since Coach Jackson had named him starting quarterback. "You're slow," the coach had told him laconically. "And your arm's no better than average. But you're smart, and you don't rattle. Most of all, you're not just a leader—you're a *born* leader."

This, Corey realized, was a new thought. Curious, he asked, "What's the difference?"

"You never look back to see who's following you." The coach cocked his head, as though studying Corey from a different angle. "Ever think about one of the academies? West Point, maybe."

Mulling this, Corey walked home on a brisk fall day. Then he looked up and saw a jet plane soaring into endless space and light, its only mark a trail of vapor. No, Corey thought, not West Point.

His appointment to the Air Force Academy came as easily as his moment of departure. He left his parents and brother at the airport after constricted hugs and awkward silences, troubled only by how small and solitary Clay suddenly appeared to him.

It was the first time Corey Grace had ever flown.

*

THE ACADEMY, TOO, came easily, as did flight school and promotion. By the time of the Gulf War, Captain Corey Grace was stationed in Saudi Arabia, restlessly awaiting the ultimate test of his abilities: to engage Iraqi pilots at supersonic speeds with such skill that he would kill without being killed.

To Corey, his F-15 was an extension of his gifts, a perfectly crafted machine with the technology in its sinews ready to do his every bidding. The only other human variable was his navigator.

Joe Fitts was a black man from Birmingham, Alabama. When Corey first met him he almost laughed in dismay—Joe's toothy smile and jug ears made him look, in Corey's reluctant but uncharitable estimate, like a guileless and even comic figure, and his loose-limbed gait suggested that he was held together by rubber bands. But, for Corey, their first flight transformed his navigator's appearance.

Joe's mind was as keen as his eyes: he seemed to know everything there was to know about his job—and Corey's. A few more flights together confirmed Corey's sense of a man whose judgment was as close to perfect as mortals could achieve; a few sessions at the bar built for thirsty officers suggested that Joe was a complicated but altogether stellar human being. And that Joe was the first black man Corey had known well confronted him with a basic truth: that whatever Corey thought of his youth in Lake City, he had been, in one very basic sense, privileged.

Joe's father was a janitor, his mother a seamstress, and their lives were molded by a time and place where the insane logic of bigotry skipped no details, right down to separate drinking fountains to keep blacks from sullying whites. Joe's parents were first allowed to vote in 1965, the year after he was born, filled with foreboding that this reckless act might leave their child an orphan. But though they were even more lightly educated than Corey's parents, Joe's pride in his father and mother was as deep as his love—they had wrung from the harsh strictures of their lives the fierce determination to give Joe Fitts chances they had only dreamed of. The sole fissure between Joe and his devoutly Baptist parents was one that he concealed from them: except when he was home, Joe never went to church.

"So you're an atheist?" Corey asked one evening.

Sitting beside Corey at the bar, Joe sipped his Scotch, regarding the question with narrow eyes. "Atheism's too much trouble," he answered. "Why put that level of energy into something you can't know? Anyone who tells you they're sure that there is a God—or isn't one—is smoking dope.

"Anyhow, it's the wrong question. Maybe there *is* a God, and he's a terrific guy—or girl, or hermaphrodite, or whatever the fuck people want to believe. I've got no objections to that. What pisses me off is when people think believing in a certain God gives them a license to crap on other people, or even kill 'em—Christian or Muslim, it makes no difference." He turned to Corey. "Ever look at those old pictures of lynchings—upright white folks with their good day's work hanging from some tree?"

"Sure."

"Notice anything peculiar about them?"

"Yeah. The black guy was dead." Corey paused, then ventured, "No women?"

"Look again—in high school I made a study of them. What you'll notice is that a lot of those mobs were dressed in their Sunday best. They were fresh from church, you see." Joe's half smile conveyed both wonder and dismay. "I've met some true Christians, and I've also met some nasty fuckers whose God is surely created in *their* image.

Overall, I'd say the correlation between godliness and goodness is kind of random. Sort of makes you wonder what history would look like if more folks had believed a little less."

But such moody ruminations did not detract from Joe's pleasure in the core of his life—a deep pride in a job well done, and an abiding love for his wife and four-year-old son. "You know why I don't want to die?" Joe admitted over drinks. "Not 'cause I'm afraid that it's the end—that all I'll be is roadkill. It's because of all I'd miss, and all they'd miss about me. It's bad enough just being stuck with you in this fucking bar."

"Funny," Corey said in an astringent tone. "When I'm with you, I don't miss Janice at all. The mere sound of your voice is like music."

Joe emitted a rueful laugh. "Yeah, I know. Let me see that picture again."

Corey laid the picture on the bar, a snapshot of his wife holding Kara. Solemnly contemplating a cake with five candles, his daughter looked taller than the four-year-old Corey had last seen, and Corey detected the first intimation of her mother's grace and beauty. As for Janice, she looked lovelier than ever; perhaps only Corey saw the rebuke in her unsmiling eyes, or knew that she had her reasons.

"Lookers," Joe said, "both of them. But it hurts to look at *mine* sometimes—Janie and Maxwell are the best wife and kid on earth, and I can't hug or kiss either one of them." Flashing a crooked grin, Joe added, "Sometimes at night that *really* hurts."

Though Corey smiled in appreciation, he felt a certain disquiet and, he admitted, a wholly unearned envy. He still wanted Janice; she seemed to still want him. But, more often than not, when they made love her soul seemed elsewhere. And all too often his daughter seemed a stranger to him, an extension of her mother.

As close as he felt to Joe, Corey chose to speak only of Kara. "I'm gone too much, I guess. Sometimes she barely seems to know me."

Usually, the mention of kids would prompt Joe to extol the miracle of child development that was Maxwell Fitts—his humor, his quickness, his astounding rhetorical gifts. But Joe was a sensitive man. With the shrewd gaze that sometimes made him seem preternaturally old, he quietly answered, "It'll come, pal. Time is all you need." He paused, then added with a certain twitchiness, "I'm tired of waiting here for this goddamned war to happen. High time they gave us the order to dust these turkeys so we can get back to the folks we love."

Beneath the words, Corey detected an unspoken fear. "No sweat," he assured his navigator. "Once this starts, you'll be hugging Janie quicker than it takes us to down the next three Scotches."

Solemnly, the two friends drank to that.

THE GULF WAR lasted little more than a month. For Corey Grace and Joe Fitts, all but the last day was a breeze.

The two men functioned seamlessly. Without compunction, Corey shot down three Iraqi planes, affirming that he loved the thrill of aerial combat. And when the head of the Iraqi air force tried to escape to Iran in a Russian-made MiG, it seemed right that Corey and Joe got the orders to shoot him down. The only trick was catching General Hussein Al-Malik before he reached Iranian airspace.

They rocketed through an electric blue sky at Mach 1.1, so fast that there was no sensation of speed. The tension lay in the tasks they had to juggle in split seconds—checking the radar; listening to the AWACS report how much closer Al-Malik was to the border; monitoring how much fuel they had burned. The balance of those factors could be a matter of life and death. The mighty jet burned thousands of pounds of fuel in a minute: once all that remained was 7,500 pounds—"bingo fuel"—their choice would be to go home or crash in the desert.

The two men were in a cocoon surrounded by endless blue sky, divorced from time and space. Though they could not see the Iraqi's MiG, they were nearly as close to his jet, the AWACS told him, as it was to the Iranian border.

"We're going to get this bastard," Corey said.

Joe watched the fuel gauge. "Twelve thousand pounds," he reported calmly. "We've got maybe four minutes."

Al-Malik was three minutes from Iranian airspace. "Time enough," Corey answered.

Moments passed with no Iraqi in sight. "Ten thousand pounds," Joe said more tautly. "We're burning fuel way faster than we should."

Corey shook his head. "The gauge has gotta be messed up."

"Maybe. But I think there's a fuel leak, Corey."

Corey felt his muscles strain, as though willing their plane to go faster than it could. "We'll get him," he repeated.

Suddenly, a speeding gray sliver glinted in the sun: Al-Malik, seconds from Iranian airspace. No longer calm, Joe called out, "We're at bingo fuel—time to turn around."

Corey kept going. "Ten seconds."

"Come on, man," Joe said tightly.

Corey counted down from ten, then pushed the button on their radar-guided missile.

In a split second the sliver was replaced by an enormous explosion, and General Al-Malik turned to particles of humanity above the Iranian border.

Corey spun the plane around.

It was a minute before Joe spoke again. "Four thousand pounds," he said softly. "For sure it's a leak. We're going to have to bail."

Corey grimaced. But there was no time for regrets. "You first," he ordered.

The cockpit opened, and Joe was gone.

Seconds later Corey bailed from the jet, plummeting headlong in a crazy free fall before the chute deployed. The parachute opened, catching air in its billows and slowing Corey's fall to a still-precipitous descent. Beneath him jagged rocks grew larger at daunting speed.

Corey jerked the wires. Too late, he realized. His feet hit rock, and then his right shoulder landed with a sickening crunch, shooting a jolt of nausea through his body. When his head hit rock, Corey blacked out.

He regained consciousness in a daze. Blinking, he saw that he was surrounded by a ragged contingent of Iraqi soldiers, and that the sun was slanted at the angle of late afternoon. Corey saw no officers—the soldier who stepped forward had a nonmilitary stubble, and his eyes betrayed a fatigue akin to madness.

Corey's broken shoulder throbbed. The man stood over him, holding a rifle with both hands.

"Speak English?" Corey rasped.

The man did not answer. With an odd detachment, he grasped his rifle by the barrel, raised it over his head, and brought it crashing down on Corey's left shoulder.

Writhing in pain, Corey asked through gritted teeth, "Where's my navigator?"

The man held out his right arm, silently pointing.

"Suicide," the Iraqi said in English. "This black man had no courage."

On a flat rock lay the severed head of Corey's friend, the sole witness to his fatal error of judgment.

THE MONTH THAT followed changed Corey Grace forever.

His captors kept him somewhere underground, in a darkness so profound that he lost any sense of time or place. The only relief from blindness was when they fed or tortured him.

Their technique was primitive but effective: using ropes as a makeshift harness, then hanging him by his broken shoulders until he screamed with pain or passed out from torment and exhaustion. His clothes stank of urine and feces. If Corey could have killed himself, he would have.

At some point one of his faceless tormentors put something, a stool or box, beneath his feet. Later an unseen hand removed the stool and plunged Corey back into agony. The pattern repeated itself, and then again; Corey began to grasp that someone had chosen to perform this secret act of mercy.

But it was not enough. For hours his mind stopped reasoning, and sleeplessness exploded into madness and hallucinations. Desperately, he focused on his wife and daughter, faces in a snapshot imprinted on his brain. "Please," he mumbled, though whether to God or Janice or Kara he did not know, "I'll be better . . ."

He began to lose all feeling in his shoulders and arms—and, perhaps, their function. With his last reserves, Corey steeled himself to resist whatever the Iraqis would demand—a taped confession, or information about a weapons system, or some other act of betrayal. Then an even more terrible fear seeped into his consciousness:

perhaps his captors wanted nothing more from him than what they were already getting. Deprived of any purpose but survival, Corey felt insanity filling a darkness in which his only sensation was pain, its only relief the dubious act of mercy that was keeping him alive to become sub-human.

Instead, they freed him.

THE PRISONER EXCHANGE took place in a blur. His captors were a rogue element of a disintegrating army, Corey learned; the Iraqis who found and freed him offered vague apologies but otherwise told him nothing. His return to America occurred in a twilight of sleep and exhaustion until, at last, he felt a different Corey Grace occupying his shattered body.

The humor revived, but his careless élan was muted by a deep, unsparing self-appraisal. And the bleakest aspect of this honesty involved Joe Fitts.

In a moment of vainglory, he had traded his friend's life for the chance to kill an Iraqi general. Miserable, he wished he could have those split seconds back, even as he faced another bitter truth: the primal Corey who had survived would not have traded his own life for Joe's. But the pledge with which Corey tried to salve his conscience—that he would imbue the rest of his life with meaning—struck him as a pathetic, even narcissistic way of seeking redemption for the death of a better man.

He could say this to no one. As Corey convalesced at Walter Reed Hospital, Janice treated him with an unvarying kindness that felt to Corey like an act of will. For Corey's part, his penance to his wife lay not in professions of love, promises of change, or gratuitous confessions of infidelity, but a new resolve to see her with clarity and compassion. But what he glimpsed in her kept him from speaking of Joe Fitts: the impeccable consideration with which Janice treated him was not informed by love. She could not even speak the word.

Perhaps, Corey thought, time would heal them, just as it might transform the solemn five-year-old who stood by his bedside into a girl who adored her father. But time was the one thing he had too much of: though his arms and shoulders would function adequately, doctors assured him, Captain Corey Grace would never fly again.

Beyond his family, and self-reflection, Corey was a man without a purpose.

Joe Fitts never left him. Corey dictated letters to Joe's parents, his wife, and even to the five-year-old Maxwell, hoping that, as the boy grew older, Corey's words would bring his father to life. Each letter, an affectionate accounting of Joe and of his stories of their family, was as comprehensive as Corey could make it in all but one respect: the nature of Joe's death, and the reason for it. "All of you," he wrote, "helped make Joe the happiest person I ever expect to know."

Corey revealed his secret to no one. He wondered if that meant there was no one to say it to; or that the permutations of Joe's death were too profound to speak; or that he was simply afraid for anyone to know the truth. Life had given Corey a pass he could no longer give himself—and, it turned out, life kept on doing so.

The president gave him a medal.

THERE WAS ALSO a medal for Joe, of course.

Joe's parents came to the White House with Janie and Maxwell. When Janie met Corey, she embraced him fiercely, as though to reclaim some part of her husband. Gazing up at him, Janie's eyes were moist. "Joe loved you, you know."

Corey tried to smile. "And he loved you more than life. He talked about both of you so much that it was like I was living in your home." He glanced over at Maxwell and saw the boy holding his grandmother's hand—the only child of her only child. "Will he be all right?"

Pensive, Janie considered her son. "In time, I think—there's a lot of love in his life. Every night I read your letter to him." Facing Corey, she added quietly, "That was a kind thing you did for Maxwell, giving him a father who was both a hero and a man. Though the world of a five-year-old's a funny place: right now the hero is more important than the man. When he leaves here wearing Joe's medal, he may believe for a time that was worth the trade."

At this moment, and for every moment until the ceremony was over, Corey wished himself off the face of the earth.

Instead, he kissed Janie Fitts on the forehead and, despite the pain in his shoulders, scooped Maxwell up in his arms. Then, for once, Corey tried to take refuge in his family.

The three adults had come—his wife, mother, and father. And Clay was there, a slim, eager boy of fifteen whose reticence in their parents' presence was outshone by his worship of Corey and his wonder at finding himself in the White House. As the Grace family clustered together in the Map Room, Clay showed an instinctive touch with Kara, eliciting the smiles she seldom granted her father. But the others, Janice and Corey's parents, milled about like strangers awaiting a train that had somehow been delayed.

When the president appeared, he was accompanied by General Cortland Lane, the first African-American to become air force chief of staff.

A lanky patrician who was himself a decorated flier, the president was both gracious and very human. But Corey was just as taken with General Lane. His unmistakable air of command was leavened by a gaze that was penetrating but warm, and his understated manner seemed less military than spiritual—reflecting, perhaps, Lane's reputation for a religious devotion as deep as it was unostentatious. Whatever its elements, Lane's force of character drew Corey to him with a swiftness that was rare.

Drawing Corey aside, Lane congratulated him, speaking in a soft voice that was almost intimate. "I'm sorry about your injuries. And about Captain Fitts."

"So am I," Corey answered. "More about Joe. Sort of makes you wonder if getting Al-Malik was worth it."

Lane gave him a long look. "Never stop wondering. It's the cost of being human." Pausing, he added quietly, "A fuel leak, the report said."

"Yes, sir."

"You're lucky to be alive." Touching Corey's elbow, he said, "I should spend time with Joe's family—"

"Sir," Corey said impulsively, "there's something I need to tell you."

Lane nodded, watching Corey's eyes. "What is it, Captain?"

"I'm no hero. I was like some idiot kid who had to win a video game." Corey paused. "That fuel leak—Joe saw it before I shot down Al-Malik. He wanted me to turn around."

Lane showed no surprise. "I'd guessed as much," he said quietly. "But what do you think I should do with that fact? Or, more important, what would *you* like to do with it?"

Corey shook his head. "I don't know."

"Then let me suggest what you should do—and not do.

What you should do is accept this medal, and then pay Joe Fitts as gracious a tribute as you can muster." Glancing toward Maxwell Fitts, Lane's voice was quieter yet. "And what you should *not* do is force his family to swap a hero for a bitter realization.

"You made a judgment in split seconds—that's what we ask pilots to do in war. Then we ask you to live with that. But no one else can tell you how."

Briefly, the general rested a hand on Corey's shoulder, and then turned to greet Joe's family.

OPENING THE CEREMONY, the president spoke with genuine appreciation, commemorating Joe, lauding Corey, and emphasizing their country's gratitude. When it was Corey's turn to speak, he gathered himself, and then expressed his thanks to the president, the military, and the parents, wife, and daughter to whom he had returned.

"I'm lucky for many reasons," he concluded simply. "But I was luckiest of all to know Joe Fitts—not just to have seen his courage, but to have felt the depth of his appreciation for the sacrifice of his mother and father, and for the gift of Janie and Maxwell." Turning to Joe's family, he said, "All of you made him the man that all of us will always love: a man who personifies all that makes our country—whatever its imperfections—worth loving."

Afterward, shrewdly eyeing Corey, the president murmured, "You may have a future in my business, Corey. You could even wind up living here."

Later, in the suite the air force had reserved for them, Corey repeated this to Janice. "Generous," he concluded. "And preposterous."

For a moment, she regarded him in silence. "Is it? I was watching you, too."

"It was all a blur, Janice. I'm not sure what you mean."

She gave him the faintest of smiles. "That's it, Corey. You don't ever appear to know, even when I suspect you do. Other people see you as someone who just *is*."

Corey clasped her shoulders, looking down at her intently. "What I care about is how *you* see me. I'm not the same, Janice. And one important difference is that I value you the way I always should have."

Janice's smile vanished. "Me?" she asked. "Or just the idea of me?"

Corey could not answer.

That night they made love slowly, as though trying to draw feeling from their every touch. Afterward, lying in the dark, Janice said quietly, "I can feel it coming, Corey. They're going to give you something else to care about."

Within a month, a delegation of Republicans came to ask whether Corey Grace, the hero, had any interest in running for the Senate from his home state of Ohio.

PART I

THE SENATOR

1

ON A CRISP SEPTEMBER DAY THIRTEEN YEARS LATER, when Senator Corey Grace met Lexie Hart, the controversy he wished to avoid did not concern his romantic life.

"The actress?" he asked his scheduler that morning. "What's *this* about?"

Eve Stansky, a pert, droll-witted blonde, was amused by his perplexity. "Life and death," she said cheerfully. "Ms. Hart is lobbying senators to vote for stem-cell research."

Sitting back in his chair, Corey rolled his eyes. "Terrific," he said. "The bill's only sponsors are Democrats; it's a direct rebuke to a president of my own party, who dislikes me already; ditto the Christian conservatives, who like me even less. This is a real winner for me." His voice took on a teasing edge. "The election's next year, the nomination is wide open, and you schedule this. Don't you *want* me to be president, Eve? Or are you just indifferent to the fate of frozen embryos?"

"You have to vote anyway, Corey," Eve pointed out in her most unimpressed voice; like the rest of his staff, she called him by his first name. "Unless you're planning to hide that day. And everyone in the office wants to meet her. The least you can do is give the rest of us a little bit of excitement."

"Has life around here really been that dull? Or have you already decided how I should vote, and hope I'll be seduced?"

Eve grinned. "I definitely know how you should vote. And no—*you're* certainly not dull. I'm just worn out from scheduling dates with girlfriends who've got the half-life of a fruit fly. Here at Fort Grace, we call whoever's the latest 'the incumbent'—except that their terms are shorter."

Though Corey smiled in self-recognition, the comment stung a little. There were many reasons why he had remained unmarried for so many years after his divorce, and not all of them—at least he hoped—stemmed from some fatal defect in his character. But this was not a subject he felt like discussing with Eve or, for that matter, anyone.

"I doubt Ms. Hart is coming here," Corey answered sardonically, "to change my life. Merely to ruin my career. Just remember that when you and I are watching the inaugural ball on C-SPAN."

As the day turned out, Corey had an unusual luxury: a ten-minute respite between a lunch meeting with Blake Rustin, the savvy political adviser counseling him about his prospective run for president, and this encounter with the actress whose mission would be no help to such plans.

Alone in his office, he did something he rarely had time to do: contemplate how he had reached this point—a genuine presidential prospect whose road to the White House was, nonetheless, filled with potholes all too often of his own making. Yet he was single, with no personal life worth the name, and too often he still felt solitary. The root of all this was captured by two photographs that pained as much as warmed him: one of Kara, now a college student in Sydney, the only visible evidence that he had ever been a father; the other of Joe Fitts, a reminder of the debt he owed to make his career in politics matter.

At forty-three, he was a better man, he could only

hope, than the one who had been Joe Fitts's friend. There was no doubt that he loved his country—America had kept faith with him, and he was determined to serve it well. Certainly his ordeal in Iraq had given him a deep sense of the transience of life, the need to live a "crowded hour," using whatever gifts God gave him to seize the moment, take risks, and make a difference—all, he hoped, in the service of something more than the greater glory of Corey Grace. Always, it seemed, he felt this driving restlessness, a clock ticking in his head, as though every moment since Joe's death had been borrowed. Nor did he worry much about making friends in the Senate if the cost was his integrity: his closest friends remained those who had served with him in the air force and shared his sense of what mattered—loyalty, perseverance, and the aim of living an honorable life.

Corey did not attempt to articulate any of this in public. It would have seemed self-glorifying, a deliberate effort to distinguish himself from his many less than courageous peers. And though he had friends in both parties, he knew very well the envy felt by many of his Republican colleagues—most of all by Senator Rob Marotta of Pennsylvania, the assiduous career politician who was the majority leader of the Senate, and who had resolved to run for president. To Marotta, as to others, Corey's arrival in the Senate had been as easy as his smile, greased by an act of heroism that seemed to induce an uncomfortable self-doubt in those never called on to be heroes. It did not help that the current president, like all presidents, tended to view disagreement as disloyalty, or that Corey, in a moment more candid than tactful, had told him that his secretary of defense's plan to invade a Middle Eastern country was "crack-smoking stupid" and a "waste of lives"; it had helped even less when events suggested that Corey was right. It didn't help that, as a bachelor, he was not required to adopt the grim pretense of devotion that characterized some political marriages. Nor did it help that, in his colleagues' minds, an all too adoring press trumpeted Corey's candor and penchant for voting his conscience. "Senator Grace," a feature in the *Washington Post* style section noted, "seems never to have bothered to craft a public persona any different from his private one." When asked about this, Corey had merely laughed. "If you're the same person twenty-four hours a day, you have a lot less trouble remembering who you are."

It was not that simple, of course—Corey's inner self, the residue of guilt and hard experience, was something he shared with no one. When he'd once remarked, "Life has taught me that there are worse things in the world than losing an election," his colleagues had assumed that he meant being hung from his broken shoulders. But his reasons went deeper than that: there is nothing worse, Corey knew, than losing yourself.

Pausing, Corey gazed at his photograph of Clay.

As far as it went, his mother had been right—his long-dead brother had lost himself by trying to be like Corey, instead of his more vulnerable, at least equally valuable self. But the fault lay far less in Clay than in his family—all of them—and in the facile scapegoating of "the other," which had marred the social environment of his country and, too often, the politics of his own party.

There were important reasons that Corey was a Republican: his dedication to national defense; his belief in private enterprise; his worry that Democrats too easily dismissed the genuine threats to America in a world of hostile regimes, fanatic terrorists, and nuclear proliferators. But he had not come to the Senate armed with a rigid set of orthodoxies; a newly voracious reader and a seeker of advice, Corey distinguished himself from many conservatives by a concern for the environment, a distaste for static belief systems, and an openness to opposing points of view. And there was something else he did not need to think about: Senator Corey Grace despised a politics that pitted one group against another, and policies that promoted the abuse of the weak by the strong.

From his first years in the Senate, Corey had been a passionate advocate of human rights. To him, the overriding reason was clear: to lead the world, America needed to stand for more than military strength or pious rhetoric. He never mentioned Joe Fitts's execution or his own torture. Nor did he ever seek to excuse the incident his political enemies used to exemplify his impulsive nature, disregard for protocol, and general unfitness to be president.

Shortly after entering the Senate, Corey, along with his chief of staff, Jack Walters, arrived in Moscow as a first step in acquainting himself with Russia in the volatile post-Soviet era. In a van driven by a Russian security man, Corey went to meet with the Russian president. Abruptly, a demonstration had clogged the street—a line of soldiers confronting young people armed only with epithets and placards. "What's this about?" Corey asked the driver.

The man shrugged his heavy shoulders. "They say our president imprisons dissenters on false charges. It is nonsense, as you know."

Corey did not know; he intended, in a suitably diplomatic way, to raise this very question with the president. But he chose to say nothing. And then, through the windshield, he saw a Russian soldier swing the butt of his rifle at a demonstrator who had just spat in his face.

Framed in the bulletproof glass like an actor in a brutal silent film, the soldier struck the man's head with an impact that made Corey wince. The demonstrator fell to his knees, blood streaming from his scalp as the soldier again raised the butt of his rifle, while his fellow soldiers aimed their rifles at the remaining demonstrators. At the second blow, Corey's hand grabbed the door handle; at the third, which caused the demonstrator to fall sideways, Corey started to jump out of the car.

Jack Walters grabbed his arm. "No."

Corey broke away. Pushing through the crowd, he saw the soldier raise his rifle butt yet again. *"Stop!"* Corey shouted.

He felt the driver and Jack Walters pin his arms behind his body. The driver called out in Russian. The soldier, rifle frozen above his head, stared at him, then at Corey, and slowly lowered his weapon. To one side, Corey heard the distinctive clicking of a camera.

For a moment the tableau before him was almost motionless: the soldiers with their rifles aimed; the demonstrators recoiling; the fallen man in a spreading pool of blood. Then the driver spoke again; two soldiers came forward, picked up the victim by his arms and legs, and carried him away.

Breaking free, Corey walked back to the van.

For the rest of the drive Corey gazed out the window, gripped by an anger so palpable that no one chose to speak. His next words were to the Russian president: "Sorry to be late. But I was held up watching your soldiers try to kill someone for spitting."

The story, and the photograph, gained currency as the years passed. Among some colleagues it was whispered that Corey was too rash, too prone to the sort of impulsive behavior that might have provoked an international incident had that day in Moscow taken a different turn. "Leadership," a *Wall Street Journal* editorial writer had opined, "requires far more than courage." And the closest allies of Rob Marotta gave the story an even darker tinge: however human Corey's instincts, the month of torture had unhinged him. "Making Corey Grace a senator was one thing," Marotta had supposedly remarked. "But do people want to put a hothead's finger on the nuclear trigger?"

At that moment in Moscow, believing a man would die, Corey could have done nothing else. Nor would he change this now. But thirteen years later, awaiting Lexie Hart, he understood too well what else he had done; he had helped elevate his antagonists' distaste for his independence into a nobler cause: the statesmanlike conclusion that Corey Grace should never become president of the United States. And for Rob Marotta, every deviation from convention, each defiance of party orthodoxy, was added to the bill of particulars he was building against his rival.

The door to Corey's office opened. "Ms. Hart is here to see you," Eve Stansky announced brightly, and Lexie Hart walked into Corey's life.

BY NOW, COREY Grace had more than sufficient experience with women—just that spring, to the titillation of Washington and the considerable amusement of his staff, *People* had named Corey one of the fifty sexiest men alive. But entering his office with a brisk handshake and swift smile that did not quite reach her eyes, Lexie Hart had an electric beauty, a carriage that somehow made her seem separate, withheld from others in some mysterious way that no magazine cover could capture. For Corey, her impact was as vivid as the first time he had met Janice, save that Corey was older, more perceptive, and a good deal less impulsive.

Motioning Lexie to his couch, he sat across from her in his favorite wing chair, swiftly taking inventory of the components that made her so compelling. She was slender and graceful, and the erect posture of a stage actress made her seem taller than she was. Her curly hair, cut short, accented features that carried a hint of imperiousness—high cheekbones, cleft chin, full lips. But it was her eyes that struck him most: their cool gray-green, surprising in an African-American, suggested the wary intelligence of a woman who employed her powers of observation as a weapon or, perhaps, a defense. Or so Corey imagined—instinctively he grasped that Lexie Hart would be a difficult woman to truly know.

With a quick smile, Corey said lightly, "I understand you've come to rebuke me for my silence on stem-cell research."

Her own smile was as slight as the shake of her head. "I've come to reason with you, Senator. If you experience that as a rebuke, it's only because you know that anyone who's really pro-life should care about the living."

The comment was so pointed that Corey nearly laughed. "I guess you don't mean to make this easy for me."

"I can't. The president is opposed to expanding stem-cell research. So are most senators in your political party. My information is that it may come down to one or two votes—or maybe just yours." Leaning forward, she spoke with quiet passion. "You can make a difference in the life of someone who can't move his limbs, or keep them from shaking. Or a woman who can't remember the daughter she gave birth to, even if that same girl is holding her hand as she looks into her eyes for a trace of recognition."

She was an actress, Corey thought at once, with an actress's ability to draw her audience into whatever world she cared to create. Less easy to account for was Corey's near certainty that *this* performance was personal. "Your mother?" he asked.

Briefly, Lexie hesitated. "Has Alzheimer's. There's no way back for her. But you can help keep other people from living in my mother's twilight zone. And not just that, Senator. I'm sure you know the science—embryonic stem cells have the potential to reverse diseases like Parkinson's and type 1 diabetes, and to repair spinal injuries that cause paralysis. How can a decent society turn away from that?"

"Oh, I think *you* know the moral argument, Ms. Hart. For many of my colleagues, life doesn't start at birth. So any component of life, like a fertilized embryo, is entitled to protection—"

"A frozen embryo," Lexie interrupted with a trace of asperity, "is not a life, and the leftovers in fertility clinics never will be. A humane society can make that distinction without opening up the floodgates to genocide and euthanasia."

She intrigued him enough, Corey realized, that he wanted to move her off her talking points—or, at least, persuade her that he was not a fool. In an even tone, he countered, "A humane society, some would say, knows that a fetus *is* a life, and values it too much to play God. But without knowing you at all, Ms. Hart, I'd bet my town house you're pro-choice, and don't distinguish between a frozen embryo and the fetuses you and I once were before we escaped the womb."

At this, Lexie sat back, arms resting at her sides, her cool eyes now appraising him. "Even if that were true, or fair, *you* can surely make that distinction. So please don't use my supposed beliefs as a reason for not considering your own. A petri dish is not a womb, and an adult with

Parkinson's—I think we can both agree—is certainly a life. Or are you one of those pro-life folks who love people only till they're born?"

Even as he chuckled, Corey realized that he found her lack of deference engaging. "Tell me about your mother," he asked. "I've never known anyone with Alzheimer's—for better or worse, I guess."

As she folded her hands, looking down, Corey sensed her deciding how much to reveal. "It's terrible," she said at length. "When I sit with her, it's like being in the presence of death. I have this instinct to whisper, though it wouldn't matter if I shouted. She's living so deep inside herself that the simplest things, like eating a sandwich, can take minutes or even hours. It'll just remain in her hand, unnoticed, and then her hand moves to her mouth again, her eyes still dead, as if the hand has a life of its own.

"I try talking to her, of course. But I can't know if my voice stirs memories, or whether it's like the drone of her television." Lexie shook her head. "The night I won the Oscar, her nurse turned it on for her. During my acceptance speech, the nurse said, my mother began blinking. I like to think that, for a moment, she knew me. But there's no way she fathomed what I'd achieved."

Her voice, Corey thought, held the disappointment of a child proud of an accomplishment she could not share. "When did this start?" Corey asked.

"Seven years ago. But each stage of the disease brought something more. First came the endless list making as she tried to remember chores; then the staring at my father's photograph, trying to remember *him;* then the day she could not remember him at all." Her voice became soft with resignation. "For a time after that, I was still me. Then she thought I was a friend she'd known when she was six. Then the friend, too, was forgotten. The simplest choices upset her. And then, just before she lost the power of speech, nothing upset her anymore. Her eyes turned as blank as marbles." Lexie sat back, as though distancing herself from her own emotions. "You and I have been debating human life. Our memories are what make us human, Senator. This disease took that from my mother."

Corey studied her for a moment. "There are those who say we don't need human embryos to combat Alzheimer's —that adult stem cells are sufficient."

Swiftly, Lexie left the personal behind. "That's non-sense," she answered. "It's a triumph of the culture wars over science, where the moral status of embryos is more important than human suffering, or scientific fact. Adult stem cells are a diversion—the science just isn't there."

"Nor," Corey responded, "can you be sure about embryonic stem cells. We're talking about hope, not certainty. Your side still doesn't know if any of this will work, does it?"

Lexie shrugged her concession. "Not for sure. But those who are already suffering feel desperate for some break-through." Her face turned soft. "A few years ago I sat with Chris Reeve when he testified before a House committee. Chris really believed stem cells would cure him. Seeing all his hope I couldn't help being sad—knowing what I knew, I never believed that Chris could make it for that long.

"But responsible scientists, including Nobel Prize win-ners, believe that fetal stem cells have real promise." Her smile was brief and pointed. "You know way more about the subject, Senator, than you've been letting on. Far too much to support your party leaders with a clear con-science. Rumor says you have one."

For a moment, Corey looked back at her in silence. Then a knock on the door interrupted them, and Jack Wal-ters leaned inside. "Sorry," he told Lexie; to Corey he said,

"Time for that committee meeting. Your day of reckoning with Alex Rohr."

"Be with you in a couple." Turning back to Lexie as the door shut, Corey asked, "Do you know Alex Rohr?"

"Enough to know that he's despicable."

"How so?"

Lexie's eyes were cold. "The way a lot of powerful white men are despicable. They think money and position entitle them to anything they want."

The chill in her tone piqued Corey's curiosity. But there was no time to pursue this. "I don't want to seem like Alex Rohr," he assured her. "But it doesn't feel like we're quite through yet. Could you break free for dinner?"

Lexie's eyes narrowed, her expression less hostile than speculative. Then she slowly shook her head. "I'm afraid we'll have to finish up by phone. Tonight I've got more commitments, and I have to be in L.A. tomorrow morning. I won't be back until the vote."

Corey hesitated, trying to decipher whether the last sentence was an opening. "Maybe," he said, "we could get together then?"

She gave him a look that combined amusement with curiosity. "I *might* be persuaded," she finally answered. "Depends on how you vote."

She shook his hand again, holding it for a brief moment while she looked into his eyes. Then she thanked him for his time and hurried off to her next appointment.

2

In the bowels of the Capitol, Corey rode the Senate subway to the hearing room, listening to Jack Walters worry aloud.

"You really want to do this?" Jack inquired glumly. "I mean, Alex Rohr merely controls a string of newspapers, two major book publishers, half of conservative talk radio, and the highest-rated cable news station in America. All of which he can use to cut you to pieces."

Nettled by Jack's persistence, Corey looked up from his notes. "So now we're supposed to give this bastard control of our leading Internet provider? That's really what we need—an America where Alex Rohr tells everyone what to think."

"Enough Americans," Jack rejoined, "already think whatever Rohr wants them to. Why make yourself this guy's enemy?"

"Maybe because he needs one."

"Fine, but why does it have to be you? Look, Rohr not only can influence millions of people, he can raise millions of dollars to finance whatever presidential candidate sees the world his way. And now you want to get *in* his way." Jack looked at Corey intently, his face etched with frustration. "Rohr's already pissed about your great crusade to keep money out of politics. To deliberately pick another fight with this guy suggests you don't know when to stop."

"I'll stop whenever Rohr does." Reading his friend's

expression, Corey spoke with a weary fatalism. "As a matter of politics, you're right—I need Rohr coming after me like I need a second navel. I'd be thrilled if anyone else in our party tried to block him. But Rohr personifies everything that's going wrong with this country—"

"Everything?"

"Damn near. His guiding belief is that he needs more—more money, more power. He'll favor Republicans only as long as we give him what he wants: a media monopoly, immunity from lawsuits, lower taxes, and new ways of amassing wealth.

"The last time Rohr honored the Senate with his presence, he wanted the right to set up his own broadcast network *and* buy a string of TV stations. Some of us started balking. So Rohr effectively bribed our former majority leader with a huge book deal worth hundreds of thousands more than his moronic screed was worth.

"You remember what happened next: our peerless leader slipped Rohr's bill through the Senate before anyone realized that Rohr had bought him off. And when the stink from *that* got too great for our leader to run again, Rohr hired him to front a talk show on Rohr News, where, funnily enough, he shills for Rohr's pet causes." Corey shook his head. "Call me naive, but when they first asked me to run for the Senate, I was in awe. Becoming a senator seemed like something fine, where people would trust you to help make our country a better place. I haven't quite accepted that I'm a whore with a fancy title."

Resigned, Jack shook his head. As they entered the hearing room, Corey rested a hand on his shoulder. "Cheer up, pal—the coverage should be terrific. There are still a few networks and newspapers Alex Rohr doesn't own."

*

As Corey took his seat next to Senator Carl Halprin, the testy veteran who served as committee chair, a glance around the room proved his estimate correct: the hearing was standing room only, with reporters, cameramen, and photographers lined against the walls. As Alex Rohr entered the room, the cameras began snapping.

Rohr took his seat at the witness table, flanked by two lawyers who specialized in media ownership. With his smooth face, slicked-back brown hair, and a hand-tailored suit that fit his trim form perfectly, Alex Rohr looked as sleek as a seal. But what struck Corey was his expression: closed off and yet self-satisfied, with an expression in his dark eyes that suggested disdain for this tiresome necessity. Rohr scanned the panel of senators, his gaze lingering on Corey. "The staff thinks you're looking to make trouble," Halprin murmured to Corey.

Though Corey smiled, he kept watching Alex Rohr. "Not for you, Carl."

THE INITIAL QUESTIONING after Rohr's statement—first from Senator Halprin and then from Senator Rives, the ranking Democrat—confirmed what Corey suspected: most Republicans would line up with Rohr, most Democrats oppose him. Which made Corey the wild card—or, in Carl Halprin's estimate, the joker.

"Senator Grace," Halprin asked in a neutral tone, "do you have any questions for the witness?"

"I do." Looking up from his notes, Corey paused, as if a new thought had struck him. "Let me ask you a philosophical question, Mr. Rohr. How much is enough?"

Though one corner of his mouth twitched in ironic comprehension, Rohr feigned puzzlement. In his careful Oxbridge accent—which, Corey privately asserted, Rohr had learned by watching tapes of *Masterpiece Theatre*—Rohr replied, "I'm sorry, Senator Grace. But I'm not quite sure what you mean."

"Then let's define 'enough.' According to this committee, you own five magazines; three major film studios; a home-video company; a cable provider; four record labels; two publishing houses, one for general-interest readers and the other for conservative Christians; a major broadcast network; the highest-rated cable news network; the nation's largest newspaper chain; and one hundred and nineteen talk-radio stations." Pausing, Corey flashed a smile. "Forgive me if I've omitted something—we have a hard time keeping up. But would you say that this laundry list qualifies as 'enough'?"

Rohr spread his hands. "In the America I came to, of which I am now a citizen, the operative words were 'freedom' and 'opportunity'—"

"Then you surely agree that all Americans should have the 'opportunity'—not to mention the 'freedom'—to read, watch, or listen to news provided by someone else."

"Senator," Rohr countered with a soft laugh, "they *can*."

"Less so all the time, Mr. Rohr. In St. Louis, for example, you own the daily newspaper, two of the major TV stations, the principal talk-radio outlet, and the local magazine. The citizens of St. Louis didn't wake up and decide one day to give you a semimonopoly; *we* in the government let you gobble up their media." Corey leaned forward. "In the brave new world that you've created, a single corporation—RohrVision—dominates the local media in *most* American cities. It seems pretty clear that you'll *never* say 'enough.' So when do you think *we* should?"

"That's a rhetorical question," Rohr countered with an ironic smile. "To which, I somehow sense, you're about to provide an answer."

"I probably should," Corey said coolly. "After all, I'm a United States senator, and you're merely rich. So it's important that we both remember the difference.

"'Enough,' Mr. Rohr, is what you already own. 'Too much' is what you're here for now: control of America's largest Internet provider."

Next to him, Corey detected Halprin shifting impatiently in his chair. But Corey had ten minutes left, and he fully intended to use them. Knowing this, the reporters in the room were alert, looking from Corey to Rohr. "I humbly disagree," Rohr answered. "All that will happen is that Netcast will provide twenty-five million Americans with better and cheaper service."

"Not *all*, I think." Corey's voice became sharper. "Here's what else you can do. You can make it easy for customers to get to Web sites that reflect your political point of view. You can make it harder to get to Web sites that don't. You can charge prohibitive fees to Web sites that displease you. You can even block users from going to them at all. You can hamper Internet fund-raising for candidates whom you oppose. And, on the theory that, in your America, RohrVision needs still more profits, you can steer customers to movies, games, and music owned by other arms of RohrVision. You can even steer them to a Web site you acquired last month: Hook-Up, which openly facilitates solicitations for underage sex—which, I have to admit, is pretty broad-minded for a man who just published a Christian book called *Bringing Your Kids to God*."

Sitting up straighter, Rohr responded in a low, chill tone. "Forgive me, Senator, if I find that litany insulting."

"How exactly? Because you thought I was suggesting that you personally troll Hook-Up? It's hard to know what else you could mean, given that you've lowered the standards of journalism in every media outlet you've acquired. Not to mention the standards of this body—"

"Senator Grace," Halprin interrupted.

Still watching Rohr, Corey said, "Indulge me for a moment, Senator. Mr. Rohr claims to find my 'litany' insulting. And yet he's spent millions in lobbying fees trying to persuade the Senate to reject a bill that would ban his company from abusing Netcast in precisely the ways I just enumerated." Leaning forward, Corey asked Rohr, "That much is true, isn't it?"

Rohr glanced toward one of his lawyers, a slight, bespectacled man who, to Corey, had the face of a mortician. As Corey and the onlookers waited, the lawyer whispered in Rohr's ear. "Senator," Rohr said testily, "I fail to see how vigorous advocacy of a legitimate point of view lowers the standards of the Senate. And I remind you that other independent voices—including Consumers for Internet Choice—are prepared to testify regarding the benefits to customers should we acquire Netcast."

Suppressing a smile, Corey asked, "So you've never once attempted to mislead us."

Glancing toward his lawyer, Rohr looked, in Corey's estimate, less like a seal than a ferret. "Absolutely not."

"So tell me, Mr. Rohr, who funds that 'independent voice' that is about to help us out—'Consumers for Internet Choice'?"

Silent, Rohr scrutinized Corey as the lawyer-mortician whispered in his ear. "I hope you're not just finding out," Corey added with an air of solicitude. "It took *my* staff three weeks."

From someone in the audience behind Rohr came a brief, nervous chuckle. At Corey's left, his friend and colleague Chuck Clancy shot him a sideways grin. "I'm informed," Rohr said grudgingly, "that some funding may have been provided by a subsidiary of RohrVision."

"You're 'informed,'" Corey repeated with mild incredulity. "So you didn't know that RohrVision was funding this group until I asked about it?"

With quiet pleasure, Corey watched his quarry weigh the risks and benefits of perjury. In a monotone, Rohr answered, "I don't recall knowing about my company's involvement."

This time the laughter was mildly scornful. Though Rohr did not turn, his face was a frozen mask. "Well," Corey said dismissively, "you've been busy, what with acquiring Hook-Up and introducing our kids to God. A small matter like trying to mislead the United States Senate could easily slip your mind."

As Rohr flushed, the decorum of the audience broke down in yet more laughter.

Rohr, Corey was certain, understood that this moment of humiliation would make the evening news. And Corey knew two other things: that, for the moment, he had made Rohr's newest plans radioactive, and that Rohr's enmity would follow him far longer. For Alex Rohr, worse than being thwarted was being made to play the fool.

"Thank you," Corey told Rohr politely. "That's really all I wanted."

3

"It's done," Corey told Blake Rustin coolly.

Restless after the hearing, Corey walked with Rustin along the Ellipse. Bespectacled and bald, his chief political adviser gave him a shrewd sideways glance and, as Corey intended, chose to drop the subject of Alex Rohr. Instead Rustin contented himself with matching Corey's brisk pace, waiting to prod his most important client on the subject that permeated their every conversation: whether Senator Corey Grace should run for president.

"So why am I going to this thing tonight?" Corey inquired at last.

"Good question," Rustin said tartly. "Seeing how you refused to speak. After all, it's only a chance for would-be presidential candidates to impress a thousand of the party's biggest donors."

"That's the point," Corey rejoined. "Unless the current political dynamic changes entirely, I'm *not* running. So why put myself in a cattle call with Rob Marotta, an evangelist who thinks he's God's anointed, and three governors who, at most, are angling for America's traditionally most pathetic office, the vice presidency.

"Besides, the donor classes are already lined up behind Marotta, hoping Rob will cut their taxes even if it drives America into bankruptcy. All I'd want to do tonight is say what they don't want to hear: that the tax cuts we already gave them are crippling the government, screwing seniors and the poor, and saddling our grandkids with debt—none of which they seem to care about. Be glad that I'm so bashful."

Rustin stopped walking and stood, hands on hips, shaking his head in a pantomime of despair. "I've been doing this for twenty years, Corey, and I've helped all sorts of candidates win races they deserved to lose. But you know what working with you is like? It's like watching a fucking oil well spill oil all over the ground—a complete and pointless waste of resources. I just stare, helpless, and all I can do is cry."

Corey grinned. "That's really touching, Blake."

"So can't you at least get married? Preferably to a war widow with two wholesome and adoring kids. Most normal men would find thirteen years of romantic conquests sufficient."

Corey felt his good humor slowly fading. "When it comes to my love life, people give me too much credit. Anyhow, I didn't plan that part. It just happened, a day at a time."

As they resumed walking, Rustin fell silent. Corey watched the late-afternoon shadows lengthen and, against his will, recalled a time when, unschooled in love by anything he saw in his parents' marriage, he had imagined himself capable of better.

JANICE HALL WAS the commandant's daughter.

The first time Corey saw her, at a formal ball in the fall of his fourth year, she was someone else's date. But even gliding in Bob Cheever's arms she was the image of the woman he had wanted but never found: tall and elegant, with a widow's peak and long brown hair that framed a face he could not stop watching—a perfectly formed chin, even lips, high cheekbones, and, most arresting to Corey, cool gray eyes that at once suggested challenge and vulnerability, the need to hold something back. He stared at her across the room until, inevitably, she saw him.

There were other things she could have done—pretend not to have noticed or redirected her glance in shyness or annoyance. Instead, her face resting on Bob Cheever's shoulder, she gazed back at Corey as though daring him to look away. Though it might have been mere seconds, the moment seemed frozen, a still photograph of desire imprinted on Corey's mind. And then the dance ended, and the girl seemed to remember Bob Cheever. But for Corey, his own date, currently occupied in the ladies' room, was already consigned to history.

"Who's the girl with Cheever?" he asked Jerry Patz.

Jerry told him. "Cheever's afraid to touch her," he added. "Can you imagine fucking the commandant's daughter?"

For the rest of the evening Corey danced with his date and joked with his peers, acting as though the commandant's daughter had vanished from his thoughts. Only at the end of the evening did he contrive to brush her shoulder as they passed. When she glanced at him, he saw that she was as aware of his presence as he was of hers.

Under his breath, Corey said, "I'll call you."

Janice's level gaze did not waver. "Is this about me, or my father?"

"You."

For an instant, Janice hesitated. And then she murmured a telephone number and turned away.

Two days later, Corey called her. Coolly, she told him, "My father says you can come for dinner."

This was not what Corey had envisioned. Nor had he anticipated that when he arrived at the commandant's house in crisp military dress, General Hall, a widower, would be in Washington and his daughter would be alone.

When Janice opened the door, her father's house was nearly dark. Corey entered, and then she closed the door behind them.

"So," Janice said softly, "is this what you wanted? Or dinner with Dad?"

Corey could feel his own pulse. Pushing aside his misgivings, he answered, "This."

He reached out for her, cradling her against him as he smelled the freshness of her skin and hair. She held her body separate, neither yielding nor resisting. But when Corey kissed her neck, she quivered and then whispered, "God, you are so not what I wanted."

For Corey to ask why, he sensed, would destroy his chances of possessing her. Instead he cupped her chin, kissing her softly, until the resistance of her body dissipated with a slow intake of breath.

As they kissed, Corey found the zipper of her dress. Her back felt cool, a slim sculpture of perfection. He no longer thought of consequences.

When they were naked, Janice led him to the living room.

They made love on the floor, Janice moving with him and yet silent, as though she had willed her soul to depart her body. Even before she cried out in ecstasy or anguish, Corey somehow knew that her eyes, though averted from their act, were closed.

Her first quiet words, oddly toneless, answered the question he had not dared to ask. "My mother was a drunk. Not because she liked the taste of it, but because she hated this life. Suicide was her ultimate escape."

The bitter story evoked in Corey his clearest thought: they were both escapees, but running in different directions. "I'm not your father," he answered.

She turned to him, and he felt her search his face in the

darkness. "Maybe not," she said. "My father was faithful to her."

Unsure of what to say, Corey held her close. When they made love again, to his surprise it was Janice whose touch signaled her desire.

The next time he came for dinner, her father was home.

In his quiet way, General Hall seemed pleased. Perhaps, Corey guessed, he saw his daughter's involvement with Corey as a form of acceptance or, maybe, forgiveness.

Perhaps they were in love.

They certainly had chemistry. Between bouts of withdrawal, Janice was a match for him: she was not only bright, an honors student at Colorado College, but funny and sometimes scarily perceptive, with a candid and somewhat jaundiced humor that cut to the core of most human situations. And she was beautiful in a way that turned heads, and that always gave Corey that same jolt of recognition and surprise he had felt the first time he had seen her. On a spring afternoon, Corey reached for her hand across a picnic blanket and said what he believed: "We're supposed to be together."

Janice studied him, her smile suddenly wistful. "A life sentence, you mean? Then God help us both."

Two months later, a week after Janice's graduation, they were married in the chapel of the Academy.

By then Corey's flying career had begun its swift ascent. He craved the feeling of flight, a thrill unlike anything he had experienced on earth. Blessed with reflexes and hand-eye coordination that even his instructors found impressive, Corey shot through flight school at the top of his class. Within a year, Janice was eight months pregnant and Corey, immersed in flying F-15s in Thailand, had spent an evening with a fetching Thai girl that meant—or so he tried to tell his conscience—only that he was far away from home.

Repentant, he returned for the birth of his child.

They had saved the gender for a surprise. But Janice, perhaps disoriented by childbirth, greeted her newborn daughter with a pensiveness so deep that it reminded Corey, somewhat uneasily, of the night they had first made love.

Returning from an errand four days after Kara's birth, he approached the bedroom of their apartment and heard Janice's voice. Staring into their daughter's bassinet, Janice did not see him. "Not again," she promised Kara. "Not for you."

Corey had gone back to Thailand without asking what she meant.

"ALL I CAN tell you," Rustin said now, "is that—and I speak as a student of politics and a scholar of history—no single, divorced man has ever been elected president."

"Someday there'll be a first time," Corey responded. "Anyhow, I won't be scaring up a wife for you by the election, Blake. As for marriage, I seem to recall having tried that."

Hands shoved in his pockets, Rustin shrugged. "Maybe we can sit," he suggested after a time. "Some of us don't think talking politics requires aerobic exercise."

They found a bench facing the Reflecting Pool, which ended at the Lincoln Memorial. With the arrival of the fall weather, Corey missed seeing as many families, the kids often tired or cranky yet sometimes filled with wonder. But there was something in the setting—perhaps the glassy reflection of the water—that soothed his often restless spirit. "As to why you're attending tonight's event," Rustin reminded him sardonically, "I want you to consider who else our Grand Old Party has to offer America. Leaders in the noble tradition of Abe Lincoln: Senator

Rob Marotta and Governors George Costas, Sam Larkin, and Charles Blair. It's a time for greatness—what with terrorism, a failed war, deep economic uncertainty, and the growing threat of a nuclear apocalypse—and the Republican Party stands ready to answer the call."

Corey gazed at the water, shimmering with the reflection of two joggers running past them, the woman glancing swiftly at Corey. "It's sad, I know. I'd feel a lot better if Cortland Lane were running."

"Lane was right," Rustin said flatly. "The country isn't ready to elect an African-American. Certainly our party isn't."

Corey shook his head. "I disagree, at least about Cortland. I think Americans are ready for a candidate who transcends race, and who they can actually imagine as president."

Rustin shrugged. "Anyhow, Lane's out of it. But if it's novelty you're looking for, there's always the Reverend Christy."

"Terrific."

"Over ten million people watch him," Rustin remonstrated, "and half of those think he's God himself. The man's serious, Corey."

Pensive, Corey remembered the first and only time he had encountered Bob Christy, and the reverberations that had followed. "Christy," Corey answered softly, "has been serious for a while."

"He's *more* serious now. And he turns issues like stem cells into dynamite—because he *believes,* truly and absolutely, in the version of morality he preaches. For a whole lot of people, he's America's last hope in uncertain times—God's regent, meant to rule us in God's name until the Messiah comes again. And those who follow him are God's new chosen people."

Corey shook his head. "There's a political ceiling on the Apocalypse. Except maybe in states like South Carolina, the man won't break twenty percent."

Rustin turned to squint at him. "Even twenty percent can change the outcome. And Christy's got an instinct for power. Got time for a quick story?"

"Sure."

"Before you entered the Senate, when Christy was already on the rise, the president started holding prayer services at the White House. I was the president's political director. So one day, Christy calls to ask if he can preach some Sunday.

"I'm not a complete fool. So I said, 'Yeah, sure—as long as you wouldn't mind giving us your mailing list.'"

Corey laughed. "After all, you were all on the same team: the president, Christy, and God."

"Exactly. But then Pat Robertson got wind of it and called me to raise hell—there was no way, Pat said, he'd put up with us giving his prime competitor the chance to brag that *he's* the president's preacher.

"I had to call Christy back. To say he was offended doesn't cover it—not only did he not give us the mailing list, but he used it to start the Christian Commitment." Rustin allowed himself a rueful smile. "That was the day, I always thought, that Christy decided, 'If I can't preach to the president, I'll *be* president.'"

"A nice story, Blake. It illuminates Christy's spiritual nature."

"Christy's complicated," Rustin cautioned. "He truly believes the sky is falling. But he also believes in power. He's tough, charismatic, and one helluva businessman—from his TV program to a string of Christian theme parks, everything he touches mints money. All of which, in his mind, is another sign of God's approval. And all of which can help him finance his own campaign."

"Money's not enough," Corey objected. "Look at Ross Perot."

"Perot got nineteen fucking percent, Corey—and that was *after* people figured out that he was certifiable. And even when Christy says things that *are* nuts, he doesn't *seem* nuts. He's like the grandfather who worries for his grandkids—you just know that he'll take care of things. And he's an opportunist in the finest sense. Remember when that judge in Mississippi moved a marble statue of Jesus into the state supreme court at midnight?"

"Sure. They damn near had to jackhammer Jesus to get him out of there. The judge became a national celebrity."

"Well, Christy put him up to it, and then made that marble Jesus the center of a fund-raising campaign that netted the Christian Commitment another twenty million. On his TV show, Christy started railing against godless federal judges and the separation of church and state, and in favor of putting the Ten Commandments in every courthouse in America. Which, by the way, registered sixty-four percent in favor in the latest Zogby poll." Rustin stood, stretching his congenitally aching back. "So don't sell the reverend short. What he offers folks is not just hope, but certainty. You don't need to think or wonder or question anymore—all you need is to interpret the Bible literally. By shunning sex, science, and the sixties, you not only save yourself and your kids, you can also save America from hell. If *you* bought the premise, wouldn't you find it kind of tempting?"

Corey grimaced. "My mother already does."

"And how does *she* feel about stem-cell research, pray tell?"

"Against. Ever since the show where Christy claimed that God told him to oppose it." Corey shook his head.

"At least when God speaks to *me* I've got the sense to know it's a long-distance call."

Arms folded, Rustin gazed down at him. "Christy's God is always at his side, and wants him to be president. The question is whether Bob's pragmatic enough to transform his Jesus into a tax cutter who wants to give greedheads like Rohr whatever they want. If Christy reaches out to *them*, his God is giving him some very shrewd advice."

Slowly, Corey nodded. "The Alex Rohrs of the world can get their daughters or girlfriends an abortion anytime they want. If Christy could give them whatever else they want, they'd be pleased to let him repeal the theory of evolution as long as he doesn't come to dinner and fill their own kids' heads with nonsense."

"Should Christy forge an alliance between the dollar and the cross," Rustin answered, "it's conceivable that he could start a cultural revolution. But a *real* revolutionary would notice that the way Alex Rohr makes money, including things like Hook-Up, is antithetical to everything Christy stands for. So which is Christy—a revolutionary or a cynic as mercenary as Rohr?

"That's why we're going tonight. I'm rooting for a revolution. No compromise with sin or Rob Marotta."

Though he thought he knew the answer, Corey decided to ask the unspoken question at the heart of their conversation. "Just what does all this have to do with me?"

Rustin laughed softly. "Everything. Just like it does for Marotta.

"The Darth Vader of American politics, Magnus Price, helped get Christy started. Then Price dumped Christy for Marotta, reasoning that an extremely smart career politician was more likely to listen to him than to God." Pausing, Rustin spoke slowly and emphatically. "To Christy, Price is a Judas. So Christy hates him and, by extension,

Marotta. And if Christy runs he'll drain support from Marotta and create an opening for someone else.

"Marotta knows he has to keep Christy from running, or from having an excuse to run. That explains why Marotta absolutely needs to defeat stem-cell research—to co-opt Christy or, at the least, some of his ardent followers." Smiling, Rustin added dryly, "But I really don't have to paint you a picture, do I?"

"No," Corey answered. "Neither man particularly likes me, but I'm important to their ambitions—like it or not. Starting with my vote on stem cells."

"Like it or not," Rustin repeated softly. "And whether today's celebrity visitor, Ms. Hart, likes it or not. This is about more than frozen embryos, Corey. It may well be about whether you ever get—despite the odds—what I damned well know you want: the presidency.

"Our party got its ass kicked in the last congressional elections—we'd even lost the Senate until Bob Hansen dropped dead and got replaced by a Republican, making Marotta majority leader. There's a new opening for you: someone who talks to the common interest, not just to the extremes. But the tension between the party's money people and the religious right has to boil over to give you a real chance. That's where Christy comes in."

Sorting through his conflicting emotions, Corey regarded his adviser in silence. And then the central reality surfaced yet again: what Bob Christy chose to do was also important to *his* ambitions.

"I'll think about it," Corey said.

4

With an amused detachment, Corey glided through the cavernous hotel ballroom, crowded with round tables that would seat the affluent men and women who had paid ten thousand dollars a head to hear five would-be presidents audition for their favor.

This event was central to what Blake Rustin called the "money primary," where candidates strained and sweated to please the affluent electors who voted with their checkbooks. The donors, self-satisfied or curious or just congenitally loyal, were prepared to judge which candidate pleased them most, while the candidates hoped to amass enough donors and dollars to scare off their opponents before a single vote was cast. It was cocktail hour, and the attendees stood in an open space reserved for mingling. The largest donors—those with a network they could e-mail to raise hundreds of thousands in a week—held court like princelings while the candidates sought them out. Corey saw Rob Marotta spot Walter Prohl, a German immigrant who had founded an auto-parts empire, calling out, *"Prohl-sy"* with more enthusiasm than Corey suspected he felt. Prohl-sy mustered a crooked grin, his shrewd gray eyes seeming to weigh and measure the benefits of stringing Marotta along for a few more weeks or months versus the leverage he could extract through a more immediate commitment.

"What a system," Corey murmured to Blake Rustin.

Eyes glinting with humor, Corey kept moving, taking

in the bejeweled women flush with the glow of manicures, skin treatments, massages, Botox, and whatever their plastic surgeons and personal trainers could do to slow the ravages of age. Next to them their husbands—secure enough in their gender and status to let nature take its course—spoke with placid authority. This was not Corey's crowd; he had devoted almost a decade to limiting the influence of money in politics, and many here had disliked him since the day he had remarked, "Bribing politicians with donations is the only way the wealthy can offset the ill effects of letting ordinary people vote." It wasn't that the celebrants here were malign, Corey thought—they no doubt cherished their kids and grandkids, relishing their joys and triumphs and grieving for their weaknesses and failures. What troubled him was their pervasive lack of interest in any world beyond their own. Too many of those present, Corey had long since learned, believed that their great contribution to America was simply to be themselves.

"*Corey.*"

Turning, Corey encountered Magritte Dutcher, the fiftyish ex-wife of a cosmetics magnate, her red-dyed hair coiffed into immobility, her face so smooth that a grasshopper could have ice-skated across her forehead. The avid glow in Magritte's large green eyes, Corey knew, came not just from vodka but from a love of power so intense that it had a certain majesty. This passion had recently been manifested by Magritte's invitation to Corey, after another such event, to spend a romantic evening on her ninety-foot yacht, one of the many spoils of her divorce. Corey had been grateful to have a semiacceptable excuse: an early-morning flight to Baghdad. Kissing her proffered cheek, Corey said, "If I were Cary Grant, Magritte, I'd say you look divine."

Magritte gave him a glance that combined skepticism and amusement. "Cary Grant was gay, you know."

"No kidding? So *that's* my problem."

Magritte's cupid's-bow mouth turned up briefly. "Somehow I don't think so—although half the closets in Washington are filled with gay Republicans. So tell me, how *was* Iraq?"

What the hell, Corey thought. "Terrific," he assured her. "Ever since we liberated them, the Sunnis and Shiites have been free to kill each other in droves. It's the ultimate Jeffersonian democracy, combining First Amendment freedom of expression with the Second Amendment right to bear arms. Everyone here should see it."

Magritte laughed softly. "You know what your 'real' problem is?"

Corey smiled. "Not a clue. So please don't keep me guessing."

"You're too real to be president. You're the only dead-certain loser I ever wanted to fuck."

Corey kissed her on the cheek. "That," he told her, "may be the most honest thing anyone says all night."

Corey hadn't counted on Bob Christy.

COREY AND BLAKE Rustin were seated with six of Rob Marotta's ardent backers, three married couples whose deepest passion was engineering yet more tax cuts—the party establishment's tacit reprisal for Corey's acts of heresy. His only real company came from Rustin and his own unspoken reflections, punctuated by the gelid stare of Alex Rohr from a nearby table.

"It's clear you've made another friend," Rustin whispered in his ear.

Corey held Rohr's gaze until his antagonist turned away. "Yeah," Corey answered. "It's this gift I have."

On the dais, the GOP's national chairman praised the current president's courage and conviction before introducing the candidates. The three governors would speak first, then Christy; Rob Marotta was last. Though Rustin had nicknamed the governors "Larry, Curly, and Moe," Corey found all three more depressing than amusing. The first, Governor Charles Blair of Illinois, while handsome in an antiseptic way, was so completely bereft of substance that in his eagerness he reminded Corey of an applicant for an entry-level job. George Costas of New York was so ungifted as a speaker that his attempts at fist-pounding emphasis seemed robotic instead of rousing. The best of them, Sam Larkin of Mississippi, was folksy, amusing, and completely unable to shed the whiff of corruption and rascality that, despite his professed devotion to the Lord, was accented by hand-tailored suits and a florid drinker's face.

"They should have called this event 'The Decline of the West,'" Corey murmured to Rustin, just before the Reverend Christy took the stage.

FROM THE MOMENT Christy began speaking, everything changed.

Corey had not seen him in person for fourteen years. Christy's hair was steel gray now, and his expensive suit could not conceal an ample paunch. But he had the same magnetic aura of caged energy, now placed in the service of a moral vision so absolute that he made the previous speakers seem like dwarfs.

"Shame on us," he began in a melancholy rumble. "Shame on our party, and our country."

The change in tone was so profound that Corey felt instantly alert. "My God," Rustin murmured, "what's the reverend going to do?"

Christy stood tall, his voice and bearing that of a leader who brooked no doubt. "Worse, we *know* better. We know the difference between the America many of us were born in, a land of faith and family, and the moral cesspool we live in now. And no amount of material wealth can obscure the speed of our decline.

"We have nightclubs where you can witness sex acts live, schools that tolerate drugs but abolish prayer, women who murder babies in a holocaust that dwarfs the work of Adolf Hitler, a government that opposes moral values rather than protecting them." Pausing, Christy swept the room with a commanding gaze. "And, worst of all, a cultural and economic elite that defines the quality of our existence in terms of the material, *not* the spiritual . . ."

"The people in this room," Rustin whispered with satisfaction, "are going to take *that* personally."

As Corey looked around, the audience seemed stunned. Despite himself, Corey began to feel a perverse admiration for the sheer nerve of this performance. "No government," Christy said in a disdainful voice, "has ever made a dead man rise. And no cut in the estate tax will save us from our spiritual death." Abruptly, Christy lowered his voice to a hush that, nonetheless, carried to the back of the room. "Our hope of redemption rests with God alone. And every moral challenge we face can be resolved in only one way: by following the laws ordained by God Almighty."

Letting this statement linger, Christy paused before asking, "So what in God's name is wrong with our society? Why is it imperative to preserve a national park but not a frozen embryo?"

As nervous chuckles broke the silence, Corey's table-mates—Marotta's funders—listened in stone-faced silence. Glancing about the room, Corey spotted Rob Marotta, his saturnine face watching Christy with an expression that showed nothing. "What kind of government," Christy asked, "saves one unborn baby through heroic measures, then casually kills another as though it were a rodent in a pantry? What kind of a society converts Adam and Eve into Adam and Steve?" A ripple of laughter rose before Christy finished with "And yet I'm sure that many here tonight are guilty of what I call moral relativism—that tired excuse: 'I have a relative who's gay.'"

There was another spurt of nervous laughter. But Corey did not smile—*this*, he thought, was where Christy's vision led: more division, more repression, more pressure on Rob Marotta to meet the harsh requirements of Christy's God. At the corner of his eye, Corey saw a young Republican senator he'd known for years, a thoroughly decent man, fretting with his napkin as his deepest fear consumed him: that his furtive homosexuality would come to light.

"Marriage," Christy thundered, "is not a cul-de-sac—a dead end whose only purpose is sexual pleasure. And if this party uses the deep moral concerns of Christians simply as a way of securing votes, then Christians will rise up and say, 'Quit treating us like a mistress and start respecting us as a wife. For hell hath no fury like all-too-patient Christians too often scorned.'"

The challenge was so startling that some in the audience responded with a spattering of oddly fearful applause. Rob Marotta, Corey noticed, cast a restive glance at his watch, like a man who wishes the evening to be over but dares not speak or move.

"Let's be honest," Christy said in a suddenly confiding tone. "There are those in the establishment of our party who have a secret disdain for Bible-believing Christians. They even hire advisers to teach them phrases like 'wonder-working power,' in the hope that if they speak to us in code, unbelievers will not notice." Christy leaned forward, speaking slowly and emphatically. "It is time for Christians to say clearly that we mean to make this the party of God, not the party of greed. And yes, that we want your children, and that *you* should want us to have them."

As Rustin emitted a low whistle, a rapt silence enveloped the audience. Looking at Marotta, Corey noted the utter stillness with which he awaited Christy's next pronouncement. But Christy's gaze had fixed not on Marotta, but on someone else. "Nor," he said in a cold, clear voice, "will Christians serve the ambitions of media magnates whose sole concern is lining their all-too-ample pockets." Pausing, Christy stared at Rohr, his voice suddenly filled with anger. "Such men should now be warned: we will turn off your programming, abandon your movie theaters, shun your music, boycott your businesses, and take back our children. And then your grip on our nation will end for good."

Narrow-eyed, Rohr stared back at Christy, ignoring the scrutiny of others. Leaning toward Corey, Rustin whispered, "Bad day for your boy Alex . . ."

"It is time," Christy repeated, "for *all* of us to choose. Only last year, your so-called leaders lost effective control of Congress because they ignored the prayers of conservative Christians. So please be warned.

"Days from now, the United States Senate will decide whether to give its blessing to stem-cell research. Some believe that this is a tempest in a petri dish. *It is not.* Every one of these embryos is a human being waiting to be born. It is not our province to *take* life—even if we propose to *save* life." Pausing, Christy said emphatically, "That power belongs to God alone. So to those who would be president, I say, Defeat this law, or step aside."

"Marotta," Rustin whispered to Corey, "had better

protect each embryo like it was his first-born child."

Rustin was right, Corey knew; Christy was laying down a marker for Rob Marotta. "Perhaps," Christy continued in a dubious tone, "one of the men you've heard from—or *will* hear from—is the leader Christians are praying for.

"If so, we are blessed. But if not, Christians *will* look elsewhere."

Tense, the audience awaited a pronouncement that, if made, could utterly transform the race. "There are those in our party," Christy told them, "who claim that for a minister to seek high office will only hurt our cause.

"To them I say, Rest easy. For if Jesse Jackson and Al Sharpton did not manage to kill American liberalism, conservatism has nothing to fear from *me* . . ."

As sudden laughter rose from the audience, Corey saw Rob Marotta allow himself a brief, ironic smile. "Perhaps," Christy suggested amiably, "those particular spiritual leaders did not quite match the nation's needs. Or perhaps, in these more perilous times, Americans at last are ready for a different servant of God."

This last phrase, to Christy's credit, was delivered with a certain humor. "For now," he concluded simply, "I implore you to help make our beloved country what God intended it to be."

Abruptly, Christy stopped, his head bowed as if in prayer.

For an instant there was silence. Then applause rose from Christy's listeners, slowly building—perhaps reflecting courtesy, perhaps fear, but perhaps, Corey suspected, a new respect. "Think he'd settle for vice president?" he dryly inquired of Rustin.

"Maybe." Still watching Christy, Rustin's eyes seemed brighter than before. "This much I know: if God wants you to be president, He'll tell the Reverend Christy to run first."

5

AT A LITTLE PAST ELEVEN THAT NIGHT, SENATOR Rob Marotta and his chief strategist, Magnus Price, met with Alex Rohr on the roof deck of the Hotel Washington. From the outset, Marotta felt on guard: as wary as he was of Rohr, that Price had urged this meeting made him warier still.

Their corner table had a panoramic view of the Washington Monument and the Lincoln and Jefferson Memorials; much closer, the White House was brightly etched against the dark night sky. "Place sure looks noble," Price drawled with a smile. "All that moonlit marble with no people to screw it up. If you're dumb enough, or drunk enough, you'd almost forget this place is the ultimate proof that Darwin was right—only the fittest, and the meanest, survive. To get to be a statesman, you first gotta be a prick."

"So what's Bob Christy?" Rohr asked sharply.

This was a sore point, Marotta understood. "A botched experiment," Price answered with a rueful tone. "Tonight was like watching Frankenstein escape. For thirty years I've busted my ass to bring Christians into the tent—including Christy—and now he's so delusional he thinks he owns the tent."

Price's laconic manner, Marotta knew, belied the man's frustration. In Price's grand design, he was the orchestrator of the Hydra, through which the various tentacles of the party—business, Christian conservatives, right-wing media, and advocacy groups from the gun lobby to the tax cutters—combined to dominate America's politics and culture. "The whole idea," Price continued, "is to make sure each stockholder in our enterprise helps get the others what they want. The rich folks and the Bible-thumpers don't gotta love each other—they just gotta help each other. Nobody's bigger than the whole.

"Problem with the Reverend Bob, Alex, is he's getting himself confused with God. And God don't go to meetings, or work through coalitions. Bob's God, to my lasting sorrow, just isn't a team player."

"So what are you going to do about him," Rohr cut in, "when the senator's running against this bastard in the primaries?"

"*If*," Price amended. "That's where Rob is gonna need all the help you can give him." Pausing, Price smiled across the table at Marotta. "I ran my own little poll after the last election. Rohr News persuaded ten percent of its viewers to change their vote and support the president. Despite his modesty, Alex here's a kind of genius. Maybe he'll treat you to what I call his 'theory of postmodernist media.'"

Rohr did not smile; to Marotta, who knew him only casually, Rohr gave off the chill of a man who disdained anyone whose success, as did Marotta's, required a measure of human warmth. Shrugging, Rohr told Marotta clinically, "The old model was that news is fact, and objectivity the ideal. Today's truth is that 'news,' like anything else we sell to the public, is a product.

"Our news product isn't some abstract notion of truth, or even reality. It's a story—consistent and repetitive, with a message that's emotionally fulfilling to the viewer." He flashed Marotta a smile that was no smile at all. "We mislead no one. Turn on Rohr News, and you're getting exactly what you want. I can help you feel better about this war, or fighting terrorists, and you don't have to think about them anymore. If we also use that power to promote our friends and advance our interests, so be it. News is a business, not a public service."

Looking directly at Marotta, Price cupped his Pepsi in both hands. "Fortunately for us all, Rob, Alex's interests and ours are aligned. Your interest is in becoming president." Price allowed himself a wispy smile. "Through Rohr News, millions of Americans will begin to *see* you as a president—principled, rooted in deep religious values, and Churchillian in your resolve to save America."

The sardonic undertone nettled Marotta; listening to these two pragmatists discuss his future, he felt less like a senator than a bottle of shampoo. Seeking to restore the balance, Marotta asked sardonically, "If I'm Winston Churchill, who do you get to be, Alex? Citizen Kane?"

"Kane wanted to be president," Rohr replied with imperious calm. "All I care about is an economic policy that rewards my enterprise, and a political system that respects my interests."

Price shot Marotta a cautionary glance. "Nothing wrong with that," Price said easily. "Alex helps because we believe as he does. And because he's in a position to help."

Nodding, Rohr gave Marotta the same cool smile. "News, as Magnus often tells me, is the software of his message machine."

Marotta glanced at Price. With his sloping belly, thin sandy hair, and mask of shrewd self-satisfaction, Price reminded Marotta of the archetypal sly southern lawyer of film and fiction, except that he was far more dangerous—including, whatever his exceptional gifts, to Marotta himself. "And the purpose of that machine," Price elaborated in an amiable tone, "is not to persuade our opponents, but to shrink their nuts to the size of raisins. That means pounding home the message that they're weasely and effete; godless; spineless and morally lax; beholden to deadbeats, gays, illegals, and, worst of all, liberals; pathetically cowed by Arab murderers; utterly unable to defend our country or our families; and, altogether, the losers in Darwin's lottery. I mean, who would want to be one of *them*?"

Rohr laughed softly. "Message," Price continued with a smile, "takes money, organization, *and* ideas. We've got them all: two hundred foundations and four hundred advocacy groups spending almost one billion dollars a year to advance the ideas we all believe in: lowering taxes, curbing lawsuits, fighting environmental extremists, ending affirmative action, and, critically, turning conservative lawyers into judges who'll control the American legal system for decades to come." Price smiled approvingly at Rohr. "Alex is helping us change the legal, political, and economic landscape of America."

"Christy," Marotta pointed out, "doesn't seem all that enamored with your vision."

Price sat back, taking in the nighttime panorama lit before them. "Christy," he said at length, "is my only mistake in an otherwise inspired notion—to persuade Christian voters to help underwrite our power by focusing on issues that don't cost the likes of Alex a fucking dime.

"Prayer in school—if we ever get it—is free. So's a ban on abortion. Alex doesn't run honeymoon cruises, so banning gay marriage won't dent his bottom line. But all of that means so much to these pious folks that it would ruin your day to deny them."

"There's also soccer moms," Marotta responded. "The suburban moderates—the ones who deserted us in droves in the last congressional elections. Strangely enough, they're still looking for a 'kinder, gentler' party than the one you have in mind."

"That's what black Republicans like Cortland Lane are for," Price replied. "You put them in the cabinet—not because black voters will love us, but because it makes white folks of good intentions *feel* so much better. And, once again, it's *free*.

"Though they're a problem, middle-of-the-roaders are still eclipsed by conservative Christians, especially in Republican primaries." Turning to Rohr, Price asked, "You know what the most accurate predictor of voting was in the last two presidential elections?"

Rohr shrugged. "Illiteracy?"

Chuckling, Price shook his head. "Religion. Two-thirds of regular church attendees voted for us. You're not gonna win elections if all you've got is atheists and agnostics. And *I*, to my lasting credit, figured that out in the 1970s.

"Thirty years ago, Alex, conservative Christians were like a seven-foot-tall basketball player with no experience—scary in their potential, but not a real factor in the game. They didn't even vote. But I could see all that potential—if I could persuade the party to reach out to them, we'd change the game entirely." Turning to Marotta now, he said, "Back in South Carolina when I was a kid, the rich folks got the votes of poor whites by pitting them against the blacks. But racism became less cool—blacks started voting, so establishment whites had to pick their spots and speak in racial code. But I . . ." Here Price paused, holding one finger in the air, "*I*, Magnus Price, figured out a whole new and more uplifting way to reach out to ordinary white folks—by signing up their God. Now Christian conservatives are over forty percent of the entire electorate. And *we're* still sitting in the catbird seat unless Christy fucks it up."

Rohr frowned. "How, exactly, can this clown accomplish *that*?"

"Because the whole design depends on keeping Christian conservatives and capitalists like you united. That's the beauty of Rob Marotta's candidacy—he shares your beliefs while being genuinely religious.

"But Christy sees a contradiction: entrepreneurs like you live off the 'debased popular culture' he rails against on television. That's why his speech tonight made me shiver." Price paused, his expression hard. "If Christy runs for president, it'll be mammon versus morality—our nightmare scenario. If Christy beats Rob in the primaries, he'll lose the general election—most voters still won't go for President Elmer Gantry. But even if Rob beats Christy, the party's gonna be divided . . ."

"I'll beat Christy," Marotta told him. "And with all due respect, I'd do that with or without the two of you."

"Today you would," Price shot back. "But suppose fucking Al Qaeda blows up Notre Dame stadium at halftime? *That* could unleash a craziness only God could fix. And God, as we know, speaks through the Reverend Christy—"

"So how do we keep him from running?" Rohr interrupted.

"By anointing Rob—endorsements, favorable polling, pledges from donors, the whole drumbeat of inevitability." Price placed a friendly hand on Marotta's shoulder. "*And* by reminding Christian conservatives that Rob's as committed to them as Christy is. That means fighting gay marriage, promoting prayer in school, and promising judges who know that 'our rights came from God Almighty.' Then we can float the message that the presidency isn't an entry-level job. Trust me, a lot of other evangelists will be glad to hop on board."

"Why?" Rohr asked.

"Think *they* want their chief competitor in the religion-for-profit game to become the president of the United States? They'll help spread our message: 'Bob's running to expand his mailing list,' or 'Bob's confusing himself with God,' or 'What does Bob know about dropping the hammer on fucking Iran?'

"We need Christians to believe that Christy's a self-serving egomaniac and that his candidacy is an embarrassment to the good religious people who just want to protect their families." Eyes fixed on Rohr, Price finished: "You can spread the word through Rohr News, talk radio, newspapers, and whatever else you own. After Christy's performance tonight, you oughta have the motivation. Do you?"

"If Rob wants me to." Rohr turned to Marotta. "All I want, Rob, is what Magnus tells me you believe in—a government that doesn't hamstring wealth creators."

Marotta understood immediately that this was a crucial moment: he was seated between two arrogant men who believed that they controlled his future, and who needed to know that he—like Christy—could not be controlled. "This is all very nice," he said with an edge in his voice, "and I'd be very grateful if you'd support me. But you're forgetting a couple of details. The first is that I'm where I am for a reason, and I got here without you. If our beliefs coincide, fine. But I'm going to trust my instincts and run my own campaign." Pausing, he looked from Rohr to Price, underscoring his words. "The second detail is all the things you don't control. Starting with stem cells."

"True enough," Price responded. "Seems like they're Bob's excuse for running."

Marotta nodded. "If we lose that stem-cell vote, he runs."

"If *you* lose, Rob—you're the majority leader." Turning to Rohr, Price asked, "Suppose we find some scientists to say the whole stem-cell thing is bogus. Think you can give them airtime?"

"Of course," Rohr answered with a trace of impatience. "But if you'll forgive my amateur opinion, you're overlooking the biggest problem of all."

"I haven't forgotten," Marotta said softly. "Corey Grace."

Nodding, Rohr repeated with equal softness, "Corey Grace."

"He's surely a problem for *you*, Alex—the phrase 'Hook-Up' comes to mind." Marotta's voice turned cool again. "So let me spell it out for you. In effect, Grace is a creature of Christy. If Christy enters, siphoning off Christian votes, that's Grace's invitation to run—"

"Not if *I* can help it," Rohr interrupted harshly. "I don't want that careless sonofabitch anywhere near the White House. No one I know wants him."

"Which," Marotta answered dryly, "absolutely breaks his heart. Corey lacks what you might call the normal incentives. Including any discernible interest in how you feel about him."

Rohr fixed the senator with a hard stare. "Isn't there anything you can give him?"

"Nothing I've been able to identify."

"It's better not to even try," Price interjected. "Why give our hero ideas?"

"He already has them," Marotta said flatly. "I was watching him during Christy's speech, and he looked absolutely chipper. Whenever he looks like that, it's a lousy day for me. In his heart of hearts, Corey is certain that he should be president of the United States, and he knows that his only chance depends on the Reverend Christy."

Rohr stared at his drink. "Let us pray," he said in a tone of disgust.

"Oh," Price answered with a smile, "I think we can do better than *that*."

6

THE DAY AFTER CHRISTY'S SPEECH, COREY MADE A point of watching his daily television show.

Perched in front of the television in Corey's office, Corey and Jack Walters ate Reuben sandwiches. Head bowed, Christy stood alone on a soundstage. "Thank you, Lord," he intoned, "for causing Hurricane Sarah to veer away from our beloved state of Virginia . . ."

"Problem is," Jack remarked, "it's about to hit Long Island. Seems like Christy's pull with the Almighty is strictly regional."

Corey shrugged. "Hitting Long Island is part of God's plan."

On the screen, Christy raised his head, his voice thick with emotion. "I can feel the presence of God today, hear the stirrings of His people. In the words of John F. Kennedy, 'Here on earth God's work must truly be our own.'"

"God's one thing," Jack opined, "but channeling JFK is shameless."

Intently watching the screen, Corey held up his hand to ask for silence. "I'm facing a great decision," Christy told his audience. "Should I run for president, or should I resist the siren song of temporal power? Please, I remind you, tell your Senate to spurn the abomination that is stem-cell research. Most of all, keep our country in your prayers."

Jack gave the screen a blank, puzzled look—though his appearance was guileless, Jack had seen two decades of

Senate infighting and was used to gauging politicians thoroughly grounded in this world. "This guy really *is* from some other planet. Didn't you tell me you'd once met him?"

For a moment, Corey was silent. "Our paths crossed," he amended. "We never actually met."

He said this dismissively, as though the memory were of little moment. But this was far from true—for reasons too personal, and too painful, ever to reveal to Jack. When Jack turned back to watch Christy, Corey's gaze, inevitably, lit on the photograph of his brother, Clay.

Throughout the rest of the program, Corey was silent. When it was over, he left to meet the adviser he valued most.

"I'm THINKING ABOUT running for president," Corey said bluntly. "And I still don't get Bob Christy. Never have."

Standing at the helm of his powerboat, Cortland Lane steered them at a leisurely pace down the brown-blue waters of the Potomac. Even here, Corey thought, Lane's close-cropped steel-gray hair made him look more like a general than a recreational boater. But at sixty-four, Lane was now retired: four years before, while he was secretary of state, his quiet but persistent reservations about the president's Middle East policy had led to his resignation. Yet Lane was still so widely admired that some in the party, and many around the country, had hoped aloud that he would run for president.

Instead, Lane had withdrawn from public life to pursue his lifelong interest in religion at Harvard Divinity School. Over the years, Senator Grace had sought Lane's council, first on military matters, then on foreign policy, until the general who'd once daunted Corey had become a friend.

But the purpose of this meeting was unique: to seek Lane's thoughts on the intersection of politics with religion—a subject, Corey readily conceded, to which he had never given enough thought.

Scanning the water, Lane inquired, "What precisely don't you 'get'?"

"His whole worldview." Corey took a sip from a bottle of mineral water. "To me, Christy's a cousin of Alex Rohr, a man who seeks power by narrowing the American mind. And he's succeeded to the point where you damn near can't admit you believe in Darwin and hope to *win* our party's nomination.

"As far as I can tell, he's never read *On the Origin of Species*. To him, the Flintstones are a documentary—people living with dinosaurs. I find that incredible."

In profile, Lane's mouth showed the trace of a smile. "A word of caution, Senator. First of all, more Americans believe in the Virgin Birth than the theory of evolution. Second, Christy is nothing new: evangelists have been in and out of politics for the last two hundred years, mostly to advance progressive causes like abolition and women's suffrage."

"*And* the temperance movement," Corey pointed out. "In that inspiring episode, they set out to make us sober and wound up giving us Al Capone."

"True enough," Lane conceded. "That was one of the things that helped drive them to the political sidelines. But the biggest factor was the Scopes monkey trial, where the great fundamentalist William Jennings Bryan prosecuted a high school biology teacher in Tennessee for implying that monkeys were, in fact, our ancestors."

"When I saw the movie about Scopes in high school," Corey said, "I thought it was a comedy. But now they're running the government—albeit with the help of that southern-fried Machiavelli Magnus Price."

Steering to avoid a water-skier, Lane was quiet for a time. "Magnus," he said at length, "may think he's Moses. But it all began with the sixties, and a chain of social shocks that, in Christy's words, 'caused the believers to awaken from their trance'—abortion, drugs, promiscuity, flag burning, gay teachers, and barring prayer in school. To Christy, these issues symbolized the moral and intellectual arrogance of a self-selected liberal elite toward ordinary Americans. I'd think a boy from Ohio would grasp *that* well enough."

"I do," Corey said softly. "I'm my parents' son, after all."

Nodding, Lane asked, "They still don't know about your brother, do they?"

"No." Corey paused. "Last night I had a flashback in the middle of a thousand donors, most of whom can't stand me. Suddenly, I just looked at Christy and thought, You helped kill my brother, you sanctimonious bastard."

Lane stared straight ahead. "Not your parents?"

"Them, too. My mother's still convinced that Christy and the Bible have all the answers." Voice rising in frustration, Corey added harshly, "My God, Cortland, the Old Testament God is a psychotic monster. Now even Jesus—if you believe people like Christy—is coming back as an avenging angel to slaughter all the bad people. What am I supposed to do with *that*?"

"Detach yourself." One hand on the wheel, Lane faced him. "Years ago, you learned to perceive Christy as a messenger of hate. But to his followers, he's only trying to defend their families and their country against a government bent on destroying the moral fabric of our society. And it's pretty hard to argue that AIDS, familial breakup, and sleazy popular entertainment are changes for the better."

"Who thinks *that*?"

"So what are you going to do about it? At least Bob Christy has an answer."

"Yeah," Corey replied. "The Apocalypse."

"That's the point. In Christy's mind, he's a patriot, trying to save the America of God's design before we—quite literally—commit suicide. Tell me this: do *you* think we're on the brink of a national decline?"

"Yes."

"So do I. And so does Christy. I'd say most religious conservatives, just as we do, fear for our society in the here and now. For example, wouldn't *you* feel better if there were fewer divorces?"

The question, Corey suspected, carried a trace of the personal: Lane's wife's battle with depression, he had confided, had come to shadow his own marriage. "Depends on the marriage," Corey answered. "Some days I'd just feel better if *I* weren't divorced."

Lane turned to him. "When *was* the last time you heard from Kara?"

"Two months ago—in a postcard. I was so pathetically grateful I wrote her a four-page letter, the kind of newsy thing that you'd put in a fucking Christmas card. But then it's hard to communicate with a daughter who's grown up half a world away."

Looking to their right, Lane studied the Pentagon, his old workplace. "Open to trying again?" he asked. "Marriage, I mean."

"In theory. There are good reasons why I haven't."

"In that case, I give you credit for placing principle above ambition. As I'm sure Rustin has told you, we haven't elected a single man as president for a century and a half or so. As for an avowed agnostic, never."

Corey cocked his head. "What makes you think I am one?"

"Agnostic? Or avowed?"

Pondering this, Corey thought of his friend Joe Fitts, explaining his unbelief over a glass of Scotch. "I've never been sure."

"You'll need a better answer if you decide to run for president. Within our party, the religious are as essential as the money people."

"Oh, I know," Corey said. "I've come up with a slogan for Marotta's campaign: 'Out of Rohr's wallet and into *your* bedroom.' Or, for that matter, your freezer. That's why we've got this stem-cell debate—Marotta is being forced to love frozen embryos as much as Christy does."

Briefly, Lane laughed. "What *are* you going to do about that one?"

Unbidden, Corey thought about Lexie Hart. "It's tricky."

"No doubt." Lane faced him now, his expression troubled. "For your own sake, Corey, you need to find a way to talk to Christy's people. *And* to people like me, who believe deeply in God—though perhaps a different one—and believe that mankind is lost without a spiritual dimension.

"You *have* one, I know. But it would help you to acknowledge, if only to yourself, that most of Christy's followers are as sincere and idealistic as Magnus Price is cynical and calculating. That's why they often find it hard to compromise. And putting aside frozen embryos, you and I both know that a fetus is the beginning of a life."

Corey felt himself smile. "Funny, I made that point just yesterday. Unfortunately, to a woman who's also a liberal. Bad timing."

Lane's eyes lit with interest. "Lexie Hart? I saw she was making the rounds. Tell me, is she as gorgeous as she looks on-screen?"

"At least. But what struck me is how smart she is. And complicated, I think."

"The best ones often are, in my experience."

This tacit reference to his wife's depression triggered another thought. "Tell me why," Corey ventured, "we always talk about *me* when the presidency comes up."

Lane's smile, Corey thought, was faintly melancholy. "Because nothing else makes sense."

"You might have been president, Cortland. You still could be."

Lane slowly shook his head. "The time for me has passed," he answered. "And probably never was. I just hope that yours will come."

DRIVING BACK TO his office, Corey found he had much to ponder: the lingering toxin of racism in politics, the ways in which politicians invoked, or abused, religion. And then, as Corey knew they would, his thoughts—and his memories—fixed on his dead brother.

7

IN THE MONTHS AFTER HE HAD LEFT THE AIR FORCE to pursue a Senate race, Corey came to accept that, however hard he tried to reach his six-year-old daughter, his interactions with Kara were far less warm than those with his teenaged brother, Clay.

Perhaps the ever-observant Kara had learned to treat him with reserve by watching her parents' marriage. At the urging of his political patrons, Corey and Janice had returned to Lake City—as one adviser put it, "to the place and people who made you who you are." But whereas Corey—newly chastened by Joe Fitts's death and the captivity that followed—tried to view the town and its citizens with a more tolerant eye, Janice saw it with a merciless clarity, a place in which the symmetrical rows of bungalows symbolized a stifling conformity of thought and action made worse by the well-meaning but constant attention of ten thousand fellow citizens. "It's like an air force base for civilians," Janice said tartly. "I'm still in temporary housing, and I'm still the general's daughter."

Nor did she mesh well with Corey's family. Not that this would have been easy: Hank Grace was still the burly and suspicious man who drank too much and spoke too little; Nettie still reacted to her husband as warily as she did to life outside the narrow confines of the known. But, to Corey, Clay was a surprise.

Twelve years younger, Clay owed his existence to a failure of birth control, and seemed to view his place in the world as equally tenuous. To Corey's amazement, Clay's bedroom was a virtual shrine to his older brother, jammed with Corey's high school trophies, pictures of Corey in uniform, news clippings of his return. When Corey had first seen this, he had turned to Clay with an ironic comment on his lips, then stifled it—in his brother's large blue eyes, he saw a boy far too sensitive for the tough humor of a cardboard hero.

At sixteen, Clay was suspended between gangly and sinewy and, Corey suspected, between identities. Clay seemed to have tackled every high school enterprise Corey had mastered—athletics, dramatics, and student office—with great determination, but much less success. Still, in Corey's estimate, becoming his avatar gave Clay a serviceable interim identity, though it could not insulate his brother against the harsh judgments of their father. "The boy tries," Hank Grace told Corey with mild disdain. "But Clay will never be like you."

"*I* wasn't me," Corey said, "until my plane ran out of fuel and I got myself captured by the Iraqis. I just hope Clay doesn't have to kill someone before you learn to love him."

That Corey was referring to Joe Fitts was something Hank would never know. Perceiving that, in a fundamental sense, both Clay and he had always lacked a father, Corey set out to be, at least, a good brother. Despite Corey's busy schedule, he and Clay played catch and shot baskets together, those male rituals that do not require talk to communicate caring. "Time for us to catch up," Corey said laconically. "When *I* was seventeen, you were five, and a football would have knocked you over."

Clay soaked up this attention. His bright smile came more often in Corey's presence, and his own sly humor began emerging. "It's like eating with cavemen," Clay said of dinner hour with their parents. "Only without the dialogue."

But with his peers, especially girls, Clay himself seemed at a loss for words. Entering his senior year, he was similar to Corey only in the fierceness of his newly declared ambition to enter the Air Force Academy. "It's a hard life," Corey pointed out. "Even harder on families."

"I want to fly," Clay answered simply. "Like you did."

That his tone made it sound less like a passion than an escape struck a chord in Corey—though whether Clay was escaping his parents or himself, his older brother could not tell.

HIS MOTHER HAD wanted Clay to attend Carl Cash University.

"What the hell is that?" Corey had inquired of Clay. "A school for Bible-thumpers or snake handlers?"

"Both," Clay snorted. "It's in South Carolina, and they believe that God created the world in a week. But even better is what they don't believe in: drinking, smoking, dancing, or interracial dating."

"What about interracial lynchings?" Corey asked.

But religion, Corey swiftly learned, was no laughing matter—either in his parents' home or, increasingly, in his travels around the state.

As a speaker, Corey was natural and engaging, able to slide by on patriotic boilerplate while he boned up on the issues and built relationships with the party faithful. Despite his success, he wondered at his motives. Would his ascension to the Senate, if it occurred, be a fluke—an ironic and ultimately empty reward for having ignored Joe Fitts's plea—or would it serve some higher purpose? One night, fielding questions at a Kiwanis meeting in Chillicothe, Corey encountered a woman quite certain of what that purpose should be. "To serve God," the woman told him flatly.

Eyeing those around her, Corey felt more perplexed than his audience appeared. "There are many ways to serve God," he parried politely. "In what way do you mean?"

"God's way," the woman said, with a touch of impatience. "To run our government according to a literal interpretation of the Bible. It's like the Reverend Christy says—if it's good enough for God, it's good enough for the United States of America. You were saved for a reason, Mr. Grace—to save America from sin."

"Did I get by with her?" Corey asked Hollis Spencer as they drove away.

His new campaign manager slumped back in the passenger seat, gazing upward as though communing with a deity he could only dimly see. The silence grew; at first, Corey took this to be the musings of a veteran political strategist who had taken Corey on as a favor to the party and was still unsure of what lay behind his eminently salable surface.

"Who knows," Hollis said at last. "But I'm seeing more people like this woman, who only care about right-to-life, prayer in school, banning sex education, teaching creationism instead of evolution, and, for some weird reason, the right to bear arms. Turns out Jesus was a gun nut." When Hollis turned to Corey, his face was grim. "I'm beginning to think you'll draw a primary opponent—a Christian conservative who speaks this woman's language. You don't meet the Reverend Bob Christy's litmus test."

"Who the hell," Corey inquired in exasperation, "is Bob Christy?"

Hollis gave him a pitying smile. "Ask your mother, Corey. She'll know."

*

"THE REVEREND CHRISTY," Corey's mother informed him after the prayer with which she now began each meal, "saved my life."

Bob Christy, it transpired, had a daily television show that emphasized personal stories of redemption inspired by belief in an inerrant God. And as crabbed as Corey found his mother's worldview, he noted that she now dealt with the life fate had given her a good bit more serenely.

"The Reverend Christy," Corey contented himself with saying, "may want to save the state of Ohio from me."

"Then you should ask yourself why," his mother responded primly.

Janice silently stared into the middle distance, as if she had discovered herself in an insane asylum that made her dreary job in the Lake City Library seem like a work-release program. Hoping to please his wife, Corey took Kara to a nearby park after dinner, first reminding Janice that life in the nation's capital would prove far more enriching. "With you running back to Ohio every weekend?" Janice asked. "What about pacifying the Reverend Christy and his followers? You only get to stay in Washington if the home folks send you back."

It was true, Corey conceded to himself as he and Clay, who had come along, pushed the subdued Kara on a swing until Clay's failed attempts to "catch" her elicited peals of laughter. "You're a better dad than I am," Corey told him dryly. "If you ever learn to make your bed, you'll make some lucky woman absolutely ecstatic."

"Can't I be like you," Clay asked, "and make a few unlucky girls ecstatic first?"

Corey put his arm around his brother. "All in due time," he said in his most avuncular manner. "First you have to call them."

But Clay, as Corey remarked to Janice, seemed to be long on theory. And the night before Clay's first date, a tragedy occurred, one so traumatic that the cancellation of the dance was as inevitable as it was trivial: the murder of Clay's favorite teacher, Vincent Morelli, by one of Clay's own classmates.

IT HAD HAPPENED after dark. Johnny Wall, a burly football player, told the police that Mr. Morelli had lured him to the wooded recesses of Taylor Park with promises of marijuana, and then solicited oral sex. The fatal beating, Johnny insisted, was fueled by shock and fear, and only after Morelli had touched the crotch of his blue jeans. But the police found no marijuana. Instead, their search yielded a discarded wad of twenty-dollar bills; the autopsy revealed traces of semen in the teacher's mouth and throat. The only rational conclusion, Corey suggested over dinner the following evening, was a transaction between buyer and seller that had spiraled into an incendiary self-disgust.

"What does it matter?" Hank Grace bit off each word. "He chose the wrong kid and got himself killed. Good riddance."

Clay stared at the table, his jaw clenched tight. "Are you saying Morelli deserved to be murdered?" Corey asked their father.

"I'm saying he took his chances, and that it's better this fairy's dead than teaching in our school. But now, they're giving him a funeral at the Catholic church like he's some kind of martyr."

Janice studied Corey's father as if he were a specimen on a slide, while his mother clasped her hands in an attitude of prayer. "Not a martyr," Corey responded evenly. "Just dead."

Hank Grace shook his head. Eyes on the table, Clay murmured, "I'm going to Mr. Morelli's funeral."

"Clayton," his mother said in quiet reproof, "you don't want to be seen as approving of such a thing. Homosexuality is a sin."

"So's murder." Clay's voice trembled faintly. "I don't like fairies, either. But I don't think you can judge a good man by the worst thing he ever did."

This simple statement induced a merciful silence. Across the table, Corey regarded Clay with new respect.

But, for the Grace family, this was not the end of the matter. Two weeks later, Corey's new primary opponent appeared at a rally in Taylor Park organized to support Johnny Wall. Far more surprising—and, to Nettie Grace, gratifying—was the identity of the principal speaker: the Reverend Bob Christy himself.

BORDERED BY THE verdant woods that had proven lethal to Vincent Morelli, the grassy expanse of Taylor Park encircled a filigreed white gazebo, a self-conscious but charming piece of Americana that always featured a local band on the Fourth of July, and around which several hundred people had now clustered to hear from the Reverend Christy.

Standing with his parents and brother, Corey appraised the crowd. The younger, more caustic Corey might have seen sheer meanness beneath the Rockwellian veneer, smug citizens drawn by mindless fervor to hear a charlatan dispense pieties that, to the unthinking, might somehow pass for thought. But now the more reflective man saw a tapestry of different needs and motives. Many who had gathered, like his mother, surely felt that Bob Christy had made their lives more hopeful, summoning a higher purpose from the random or mundane. Others—like his senior-prom date, Kathy Wilkes, glancing sideways at Corey as she held her newborn son—were no doubt moved by an emotion their teenaged selves would never have imagined: the countless ways adults learn fear by having their own children. Still others, Corey knew, were drawn by the murder itself, some by anger or hatred. But many more had come out of loyalty to Johnny Wall and his parents, or out of sheer bewilderment at what had befallen him, or might next befall someone they loved.

Last were the foot soldiers of the Christian Commitment—the nationwide group newly formed by Bob Christy to fuse political action with his brand of Christianity, and who now formed a base of support for Corey's opponent in the primary election. Their placards momentarily discarded, they knelt in a circle, praying. Glancing toward his mother, Corey saw her regard them with an expression close to longing: but for the fissures within her family, Nettie would have joined them.

Clay, too, was observing Christy's followers. "What did you ever do to *them*?" he asked.

"Not be one of them," Corey answered. "Seems that's all it takes."

THE SPEAKERS WHO preceded Christy were a disparate lot: Johnny Wall's father, so mortified that he drew the audience closer; then Johnny's lawyer, whose attempted sound bites were marred by the odd malapropism; then Corey's primary opponent, George Engler, a real-estate agent from southern Ohio with a Chamber of Commerce assurance that, Corey judged, would translate best in small groups of the like-minded. But Engler seized the chance to associate himself with the Reverend Christy through a florid introduction that somehow glorified them both. "I am truly humbled," Engler concluded, "to introduce a man as central to my family as he is to the moral life of America—a man whose mission it is to bring *all* families closer to our God until we become, in his own eloquent words, 'a nation with the soul of a church.' "

The Reverend Christy, Corey perceived at once, was a natural.

Corey had watched him briefly on television: humorous, affable, and yet imbued with a certainty that could infuse his tone with steel, Christy had seemed so three-dimensional that he almost popped through the screen. In person, his tall, bulky form prowled the gazebo with a caged energy and yet surprising grace, his resonant voice an instrument with as many notes as the man had moods—passion, scorn, tenderness, love, and longing for transcendence. Christy could recite the list of ingredients on a cereal box, Corey judged, and move most listeners to rapture—his own mother's eyes had taken on a sheen of wonder. But most impressive to Corey was that Bob Christy seemed to mean every word, including those calculated to short-circuit Corey's career in politics.

"There are those," Christy informed the audience, "who believe that Christian principles have no place in our government—"

"No!" one of his followers called out.

Smiling, Christy held up a hand. "Many are good people who sincerely feel that God's kingdom resides in the air, or in a church, or in our homes—but that our *schools,* or our *Congress,* are not the Lord's domain. But too many others, by mere silence, lend aid and comfort to this misguided mode of thought.

"I'm not here for political reasons. I'm here with all of you to stand up for Johnny Wall and, through Johnny, for all young men endangered by predators—even the very teachers to whom we entrust their minds—who would enlist them in a lifestyle that steals their souls and takes their lives."

"Sound attractive?" Corey murmured to Clay. But although their father was scowling with the displeasure he felt at being forced to suffer anyone's high-flown sentiments, Nettie Grace was nodding, a reflex of which she seemed unconscious.

Microphone in hand, the Reverend Christy paused to survey his audience, many drawing closer, a few casually sprawling on blankets. "What moral leader," Christy demanded to know, "can remain mute in the face of such a scourge? And yet George Engler's opponent in the Republican primary chooses silence, even when this terrible perversion comes to his very doorstep."

"*Coward,*" someone else called out.

The Reverend Christy held up a meaty hand. "Corey Grace," he remonstrated, "is a genuine American hero. Anyone who loves our country owes this man our heartfelt thanks. But it would be morally wrong to thank him with our votes.

"We invited Captain Grace to speak here today. He declined, saying through a 'spokesman' that he did not want to 'politicize an ongoing legal matter.'" Christy paused, letting his verbal quotation marks linger for an artful beat. "But we are not asking him to take sides in a 'legal matter,' but to speak out against a sin—"

"*Amen,*" someone shouted.

As a few people around them turned to glance at Corey, Nettie Grace began staring at the ground. "I'm told," the Reverend Christy called out, "that Corey Grace is with us today. So I say to him, Corey, my friend, come home—not just to Lake City, but to God."

Were it not for the scrutiny of others, Corey would have laughed aloud—the man was that good. "Because *all* of us here," Christy went on, "are *all* God's children. And that is why we cannot allow *our* children to be lured from the natural order ordained by the Almighty."

Briefly, Christy bowed his head. "A man died in this park," he said in a tone that combined sadness with admonition. "Some now call it a hate crime. But what caused this tragic act was a young man's revulsion for a crime against God. As we know from the first chapter of Romans, an entire city was destroyed because of it, and the sin of homosexuality named for what it is: an abomination." Eyes closed, Christy raised his head, words hovering above the silent crowd as he concluded in a hushed but resonant voice. "I pray for all those who have chosen the gay lifestyle to feel shame. For to embrace homosexuality is to embrace death—the death of our children, and of our culture."

Turning to his mother, Corey saw tears trickling down her face, then noticed that Clay was watching her. "I need to get out of here," Clay said with quiet vehemence. "Not just this place—this life."

THE NEXT DAY Corey called General Cortland Lane and, after an awkward beginning, turned to Clay's candidacy for admission to the U.S. Air Force Academy.

"He's a legitimate candidate," Corey assured the general. "I've asked around. Clay's already passed the qualifying test and done well in his interviews. But there are only three picks in our district, and the Academy ranks Clay fourth."

In the silence that followed, Corey imagined General Lane weighing the justice of such a request. "He's a good kid," Corey insisted. "If he's admitted, I know he'll never let the air force down."

"Let me see what I can do," Lane said at last. "Tell me,

Captain, how are *you* getting along? All right, I hope."

"More or less," Corey answered. "Having a purpose helps."

The day after Corey defeated George Engler in the primary—albeit by a narrower margin than Hollis Spencer would have liked—Clay was appointed to the Academy. "Did *you* have anything to do with this?" Clay asked his older brother.

"Not a thing," Corey answered with a smile. "I'm a civilian now, remember?"

TWO NIGHTS BEFORE Clay left for the Academy in June, Corey took him out for dinner at one of Cleveland's plusher restaurants. When Corey ordered Scotch for both of them, no one seemed to mind.

Cautiously sipping his drink, Clay asked, "So what will the summer be like?"

Warm with the glow of Scotch and brotherly celebration, Corey sat back, pondering how to explain what, to Clay, might seem like the rites of some aboriginal tribe. "It's part ritual," he began, "and part indoctrination. One purpose is an exorcism of ego, meant to grind down the hot shots who enter the Academy.

"The abuse is mostly run by upperclassmen—grueling exercise, cut-throat sports, and endless harassment designed to run you ragged while they scream at you from dawn till dark. At five A.M. it starts all over again when they roust you out in a zombie state for a brisk four-mile run. And so begins another day, until the days begin to blur." Watching his brother's face, Corey decided that it was time to temper this narrative. "The thing to remember is you're not alone. Everyone's miserable—after the first week, almost everyone wants to pack it in.

"But no one does. For one thing, no one wants to face

the folks at home." Reaching across the table, Corey patted his brother's arm. "The secret to survival, pal, is remembering that it's a game. Some of the upperclassmen are pricks, it's true—it's open season for low-grade sadists. But even they serve the cardinal purpose of the game: to make you accept the discipline men need to survive in war, and to bond you with your classmates irreversibly. Some of the guys in my class will be friends until I die."

For a long time Clay gazed at his drink. "I guess I'm a little afraid," he said at last.

"You don't need to be," Corey assured him comfortably. "All you're going to be up against is other guys like you."

Precious months later, Corey learned to his sorrow that this was not quite true.

8

THE DAY BEFORE THE SENATE HELD ITS DEBATE ON stem-cell research, Senator Rob Marotta paid a rare visit to Corey's office. With a smile so strained that Corey found it painful, Marotta spread his hands in a gesture of resignation. "This is about the stem-cell issue, of course. I need your vote here, Corey."

Corey felt a certain sympathy; he knew too well how much Marotta disliked asking, and that Marotta resented what he saw as Corey's all too easy rise to prominence. In Marotta's mind, *he* was the one who had tackled the hard jobs—doing favors without end, speaking at their colleagues' fund-raisers, mastering the rules and culture of the Senate—while Corey saw himself as above such striving. That was the crux of their estrangement: to Marotta, Corey was not serious about the world as Marotta defined it; to Corey, Marotta was serious about everything but what mattered most—a cause to match his talent and ambition. And so they were fated to be antagonists. In Corey's gloomy appraisal, it was quite possible, in the end, that one might do great damage to the other.

"Are you sure?" Corey asked.

Marotta studied Corey closely. "The vote can go either way," he conceded. "You're hardly the sole determinant, but three or four other senators are watching to see what you do. As is the president."

Corey shrugged. "Then I'd better be sure the president's right."

Normally, Marotta's somewhat saturnine appearance was relieved by a boyishness appropriate to his age—the same as Corey's—and an ability to conceal his emotions with an air of composure and calm. But the sour smile at one corner of his mouth suggested that he found Corey's answer arrogant and disingenuous. "What's 'right,' here, Corey? No one knows for sure that fetal-stem-cell research isn't a total pipe dream. Why not wait for methods that don't compromise how we value human life?"

"Because people are suffering now. Ever known anyone with Alzheimer's?"

Marotta hesitated. "Maybe. We're starting to think Mary Rose's mother may be in the early stages."

"Wouldn't you like to help her?"

"Based on what? Guesswork? We're Catholic, and for us the sanctity of life is nonnegotiable." With a self-deprecating smile, Marotta added, "That's why we've got five kids, aged seventeen to three."

Corey returned his smile. "And here I'd thought you'd flunked Bob Christy's favorite program: abstinence-only sex education."

The mention of Christy, however light, banished all good humor from Marotta's face. "Politically speaking, that brings us to the crux of things. Christy's made this vote about himself."

"He's hardly unique. Ask the president, and it's about *him*. I'm sure you believe that *I* think it's all about me. Why isn't it about some infant with a spinal disease?"

"If Christy runs," Marotta said flatly, "he splits the party, and maybe helps elect a Democrat. That can't be what you want."

Corey laughed. "Hardly. It's been at least six years since I saw the slightest sign that the Democrats are fit to govern anything."

"So why give Christy an excuse to help them out?"

Leaning on his elbows, Corey propped his chin on steepled fingers, gazing at his rival intently. "There's something off about this conversation, Rob. We've managed to reduce a question of human suffering to the parochial political problem of how to pacify an evangelist who's blackmailing us on television."

"*That*," Marotta snapped, "involves a whole lot more than stem cells. This is still your party, Corey—the president is our party's leader, and I'm its leader in the Senate. If you divide our party, you're at risk of becoming a very sorry man."

At this not so subtle threat, Corey felt the anger rise within him. "With respect," he said softly, "that's spoken like a man who's never learned what 'sorry' means."

Marotta considered him. "So why don't you explain it to me."

"I'll never have time enough, Rob. Just accept that it involves living with myself. I'm deciding this one on the merits."

OF COURSE, IT was not that simple: within the hour, the president of the United States called. Corey made no commitment; hanging up, he pondered the risk of deepening the president's antipathy. As Marotta had implied, Corey could expect to be in politics long after the president was gone, but the incumbent retained considerable power to ensure that the next president would not be Corey Grace.

A familiar voice from the television distracted him: in the last few days, Jack Walters had made a habit of watching Bob Christy's weekday show. "We are monitoring the Senate closely," Christy assured his followers, "to determine whether Senator Marotta and his fellow Republicans will defeat this ungodly tampering with life."

"Ever wonder," Jack asked, "why *Christy* hasn't lobbied you?"

Corey cocked his head in inquiry. "What makes you think that Christy wants me to vote against?"

As Corey watched the television, Eve Stansky walked in. "Lexie Hart called. She's wondering whether she should hold dinner open after tomorrow's vote."

Surprised, Corey laughed. "Tell her to watch the debate. She'll find out when I do."

WHEN COREY ARRIVED on the Senate floor, the gallery was packed, and Lexie Hart sat in the front row.

Corey looked up until she saw him. Even at this distance, he could read her anxiety and doubt.

Senator Rob Marotta opened the debate. "A frozen embryo," Marotta argued forcefully, "is the moral equivalent of a fetus, summoned into being so that a married couple can fulfill their sacred purpose of bringing life into their world. But now, the proponents of this science project propose to *create* life to *destroy* life."

Pausing, Marotta scanned his colleagues' faces. "There are over four hundred thousand frozen embryos. Unleashing scientific experimentation on so many potential lives is the moral equivalent of mass murder—no different than abortion on demand.

"There are always 'good reasons,'" Marotta continued with disdain, "to destroy a human fetus, and now there are other 'good reasons' to destroy a human embryo. But there will never be a reason good enough to allow us to play God."

Watching Marotta, Corey judged that his delivery, unusual in its fervor, was intended to match Christy's passion. "And where does it end?" Marotta asked. "Do we begin to tinker with the cells—or even the genetic makeup—of babies? Do we create 'research infants' to satisfy whatever experiment we dream up? Do we begin to wonder if human cloning is truly so unthinkable?" Abruptly, Marotta's voice rose. "Are we edging closer to the day when our moral preceptor is not God, the Father of us all, but Josef Mengele, the father of Nazi experimentation in the laboratory that was Auschwitz?"

Glancing up, Corey saw Lexie Hart's expression, a stoic mask. "Life is precious," Marotta said with sudden quiet. "We forget that at our peril."

COREY HAD WRITTEN the speech himself. When his turn came, after an hour of debate, he felt the close attention of the other undecided senators—Lynn Whiteside and Timothy Cole of Maine, Brian Kell of Rhode Island, and, to his surprise, Chris Lear of Nebraska.

"In the last few years," Corey began, "we have seen a development almost as disturbing as the horrors cited by Senator Marotta: the politicization of science, in which decisions that affect the health and welfare of Americans are based on bogus data and political calculation.

"We've heard that global warming doesn't exist. We've seen appointees to scientific agencies whose ignorance is matched only by their partisan zeal. We've even meddled in the familial tragedy of a literally brain-dead woman. And, in the end, all of this is as inhumane as it is pointless."

A few rows ahead, Marotta turned to watch him. But Corey was more conscious of the other Ohioans who had stood at this desk and whose names were carved inside: Warren Harding, who became president because he was so pliable; Robert Taft, perhaps worthy of becoming president but too principled to be another Harding. Corey also knew—and this both tempted and troubled him—that what he was about to say could help make, or unmake, the *next* president. "Politics," Corey said, "can no more block legitimate scientific progress than the anti-scientists of the Renaissance could stop Galileo from changing our conception of the universe. We cannot halt the advance of human knowledge—we can only damage human beings."

After pausing, Corey spoke quietly to his colleagues, as though unmindful of the galleries. "With due respect to Senator Marotta, I believe that most Americans can distinguish living fetuses from frozen embryos that would otherwise be discarded. Just as I believe that we, as senators, know that conducting Nazi experiments is different from relieving human suffering."

At once, Rob Marotta was on his feet. "Senator Grace," he asked sharply, "may I ask a question?"

Though unusual, this intervention was no surprise to Corey. "Of course, Senator."

Marotta held aloft a binder. "Collected in this binder are articles by scientific experts stating that embryonic-stem-cell research will yield no medical benefits. Are you familiar with this research?"

"I am, Senator. Just as I'm familiar with the doctors who claimed that Terri Schiavo had a functioning cerebral cortex." As a spasm of nervous laughter came from the galleries, Corey continued. "Let me suggest that you postpone this vote a week; give those binders to the most recent winners of the Nobel Prize in medicine, Drs. Carole Lauder and Joseph Di Santi; and advise the Senate of their conclusions. Having consulted with both, I know they'd be willing to help you."

Though Marotta looked startled, he swiftly recovered. "Experts will always disagree, Senator. Our obligation is to place ethical considerations above scientific benefits that may not ever exist."

At the corner of his vision, Corey saw Senator White-side shake her head, and knew that Marotta had lost her. "My offer stands," Corey said dismissively, and turned from Marotta to his colleagues. "In the gallery," he said, "are many who hope this research will someday stop their suffering, or spare others what they or their loved ones have already suffered. We cannot tell them in good conscience that human beings must suffer or die to protect an embryo that will never become a life—let alone as human sacrifices to political expedience. Nor, in my theology, does the God we purport to believe in require this."

The gallery burst into applause, swiftly gaveled down by the Speaker pro tempore, a venerable Montanan who was Marotta's ally. "And so," Corey concluded, simply, "I will vote in favor of stem-cell research."

THOUGH THE VOTE was fifty-seven to forty-three, Corey felt no elation. Returning to his office, he was certain that his relationship with Marotta would become more difficult yet, and that the media—with some justice—would focus on the role of presidential politics in Corey's own decision.

On his chair was a single slip of paper with a cell-phone number. "She's free for dinner," Eve had written. "Call her."

9

As the maître d' guided Corey and Lexie Hart to a corner table at Tosca, he felt a level of attention more intense than usual. After they were seated, he remarked, "Seems like I'm particularly fascinating tonight. What could it be, I wonder?"

A smile flickered at one corner of her mouth. "Some people," she said, "may think this isn't a presidential thing to do."

Corey laughed. "Depends on which president, I suppose."

Their waitress arrived, seeking assurance that Lexie approved of their table. Instantly, Lexie became so responsive, so concerned that the young woman not be anxious, that Corey saw her from a different angle. The other thing he noted was that Lexie, asked if she cared for a cocktail or wine, ordered mineral water instead.

As Lexie raised her glass, she told him with a smile, "I want to thank you for what you did today. However complex your motives may have been."

Corey looked at her askance. "You're not easy, are you?"

"Not since the day I was born. Or so my mama used to say."

Corey hesitated, then touched his glass to hers. "To Mama."

Briefly, their eyes met. "Yeah," she said softly. "To Mama."

To others, Corey realized, this moment might seem more intimate than it was; two couples at a nearby table were sneaking looks at them, then whispering among themselves. "So what makes you think all this interest is about me?" Lexie inquired. "You do have a certain reputation, you know."

That again, Corey thought; though he tried to shrug off such comments, this one fed his pervasive sense of being misapprehended. "So I hear. And all richly undeserved."

Her gray-green eyes appraised him, and then she seemed to catch his mood. "If there's one thing I understand, it's being the object of other people's fantasies. That's the business I'm in. I guess it doesn't help that you look like *you* should be in it, too."

Suddenly Corey experienced himself and Lexie less as a couple whom others might misapprehend than as two people who might define, in the next few sentences, whether their interaction would be trivial or truthful. "I joke about this," he told her. "But I look at the guy in *People,* and he doesn't seem like me."

As Lexie gazed at him silently, he registered her indifference to the usual social lubricants—the too easy laugh, or chatter intended to ward off an awkward silence. "So people just misunderstand you?" she asked.

This could have been a gibe or just an invitation to say more plainly what he meant. Perhaps out of loneliness, perhaps because she challenged him, he yielded to the impulse to be candid. "I don't know you at all, Lexie. After tonight, I'll probably never see you again. So I've got nothing to lose by being honest.

"I've had one experience with marriage, and I blew it. First, I was unfaithful; then I entered politics—it's hard to know which was worse. Maybe Janice was wrong for me, but I was no prize husband. Or, as it turns out, father."

Lexie's dubious look had vanished, Corey noted, encouraging him to continue. "So now I'm a senator in a town filled with women obsessed with politics or power, some of whom may fantasize about my future prospects. It's hard to find that kind of interest heartwarming, or even take it personally. And ever since leaving the Academy, I've lived an itinerant life, and still do—speeches here, a fund-raiser there, some crisis du jour or another. Maybe I'm congenitally restless. Whatever the cause, and however rotten I may feel about this, it's never added up to a second marriage.

"So I date, and sometimes a woman will stay over—maybe even because she likes me. That's how I get by."

Lexie placed a finger to her slightly parted lips. "You sure know how to sugarcoat things, Senator. Ever think about giving it up?"

"Dating?"

Lexie laughed softly. "Politics."

"What else would I do? Every now and then I'm offered the CEO job at some ersatz Halliburton that lives off government contracts. They sure as hell don't want me for my keen grasp of free enterprise; the idea is that I'd cash in my reputation and my contacts, buying dinners for government procurement officers or buttering up former colleagues—half of whom I'd never speak to voluntarily." Stopping himself, Corey smiled. "The simple truth is that I care about what I do, and I'm way too young to retire. So I'm stuck."

"In the Senate?"

"Seems like. Even though, more days than not, I feel like a man in a catatonic trance—unable to speak or move, but perfectly aware of everything around me. Including that our country is a shambles, and my party's still a devil's bargain between fundamentalists and the wealthy. It's pretty hard to watch."

"You're more than a bystander," Lexie demurred. "You carried a lot of people on your back today."

"Which was nothing but symbolic. Truth to tell, you were lobbying for a bill that'll be dead on arrival. The president will veto it as soon as it hits his desk. All I did was make more enemies."

Her smile reappeared. "Not *all*," she replied. "You also roiled the political waters. There's a job opening up next year, one where you could try to change everything you dislike."

Corey toyed with his glass. "I know that," he said finally. "And everyone else has always known it. That's another reason Janice left me. She knew the price I'd pay, and that I'd be willing to pay it."

"Then maybe you've paid it already."

"Maybe so."

The waitress arrived to take their orders. When she left, Lexie sipped her water, momentarily silent. "So *are* you running?" she asked. "You've got a great story, as they say at pitch meetings, and charm to burn. You even do candor well, and the people I meet are just dying for a little of *that*."

"You make it sound like auditioning for a part," Corey answered. "If I ran for president and got slaughtered, I'd lose whatever influence I have as someone who *might* become president. Today's suicide mission illustrates the problem. In a single vote I managed to further estrange the current president, piss off the Senate majority leader, and incense a boatload of Christian conservatives. Put them all together and it adds up to a death wish."

"Isn't that part of your charm?"

"Enough of the amateur hour," Corey protested with a laugh. "You know just enough to be dangerous, Lexie. So let's explore reality.

"Rush Limbaugh's beating me around the head and ears. Marotta's nailed down the money people. The gun nuts, creationists, anti-environmentalists, and other members of the party's flat-earth coalition hate me like some dread disease. And the people who like me, the moderates and good government types, have been shunted to the margins or left the party altogether." Despite himself, Corey felt his frustration breaking through. "Do I want to be president? Sure. But I'd have to launch a holy war for the soul of the Republican Party, trying to wrench it away from the Christys and Marottas and into my version of the twenty-first century. The people behind Marotta, like Alex Rohr and Magnus Price, don't give up power voluntarily–you'd have to pry their fingers off the wheel. The campaign would be bloody and brutal, an absolute cesspool. And I'd lose."

Taking another sip of mineral water, Lexie regarded him over the rim of her glass. "What about a third party?"

"I've thought about it. But no one's ever done that and won. And if I *did* win, both parties would make it impossible to govern." Smiling, Corey added, "I'm sure all this is fascinating. But as George Hamilton would say, 'Enough about me.' Why don't we turn to *your* life for a while?"

The look she gave him was not inviting. "What part?"

"Take your pick. The scholarship to the University of South Carolina, the two years in the Peace Corps, your time at Yale Drama School, your stellar record of activism in causes rock-ribbed Republicans despise. Maybe your star turn as the first black Lady Macbeth on Broadway, or how it felt to win an Oscar." Corey grinned. "So much to choose from. Personally, I'm most interested in your marriage. Seems only fair, doesn't it?"

Lexie raised her eyebrows. "Guess you Googled me."

"Yup."

At this moment, dinner arrived. "I'm flattered," Lexie informed him. "And hungry. The story of my life can wait."

DINNER AFFORDED HIM time to study her more closely. Like much else about her, Lexie's appetite was straightforward: she savored her filet mignon without any pretense of reserve. But Corey continued to sense that there was a considerable part of her that, for all her poise and confidence, she chose to withhold from others. What eluded him were the reasons, though there were many possibilities—starting with the fact that she was black.

Clearly she was beautiful: her high cheekbones and almond-shaped eyes betrayed, he learned, a trace of Native American ancestry. But what drew him was her hyperalertness, a mixture of thought and feeling constantly at work—watchful eyes, a quick tongue, a smile that flashed and vanished but conveyed a myriad of emotions. Knowing this woman could be well worthwhile but, even were it possible, the process might take years.

As they finished dinner, Corey asked, "Don't talk to the press much, do you?"

"No-o-o," she answered in a tone of satiric horror. "Maybe I'm like my Blackfoot ancestors, who thought a photograph would steal your soul."

"And yet you're a celebrity."

"True. But that's the price tag for doing what I want to. So I pay it."

Corey took a sip from his glass of wine. "Did the price include your marriage?"

Lexie studied the table, pondering her answer or, perhaps, deciding whether to answer at all. "Ron was a screenwriter," she said at length. "He was black, well educated, and seemed to have the same values I did. And we were both at the beginning of our careers, more hopeful than successful.

"Overnight, it seemed, I broke through—parties, premieres, the things that happen when you're on the rise. Suddenly Ron was 'Mr. Hart'—he never knew why he got the jobs he did, especially when nothing he wrote became a film."

Abruptly, she stopped. "Then what happened?" Corey asked.

Lexie gave a small movement of her shoulders. "Our marriage became a cliché: one night I flew back early from a movie set in Paris and discovered he'd been cheating on me. Suddenly it was over—Ron believed he'd found love at last."

"Sounds like the price of celebrity to me. Or maybe the price of his insecurity."

Lexie returned her gaze to the tablecloth. "Maybe both. But all Ron said was, 'You're not home to me, Lexie. There's something about you I can't touch.'"

Though soft, the words seemed to bear the weight of her own self-doubt. "Do you think that's fair?" Corey asked.

Lexie shrugged again. "These days, it's so hard for me to know. People think I can have any man I want. But it's not that simple—I seem to scare men off, or make them feel small. And I don't mean to."

For an instant, Corey felt her solitude, and chose to lighten the moment. "Look at yourself," he admonished with a smile. "You're way too beautiful, and way too smart. What's the average pitifully insecure male supposed to do with *that*?"

Though her own smile was rueful, Lexie seemed relieved at being probed no further. "Mama always said I had a mouth on me. Sure got *that* right, didn't she?"

Corey was quiet for a moment. "After dessert," he suggested, "why don't we take a walk. Seems like we've got the night for it."

Briefly, Lexie regarded him across the table, and then gave him something close to a genuine smile. "Guess a walk couldn't hurt us, could it?"

10

"South Carolina," Lexie told him, "is a funny place—filled with bigots, evangelists, storytellers, some truly wonderful folks, and more crazy people than you can count. But it still feels like home to me."

They had walked for a time in the cool of a late September night, and then sat on a park bench near Lexie's hotel, gazing at the traffic through the shadowy branches of trees. "Your home," Corey remarked, "is also the site of a critical primary election, and about the dirtiest politics you can find. A lot of it involving race."

"You don't need to tell *me*, Senator—it wasn't easy growing up there. But now my uncle's a congressman, and I'm South Carolina's reigning Citizen of the Year. So I guess we've made some progress. Or maybe it's more that *I* have."

Corey looked at her sideways. "When did you start acting?"

"Early." In the shadows, Lexie's smile seemed reflective. "It was sort of sad, really. Acting was my escape."

"From what?"

"Daddy had a heart condition—the next heart attack, the doctors said, would kill him. The message I got from Mama was, 'Be good, be quiet, keep your daddy's world a certain way, or maybe you'll be the thing that does him in.'" She slowly shook her head. "When I look at pictures from that time, I see this skinny, sad-faced girl.

"What I remember is withdrawing. I'd go sit under that

mossy tree in the backyard and read for hours, lost in my own world. I bet I was the only nine-year-old black girl in Greenville who cried over *Wuthering Heights*. Then I discovered acting, and how you could turn into somebody else."

"Was there a particular 'somebody' you liked best?"

"Yeah," Lexie answered with a laugh. "A bit part in *The Crucible*—a teenaged girl in the grip of hysteria. I got to scream, right out loud, and it wasn't going to kill my daddy. And I realized I felt freer on the stage than I'd ever felt off it.

"A part of me still does. I can be in a play, acting in front of friends who've come to see me, and then have nothing to say to them afterward. *Macbeth* was like that. But most of the time I know how to turn it off—I go home now and I'm Lexie Hart, not somebody else."

The story intrigued him, both for its own sake and because, Corey guessed, she seldom talked about herself. "But is acting still an escape for you?" he asked.

"Yes and no. Maybe politics is vicious, but my form of make-believe comes with its own harsh reality—Hollywood can be like the world's meanest high school, filled with some of the most treacherous people on earth. And I'm almost thirty-seven. If you're a woman and over thirty, you can be obsolete in a nanosecond." Briefly, she glanced at him. "Some days you feel pretty much alone. But then what do they say about Washington: 'If you want a friend, get a dog'?"

Corey laughed. "I'd just have to pay someone to take care of it. So how do you deal with all that?"

Lexie contemplated the grass at her feet. "By limiting my own success, in a way. After I won the Oscar, I didn't want to be hijacked by the machine, posing for every magazine in somebody's designer gowns, or making bad, expensive movies pitched to eighteen-year-old guys." She shook her head and smiled. "Though there *was* one where I fired a laser gun and said, 'Take that, furball.' Every now and then, you just have to take their money—if only to pay for work that matters more.

"But mostly I pick films that will stretch me, even if nobody sees them. I guess it's like what you said about deciding to run for president: I don't want to do what other people expect me to do and wind up earning their contempt for doing it. Or maybe feeling contempt for myself." Lexie paused, then finished softly: "What I can never figure out is whether that makes me proud or just afraid. Ever ask yourself that question?"

"All the time."

They fell silent together. It struck Corey how alike their worlds were—perhaps *they* were—and yet, in many ways, how different. "What's the hardest part," he asked, "being a woman or being black?"

Lexie responded with a mirthless laugh. "In Hollywood or in life?"

"Both, I guess."

She turned to face him. "Life's a bigger subject than we've got time for. But, as in life, race is the hardest thing in Hollywood.

"That can't be a surprise to you. The number of roles for white actors versus black is a lot like the ratio of white to black senators—ninety-nine to one, the last time I looked." Her voice became flat, and perhaps a little weary. "If you're a woman, getting older, *and* you're black, you just have to keep fighting for good parts.

"Some of the trouble is that the male writers who dominate the film business don't create credible women—let alone black women—so much as recycle old stereotypes. Or maybe *their* stereotypes: sign up to play somebody's mother, and it turns out you're playing *their* mother. So you just try to find the humanity in whoever you've agreed to be."

"And when you're *forty*-seven?"

Looking at him more closely, Lexie said, "I've been talking a lot, Senator—"

"Corey."

"Okay, Corey," she said in a slightly sardonic tone. "Feels like I've been performing a monologue. How much of what I do can really interest you?"

How could he penetrate, Corey wondered, the layers of her mistrust? "Pretty much all of it," he answered. "So now I find myself wondering what's ahead for you."

After a moment, she shrugged. "Producing films I care about—maybe directing them as well. But I'll need financial backing. And the moneymen in film are often as crass as they are powerful. Alex Rohr, for example—he's where our worlds connect.

"Beyond that, I'd like to do more plays. They can be wonderful—every night, the same character turns out a little different." Glancing at Corey, she said, "And politics, of course. For me, that started as early as acting did."

"Because of civil rights?"

"That, and just plain being poor." Her voice softened. "Mama always loved the Kennedys, the idea that rich folks somehow cared about her life. So I learned to connect government with lifting people up—that we had this obligation to see to one another.

"As a celebrity I've got the power to do something—at least until the fame runs out. But fame has also made me careful." Pausing, she pulled her suit coat more tightly around her shoulders, as though warding off a chill. "There are plenty of people in your business I don't like at all. But I know how hurtful it can be to live your life in public. So I try very hard to keep focused on the issues, even when politicians come after me—or my industry—in a personal and nasty way."

"You're a bit of a target," Corey responded. "Personally, I don't much care if some actor decides to go off on *me*. But I care a lot about the kind of crap the entertainment world inundates our kids with. That's where Christy and I can find some common ground."

"Even about censorship?" Lexie asked pointedly.

"Not that. But I sure as hell think your industry can do better than it does. I also think you know it." Corey felt the cell phone vibrate in his pocket, the silent ringing used to alert him to what, at this hour, was some no doubt urgent message. "Look," he added in a mollifying tone, "the sins of show business aren't about you and me. I just didn't feel like sitting on my opinions."

"Oh, this much we agree about—my industry can do a *whole* lot better by black people than the kind of trash they make about us. There's a movie I want to produce that's all about that. Assuming I can ever get it off the ground."

Judging from the frustration in her voice, this was as important to her as anything she had mentioned. "Tell me about it," Corey requested.

Slowly, Lexie shook her head. "It's a long story, and it's getting late."

Disappointed, Corey shrugged. "Perhaps next time, then."

For a long time, Lexie held his gaze. "Maybe it's what you've been asking, and what I've chosen to tell you. Or maybe it's just me. Whatever, I'm feeling the need to be honest.

"You seem like a decent guy, Corey. I've enjoyed tonight, and I'm very grateful for your vote today. But I can't stand your political party—to me, it's carried the stench of racism and privilege ever since most of the segregationists in South Carolina made it their new home."

"I didn't invite them," Corey interrupted. "And I don't like them."

"Still, they're part of the company you've chosen to keep." Though Lexie's voice softened, her tone was firm. "Maybe, on some things, we could agree to disagree. Maybe all this sounds incredibly bizarre to you—my own personal brand of bigotry. But race cuts deep for me. If I have to argue with somebody about it, or ask them to consider what I've been forced to think about since the day I figured out I wasn't white, it's way too much to take on."

Nettled, Corey stood, hands jammed in his pockets. "So people can never change or grow, and all Republicans are alike? That's pretty condescending. Why not just let the two of us be people?"

Folding her arms, Lexie said quietly, "As you acknowledge, you're a busy man with large ambitions. So why does it matter to you? Do I symbolize some sort of outreach program, or am I today's new challenge?"

The question had just enough truth to sting Corey and, for a moment, silence him. But the answer that came to him felt like a deeper truth. "I really can't explain this, Lexie, and I'll be damned if I'll jump through hoops for you. But somehow it feels like *you* matter—*you*, not some random African-American, Oscar-winning movie star. I can't imagine spending time with you and just going through the motions. And at the risk of sounding conceited, I'm big enough for you."

Even in the moonlight, Corey could detect her smile of skepticism. "Because you're a senator?"

"Because you don't scare me. I'm not even particularly in awe of you. That leaves me free to like you and, believe it or not, take a genuine interest in how you see the world—including my world. I may even be capable of sorting out your unbelievable defensiveness from your incredible lack of tact. So, yes, I think I'd like to see you again."

For a long time she simply stared up at him. Then, standing, she touched his sleeve. "Walk me back, okay?"

They walked three blocks in silence, alone on the empty sidewalks. Only at the hotel did the doorman, trying hard not to stare, remind Corey of what they both could never escape.

Turning, she looked at him, her gaze direct and steady. "Thanks for dinner," she said. "If I came off too harsh, I'm sorry."

Once again, Corey felt the cell phone vibrating in his pocket. "Not too harsh. Just someone who doesn't know me.

"Maybe you never will. But I promise not to see the next dinner as a Tracy-Hepburn film where I help you discover your inner girl—let alone your inner Republican."

Lexie gave him a last fleeting smile. "No chance of that," she said and then, turning, vanished as the doorman whisked her through the entrance.

Pondering her meaning, Corey resolved to find a cab.

It took him five minutes to flag one. Only as they neared his town house did the sight of the Capitol, a glowing dome in the darkness, remind him to check his messages.

There were three, all from Blake Rustin: Bob Christy, Rustin had it on good authority, was planning an announcement next week. "You flushed him out today," Rustin said with palpable satisfaction. "I'm pretty damn sure he'll run. After that, the only question is how badly he damages Rob Marotta, and what that does for you."

11

On the first Tuesday in October, Corey and Blake Rustin watched the Reverend Bob Christy make his "special announcement."

Christy sat in an overstuffed chair on the set of his TV show, speaking without notes as the camera framed his face. "For forty years," Christy said gravely, "I have watched our own government precipitate our nation's moral decline.

"The day it began still burns in my memory. I was in divinity school, watching the news, when Walter Cronkite told us that the United States Supreme Court—the so-called protector of our liberties—had barred America's children from beginning their school day with a simple prayer to our Creator." Christy's voice thickened. "Tears came to my eyes. And yet I did nothing."

"He's running," Rustin said.

Christy leaned forward, his face filling the screen. "Ten years later, that same court told American women they had the right to *murder* their unborn children. And I realized that these nine judges had become the high priests of our government's new 'religion'—a secular humanism that knew no boundaries and saw no need of God."

Sipping black coffee, Corey imagined his mother watching. "The man's good," he told Rustin. "You can agree or not, but he has a gift for touching the nerve endings of our social disquiet."

"I had always disdained politics," Christy went on, "until I realized that our *politics* disdained our *God*.

"How could God, I asked myself, ordain our form of government and then be indifferent to its works?" Christy's voice became low and stern. "But it was *we* who had become indifferent, heedless of our duty to ensure that America obeys God's laws.

"Ever since that awful day when the Supreme Court sanctioned murder, millions of ordinary Americans have risen to fight a godless government that asks us to accept rampant divorce, sexual promiscuity, gay marriage, the relentless eradication of God from public life, and a contempt for life itself so profound that we dismember babies in their mothers' wombs." Christy's eyes moistened, and his mobile features appeared to sag with the weight of grief. "The outcome of this great battle remains in doubt. Two weeks ago, in the United States Senate, a group of renegade Republicans joined with Democrats to approve a death sentence for four hundred thousand potential lives who cannot speak in their own defense. Imagine what they would say if we could hear them."

Christy paused, shaking his head in reproof. "It's all of a piece, whether abortion or stem-cell research. But this much is obvious: everyone who believes in abortion has already been born. Perhaps they do not see that a society that allows them to select which babies will die can also decide which old people will live."

"This is where I get off the train," Corey observed. "Trying to cure paralysis doesn't lead to euthanasia."

Briefly, Christy closed his eyes. "For two weeks," he said in a hushed voice, "I have prayed on what to do. In the millions, you have shared with me *your* hopes and prayers for our beloved, wayward country.

"I have heard your voices and, I humbly believe, the voice of God Himself. And so the journey I began forty years ago has led me to this awesome day." Slowly,

Christy's eyes opened, and he spoke in a husky tremor. "Today, grateful for your blessing, I declare my candidacy for president of the United States . . ."

"That tears it," Rustin said cheerfully. "Marotta's world just stopped spinning on its axis—"

Corey's cell phone rang. Standing, Corey glanced at the number on his caller ID and wondered whose area code was 310. And then he knew.

Answering, he said quietly, "*This* is a surprise."

Rustin turned to look at him. "I don't exactly know how to say this," she told Corey, "but I've been thinking about you a lot."

"And I you." Swiftly, he gathered his thoughts. "Where are you?"

"On Martha's Vineyard. I've rented a place here until next week." She paused, then added, "I was wondering how you'd like the guesthouse."

Corey hesitated, mentally scanning his calendar as he tried to assess the risks and the rewards of spending a celibate weekend with this particular instantly recognizable woman. In a tentative voice, she said, "I know you're busy . . ."

Abruptly, Corey decided. "Too late to head me off. Just tell me how to get there."

Her laugh conveyed relief, as though she had feared rejection. "There are airplanes that fly from Boston. Sort of like the one the Wright brothers used—one pilot and a couple of propellers."

"I've flown worse," Corey answered.

Hanging up, he found himself smiling at Bob Christy. "Who was *that*?" Rustin asked. "Here's Christy trying to make you president, and you look like you just had a lobotomy."

Corey felt his face close. "Unless *I* run for president, Blake, my private life's my own."

12

THREE DAYS LATER, COREY FLEW TO MARTHA'S Vineyard. He told no one of his plans; nor did she meet him at the airport. Whatever else, they'd agreed, it was better to get him on and off the island without creating problems for both of them.

The place she had rented in Chilmark was an eccentric rambling structure that seemed to have been constructed at different times in clashing architectural styles. Parking his rental car, Corey, as instructed, searched for her out back.

He found her lounging on a patio facing a grassy field that led to the white-capped waters of the Atlantic Ocean glistening in the midafternoon sun. Dressed in blue jeans and a wool sweater, Lexie held a book on her lap, reading so intently through half-glasses that she reminded him less of a movie star than an unusually attractive doctoral student. "Hi," he said.

She started visibly and then, almost at once, laughed at herself. "Sorry," she said. "I spook sometimes. Guess I got lost in this story."

"What is it?"

"A novel by a young Nigerian woman, based on the death of a writer hanged for exposing his government's dealings with an oil cartel. The author wrote it because no one seemed to remember him." Rising, she briefly touched Corey's arm. "Anyhow, welcome."

"Thanks." Hands in the pockets of his khaki pants,

Corey eyed the house. "What's the history of this place?"

"Eccentric. It was built by a local artist as a kind of rustic camp. When he began selling paintings, he started adding rooms whenever the whim struck him." She waved an arm toward a sunroom that jutted from the house like a trailer that had been blown there by a hurricane. "As you can see, the man's sense of proportion was confined to his art. But the views are great, and most people don't even know this place is here." Smiling, she added, "Besides, I kind of *like* the house—it reminds me of this old rag doll I kept patching up until her button eyes were different colors and all her arms and legs were crooked. Somehow, I feel like I can't abandon it."

Something in the story struck him as characteristic—it was easy to envision her as the child who wove fantasies beneath a mossy tree. He was surprised to realize that, whatever the cause, she seemed more accessible than the guarded woman he had met in Washington.

"Care to show me around?" he asked.

Leading him from room to room, she pointed out a mishmash of fixtures and furniture as quirky as the house itself. The tour ended on a second-story deck that commanded a panoramic view of the ocean on this Indian summer day. "And here's the ocean," she said appreciatively. "Another reason I come here."

"How did you find this place?"

She leaned against the railing, gazing across the sea grass at the water. "I'd always heard of the Vineyard—the town of Oak Bluffs was a center of the abolitionist movement, and it's become a haven for black intellectuals, or just black families looking for a socially comfortable place to vacation. Spike Lee lives there on and off. But years ago, when I first decided to come here, Spike's place was occupied, and I desperately needed to be alone. *This,*" she finished quietly, "was alone."

Corey joined her at the railing. "Was there some crisis?"

She seemed to ponder the question. "A mini-crisis of the soul, I guess. Ron and I had broken up the year before, and I was drifting, still hurt, still not knowing what had happened to us. So I did about the dumbest thing I could have done—I had an affair with a costar."

"Dumb?" Corey asked. "Or human?"

"Dumb," she said emphatically. "And potentially hurtful to people other than me. Specifically, his nice blond wife and three blond kids."

"Maybe so," Corey allowed. "But I know a little about this subject. It was *his* marriage, after all."

"So I told myself. But I knew better than that, just like I knew what was happening to us both." Her tone filled with regret. "We spent two months filming in Corsica—no role you can play is as unreal as the atmosphere on a movie set. You don't take out the garbage anymore. Everything you say is funny. And you're intensely involved with people who, like you, are totally removed from any reality except the story that's become your common obsession. In this case, a love story.

"If you want a completely romantic, affair-spawning environment, that's about the best there is. And the problems are so obvious." She turned to him. "What makes sense on location makes no sense in life. I turned to this man for reassurance—that I was a desirable woman whose sexuality was merely dormant. And I could have ruined the perfectly okay marriage of a guy I was using to try to make *me* whole.

"So I broke it off, and came here to reflect. By the time I left, two weeks later, I'd regained some semblance of balance. I've worked to hold on to that ever since."

The story, Corey sensed, was one of the puzzle pieces

that made up Lexie Hart. But it was only one piece, and he was certain he had much more to learn. As she studied him, a trace of doubt surfacing in her eyes, Corey wondered if she had somehow read his thoughts.

"Now that you're here," she said. "I'm not quite sure what to do with you."

"Easy," he answered. "Feed me."

THEY SET OUT for the fishing village of Menemsha, where, Lexie promised, they could grab the best cooked lobster on the island. "Speaking of unreal," Corey remarked, "you know you're living right when lobster's your idea of takeout."

Smiling, Lexie focused on the two-lane road that wound past the stone walls and grassy fields that, for Corey, typified New England. "You'll be back in your own unreal world soon enough," she said. "Was it hard to get away?"

"From my staff, for sure. Also from presidential politics—I'm afraid I'll be devoting some of our time to figuring out what I should do. I guess you saw that Christy's running."

"And I guess you're not surprised," she answered wryly. "Not since I persuaded you to go after all those embryos Christy's sworn to protect."

Corey turned to her. "What do you make of him?"

"Christy?" The shoulders beneath her wool sweater briefly twitched. "Maybe the man's sincere. But I listen to him, and just can't help but think back on all the preachers in my childhood who knew, absolutely knew, that the Bible forbade our races to mix, and whose fundamentalist God hated me and mine.

"When I was maybe seven, my mama looked after a white boy about my age. I had this baby crush on him.

One day Mama told me, 'Don't be so attached to Stevie. Someday that boy may grow up to call you "nigger."'

"He more or less did. He also grew up to be a preacher." Pulling down the sun visor, she said, "Christy fights for the unborn like there's no tomorrow. But once black kids get born, he doesn't have much to say about how they're housed or fed or educated—just a bunch of pious stuff about 'our common pathway to eternity.' Between birth and death, I think he sees us not at all."

When they got to Menemsha, Corey went to the fish market, and Lexie stayed in the car. He wondered if that made her feel as strange as it did him.

THE PLACE SHE took him was accessible only by a dirt road so uneven that it caused Lexie's Jeep to vibrate with each jolt. But once they reached the sandy trail leading through sea grass to the rise from which the beach descended, he understood why they had come.

Blessed with a western exposure, miles of white sand and half-buried rocks stretched toward the red-clay promontory on which the Gay Head lighthouse stood, a distant shape against the cobalt blue of early evening. Across the sparkling water that swept to the Elizabeth Islands, a lowering sun backlit a skein of clouds, filtering the light that caught the whitecaps and tinted the varying colors—green sea grass, aqua water, gray rocks, brown sand—with a filmic sepia tone.

"Beautiful," he said.

Lexie nodded. "For me, the real draw's the ocean. I can watch the water for hours and never know where the time has gone."

They spread her blanket between two rocks that provided shelter from the breeze. While Lexie arranged their meal—lobster, French bread, a fresh salad—Corey opened a bottle of mineral water, feeling both the strangeness and the stimulation of being alone with her. Filling her paper cup, he inquired, "What should we drink to?"

"I don't really know," Lexie said, covering her hesitancy with a smile. "Confusion, maybe. Or ambiguity."

"Oh," Corey said lightly, "*those* I live with every day."

They sat quietly for a time, eating lobster coated with butter and lemon. "I did wonder, though," Corey said at last, "what moved you to invite me."

"I wasn't going to," she answered with a slight laugh. "First I had to check your voting record and read a few of your speeches."

Corey studied her more closely. "You're *serious*, aren't you? That wasn't a joke."

The complex look she gave him was a mix of amusement, embarrassment, and defiance. "I *told* you how I felt about Republicans. But there's not much about *your* record that I could quarrel with. I especially liked the speech in which you called opposition to the Voting Rights Act 'genteel racism disguised as the pious belief that equality has arrived.'" She smiled briefly. "Though you've still got a ways to go, seeing how you belong to a party financed by rich white guys like Alex Rohr, whose basic premise is that we should make them even more entitled than they are. Sure you don't want to just ditch these people?"

"Ditch them?" Corey answered with a smile. "I'm their salvation. They just don't know it yet."

She shot him a look of skepticism. "We really *do* need to talk about that. But maybe I should have patience enough to let you eat."

They finished their meal in amiable silence. Leaning back against a rock, Corey watched the sun light the clouds bright orange as it slipped beneath the water. "This film project of yours," he asked, "would you mind telling me about it?"

Lexie frowned. "Describing it makes me feel superstitious. Like if I talk about the story, it will never become a movie—that somehow it'll be taken from me. Paranoid, I guess."

"No, I think I understand."

Darkness began to envelop them. Then, to Corey's surprise, she said quietly, "It's a normal coming-of-age story, in a sense. Except that the boy involved is black, and sixteen, and caught between his brother's gang life and all the potential he has to grab hold of a different future. It's not an uplifting story—I want people to see the truth. And here the truth means tragedy.

"We've lost three generations of young black men, and all politicians can think to do is jack up the penalties for crack cocaine." Her voice remained quiet. "There's surely more 'white America' can do, but much more we need to be doing for ourselves. That's what I'm trying to say."

Moments passed, their silence seeming more intimate than before. Behind them, Corey noticed, a quarter moon had materialized above the sea grass. "If you were running for president," Lexie finally asked, "would you have come?"

In the darkness, he could not read her expression. "I don't know," he said. "There's more in that question than I can easily answer."

"Well," she responded softly, "at least that's honest."

They fell silent again. When Corey reached for her hand, she did not try to remove it. Her skin felt warm to the touch.

13

THEY SPENT THE WEEKEND HIKING, KAYAKING, running on the beach, and talking about whatever struck them, whether trivial or serious. The only time they parted was at night, the long stretches when Corey found himself awake—conscious of her closeness, wondering if she, too, was thinking of him.

On Sunday afternoon, they climbed the winding trail to Waskosims Rock. Sitting atop the hill, they took in a sweeping vista of woods and fields; the leaves were turning, and the oak trees were burnished with red-orange as far as Corey could see. The woods had once been farmland, Lexie told him, until the farmers had moved on and nature had reclaimed the land; the old stone walls that threaded the woodland were the last signs of that agrarian past. "All through New England," Lexie said, "there's this feeling of abandonment, of people who simply vanished. To me it feels almost druidical, like I'm visiting Stonehenge—walls slowly crumbling, markers in untended graveyards leaning at odd angles, with the names half-erased by wind and weather. I'll stop at one of those places and think, Who *were* these people? What were they like?"

Corey smiled. "You do that a lot, don't you? Imagine other people."

"Are you saying that's a bad thing? Or just weird?"

"Neither. It's just that sometimes I think that's what this country's dying from—a massive failure of empathy and imagination."

She turned to look at him. "How so?"

"Where do I start? Take politics as practiced by Magnus Price: inflame your supporters by defining those who don't think like they do as the enemy, hell-bent on tearing down the 'real America,' until half the people in this country hate each other, and the rest think politics is so toxic they don't even bother to vote. Or take the media as perverted by Alex Rohr, which teaches you to despise people you don't even know. It's all a cynical exercise in marketing—find your demographic, and then exploit it." Corey's voice was etched with frustration. "In the America of Price and Rohr, voters are lab rats in a political-science experiment, programmed to be even more frightened of 'the other' than the folks I grew up with—Lord knows that my own parents certainly are. But they're really not much different than the liberals on both coasts who call them 'flyover people,' making no effort to imagine how the world looks to them. Instead of *seeing* one another, we've started living in gated communities of the mind created by jerks like Price and Rohr. It makes me want to puke."

Lexie's eyes widened in mock surprise, and then she began to laugh. "That's quite a speech, Senator Grace. How come you've only given it to me?"

He shook his head. "I'm tempted, all the time. But it would be the last nail in my political coffin. Besides," he added wryly, "it'd probably come off like a talk-show rant—totally unpresidential. Or so my advisers tell me."

Lexie grimaced. "Because truth is a terrible thing, right? We need our leaders to be robots, 'cause we're too dumb to elect real humans. Next time I hear some failed presidential candidate say, 'Next time I won't let my handlers keep me from being me,' I'm throwing a brick through my TV screen."

"But that's exactly what Democrats *do*," Corey rejoined.

"They haven't nominated a human in years—just androids whose speeches sound like a tape recording spliced from focus groups. I'd ask where the hell you find these people, except I know—the Senate."

Lexie's eyes glinted with the amusement that served as a warning of some conversational laser. "All that's very interesting. Especially the part where I found out for the first time you're actually not an orphan. So how come I never hear any heartwarming anecdotes about Mom and Dad—or brothers and sisters, for that matter? Or are you like me, an only child?"

Corey felt the question transform his mood entirely. Turning from her, he gazed at a farmhouse in a distant clearing. "I am now."

"What does that mean?"

"That it's a very long story, with a very bad ending."

"Would you like to tell me about it?" she asked quietly.

For an instant, Corey thought of Clay as he had last seen him, then felt Lexie watching his face.

"If it's all *that* bad, Corey, don't. I understand about secrets. But I'm also better at keeping them than you could possibly know."

His own emotions, Corey realized, were a minefield of contradictions: the desire to break his silence as deep as his desire to preserve it; the fear of how he might appear to her, both as a senator and a man; the mixture of hope and self-contempt as he perceived that baring his soul might draw her closer. "Corey Grace," he murmured at last. "Such a sensitive guy. Not all shut down like your ex-husband."

"What do you mean?"

"That I don't want to use my brother's death."

Lexie shook her head. "If you think I'm going to sleep with you as payback for opening up, forget it. I'm talking to you as one human being to another. What you do with that depends on whatever else it is you need."

Corey stared straight ahead, feeling a constriction in his chest. And then, without inflection, he began to tell her what he had never told anyone.

14

AFTER THE GRUELING DAYS AND EVENINGS OF HIS first campaign for the Senate—a blur of airports, buses, motel rooms, and, above all, people who were skeptical, or avid, or simply wanted to see or touch him—Corey Grace relaxed by reading his brother's letters from the Academy.

Corey was good at politics, he now understood—in part because he had begun to rebel at regurgitating pat talking points, relying instead on candor and his increasing mastery of the issues. But the campaign was not easy: his opponent was skilled at implying, without quite saying so, that Corey's lone qualification for the Senate was crashing an expensive airplane—a sentiment that not only earned Corey's private agreement, but that reminded him, as if he needed reminding, of Joe Fitts and his family. And he was also lonely: Janice rarely appeared with him. When she did, although her graciousness was impeccable, Corey understood that he was watching an ironic and thoroughly self-aware performance as a species she disdained—the general's perfect wife—which, in Janice's case, involved a haunting impersonation of her own dead mother. So, at first, reading Clay's letters was a welcome relief from solitude.

With laconic fatalism, Clay cataloged the initial phase of becoming a "wad": they took your belongings, shaved your head, jammed you into a room with three other guys for a few hours of sleep, and woke you up by banging

garbage cans with sticks. Clay started waking up five minutes before the others, and he'd lie there dreading the
banging of the cans; accustomed to sleeping eight hours
or more, he now was lucky to get five. At the brink of
exhaustion, Clay described his equanimity slowly fraying,
his demeanor becoming numb and robotic—all of which
seemed normal to Corey, except for a recurring theme in
Clay's more recent letters.

Their focus had become an upperclassman named
Cagle.

To Clay, Cagle was the embodiment of unreasoning
malevolence. Clay described Cagle's animus as being
directed less toward him than a classmate identified only
as Jay, but with whom Clay seemed to identify so closely
that, troubled, Corey began to wonder if Jay was a pseudo-
nym for Clay himself.

Cagle had made Jay his special project. He woke Jay at
night to run wind sprints until he vomited, or do push-
ups in a field turned to muck by a sprinkler system until,
muscles twitching, Jay collapsed face-first in the mud. At
meals, Cagle required Jay to hold his knife and fork at a
forty-five-degree angle, sitting upright with his body three
inches from the back of the chair; Cagle peppered him
with so many questions that it became impossible for him
to eat and Jay, already thin, seemed to become slighter
with each passing day. Reading the letters, Corey envisioned an upperclassman who reveled in tormenting
cadets, but who also sensed in Jay something that so
inflamed him that he had resolved to drive his victim out
of school. If the ostensible point of the abuse was bonding
classmates, it was surely working—Clay's letters described
his efforts to buck up his flagging classmate, trying to
stave off the prospect of a nervous collapse. But Corey
began to worry about Clay himself. "Watch your buddy,"

he advised his brother, "but also yourself. Your survival isn't tied to Jay's."

When the summer of indoctrination ended, Corey felt a deep relief. His brother had survived.

Clay stopped mentioning Jay. But as the fall began, Cagle resurfaced in Clay's letters, this time as a petty tyrant who conducted random "room inspections" at odd hours, breaking Clay's and his roommate's sleep to scour the room for imaginary contraband. In letter after letter, the raids were so unpredictable, yet so frequent, as to border on obsession. Though sometimes couched in humor, Clay's letters gradually took on an increasing tone of darkness, one focusing on a cadet who, abruptly cracking up, had been talked out of jumping off the roof of a building, another on two female cadets who had vanished overnight amid whispers of lesbianism. "No one ever talks about them," Clay wrote. "But last night I lay awake wondering what they told their families."

Without responding to these stories, Corey sent back a letter of encouragement. "We're all proud," he told Clay. "Dad's actually begun bragging about you, and Mom's given up on exiling you to Carl Cash University. Maybe next year you'll even have time to get laid."

Two days later, in mid-October, General Hall's successor as commandant tracked down Corey by telephone at a hotel in Toledo. There was no good way to say this, General Pierce told him somberly—his brother had killed himself.

For a long time Corey could not speak.

"How?" he finally asked and felt himself shrivel inside at the inadequacy, the sheer stupidity, of his question.

"By jumping off the roof of his dormitory." The general paused. "It's five stories, you'll remember, with concrete below."

Corey felt his eyes close. "What have you told my parents?"

"Nothing. We wanted to call you first. As a courtesy to someone we all respect, for whatever help it is."

Corey forced himself to think ahead, the reflex of an officer. "Please don't contact them," he requested. "I'm coming out there myself."

"Make it soon," the general responded soberly. "I'm not comfortable sitting on this."

"I understand." Corey hesitated, then asked, "Before Clay did this, did you have to talk another cadet out of jumping?"

"No," the general answered in a puzzled voice. "Where did you hear that?"

Sitting down on the edge of the bed, Corey felt sick. The letters had been a window into Clay's own torment, marbled with clues that Corey had overlooked. And then, as the whole, horrible truth seeped from his subconscious, Corey grasped the reason he wished to keep his parents clear of this.

"I'll be there tomorrow," he promised Pierce.

COREY HAD NOT returned to the Academy since graduation.

Once he was there, his memories were curdled by Clay's death. The Terrazzo level of the campus, a thousand feet above Colorado Springs, offered Corey's favorite vista, a majestic view of the Rockies that had always made him ponder the miracle of flight. But even amid this grandeur, the campus now seemed cold and antiseptic. Arms folded, he gazed at his old freshman dorm, so recently home to his brother. Another memory returned to him: the cadet in his class who, fearful of returning home as a failure, had jammed a pencil in the barrel of his

M-1 and shot himself in the eye. But all he had done was blind himself, and now Clay's eyes, too, were sightless.

Corey drove to the morgue.

His brother lay in a drawer, his skull crushed, his face bruised and distorted by the impact of his fall. His death had required a grim resolve—he had jumped headfirst, a witness said, a near-perfect dive guaranteed to break his neck. Hand trembling, Corey gently traced the bristles of his hair.

"I'm sorry," he whispered. "I never knew."

BEFORE VISITING THE commandant, he asked to see Clay's room.

The commander of Clay's squadron, Major Kelleher, escorted him in silence. The room was as Spartan as Corey's own had been: a tile floor, a closet, a sink, a chest of drawers, two steel-frame beds. But this room was absolutely bare.

"Where's Clay's roommate?" he asked.

Kelleher seemed transfixed by the empty beds. "Gone."

Corey was no longer surprised.

THE COMMANDANT COVERED his embarrassment by recounting the facts in clipped military fashion.

One week ago, shortly after two A.M., an upperclassman holding a flashlight had conducted a surprise room inspection. Throwing the door open, he'd captured in a beam of light an act that called for expulsion: Cadet Clayton Grace as he performed oral sex on his roommate.

Corey listened impassively. "This upperclassman," he asked, "does his name happen to be Cagle?"

The commandant's lips pursed. "I'm afraid that's confidential."

"Then tell me this," Corey inquired softly. "When your

nameless cadet turned in Clay to Major Kelleher, did he still have an erection? Or did he jerk off first?"

Pierce's eyes narrowed. "Your point?"

"That the sickest cadet in this story isn't the one who's dead. I'd think very hard before I made this man an officer."

"The upperclassman broke no rules," Pierce answered in a monotone. "Your brother did. Any cadet in this man's place would be honor-bound to turn him in."

"But not every cadet, General, would *be* in this man's place."

The general's silence, Corey sensed, was meant as a sign that he understood this. "So his roommate's gone, too," Corey said at length.

"Yes. He accepted what we offered Clay—an administrative discharge for reasons that will, to the best of our ability, remain confidential."

"At least as confidential," Corey amended, "as your vigilant upperclassman cares for it to be."

Pierce contemplated the desk as though pondering how much to say. "This upperclassman was reminded of our policy. But, yes, your brother expressed that concern to Major Kelleher."

Corey tried to imagine his brother's turmoil. "How did Clay act?" he asked.

"Frightened—much more than his roommate, Kelleher thought. When we quarantined them—separately, of course—during the time needed to resolve the matter, your brother stopped eating."

"And you didn't watch him?"

The general's eyes were veiled. "Not closely enough, it seems."

It was pointless, Corey told himself, to turn his guilt and self-disgust on General Pierce. "I'd have thought,"

Corey told him softly, "that Clay would leave a letter."

"Not that we've found." Pierce frowned, then added, "According to Bill Kelleher, he did express a terrible shame, and a deep fear of exposure. He was certain that your parents would reject him—"

"Why didn't you call me then, for Christ's sake?"

Pierce gazed across the desk. "He implored us not to. You were a hero, he told Bill—and a hero or a senator doesn't need a 'fairy' for a brother."

Head bowed, Corey touched his eyes.

For numberless seconds, he sat there, barely conscious of the man across from him. Looking up, he said wearily, "Then at least you can honor Clay's request."

"In what way?"

"With secrecy. He was right about our parents."

Pierce nodded slowly. "As far as our records go, and subject to review by General Lane, I think we can all agree that your brother was depressed. As to his roommate, I can only assume that he'll stay quiet. I take it you don't know him."

Corey felt the final piece fall into place. "Only that his name was Jay."

Pierce nodded. "We'll have to leave it at that, then. As you can appreciate, everything else about him is confidential. He has to live with this, too, you know."

With sickening finality, Corey absorbed how completely he had misperceived his brother's letters. "Yes," he answered. "I know."

HIS CAMPAIGN SUSPENDED, Corey accompanied Clay's body back to Ohio.

TV cameras waited at the evangelical church chosen by Corey's mother, present to record the loss suffered by the military hero and his family. Janice was quietly supportive to Corey and his parents, all edginess banished; though she said nothing of herself, it was clear that Clay's death echoed with hard memories of her own mother's suicide and that, for her, it was a tragedy beyond redemption. This was how Corey felt; the service itself, which was focused more on exalting God than evoking the eighteen-year-old boy in the coffin, only deepened his own misery. His father sat next to him, mute and uncomprehending, a soul in life's harness; mystified and vulnerable, Kara held her mother's hand. Only Corey's mother seemed to find comfort in a service that sharpened Corey's distaste for Nettie Grace's overweening God.

They buried Clay on a gray fall afternoon, in the last open corner of the cemetery that would someday hold his parents—but not, Corey had decided, himself. Even now, he reflected bitterly, his brother was alone.

They returned to his parents' house, the family and a few friends, exchanging well-meant reminiscences as the gathering dwindled until the Graces were alone with Nettie's scrapbook of old photographs. Her religious conversion, Corey perceived, had caused a fault line in the album; before, the photos of Corey and Clay were neatly inserted in the plastic sheets; after, most remained in their packages, unopened. The Reverend Christy had turned Nettie's thoughts to a better place.

Now, her eyes filmed with tears as she looked at the snapshots of Clay, so slender and uncertain looking compared to the insouciance that leapt from pictures of the teenaged Corey. Suddenly, her thin frame seemed to quiver. Looking up from the album, she said to Corey in a voice thickened by grief and helplessness, "Didn't you *see* him, Corey? You never should have encouraged him to enter that terrible place. He died from trying to be like you."

Stunned, Corey's first impulse was to issue some

scathing rebuke—about her own blindness, or bigotry, or the fact that surely Clay was lucky to be in the arms of God. But he said none of that. Nor did he tell the truth; overcome by the tragedy that had brought them here, rooted in a family maimed by its failures of empathy or comprehension, Corey simply gazed at her, determined only to make this day no worse.

For seconds no one spoke. Turning to Janice, Corey saw her look of quiet compassion. "I think it's time to go," she said.

As they left, she entwined her fingers in his. "She shouldn't blame you, Corey."

For an instant, Corey wanted to tell her why Clay had taken his own life. But, however raw Corey's feelings, the impulse died. "Let her," he answered softly. "It's all she's got but God."

THAT NIGHT, AS he sat in the darkened bungalow Janice and he had rented, the phone rang. He considered not answering, and then, acting on instinct, did.

"Corey?" The voice, deep but gentle, was somehow familiar. "This is Cortland Lane."

Startled, Corey was slow to reply: Cortland Lane was now chairman of the Joint Chiefs of Staff, with worries well beyond the suicide of the late Cadet Clayton Grace. "Hello, General. I guess I know why you're calling."

"And I apologize for calling so late. But I wanted to tell you personally how sorry I am for your loss."

"Thank you," Corey answered. "It's been hard. I helped Clay get in, you remember."

"I remember. I also know how hard this is on your parents."

This, Corey knew, was his opening. "Not as hard as it could be."

"I understand. So let me assure you that it will get no worse for them. At least as far as the air force is concerned."

Corey felt a surge of relief. "Thank you, sir."

After a brief silence, Lane asked, "So what will you do now?"

Unsure of how to interpret the question, Corey answered, "I don't really know. It's hard to imagine waking up tomorrow, let alone campaigning."

There was another brief pause. "As a military man, Corey, I'm not supposed to care who wins. But I do. The day we met, I said you'd have to find your own way to live with Joe Fitts's death. Perhaps you've found it—as a senator you can do the country some real good. And losing will make *this* loss no better."

Four days later, Corey resumed his campaign.

Each appearance required an act of will. But in early November, at the age of thirty, Corey Grace was narrowly elected to the Senate.

15

LEXIE LISTENED IN SILENCE. WHEN AT LAST COREY turned to face her, her expression was dispassionate, as if nothing he had told her was in any way remarkable.

"So you never told your parents?"

"I never even told Janice."

Lexie studied him. "Do you know why?"

Corey leaned forward, arms resting on his knees as he stared at a patch of dirt. "What I told myself," he said, "was that teaching my homophobic parents a moral lesson was cruel—if they wanted to blame me, that was the price of compassion, and probably fair enough at that.

"As for Janice, I worried there might be some edgy night, maybe after a drink or two, when she zinged my mother with the truth. So it was better just to add another brick to our wall of silence. Or so I told myself at the time."

"And now?"

"Now I wonder. As long as my parents are living, I've got the same excuse. But there's something more to this.

"Right now, a lot of people see me as a 'good Republican' when it comes to gays. And what's my big contribution? I don't actively hate them. I don't beat the drums against gay marriage. I barely say anything, actually." Corey's voice turned harsh. "If I tell the truth about Clay, I've got no excuse for not confronting Christy and Marotta about victimizing people for who they were born to be, or for not labeling all their crap about protecting the sanctity of marriage the joke that it is. I mean, does anyone really think that Janice and I got divorced because we figured out that ten years later guys would be marrying each other in Massachusetts? Not only is it bullshit, but it's *exactly* the kind of calculated cruelty Price and Marotta profit from ginning up. They're generating hatred against gays as surely as Bob Christy helped push my brother off the roof—except that Christy may actually believe what he's saying." Corey's voice flattened. "That's what *I* believe, Lexie. And if I said it in public I'd be absolutely dead as a presidential candidate—over with, as in 'stick a fork in Corey Grace.' That's a pretty good reason to leave my brother behind."

"But you haven't."

All at once, Corey felt drained. "No. Clay's still with me. Only now he knows that I'm a coward."

Lexie considered him, silent.

"Say something," Corey demanded.

"About what? We're not defined by any one thing we're done—or haven't done. The truth about most people is more complicated than that." Pausing, she finished softly, "And kinder, I hope."

After a time, they began their slow descent to the wooded trail below, quiet until they reached the parking lot. Lexie turned to him, hands in the pockets of her sweatshirt. "You're only forty-three, Corey. You've got time to sort it out."

THE LATE-AFTERNOON FOOTBALL game pitted the Cleveland Browns, Corey's team, against the Pittsburgh Steelers. Sitting at the kitchen counter, Corey and Lexie ate salmon steaks and watched the Browns take a brutal pounding. But the game, Corey knew, was Lexie's way of leaving him in peace.

Shortly before halftime, his phone rang. "You watching CNN?" Rustin asked.

"Not if I can help it."

Even on the telephone, Corey could hear his adviser exhale. "Get back to Washington, Corey. Marotta's declaring tomorrow, and it's time to get moving. You've got no real campaign infrastructure or fund-raising operation—"

"I can raise money on the Internet," Corey objected. "I've got the name recognition to do it, and supporters on Wall Street who honestly care that our country's going off the cliff. So don't push me, Blake—I can wait a while longer."

Lexie, Corey saw, was trying to focus on her salmon. "Why risk it?" Rustin asked. "What will you know in a month or two that you don't know now? We both know you want this more than anything in the world."

"Do 'we' now," Corey said sardonically. "How nice for both of us—"

"Where *are* you, for Godsakes?"

"In Palm Springs with my lover, Michael, who looks fetching in the feather boa I just bought him. Using my own charge card, by the way, so Price will know where to send the reporters from Rohr News." Pausing, Corey finished tersely, "I'll be sure to watch Marotta. The rest can wait till I get back."

Hanging up, he clicked the television off. Lexie looked up at him, her expression indecipherable. "Do you think any less of me?" he asked.

"For what?"

It took Corey a moment to realize that in her mind, and perhaps in his, the question did not refer to Clay alone. "Whatever."

"No," she answered, and then amended this with a smile. "At least not yet."

That night, Corey lay awake, wishing she were close. But what he might say or do, and how she might respond, was as unclear to him as what his future held.

16

AT SIX A.M., ROB AND MARY ROSE MAROTTA sat drinking coffee at the breakfast table of their modest home outside Pittsburgh.

In one sense, this was typical, part of the fabric of their marriage—Rob, restless and unable to sleep; Mary Rose, despite her own weariness from the various demands of their children, stirring herself from the warmth of their bed to serve as a sounding board. But today was different: in four hours, he would declare his candidacy for president of the United States.

Despite this, Rob saw the two of them clearly: he in his robe, the thick black hair on his crown standing up in the way that amused Mary Rose, who, as she did so often, appraised him with a look combining keenness with affection. She battled with her weight now, and the fifteen extra pounds blurred the gamine face that had charmed him at age nineteen, but the girl he had fallen in love with still shone through the woman who had been his partner for twenty-four years of marriage. Whatever good fortune Corey Grace enjoyed, Rob told himself, he would not have traded this moment for the best moment of Grace's life.

Putting down her coffee mug, Mary Rose touched his wrist. "Once you start speaking," she assured her husband, "people will feel what they always do—that they're listening to someone smart and solid, who can meet whatever challenges we face. That's what people need so desperately, Rob—to feel safe."

Rob felt himself smile. "'Solid,'" he repeated. "'Safe.' It sort of sounds like cement settling in a driveway."

Mary Rose smiled. "You know what I mean. This is about Corey, I suspect. But why worry about Corey Grace when he's not what the party wants?"

"Because he's the kind of man who lightning strikes—a risk taker who doesn't care about much of anything but what he wants to do." He stirred more creamer into his coffee. "Most everyone else in our caucus is pretty simple to decode—they want to keep their seat, and they want their dignity honored, and it's all a matter of assessing how those needs affect them on a given issue. But Corey is unpredictable. And he's a much better intuitive politician than even Magnus gives him credit for."

Mary Rose sipped her coffee, her clear blue eyes gauging her husband's mood. "Why brood over him, Robbie? He may have good looks and good luck, but the same things that perplex you about Corey Grace bother other people."

Rob sat back in his chair. "He's *already* affecting me in ways I can't help. He gave Christy his excuse to run—you don't think Grace intended that when he stuck it to me on stem cells? Now I have to pretzel myself trying to keep Christian conservatives from voting for Christy, knowing that if I 'go too far' I may give Corey an opening to the left.

"That's the reason I've moved up my announcement— to regain the momentum and keep party people from looking toward Grace. In a two-way race I'd beat him—I've got the organization, the financial backing, and I've worked damned hard to keep the major factions of our party together. But in a three-way race, who knows?"

"What does Magnus say?"

The carefully neutral tone of the question, Rob knew

well, reflected their shared but unspoken misgivings about his master strategist. "That my first job is to preempt Christy, then finish him off in the early primaries. Worry about Grace later, is the strategy. Problem is, Christy's got his own money and a hard core of followers who get him confused with God. He may wind up being tougher to kill than a cockroach."

The faint smile this elicited from Mary Rose did not conceal her worry. "Sometimes I don't know whether Magnus is Mephistopheles or only Machiavelli. But you seem to think he's right about most things."

"He is." Marotta paused, reluctant to express his deeper feelings. Then, because they were partners in everything, he did so. "The problem with Magnus is that he respects no one as much as himself. Sometimes I think he believes he could make a tackling dummy president and I'm the dummy he's using to prove it."

His wife's smile vanished. "He chose you because you'd make a fine president. And because he needs you. Without you, Magnus Price is that nerd in glasses who couldn't get a date in high school. Just be yourself."

It was the closest she dared come, Rob perceived, to expressing her deeper concern: that the 'price of Price,' as she called it, would be for Rob to become so enmeshed in tactics that he could lose some part of himself. "Only Grace gets to be himself, honey. Mere mortals have to choose their spots. The key is to remember why we're doing this."

"Because you should be president," Mary Rose answered simply. "Whenever I listen to you, I'm so proud of what you stand for. And whatever doubts you may feel, people *see* how capable you are. That's why you'll win."

Rob smiled. Though this encouragement was typical, her reassurance buoyed him—he *had* come far, and she had been with him at every step. And now, as he had first imagined as a boy, he might be within sixteen months of becoming president.

"You know what I *really* look forward to today?" Mary Rose told him. "Being off my feet for a while." She took his hand. "Let's go look at the kids, Rob. We love them even more when they're asleep."

Rob caught something wistful in her expression, the shadow of a feeling she had expressed only once. "I know we're not enough for you," she'd told him after their second child was born. "I know what you need, Robbie, and that's okay. It's enough for you to love us."

Kissing her on the forehead, he went with her to Bridget's room.

17

COREY AND LEXIE SAT AT THE KITCHEN COUNTER, watching Marotta's announcement on Rohr News. Now and then the camera would pan to Mary Rose and the children. "When the rest of us were trying to find prom dates," Corey observed, "Rob was auditioning first ladies."

"What's their marriage actually like?" Lexie asked.

Corey shrugged. "Who really knows about someone else's marriage? But as near as I can tell, Mary Rose Marotta has both feet firmly located on planet Earth. She's the clearest evidence I've uncovered that beneath the layers of calculation Marotta has a core of decency."

Seated with Mary Rose and the children were Marotta's mother, his parish priest, and the Jesuit high school debate coach who had told him that, with diligence and the help of God, he could become a senator. Recounting this story, Marotta said, "I've asked Father Frank if he wouldn't mind amending that prediction upward."

The audience chuckled approvingly. But, Corey thought, there was something strained about Marotta's humor or perhaps something too telling about his ambition for it to be tossed off as a joke. "This is the America I grew up in," Marotta said. "A community of faith and love in which the dream of a working-class family for its oldest son could become, with God's blessing, a reality."

"When you were a kid," Lexie asked, "did *you* imagine being president?"

"Never. That's part of what unsettles Rob, I think. But then my family life wasn't quite so idyllic."

Marotta's voice grew stronger. "And at the heart of that world," he stressed, "was faith. That's the world Mary Rose and I want for our children, and America's children. Not simply a place that is safe from terrorism, but a place where it is safe to worship God . . ."

"Here we go," Corey said.

"A place," Marotta continued, "as blessed by God as the America that survived a depression, defeated Adolf Hitler, and vanquished the bleak vision of a Communist system that conceived of mankind without a precious spark of the divine.

"A place where men and women—and *only* men and women—marry for the reasons ordained by our Creator: to love and cherish each other, and to give their children the mother and father a loving God intended them to have . . ."

"In other words," Corey told Lexie. " 'You don't need Christy to protect you from gays.' "

"Schools where your children can pray, go to libraries free of obscenity, learn alternative explanations for the miracle of our existence, and be taught to appreciate that our flag stands for principles too sacred to permit its desecration. A country," Marotta concluded firmly, "where parents can still direct the moral and religious education of their children. Because our war against terror depends not only on the valor of our military, but the strength of our commitment to God . . ."

Once again, Rohr News panned to Mary Rose Marotta, holding the hands of a son and a daughter to each side of her as she listened intently to her husband. "That's an object lesson in the power of a single image," Lexie observed. "Mary Rose as message."

"She's a help," Corey agreed. "But I think he's going too far."

"In what way?"

"Rob's becoming a shape-shifter. Price told him to evoke Christy, so that's what he's doing. It's a bad road to start down—the idea of a president unsure of his own identity makes voters feel uneasy."

When Corey's cell phone started ringing, he turned it off.

LATER, AS COREY and Lexie sat on the deck, gazing at the ocean on a gray and misty day, he took her hand in his. "I'm already sorry to leave," he said.

She turned to him. "Those phone calls you ignored—"

"Were from Rustin. His message was: 'What, you want an engraved invitation to run? Marotta's given you an opening.'"

"Has he?"

"He's certainly given Republicans nervous about Christy reason to be nervous about *him*, especially after we got killed in the midterm elections last year. But the money people like Alex Rohr know the score. Right now, Price is whispering into their collective ear that Rob just has to say this stuff to make sure Christy doesn't screw things up." Corey gazed at the distant gray-white spume of the surf. "The problem with that is Christy. Price's idea is to unite the godly and the greedy behind Marotta. Christy's idea, I think, is to pit the godly against the greedy in order to draw me in. If I erode Marotta's support from the other side, Christy believes, he could actually win the nomination. What Christy *doesn't* believe is that *I* could actually win."

Lexie's tone was carefully dispassionate. "What do you believe, Corey?"

"That I'm sick of politics as usual. The Democrats are so bent on holding one interest group or another that they stand for absolutely nothing. They caved in on Iraq, afraid of being called wimps. Now the war's gone south, and instead of a coherent policy all they can offer is the stirring slogan '*We're* not *them*,' and deadlines for withdrawal.

"Then there's us. A couple of inaugurals ago I saw with utter clarity what my party had become. D.C. was awash in fundamentalists, of course—I saw one bus with pictures of Jesus and the president painted on its side. But most striking was a reception for our biggest donors. The place was jammed with fat, rich guys and their wives, the women wearing more fur than I'd seen this side of an old movie about the Visigoths invading Rome. There was so much smugness in the air I nearly choked.

"At the Inaugural Address, I occupied myself by watching them. When the president gave his riff about opportunity and diversity, they rarely applauded, though a lot of it was pretty good. But then he mentioned tax cuts." Corey turned to Lexie. "Suddenly they were on their feet, screaming like their team had won the Super Bowl. They'd come to Washington to celebrate their own greed."

Lexie smiled without humor. "And that surprised you?"

"The single-mindedness of it did. That's why they don't mind giving half the store to fundamentalists—if you're rich enough, they figure, whatever else happens in society won't affect you. At least until Al Qaeda eradicates the New York Stock Exchange.

"Hell, Price and Rohr even put Osama to work for them. In the last presidential election, our slogan came down to 'Vote for us or die.' But our foreign policy was run by the dumbest, most self-satisfied bunch of white guys who ever fucked up a savings and loan—except they fucked up an entire war. So now our slogan's 'Only *we* can save you from the consequences of our own disaster.'" Restless, Corey stood. "We've got to be about something other than fundamentalism, fear, greed, and nailing Mexicans at the border. And we need to offer young people a cause bigger than themselves, maybe even compulsory national service. The air force taught me that much."

Turning, Lexie gazed at their interlaced fingers, and then into his eyes. "You're running, aren't you?"

Corey jammed his hands in his pockets. "If the party nominates me," he answered, "I'll become president. There's no Democrat who can beat me, and the people who support Marotta know it. The question is whether they'd rather risk losing than risk what would happen if I won, and what they might do to stop me."

Lexie fell silent.

THEY ATE DINNER by candlelight, talking quietly. The evening had a faintly elegiac quality; before she went upstairs, Lexie kissed him gently on the lips.

Corey tingled with surprise. "What was that for?" he asked.

"For coming. And for staying when you could have left."

Once again, Corey could not sleep.

Deep in the night, he heard a quiet knock on the door. Then it opened, and moonlight framed her silhouette.

"Don't ask," she said softly. "Just accept that I want to be here."

She stood beside his bed, still for a moment. In the darkness he heard, but could not see, her robe dropping to the floor. Then she slipped beneath cool sheets.

Silent, they lay facing each other, inches apart. Reaching for her hand, Corey felt the pulse beneath Lexie's slender wrist. He leaned forward to kiss her, gently, and then she rested her forehead against his shoulder.

They stayed like that for a time, their bodies not quite touching. Corey traced her spine with his fingertips, aroused by her closeness but knowing there must be no rush. When he kissed the nape of her neck, he felt her quiver. The scent of her hair was sweet.

As she stretched, offering more of her, the tips of her breasts grazed his chest. Corey felt a current of desire. Touch was his means of sight.

His fingers slid to the base of her spine and, palm opening, brought her closer to him. She froze for an instant, then kissed him softly on the mouth. As the length of their bodies met, the tip of her tongue touched his.

Their kiss went deeper. Then Corey's lips slid down her throat, her breasts, the taut flatness of her stomach and, finally, lower still. This new intimacy drew a soft cry from her lips. The cry, repeated, and the rise of her hips signaled her insistence that this not stop. When at last she quivered with release, her fingers entwined his hair.

As Corey entered her, he felt her gazing into his face.

They began moving together, slowly at first, then with greater urgency. At the edges of his consciousness, Corey sensed her detaching from him, as though, even as her body merged with his, some part of her had slipped away. Her cry of fulfillment sounded solitary.

Swept up in his own release, Corey no longer thought at all.

LYING BESIDE HER, he tried to sort out the reason she had come to him; despite the deep mutuality of their desire, the intense closeness had dissipated into a tangible sense of her apartness. "Talk to me," he said.

She slid away, lying on her back beside him, only their fingers touching. In her silence Corey felt the intensity of thought.

"It matters to me, Lexie. I don't want you to hide."

He heard her draw a breath. Still gazing at the ceiling, Lexie began speaking in a monotone.

18

SHE WAS TWENTY-FOUR THEN, A PEACE CORPS volunteer at the end of her tour in rural Colombia. She arrived at a regional airport, the first leg of a trip that would bring her home to Greenville for two weeks with her mother, and then on to the fresh and daunting challenge of Yale Drama School.

As she checked through security, preoccupied with imaginings of her future, two uniformed guards with handguns pulled her aside.

Lexie assumed they were looking for cocaine. She had none: intent on her studies, she had not even smoked dope in college. Only when they led her to a windowless room did she sense her vulnerability.

She looked at the men more closely. One was mustached and cadaverous; the other squat, with the face of an Aztec mask. The first guard motioned Lexie to a chair, questioning her in soft, insistent Spanish—why was she here, why did she seem afraid. At the edge of her vision, the other man, his heavily muscled back turned toward her, rifled her backpack.

She had nothing to hide, Lexie insisted. Her tongue felt thick.

Turning, the squat man held aloft a small plastic bag of white powder, eyebrows arching in his cruelly impassive face.

"Cocaine," he said. "Unless you cooperate, you will spend many years in jail."

Panicking, Lexie began to protest.

The thin man shook his head. When he unzipped his pants, his penis was already hard.

The squat man pushed her head down.

Afterward, as she sobbed, the man she had sated held a revolver to her head.

They permitted her to undress herself. Then they shoved her to a mattress in the corner of the room. She fell to her knees, begging first in English, then in Spanish.

They pushed her onto her back. As the squat man entered her, she tried to detach herself, to force her mind to separate from her body. The tears running down her face felt like someone else's.

The second man, aroused again, thrust into her. When he was done, they rolled her on her stomach for the first man's use. There were several ways, he told her in Spanish, to take pleasure from an American woman. Close to unconscious, Lexie realized through her shock and anguish that they knew at least one word of English.

Nigger, the squat man repeated harshly, and laughed.

WHEN LEXIE LEFT the room at last, each step was that of an automaton. She went to the bathroom and vomited; afterward, still weak-kneed, she tried to wash herself, as though to erase what they had done. Boarding the plane, she felt the dull ache of her body, the residue of violation.

She changed planes twice, speaking only when addressed. Feigning sleep, she curled in her seat, her back to whomever they seated next to her. She barely acknowledged offers of a meal.

Her mother greeted her at the airport, eyes welling with the joy of Lexie's return. Embracing her, she complained, "You look like a zombie, girl."

Lexie kissed her forehead. "It was a long flight, Mama. I'll feel better soon."

LISTENING TO LEXIE'S story, Corey wrapped his fingers around hers. "I didn't tell anyone," she said. "I was female, and black, too often invisible growing up. And Daddy's heart condition had taught me the habit of silence."

"Even about *this*?"

"When it mattered," she answered wearily, "I couldn't make those two men hear me, or see me as a girl anyone loved. They didn't just violate my body—they took part of my humanity. I'd become invisible again.

"All I wanted was to erase that moment forever."

SHE FOUND A boyfriend at Yale—an acting student who burned so brightly that he seemed to live at the extremity of his nerves.

"Heroin," Lexie told Corey flatly. "The perfect rabbit hole for me to crawl down. I experienced each sensation vividly, and felt nothing at all inside.

"I was company for Peter. That was all he wanted from me." Her tone became flat again. "We snorted heroin every night. I learned to function, get myself through the school year. The day it ended, I flew to Mexico and checked into a seedy hotel near Cancún.

"I called Mama to say we were on vacation, and locked the door. Then I shook and writhed and sweated until I was all dried out." Corey felt her turn to face him. "I've watched you wonder why I don't drink alcohol. In Mexico, I looked in the mirror and saw an addict, with burn holes for eyes. I never want to know that woman again."

"At least you learned something important, Lexie—that you're strong."

Lexie inhaled. "Kicking heroin was the easy part. The rest is harder to fix."

HER SEPARATENESS, AND her silence, became part of who she was.

"Even after I married Ron," she said, "I chose not to tell him. Just like you never told Janice about Clay.

"Maybe I thought Ron was too caught up in his own worries and needs to really see me. And maybe that was what I wanted: a man who, even during sex, was focused on his own desires." She turned on her back again. "In a way, I underrated him. But only in a way."

"How so?"

"After I found out he was cheating, I asked if we could see a therapist. That's when he first described for me how distant I was, as a woman and as a lover—that there was something about me he couldn't touch.

"I forced myself to tell him the story, tears streaming down my face, with a male therapist sitting between us. After I finished, all Ron could say was 'My God, Lexie, *I* didn't rape you.' That's when I knew we were done."

COREY LET MOMENTS pass, trying to absorb all she had told him. Quietly, he asked, "Why did you come to me tonight?"

"I'm not sure yet. Maybe because I think you're going to run."

"And so you decided to sleep with me?"

She turned to face him. "If you *do* run, that fact will come between us, for all the reasons we understood before I called you. And now you know another reason.

"Nothing that's happened between us gives me the right to even hope that you won't run. And I didn't make love with you to give you second thoughts." Her voice became dismissive. "Maybe accepting your ambitions is a form of self-protection. There's a built-in end to us, and it won't be anyone's fault."

Sifting through his emotions, Corey found that the thought of never seeing her again made him feel far lonelier than before. "Don't be so sure of what I want."

"You should think about that very hard," she answered evenly. "As I will."

They did not make love again. At length, quiet, she fell asleep in his arms. Sleepless, he listened to the rhythm of her breathing.

In the morning, Corey drove to the airport alone.

19

On Wednesday afternoon, Corey drove with Jack Walters to the horse country of Virginia, where his media adviser, Brian Lacey, owned a farm, a place for them to assess, without being seen or heard, Corey's chances of winning the presidency.

Blake Rustin was already there. The four men sat on Lacey's brick patio around a table covered with printouts and charts, the bones of Corey's prospective candidacy. Despite all of Rustin's prior successes, Corey knew, this was his chief adviser's chance to leave an indelible mark by placing an insurgent candidate in the White House, and his sense of urgency was matched by his preparation.

"We've done blind polling," he told the others, "describing Corey, Marotta, and Christy only by their attributes. For Corey, the key phrases are 'war hero,' 'independent,' 'defies his party on money in politics,' and 'not captive to the Christian Right.'" Facing Corey, he said, "You beat Christy by thirteen points, and Marotta by eleven—"

Corey looked at him quizzically. "Just how did you describe Marotta, Blake?"

A keen look crossed Brian Lacey's diplomat's face. "Marotta," Rustin answered, "is a professional politician with a cherubic-looking wife. His calling card is 'father of five' and 'stands up for family values.'

"You're a genuine hero, Corey. People trust you to clean up corruption, make your own decisions, and straighten out this fucked-up 'war on terror.'" Rustin placed his fingers on a sheet of data. "You risked your life to shoot down that Iraqi general, and then withstood torture at the hands of Arab enemies. That's invaluable."

Not if you saw Joe Fitts's severed head, Corey wanted to say. Instead he turned, gazing at three dappled horses cantering in a field. Briefly detached from the others, he wondered what Lexie might think of this meeting, or the truth about Joe's death.

"Blake's right," Lacey interposed. "I know you don't like to cash in on your medals, Corey. But ads with pictures of you and your navigator would have a real impact."

Corey did not respond. Turning to Rustin, he asked, "Did you run any polls with real *names* attached?"

"Of course. Among likely Republican primary voters, you're neck and neck with Christy, and only seven points behind Marotta—"

"In other words," Corey interrupted, "my fellow Republicans like my biography until they know it's me. To Magnus Price, the *real* me comes with attributes like 'soft on gays,' 'callous toward stem cells,' 'panders to blacks,' and 'indifferent to the moral concerns of Christians.' Along with charming personal qualities like 'arrogant,' 'crummy father,' and, worst of all, 'unmarried,' which leaves open the question of *which* sex I might be having extramarital sex with. In the fever swamp of the Republican right, I'm as appealing as Chairman Mao."

As Rustin scrutinized him, Corey could read his anxious, unspoken question: *Where were you last weekend, and with whom?* "I grant your problems with our party, Corey. And, yes, I wish you'd beaten Marotta to Mary Rose. But if we can get you to the general election, Americans will make you the next president of the United States."

Even in this jaded company, Corey saw the talismanic power of those words. And he felt sympathy for Rustin, whose ambitions could only be realized through his surrogate, and who could only fret as Corey decided. "Chances are I never get to the general election," Corey argued. "Why do you think Marotta and Christy are fighting for the title of God's second-born child? In primaries like South Carolina, where turnout is low, the predominant voters are conservatives galvanized by their church, Christian talk radio, and even the hit men at Rohr News."

"Not this year," Lacey countered. "This may be the year that Marotta and Bob Christy tear Price's grand design apart—a year, by the way, in which Americans are more frightened and confused than ever about how we combat terror. And they've moved the primaries up in states like New York and California, where you figure to do well!

"Who knows what happens if there's another 9/11? By the time they get through with each other, Marotta and Christy may look like pygmies compared to Osama bin Laden. That leaves you." Lacey's speech became ever more insistent. "Only *you* can get to all the young people who don't vote. Only *you* can offer hope instead of rancor and division. Only *you* have the charisma to go over the head of the donor classes, and bail this party out of the mess it's in. And this year may be the *only* year that you can change our party for good. So I ask you, Corey: do you have the right not to run?"

Once more, Corey was silent; Lacey was deeply experienced, and his instincts were as sharp as his skill at crafting a message. Watching Corey's face, Jack Walters suggested, "Let's go over the issues—gay rights, for an opener. What do you think, Blake?"

Rustin eyed Corey with a wary expression. "We have to finesse that. Corey doesn't want to be for a constitutional ban on gay marriage. The classically conservative thing to say is that we're against it but we don't need to tamper with the Constitution."

"What about civil unions?" Lacey asked. "That's trickier."

"We should be against them, at least for now. But quietly." Turning to Corey, Rustin elaborated, "In the short term, we have to pacify suburban moderates without making religious conservatives irate. The subtle message to suburbanites is 'Keep having gay cousin Arnie and his partner to Thanksgiving, and eventually we'll work things out.' I know you don't want us to be the 'mean party,' Corey."

"So you can live with my vote on stem cells?"

"Under these circumstances, yes. With Christy and Marotta splitting Christian voters, that vote on stem cells enhances your appeal to centrists." He paused, then added, "Still, you might start going to church. Some plain-vanilla denomination, like Methodist or Presbyterian—Episcopalians are turning gay men into bishops, so they're out. It could help to put out that your mom's an evangelical—"

"Mom," Corey said succinctly, "is staying where she is. If God supports my candidacy, He isn't telling her. Pray that Christy and Marotta leave her out of this."

Walters kept his eyes on Corey. "There's also affirmative action."

"Oh," Corey said quickly, "I'm against *that*."

Brian Lacey raised his eyebrows. "Really?"

"For white people," Corey amended with a smile. "From my own experience, being a privileged white guy is the biggest affirmative action program in America—anyone who doesn't get *that* isn't paying attention. So I'm absolutely against more privileges for guys like us."

Lacey's own smile was a wispy ghost. "I hope you're not planning to say that."

"Not as I just put it, Brian. But we both know that there's still a racial problem, and our party's response is slickly packaged condescension." Scanning the others, Corey said, "Look at our last convention. There were more black entertainers on the stage than black delegates in the hall—Rohr News interviewed all nine of them, I think.

"Our outreach to minorities is a joke. Someday we'll realize that sticking symbolic black folks in the cabinet doesn't cut it anymore." Standing, Corey asked, "So is everyone interested in how the world looks to *me*?"

"Of course," Rustin answered. "We all are."

"Our military is degraded from fighting the wrong war. Our political dialogue is bankrupt. Our party vamps on global warming while our kids wonder if *their* kids will still be able to breathe. And, assuming they can breathe, we'll have helped to put them as deep in debt as they are dependent on foreign oil. And what's our solution? Sticking oil wells next to caribou and reindeer." Corey began pacing. "*If* I ran for president, I'd have a very hard time not mentioning some of that. Which, in this party, is a good reason not to run.

"My compelling reason *to* run is to change our party, our politics, and this whole corrupt system, which is strangling us all. I'd run as if politics is an honorable adventure, in the belief that Americans deserve more from us than narcotic babble punctuated by demagoguery and slander." Folding his arms, Corey finished evenly: "All of you will go on, regardless of what I do. But I only get one chance, and I'm not sure that this is it."

Rustin placed curled fingers to his lips. "There are things you can do, Corey, short of jumping off the cliff."

"Such as?"

"Assembling a campaign staff. Telling potential supporters to stay loose. Acknowledging that Christy's changed the political landscape. Redoubling your appearances in early primary states like New Hampshire, South Carolina, Michigan, and California."

"What about Iowa?" Walters asked.

"A waste of time, packed with evangelicals." Pointedly, Rustin added, "*That* part's good for Christy, though. By winning Iowa he could take a piece out of Marotta."

Lacey looked at the others and then stood to face Corey. "We've all drawn straws," he said quietly, "and I get to ask the inevitable question."

"Which is?"

"Is any part of your reluctance based on something—anything—that voters would find disqualifying?"

Corey gave him a faint smile. "Voters? Depends on which ones, I guess. But there's nothing you don't know that *I* would find disqualifying."

Briefly, Lacey glanced at Rustin. "Then all of us agree, Senator. We admire you, and we want to help you to become president. But it's time for you to decide."

The three men stared at him, awaiting an answer as Corey tried to envision his life and future, the personal and political consequences of one course or another. But nothing was clear to him, and the reasons for his irresolution seemed murkier than before. "I appreciate all you've done," he told them. "And I owe you a decision. By Thanksgiving, I'll be in or out."

"Six weeks?" Rustin inquired dubiously. "It's very late already."

"Six weeks," Corey affirmed. "Put together a travel plan."

*

DRIVING HOME, COREY discovered that he could escape their importuning but not the echo of his own disquiet.

That night, unable to sleep, he called Lexie. Though she sounded surprised, even pleased, all she did was ask, "What's this about, Corey?"

"It's sort of a jumble. But I wanted you to know that last weekend was important. At least for me."

Even on the telephone, he could sense her hesitation. "Then I'm glad to hear from you," she answered. "I guess phone calls are safe enough."

20

"ABOUT RELIGION," LEXIE ASKED, "WHAT EXACTLY *do* you believe?"

Corey sat in his motel room in Nashua, New Hampshire, cell phone to his ear. "Not much," he answered. "But I do believe that there's a balance in the world: that kindness breeds kindness, and that evil comes to those who perpetrate it. God doesn't control our destiny—we do. To me, character is fate."

He could hear her reflect. "Not very comforting, my mama would have said."

"It should be. It means that our lives, and our world, are our responsibility. No one else has the power, and there's no one else to blame."

This snatch of conversation, like their others, was stolen between tight schedules complicated by different time zones: while Corey juggled his duties as senator with crisscrossing key primary states, Lexie was finishing a movie on the West Coast—a commercial project in which, to her amusement, she played a Secret Service agent who was the president's clandestine lover. "Not the First Lady," she pointed out dryly. "Even this piece of eyewash aspires to a little realism."

It was best, Corey decided, to take a pass on parsing *that* one. "Sounds right to me," he answered. "It's hard to imagine you in church-lady clothes and sensible shoes, gazing at your husband with mindless adoration."

Lexie let it slide.

That became the pattern of their conversations, ranging from the everyday and amusing—the stifling vanity of Lexie's costar; the woman in Michigan who told Corey that a male's biblical duty was to take the garbage out—to the more serious, as when Corey recounted his latest awkward phone call to the daughter he barely knew.

"I'm sorry," Lexie said, and then asked, "Did you ever think about trying fatherhood again?"

Corey hung up his suit coat in the closet of another motel. "In the abstract, yes. But there hasn't been anyone I'd try *with*. And who's to say, given my past performance and the world I live in, that I'd do any better?"

"You wouldn't, necessarily. You don't have kids just to have them, or just because your partner wants them—any more than you could fairly tell a woman who wanted children *not* to have them."

She had clearly considered this, Corey thought. "Did *you* ever want kids?"

"I always have. But eventually I realized that Ron wanted to be the only child of our marriage. He couldn't stand the competition."

Corey caught the sadness in her tone. "I guess he wasn't honest about that, either."

"Maybe I just didn't want to hear him. But no, Ron wasn't terribly honest about a lot of things. Sometimes honesty means conflict. He found that inconvenient."

This exchange lodged in Corey's mind. So the night she asked if he had resolved to run for president, he weighed his answer carefully. "Some of the indicators say that I should. The crowds are getting bigger, and the media buzz is better than I expected—for this week, at least, I'm the 'candidate of candor.' But the odds are still long, and campaigning breeds the danger of self-delusion: there's always someone to tell you you're the one, and you all too easily stop seeing the reasons you might not be. Being compared to Winston Churchill tests one's sense of balance."

Lexie laughed. "If it does," she answered, "it's all your fault. Character is fate."

Gazing out the window of his limousine, Corey found himself smiling at the darkened streets of Detroit. Her next question caught him up short. "So," she asked, "what exactly are the two of us doing?"

"Talking on the phone?"

"And I enjoy this, Corey—I even find myself scheduling things around it. But I've started asking myself where this is going."

"Does there have to be an answer?"

"I already know the answer if you choose to run. And I think you should run, now or later, if only so you don't spend your life calling yourself a coward. So why am I hanging on the phone? This isn't a relationship, really—it's not even phone sex."

"No, it isn't," Corey said. "We've already done much better."

"Oh," she said quietly, "I've thought about that, too. But that's dumb, really. It's my own fault, Corey, but you're taking up more space in my life than makes sense for me. I even wonder about who might be intercepting our cell-phone calls, and then hate myself for worrying that even talking with you will screw up your career. It's time for this girl to get a grip."

Silent, Corey stared out at the darkness.

"Corey?"

"I'm still here. So what are you doing once you've wrapped this film?"

"Going away. I've taken a place in Cabo San Lucas for the first week of November."

It sounded like a sudden decision. "Is that a strategic withdrawal?" he asked. "Or would you like some company?"

Lexie hesitated. "What would our reason be, Corey—yours *and* mine?"

"To spend more time together. Then maybe we can figure out the reason."

For a moment, all Corey heard was static. When Lexie spoke, her voice sounded tinnier than before. "Let me think about it."

For the next two days, Corey could not reach her. Then, driving to the airport for a flight to South Carolina, he picked up her message. "Here are the dates," she began. "If you've really thought about the fallout and still want to come, let me know."

Corey hit the button for her number.

LEXIE HAD TAKEN a villa at Pedregal, nestled in the hills above the harbor.

When she answered his knock, she was wearing a bikini. Corey stared at her. "Jesus," he said. "The last time it was dark."

Her expression was both embarrassed and amused. "I wasn't sure when you'd get here—I was napping on the porch. Collect yourself, and I'll show you the inside."

The top floor was open, with a porch that provided both sun and shade. When she led him there, Corey saw that it overlooked the villas below and, farther out, a palm-sheltered harbor, its color a vivid blue. As he gazed down at the rear garden, two graceful birds performed a pas de deux above the swimming pool.

"Beautiful," he said.

"And quiet. We can eat dinners in—they have a staff for that." She hesitated. "I assume no one knows you're here."

Corey still gazed at the pool. "I left under protest—

Blake's and Jack's. All they know is that I'm not in New Hampshire, where I should be, and that I'll be out of touch for a few days."

By unspoken consent, they moved on to other subjects.

That evening, a shy woman who spoke no English prepared fresh fish for them and left. They sat on the porch, unhurried, watching a cruise ship ease toward the harbor.

"What I've concluded," Corey ventured, "is that you and I are a lot alike."

She eyed him with a skeptical smile. "You think so?"

"At least our challenges are alike. For one thing, it's hard for us to find peers, and other people project onto us the things they need us to be. Not that we don't ask for that. But that leaves it up to us to remember the laws of gravity."

"That's not hard for me, Corey. I just have to remember far enough back." Sipping her mineral water, she watched the progress of the ocean liner. "People can be funny, though. One night, after I'd finished performing in a play, Ron picked me up in this old beat-up Honda Civic I was too sentimental to unload. There were autograph seekers outside; a woman who saw me getting in the car was totally horrified. 'Why are you getting in that car? You can't get in *that* car.'

"It was like I'd ruined her dream of being me. Funny thing is, I actually felt bad for her."

"Do you still have the Honda?"

"Of course," she said dryly. "During the divorce negotiations, Ron swapped it for the beach house in Malibu. I hear his girlfriend liked it there."

Carey laughed. "I'm feeling a little like Ron," he conceded, looking around them. "I couldn't afford all this."

"So pay the cook, if it bothers you. Whatever else you are, Corey, you're not like Ron."

Corey's smile faded. "Janice might disagree," he said at

length. "Whatever the case, maybe it's time to talk about my marriage. And how and why it ended."

AFTER WINNING ELECTION to the Senate, still grieving for Clay, Senator-elect Corey Grace had immersed himself in the present, building his staff, meeting more of his new colleagues, and searching for a home in Washington that Janice and Kara would like. But when he showed Janice the real-estate listings, she showed so little interest that he asked what was happening to them.

Glancing toward the small yard where Kara was playing, she led Corey to their bedroom, closing the door behind her. Sitting beside him on the bed, she stared straight ahead, a portrait of silent anguish.

"I can't go with you," she said.

"Why not?" Corey asked. "This is a new start for us."

She turned to him, her eyes filled with a pity so devoid of affection that it cut him to the core. "Because I'm in love, Corey."

There was no doubt she did not mean him. "Who is he?" Corey managed to ask.

"He's Australian—right now, names don't matter. I met him two years ago, while you were in the Gulf." Briefly, she looked away. "When you disappeared, and I thought you were dead, it all had this terrible simplicity. Then you were alive again, so badly damaged, so filled with remorse, that I thought I should give us a second chance. And I thought that if you were leaving the air force we *had* a chance."

"And this guy?"

"Was patient. I told him I couldn't leave you then, and not to think I was coming back." She shook her head in sorrow. "I tried, Corey—honestly I did, I tried as best I could. But then there was politics.

"I even tried that. But I hate the life—just like with the air force, you were gone again. What kind of life is that?" She folded her hands. "He has room in his life for Kara. He even wants more children."

Corey felt the bile in his throat. "I have to hand it to you, Janice. At least you didn't turn to drink."

His wife blanched. "No," she said in a brittle voice. "I'm not my mother. And you're not my father—I know that you had other women, perhaps a number of them. Not that it matters now."

The finality in her tone—as fatal, it seemed, as Corey's own failings—transformed his anger into an aching sadness. "Where would you live?"

"Sydney."

"And Kara?"

Janice inhaled. "I know you can make this hard for me—for us. Please don't. Please, give me the life I need—"

"It's not just about you."

"I know," she acknowledged softly. "But Kara can see you summers."

"*Their* summer, Janice, is *our* winter." When Janice looked down, he said harshly, "Let's not mince words. You're asking me to write off my eight-year-old daughter."

"I'll try to help, I promise." Eyes shiny with tears, she touched his face. "You never had room for us, Corey. Who's been Kara's parent? Who *would* be, even if I lived in Washington? Kara deserves a chance to be more whole than either of us. I think this man and I can give her that. That's something to try for, isn't it?"

Corey could find no answer.

In early December, the day before she left for Australia, he said good-bye to his daughter. Kara hugged him stiffly. Then she ducked into her mother's car; excited about her new adventure, the little girl did not look back.

21

THE REST OF THE DAY PASSED GENTLY, LEXIE absorbing what he had told her.

That night she lay next to him. When he reached for her in the quiet darkness, she turned her face to him. Her skin felt warm.

Their lovemaking was sweet and intense. Only later, awakening, did Corey realize she was gone.

Rising, he pulled on shorts.

She was standing at the railing of their porch, gazing intently at the moonlit bay. She did not see him; instinct told him not to startle her. He returned to bed alone.

When he awakened at first sunlight, Lexie had returned.

It was warm at dawn. By nine in the morning, Corey discovered, the sun had risen high enough for the porch to be a welcome source of shade. He found that he liked to sit at the table, drink a cup of strong espresso, and reflect.

On the second morning, a thin, low fog sat over the harbor, filtering the sunlight and turning a massive luxury liner into a shadowy shape that could have been an island, until, as it moved slowly toward the harbor, its features became clear.

"It's like a mystery ship," Lexie observed, hands resting on his shoulders. "So have you mapped out your day?"

"Relaxing has always been hard for me." He turned to her. "An hour ago, I realized I didn't know what time it was. In the military, I always knew: everything was hyperorganized, with the days sliced into segments and tasks. Same thing in this job—one appointment after another. Your soul never catches up to your body."

"No choice now," Lexie answered. "You're marooned. No one knows where you are, so there's no one to save you from yourself."

Corey smiled. "No one except you."

Beyond the mists, Corey noted, the water had begun to sparkle, fireflies of light on an ocean still tinted gray. "Maybe," he said finally, "I'll watch the boat."

Lexie did stretches and sit-ups, then ran for several miles down and up the stone road that wound from their villa to the main street toward town. When she returned, Corey was lying on a raft with his eyes closed, enjoying the cool water of the pool.

"Your boat's still there," she told him. "Why aren't you watching it?"

"I got to thinking, and then I figured out what's wrong with my life. Or maybe any politician's life."

"What's that?"

"You strip-mine your own resources—all your energy, intelligence, creativity. Worst of all, there's never enough time to reflect. Or maybe you're just better at that than I am."

"Maybe so."

That afternoon, in the light and shadow of the bedroom, Corey and Lexie made love again. They dozed for a while. When they awakened, the cruise ship was gone.

"Change," Corey noted philosophically. "Sometimes it's hard to live with."

Lexie smiled. "Hungry?" she asked.

FOR THE MOST part, Corey discovered, the private world they created, in which he felt suspended between past and future, was sufficient.

Sometimes he thought about politics; at others, to his

surprise, he thought of little else but Lexie. She had begun to fill his senses.

Yet they were both independent—parting, coming together again, talking, reading novels when they wished to. This shared routine, as sensual in its own way as their lovemaking, was something that, for the most part, he savored—with each day, he came to realize, he felt less solitary. But at other times he was disoriented, as if their time here was a shadowy prelude to the all-consuming life, should he choose it, of a candidate for president. He wondered if she sensed this.

That afternoon, after a late lunch, Lexie told him a story.

When she had first gone to the University of South Carolina, her uncle, then a state representative, had driven her to school. In the parking lot, he'd said, "You're at college now, Lexie, where none of us can look out for you. Things will happen to you just because you're my niece and your name is Hart. Some of it will be good. Some of it will be bad. But in the end they'll more or less even out." He paused, then finished with uncharacteristic gentleness: "But there are other things that will happen just because you're black. And these things will never even out. *That's* the reality you'll have to deal with."

Lexie had said nothing in reply. But on the day before Thanksgiving, when her uncle picked her up, she told him she understood.

Listening, Corey watched her gaze become distant. "The football team," she explained to him, "had a star running back, George Rodgers—a gifted black athlete who was a contender for the Heisman Trophy. Next to us in the parking lot where my uncle met me was a pickup truck with two bumper stickers. One was a Confederate flag; the second said 'Rodgers for Heisman.'

"My uncle was fixing to run for Congress. I pointed to the truck and said, 'Whoever owns that would never have a "Hart for Congress" sticker.'

"My uncle gave me this funny kind of smile. 'Why not, girl?'

"'At the homecoming game,' I explained, 'they introduced the first black homecoming queen we'd ever had. I was sitting near a bunch of white boys, most of them pretty drunk. When that girl was introduced, a lot of them sat there and booed. But when they introduced the football team and called George Rodgers's name, every one of them got to their feet, hollering and cheering.'

"My uncle went quiet. 'Yeah,' he said, 'It's okay for us to entertain them, but not to represent them. The real change won't come, if it ever does, until those boys die off.'"

Corey absorbed this for a time, wondering what message she intended to convey. "Earlier, I hope. If Cortland Lane had run, he might have been elected president."

Lexie looked into his face. "Corey," she said evenly, "I don't mean to make you a whipping boy for racism. But there's a reason we view this differently, one anyone else could see just by looking at us. And I think deep down you know it."

"What do you mean?"

She tilted her head. "Tell me this: why do you think we're hiding out?"

The question made him edgy. "To protect our privacy. To get the chance to be ourselves without explaining ourselves."

"True enough," she conceded. "And you know how little I want to live my life in public. But another reason is to protect your chance of becoming president."

"I don't accept that, Lexie."

"Don't you? I guarantee your advisers would, especially

whoever does your polling." She put down her iced tea with exaggerated care. "If they knew you were with me, they'd be horrified."

"Yeah. Because you're an actress—"

"Don't be disingenuous, Corey—it doesn't suit you. They'd be horrified because I'm black." Her effort to speak dispassionately was palpable to Corey. "A lot of white folks—especially in your party—would know for sure you were a 'liberal,' with 'values' unlike theirs. There'd be whispers like 'Can you imagine a black First Lady and children of color in the White House?'"

"For Godsakes, Lexie, that's what America's going to look like."

She gave him a thin smile. "We're getting a little ahead of ourselves, I know—we haven't had the baby yet. But other people will go there without us. So save the pieties about the multicultural face of America for campaign speeches, where it's safer.

"Too many of your people wouldn't want me to represent their version of America, and that'd be on their minds even if it's not on ours." Her voice softened. "My people, too. Some might like you better; others would like me less. 'What's wrong with that girl?' they'd say. 'Isn't a black man good enough for her?'

"Then there's the media. To them, I'm not 'an actress'— I'm a '*black* actress.' Why do you think I got bombarded with questions about Janet Jackson's exposed breast— because I'm an expert on wardrobe malfunctions, or maybe because I've got two breasts? Janet and I've got one obvious thing in common: we're both black." She shook her head emphatically. "So let's be real here. Put aside the actress thing, and you and I still can't be seen as people in a relationship. You're playing with fire to even be here."

Corey stood and walked to the edge of the porch.

Hands on the railing, he gazed out at the waters of the bay, a gray-blue shadow in the light of late afternoon. He felt her touch his arm. "Sorry, baby," she said. "I *did* ask you to come."

"I was just thinking, that's all. There must be a restaurant here you like."

"Come on, Corey. What exactly are you trying to prove?"

"Don't spoil the moment, all right? I'm finally paying for a meal."

She kissed him on the cheek. "Okay," she said. "Now you've made your point, and I get to be the sane one here. Thank you, but no."

He turned, taking her face in his hands. "Just how seriously do you take me? As a person, I mean."

She looked into his eyes. "As a person? Pretty seriously, I'd say."

"Okay, then. I'm seriously tired of holing up here. I was looking at the guidebook this morning and saw a place called L'Orangerie."

Lexie gave him a somewhat crooked smile. "Never been there," she answered.

THEY ARRIVED EARLY, hoping to avoid gawkers, and secured a secluded table in the corner of a beach-side garden, from which they could see two sailboats slicing the water, a trawler trolling for fish, and a lone parasailor gliding in and out of view. Lexie smiled across at him. "This really *is* nuts, you know."

"Yup." He touched his Scotch on the rocks to her tall glass of iced tea. "Anyone ever mention that you look like a movie star?"

She rolled her eyes. "Is *that* the best you can do? Because it's completely lame."

They both felt oddly giddy, Corey realized. "You do notice," he told her, "that we're acting like two kids who just cut physics class to go to the beach."

Lexie reached across the table for his hand. "Yeah," she said softly. "I noticed."

They fell into easy conversation. When the middle-aged waiter came back, scrupulously attentive to Lexie, she spoke to him in flawless Spanish. Watching, Corey reflected that she must have acquired this fluency in Colombia, reminding him of all that had happened to her. Then she turned to him, and he dismissed the thought.

Lexie chose smoked salmon and sea bass; Corey, fresh scallops and shrimp Pernod, accompanied by a chilled half bottle of Mexican chardonnay. Smiling, Lexie said, "I'm driving, I guess."

"Sure. Why do you think I brought you?"

As the appetizers arrived, Corey noted that the tables nearby were beginning to fill. He decided to focus on how beautiful she was.

She raised her eyebrows. "Why are you looking at me like that?"

"Because *I* get to—not some other guy. I like that quite a lot."

She studied him more seriously. "About that fictitious baby," she said after a time. "I know how fictitious your own life makes it. But in the long run, I want one, and my long run's getting shorter. Just so you know."

"Understood," Corey said. "As for me, no one wants their children raised by wolves."

A softness settled between them, faintly pensive. Lexie took his hand again. "I like looking at you, too."

A flash made Lexie blink. Starting, Corey glanced around them and saw a woman in a sundress stuff a camera in her purse. Seeing his expression, she mouthed,

"Sorry" and backed into the shadows.

"Oh, well," Corey murmured.

Lexie's startled look had changed to resignation. After a moment, she said wryly, "You're still okay, Senator. The back of your head looks like anyone else's."

Their entrées arrived. They focused on the food to let the feeling of invasion gradually recede. By dessert, their equilibrium recovered, they were discussing Lexie's brief career as a high school javelin thrower. "All arm," she reminisced, "and no technique. One time I nearly speared the coach."

"Ouch," Corey said, and then noted a thin, thirtyish woman standing over their table, looking hesitant but carrying a pen and a scrap of paper.

"I'm so sorry," she told Lexie. "But I saw you here, and it's my only chance to say how much I love your movies."

Lexie mustered a gracious smile. "That's so nice. And you are . . . ?"

"Carole Walsh."

"Thank you, Carole—that means a lot. Would you like me to sign that for you?"

As Lexie wrote her name, the woman looked at Corey. "I'm sorry," she said. "Somehow I feel like I should know you."

Smiling, Corey shook his head. "It's just because I'm with *her.* Don't worry, it happens to me all the time."

Reassured, the woman thanked Lexie for her autograph and returned to her table with a visible glow.

Corey grinned. "*That's* certainly humbling."

Lexie gave him an ambiguous smile. "Get used to it. Unless you get yourself elected president."

Five minutes later, they left, aware that others had begun to watch them.

*

THEY SAT ON the porch, Corey drinking brandy, Lexie with his sport coat draped over her shoulders. Quietly, she said, "I hope that woman didn't throw you off."

Corey shook his head. "I was thinking about something else."

"Politics?"

"Yes and no," he answered, and he knew that it was time to talk about Joe Fitts. "Actually, I was remembering a friend."

THOUGH LEXIE SAID nothing, her stillness revealed how closely she was listening.

"You know what I still wonder about?" Corey finished softly. "Whether Joe was alive when they cut his head off."

When he said nothing more, Lexie spoke at last. "Wasn't there an autopsy?"

"They never returned his body. That much was a mercy—his family never knew. I concealed that fact, too."

"You were also tortured, Corey. Where does *that* fit into this story?"

"Nowhere. If they'd wanted anything from me, I'd have given it to them. All I wanted was to live. But all they wanted was to make me suffer, and one of them wouldn't let me die. So I wound up a senator instead." Corey drained his brandy. "A while back, when my media guy proposed putting Joe's picture in our campaign ads, I felt like I was dancing on his grave."

"Will you let them?"

"No."

Lexie drew her chair a little closer. "I'm sorry," she said after a time. "Sorry for Joe, sorry about how you feel. But that raises something I have to ask you. Is being with *me* a way of compensating for your guilt about Joe Fitts?"

Corey felt a surge of anger. "Get over yourself," he

snapped. "For once. Just how fucked up do you think I am?" Then he stood up, his temper already cooling. He began speaking rapidly but clearly. "This much I'll give you—Joe made me think differently about race, and that affects my politics. But he did that by living, not dying.

"What Joe's *death* did was turn me into an illusion. There isn't a Kiwanis meeting in America where I won't be introduced as an 'American hero.' *That's* my edge over Marotta and Christy—only one of us was reckless and self-absorbed enough to cost a friend his life, and I'm riding it for all it's worth. *That's* the point of the story." He paused, his hands shoved in his pockets. "I'm not telling you all this because I need some black person to grant me absolution. I'm telling you because this is the ambiguous space I live in, and I wanted you to know.

"I said I didn't want you to hide, Lexie. I don't want to either." His voice went quiet. "This wasn't about race, but about us. I hope you can live with that."

Her chin gracefully resting on arched fingers, Lexie appraised him, so closely that he felt as though what became of them might depend on what she saw. At last she said, "So do you want to know what I think?"

"Yes."

"Cortland Lane was right—you made a split-second decision, and the consequences to you and your friend were different. The question is how you process that, and what you do with it in the world." Lexie paused. "The first part's hard—I understand that. But you wouldn't have done anything for anyone by turning your back on politics and the chance to become a senator. It's your appreciation of how you got there, and your desire to give it meaning, that makes you different from Marotta. And that quality is as real as the 'heroism' you're convinced is so phony. So," she finished, quoting him with the faintest smile, "I hope you can live with that."

Sitting down across from her, Corey puffed his cheeks and exhaled. After a time, he murmured, "Quite an evening, wasn't it?"

"It was," she said, and took his hand. "Let's go to bed."

THE NEXT DAY they resumed their routine.

Much was the same. Lexie ran; Corey floated in the pool. In the afternoon, when it was hottest outside, they made love in the shelter of their bedroom. After dinner, they watched an old movie, Lexie offering commentary as they nestled in an overstuffed couch. But what had happened between them, though unremarked, made the remaining two days feel richer, deeper.

Packing after their final breakfast, Corey felt the pulse of his normal life stirring, the anticipation of meetings, hearings, speeches, interviews, of time spent in airports, the quick and constant shifts of focus from one imperative to the next. But he sensed that he was leaving some part of him with Lexie. He could not remember having felt so much at peace.

He said this to her. Smiling up at him, she said, "Vacations wear off, you know. The rest is always with you."

He pondered this on the flight to Washington, still uncertain about where he wished "the rest" to take him. When he landed, reporters and photographers jammed the sidewalks. On the front page of a Rohr-owned tabloid one of them thrust out at him, Lexie was emerging from the pool as he handed her a glass of iced tea. His memory did not lie—her bikini had been stunning.

22

THERE WAS NO TIME FOR REFLECTION: COREY's choice was to say something spontaneous or ignore the shouted questions, creating an indelible portrait of embarrassment. Heading toward his limousine, he paused in front of the nearest reporter with a microphone. "Ms. Hart and I have a relationship," he said with a smile. "Many single men and women aspire to that."

"How will this affect your presidential prospects?"

"Dating?" Carey asked with feigned incredulity. "Last time I looked, there was a war on, and Iran was developing nuclear weapons." With that, he climbed into the limousine and shut the door.

He listened to several messages from Blake Rustin, each more agitated than the last. His advisers were meeting at Brian Lacey's, the final message informed him—if Corey happened to be in the area, he was more than welcome to attend. Deciding swiftly, he instructed the driver to head for the Virginia countryside, then clicked his speed dial for Lexie's cell phone. "Are you back in L.A.?" he asked.

"I got in an hour ago." Her tone was somber. "Guess you've seen."

"Yup. Still love the bikini, by the way."

"This is serious, Corey—especially for you. When I got home, reporters were staking out the place. They're going to be all over my life. You know that, don't you?"

Corey felt the adrenaline wearing off. "I do, and I'm sorry. But not about us."

Lexie hesitated. "What about *you*?"

"What were we going to do—hide forever? Actually, I'm kind of relieved."

"Is *this* really what you would have chosen? Or did you get cornered, and now you're stuck trying to brave it out?"

"I would have chosen a more graceful rollout, Lexie. But I wasn't going anywhere." Pausing, Corey said firmly. "I told them we have a relationship. That's what I want. If you can deal with the fallout, I can."

"I'll have to think about it, Corey." Her voice became gentler. "I just wish we didn't have to decide like this."

"My fault. It's the president thing—"

"What are you going to do about *that*?"

"I have no idea," he admitted. "I'm on my way to meet with my advisers."

"Bet they're excited," she said with a small laugh. "Better have your publicist call my publicist. To borrow a phrase from your world, we both have to be 'on message,' whatever the message may be."

"I know what *I* want it to be," Corey answered. "That we're a couple, and the hell with anyone who doesn't like it."

"Wouldn't it be nice," she said, "to know what we'd have decided without Alex Rohr's assistance. Or to know what will happen now that he's taken such an interest."

Corey knew what she was thinking, as clearly as though she'd said it: black movie stars were one thing; former heroin addicts were another. And he was just as certain she would never offer rape as her excuse. "We never had that chance," he answered. "But whatever I decide, this isn't just about me anymore. It's about us."

"As long as you're with me," Lexie answered, "it's *all* about us. So you need to decide whether to throw away whatever chance you've got of becoming president for a chance at whatever we might have. The unselfish thing for me to do is step away."

"Not for my sake," Corey said, and then wondered if this was quite as true as he made it sound.

"It *was* a nice getaway," Lexie said softly, and got off.

THE TABLOIDS WERE spread across Brian Lacey's dining room table.

"I don't care how good she looks in a swimsuit," Rustin said tiredly. "A lot of Republican women will take one glance at this photograph and decide you're not a leader their children can look up to."

As Lacey and Jack Walters appraised him, Corey leaned forward to scan the photographs: Lexie and Corey holding hands at L'Orangerie; eating dinner on the porch; and, of course, poolside in their "Mexican love nest."

"'Senator Grace,'" Rustin read aloud, "'attempted to conceal his identity, a stark contrast to his reputation for openness and candor.'" Looking up, Rustin said, "Rohr staked you out—the fun you had with him at that hearing came at a price. 'Girlfriend' is bad; 'black girlfriend' is worse; 'black actress girlfriend' is the fucking trifecta."

Rustin sounded as morose as he looked. "If she were Condi Rice," he continued, "you might get by with 'black.' But Lexie Hart is an outspoken liberal who symbolizes everything people loathe about the entertainment industry, right down to this skimpy swimsuit most women know they couldn't wear. Stay with her and you're dead in more primaries than not. *If* you're not dead already."

Corey glanced at him sideways. "Done yet, Blake?"

"Not quite. Most Americans want their president to be an authority figure, not some guy with a 'girlfriend' who tells him what to think. She comes to lobby you on stem-cell research—next thing anyone knows you're voting in favor of stem-cell research." Rustin spoke more evenly. "*I* know your vote helped pull Christy into the race. But Price and Rohr will make it look like a black Jane Fonda's angling to move into the White House and whisper pillow talk in our besotted president's ear."

Corey felt Lacey and Jack Walters watching him. "At the risk of stating the obvious," he told them, "I wasn't making a political decision when I went to Cabo San Lucas. And the people who'd vote against me for this would vote against me anyhow."

Turning his palms up, Rustin glanced at Lacey in a wordless plea for help. His thin face filled with doubt, Lacey spoke somberly. "I'm torn here, Corey. Most of what Blake says happens to be true, even if it's a sad commentary on our country and our party. But we're still a racially divided society.

"She might actually help you here or there—primaries like Michigan and New Hampshire, where white moderates remain significant. But in the West and the South—"

"He's dead in South Carolina," Rustin interrupted flatly. "You think Rohr's going to back off now? He'll have people hammering on Corey twenty-four/seven, until 'war hero' is replaced in the public mind by 'the guy who's fucking Lexie Hart.'" Turning to Corey, he added, "Sorry, but that's what's going to happen."

"Depends on how you spin it," Lacey responded. "Some people are suckers for romance, especially if it ripens into love. Suppose she and Corey got married?"

Rustin smiled in disbelief. "I'm serious," Lacey insisted. "It addresses the problem of running as a bachelor. It puts Corey back on the side of family values, yet eliminates the bad example of a forty-three-year-old presidential candidate having sex outside of wedlock. It will give the new Mrs. Grace a chance to use her obvious charm, intelligence, and communications skills in the service of whatever issues are good for Corey.

"Most of all, it gives Corey a chance to stand for love and marriage. And marrying a black woman would confirm that he's the candidate with guts—"

Corey began laughing.

"Did I miss the punch line?" Jack Walters asked him.

"Why don't we just get Lexie on the line and explain that marriage will be better for my image? Then one of you can pop the question." Corey shook his head. "*That* would be one of the odder proposals in the history of marriage."

"Maybe so," Lacey said. "But not in the history of politics. Lexie Hart has all the elements of a good political wife. She's poised, gracious, and articulate. She's already dealt with fame and the media—nobody needs to tell her there's no such thing as off the record—and she's learned what to give and what to withhold. She's an incredible draw in her own right, with magnetism to burn. Not even Mary Rose Marotta can compete with *that*.

"More and more people of color are crossing over into the American mainstream—Bill Cosby, Michael Jordan, Tiger Woods, Oprah Winfrey. Together, you're the best-looking couple on the planet: Jack and Jackie Kennedy, only from appealingly modest backgrounds. And in a general election, she'll help pull in new constituents you need to win, like minorities and the young." Lacey paused for emphasis. "The worst of both worlds, Corey, is where you are now—having an affair. If you love her, marry her, and the faster the better. Otherwise, you really *do* have to get out of Dodge."

All at once, Corey felt drained. Looking from Lacey to Rustin to Walters, he said, "I believe that Cortland Lane could have been elected president. You may disagree. But the political impact of my involvement with Lexie can't dictate the fate of our relationship.

"I'm seeing Lexie Hart—at least if she's still agreeable. But it's completely absurd to imagine that I'd marry her for political damage control. Even if I wanted to, *she* wouldn't."

Head bent forward, Ruskin touched his eyes. "Then don't run from it," Lacey advised gamely, "and don't flaunt it. Go out socially—but not in Hollywood. Buy her a one-piece bathing suit. Book separate hotel rooms: Rohr and Price will be all over pajama parties. The snapshot you want is of two smart and mature professionals with serious intentions."

Rustin gazed across the table, his expression bleak, his feelings of shock and betrayal so apparent that Corey felt genuine sympathy. "You would have been president," he said quietly. "I swear it."

"And now I can't be?"

Rustin's shrug was a heavy, dispirited movement of his shoulders. "I've given you my best assessment. If you're still considering a run, I'll poll it."

"Do that," Corey said softly. He was not sure whether he said this just to mollify Rustin or because some stubborn part of him could not abandon hope.

"'DATING'?" LEXIE ASKED with faint amusement. "Sounds like a step backward to me. Is your brain trust hiring a chaperone?"

Returning from Lacey's horse farm, Corey watched rain and sleet spatter the car windows. "That's where I drew the line. Seriously, Lexie, this is what I want."

"As opposed to the presidency?"

"I haven't decided." Corey hesitated. "Is that absolutely a deal breaker?"

Lexie was silent. "*I'm* a deal breaker, Corey. If your advisers knew—"

"One step at a time," Corey said. "First, I need to ask you for a date."

THEY PUT OUT a joint press release, emphasizing their regard for each other and the seriousness of their relationship.

This only increased the frenzy. Reporters from Rohr's media empire and elsewhere staked out their homes and badgered friends for comments; Marotta laced his speeches with references to "Hollywood values"; more forthright, Bob Christy called their relationship "unacceptable not because of Ms. Hart's race, but for the moral example it sets for children of *any* race." The photograph of Lexie became a staple of cable news; a virulent right-wing talk-show host accused Corey of "thinking with an organ more commonly associated with the tawdry excesses of Democratic presidents"; Jay Leno called the relationship a "bold departure from the Republican tradition of pedophilia and petty graft." Corey's e-mails and telephone calls were more unfavorable than not, including a number from Ohioans professing their regret for having supported him. Consoled by early polling that suggested Americans were, on the whole, more generous than his mail, Corey felt more pain for Lexie than for himself.

Her first trip to Washington was difficult. At Citronelle, the smiles of fellow diners were offset by the fat inebriate who, passing their table, expressed sympathy to Corey for the hard life of a politician. Nodding to Lexie as if she were a potted plant, the man said pointedly, "You have to be real careful who you're seen with, Senator."

Lexie's face went blank. Coldly, Corey answered, "I am. So please leave."

The man opened his mouth, then silently retreated. "Sorry," Corey told her.

Lexie shrugged. "He was drunk. Sober he'd only have thought it." Reaching out, she covered his hand, adding softly, "Let it go, Corey."

But he couldn't quite. The next night, at a Republican gala, well-dressed men and women vied to meet this emissary from a wholly different world, many friendly or at least polite, a few staring openly. Lexie was unfailingly gracious. "It's okay," she murmured to Corey. "We may not feel like Thomas Jefferson and Sally Hemings, but people think we are."

Only later could she tell him what she had overheard in the ladies' room of the hotel. "She's very well-spoken," one woman told a friend sotto voce. "Usually they're not so well educated." She paused, then added tartly, "Actresses, I mean."

"She does seem nice," the first woman insisted. "And even more attractive in person than on film. There must be some Caucasian blood there, don't you think?"

"Whatever race she is," her friend responded, "it's enough to make a United States senator lose his senses. At least *some* of his senses."

Sitting in the underground parking lot of her hotel, Corey watched her expressionless face for clues as to how she felt. The vignette, he concluded, was clue enough. Kissing her, he said lightly, "Actually, my senses have never worked better. All of them."

Lexie rested her forehead against his. It was then, though he refrained from telling her, that Corey Grace decided not to run for president.

23

THIS DECISION, COREY FOUND, DID NOT PUT AN end to his ambivalence.

He still did not tell Lexie, rationalizing that this might help her feel less responsible for his decision when he announced it. For another week he maintained his hectic schedule in the key primary states, torn between the vision of a relationship with Lexie unimpeded by presidential politics and dread of the letdown he would feel on the day of public relinquishment, made more bitter by the satisfaction it would give men like Rohr and Magnus Price.

Oddly, it was his mother who provoked him to move out of this twilight zone. Calling Corey over a busy weekend in New Hampshire, she informed him that she and his father worried, along with the Reverend Christy, that "carrying on with this woman is lowering the morals of our children." When Corey gently rebuked her, she implored him, "Please, Corey—try to imagine what your own brother would think of you now." Appalled by her appropriation of a boy she had understood so little, Corey answered quietly, "I really can't, Mom. And neither can you."

Hanging up, Corey reflected sadly on his distance from the woman who had borne him. But she had crystallized a larger truth: for too many people like her, his relationship with Lexie had been defined by his antagonists. Lexie did not deserve this, and he would be selfish to continue making her a target.

Later that day, when Marotta called to request a meeting, Corey understood his purpose: to suggest that, in light of Corey's new realities, his only rational choice was to support Marotta over Christy. It was then that Corey called Blake Rustin and Brian Lacey, informing them of his decision: he would tell Marotta that he had chosen not to run, and let the conversation flow from there.

MAROTTA'S OFFICE WAS on the first floor of the Russell Building, Corey's on the second. Corey walked slowly down the marble stairs. With each disheartened tread he imagined the relief and satisfaction Marotta would struggle to conceal.

Corey had reached the bottom step when he heard gunshots.

In the sunlit rotunda of the southeast entrance, a security guard lay sprawled on the marble floor as two armed men burst into the opposite end of the corridor that Corey was about to enter. Stunned, Corey flattened himself against the wall of the stairwell.

No longer able to see the gunmen, he heard their footsteps echo on the marble floor. One of the invaders spoke hurriedly in a language Corey recognized from his captivity. Across from where he hid, only the open door of Marotta's office—the last on the corridor—remained visible. Marotta's receptionist appeared in the doorway, peering out as two visitors stared up at her from a leather couch.

Caught between fear and the instincts of a fighter pilot, Corey watched the receptionist shrink back from what she saw.

The gunmen burst into Marotta's office. Framed in the doorway, one turned to the two men on the couch, unloading a burst of gunfire that caused them to twitch like puppets, blood spattering the wall. Corey stopped thinking.

As the second man cut down the receptionist, he sprinted across the corridor.

Startled by his footsteps, the second gunman spun. Desperate, Corey lowered his head and lunged for the man's stomach, disrupting his aim with an outflung arm. The man's companion spun around and fired.

Corey's head struck his target's midsection. The man's upper body absorbed the bullets; a spray of blood hit Corey's face. Reaching out, he grasped the stock of his automatic weapon as the terrorist fell across him. Sheltered by his body, Corey found the trigger.

More bullets hit the dead man's back. Thrusting out the gun, Corey fired blindly.

The weapon jumped in his hand and escaped his grasp. Frantic, Corey lunged to retrieve it.

Silence fell, sudden and eerie.

The first terrorist was sprawled with his back against one of the dead visitors' legs, blood gushing from a throat wound that had nearly decapitated him.

Crawling forward, Corey picked up the gun. *"I need help here,"* he called out.

Slowly, the door to Marotta's suite of offices cracked open. Staring at the carnage, Rob Marotta blinked at the sight of Corey's blood-spattered face.

A sudden clicking sound made Marotta flinch instinctively. Spinning to fire, Corey saw a photographer. "Don't shoot," the man cried out, and his camera kept clicking.

THE SAME PHOTOGRAPH filled the front page of every newspaper in America. In the foreground, Corey held the terrorist's weapon, his face smeared with the dead man's blood; behind him stood Marotta, peering from the doorway. The headline in the *New York Times* was almost super-fluous: "Senator Kills Terrorists in Capitol Raid." So was the subheading that followed: "Grace Saves Rival's Life as Al Qaeda Gunmen Murder Four."

Though the image was horrific, Brian Lacey could not help but note, "Marotta looks scared, doesn't he?"

They sat at Corey's conference table. Corey still felt stunned; his only statement to the media—written, not spoken—had expressed sorrow for the dead and gratitude for his own survival. His first call had been to Lexie. "I saw," she said in a near whisper. "I'm so glad I didn't lose you."

She sounded as shocked as he felt. "Do you need me to come back?" she asked.

Corey struggled for clarity. "In a day or so, I'd like that. Right now there's so much to deal with I'm drowning in it."

And he was: the police, a media obsessed with terror, a newly anxious public, cameras everywhere he went, and, invariably, the siren song of ambition—his advisers' desires, and his own need, to process the shift in the country's psychic landscape. As Rustin gazed at the photograph that Lacey was already calling "an iconic image," Rustin said, "You've been touched by the hand of God and Al Qaeda.

"Fate's an amazing thing, Corey. Two Al Qaeda sleepers can't figure out how to kill the president, and then it dawns on them that Marotta, possibly our next president, has an office with practically no security. So they go on his Web site, read his schedule, and decide to drop in. And, in the process, maybe create the *real* next president by accident—with a little help from you, of course.

"But as you always say, character is fate. Yours and Marotta's." Rustin shook his head in disbelief. "The same guy who flies to Cabo to meet an actress sprints across the hallway to jump a terrorist. And Marotta looks like he lacks the guts to open his fucking door."

And yet, even as he studied the photograph, Corey's reflections were deeply personal. He pondered about the thin line between action and inaction, between the seemingly heroic and the ostensibly craven, and, most haunting, between life and death. Rob Marotta had felt it, too. In the brief moment before the police had arrived, Marotta, shaken by what might have befallen him, had become more human than Corey had ever seen him.

"I don't know if I could have done that," he'd murmured to Corey.

Corey had looked around them at the dead. And then he, too, had given way to his emotions—a toxic compound of what Rohr, Marotta's backer, had done to Lexie and how Marotta had exploited their romance to further his own ambitions. "I wouldn't waste time on it," Corey had responded tersely, "because you'll never know. What happened is what you get to live with."

Marotta's face had closed. He had already sensed, as had Corey, what he would have to live with.

"This is a transcendent moment," Blake Rustin said now. "You didn't plan it, and the way you responded will define forever who you are. It's like Giuliani after 9/11—a remission of all prior sins."

Brian Lacey placed his finger next to Marotta's stricken face. "This is also defining for Marotta. Like few others— and unlike the snapshots Rohr's jackals took slinking around Cabo San Lucas—this photograph captures an essential truth. You're the hero, and Marotta's Humpty Dumpty. Not even Magnus Price can put him back together.

"People are afraid again. They need a real leader."

Standing, he placed a hand on Corey's shoulder. "I know this was horrific, Corey. No one knows why these things happen. But this is your time."

Corey sat there, silent, his attitude of reflection so deep it felt close to prayer. Looking up at last, he said, "And Lexie?"

Rustin and Lacey stared at him, as though stupefied by the inconsequence of the question. "Whatever," Rustin answered. "This is your chance to say what you want and realize your destiny. For Godsakes, take it."

"THEY'RE RIGHT," LEXIE told him.

An hour after Corey's return from the funeral for Marotta's receptionist, Lexie lay beside him in her suite at the Madison Hotel. They had made love hungrily, celebrating the fact he was alive. Only afterward could they discuss the larger implications of his survival.

"I know they are," Corey answered. "I also want you in my life."

Lexie touched his face. Softly, she said, "I just may be in love with you, Senator."

Corey felt a rush of feeling. "Lexie—"

"Let me finish, please." She looked deeply into his eyes. "Remember when I said a man should never tell a woman she can't have children—that no one can deprive another human being of something so essential to her life?"

Corey smiled ruefully. "How could I forget?"

"In a way, Corey, this is the same thing. A week ago whether you ran was a judgment call that could have gone either way."

"I'd already decided, Lexie. I was bowing out."

For an instant, her eyes closed. "That was then, Corey. And it was about me."

When he began to protest, Lexie placed a finger to his lips. "Then, I could have accepted that. I even could have convinced myself that it was best for you. Now, I can't." She paused, seeming reluctant to continue. "I'm afraid for you," she told him in a husky voice, "afraid some madman with a gun will shoot you because of me. Afraid of what this terrible process will do to us. I'm even afraid for me. But I can't—won't—be the reason that you don't run.

"Maybe running will put an end to us. But if you don't run, I think it will end us for sure—maybe not soon, but soon enough. Our only chance is for you to run, and for us to take our chances."

Corey felt both elation and apprehension. "But what will you do?"

"I thought about that the whole flight out here. I think it's best for us if I stay away from your campaign, at least for a while, until things are clearer to us both." She mustered a smile. "Like you, I'm not going anywhere—at least not yet. And we're pretty good on the phone."

At that moment, Corey wanted to say that he, too, was falling in love. But it was the wrong time, and he was not certain she would believe him. "Yeah," he answered. "We're pretty good on the phone."

WHEN COREY ANNOUNCED his candidacy, his parents, but not Lexie, were with him.

He stood in the band shell at Taylor Park, where Bob Christy once had spoken, savoring the irony. His father and mother sat behind him, unavoidable props in his political pageant, looking proud, discomfited, and somewhat mystified. Even they, Corey suspected, sensed what he knew all too well—that campaigning for president is the American odyssey, and the journey tests those who undertake it in ways they can only guess at, and in others they never suspect until the crisis is upon them.

He gazed out at a throng that overflowed the grass, speckled with familiar faces but swollen by the trappings of a presidential campaign: reporters, videocams, supporters who arrived on buses, a documentary film crew retained to capture footage for Corey's TV ads. With him on the bandstand were his closest friends in the House and Senate, the daring few who would have backed him even before lightning struck—notably Dakin Ford, the young, iconoclastic senator from Lexie's home state, South Carolina. Seeing Ford reminded Corey of how much he already missed her.

But this was his moment, and he rose to meet it.

"In the face of all our challenges," he said, "I call for a new beginning, and an end to the willful obliviousness to all that we must face together. We must be more than the party of business or religion. We must not seek power by dividing the country on the basis of creed or culture or even the fear of terrorism. And we must speak clearly about what it means to be conservative.

"It is *not* conservative to turn one group of Americans against another.

"It is *not* conservative to saddle our children with debt.

"It is *not* conservative to despoil the environment that our children's children will inherit. Nor is it conservative to squander the lives of our soldiers in a war that degrades our military strength." Corey's voice rose. "To conserve means not only to honor the past, but to meet the challenges of the future, leaving our country better than we found it."

Speaking these words, Corey felt liberated, if only for a moment, from fear of their consequences. During the applause that followed, he again scanned the faces before him, some familiar, most not; young, old, and, in a few heartening cases, Hispanic or black. "Give me your help and your hand," he told them, "and together we will build an American future kinder than our present, and even greater than our past."

In that intoxicating, perilous moment, Corey Grace believed that he could make it so.

PART II

THE INSURGENT

1

STUCK ON THE RUNWAY IN CLEVELAND, COREY watched sleet striking the window.

"We're risking it all in New Hampshire," Rustin said.

They sat in the front cabin of the chartered plane, separated by a cloth curtain from the section jammed with reporters. Seated behind them, Brian Lacey reviewed potential ads on a DVD player and Jack Walters scanned Corey's schedule, while Corey's new press secretary, Dana Harrison—young, African-American, hyperalert, and nominally a Democrat—worked the press in back. The campaign was two hours old.

"No appearances in Iowa," Corey said again.

"No way. We're already deep in November—starting this late you have to pick your spots. In a caucus state like Iowa, organization is key, and we don't have any. The best network is among the evangelicals, where Christy's strong." Rustin grinned. "He's opened up his mailing list to all the local preachers—two days ago, they turned out twelve thousand Christians at a pancake breakfast for Christy, praying over the fucking maple syrup. If I were Magnus Price, I'd be terrified for Marotta."

Corey shrugged. "Still," he argued, "Marotta should win. Especially if I'm not draining off support."

"*Should* win," Rustin amended. "But will he? Some nut of a billionaire who owns a Christian mail-order house has started running ads with side-by-side shots of Christy in the pulpit and Marotta peeking through his office door. Brutal.

"Plus, Iowa is pro-life heaven. Nobody loves the unborn more than Reverend Bob." Rustin sat back, loosening his tie. "New Hampshire's right for you—way more independents and moderates than people in prayer circles asking God who to vote for. *That's* where you take Marotta down."

"And if I don't?"

Rustin turned to him, head still resting on the seat. "You're finished."

Though Corey had heard this before, his competitive instinct was aroused. "Because of South Carolina."

"Yup. You need momentum out of New Hampshire to keep from getting flattened there. But if you win, we can do this." Rustin's gaze grew more intent, like someone in the grip of a compelling inner vision. "You can't sweep the primaries—impossible. What you *can* do is freeze the race—just by running you've kept Governors Blair and Costas from supporting Marotta, which puts Illinois and New York on the sidelines. If you can win enough of the primaries bunched up after South Carolina, especially California, Blair and Costas will want what we may end up wanting: a deadlocked convention where they swap their support for the chance to be VP.

"In their fantasies, you, Marotta, and Christy all destroy one another and the convention turns to one of *them*. But Blair's unseasoned, and Costas is too weak. When they see a president in the mirror, they don't notice that it's cracked."

"What about Larkin?"

Ruskin waggled his head, smiling again. "Sam personifies how Christy's screwing Marotta in the South. Before Christy came in, Mississippi was in Rob's pocket—you never had the proverbial prayer. But Christy's brand of Jesus is hot down there, and that gives Sam an excuse to play the same waiting game as Blair and Costas." Rustin's smile broadened. "Sam's hopelessly corrupt, of course. *So* corrupt he'd even sell his votes to you for the chance to be your VP."

"Forget it," Corey said. "I don't want a vice president whose desk is jammed with bourbon bottles and hundred-dollar bills."

"Oh, Sam knows that—he's too gifted a crook to be a fool. But he's looking at all three of you, and thinking one of you will need him in the end.

"You've all got weaknesses. In *this* world, Christy's got no qualifications whatsoever to be president. Marotta's too calculating—he's been running for president since the womb. As for you . . ."

Corey smiled. "Suspiciously irreligious, too unpredictable for comfort, morally unfit . . ."

"Don't depress me. Let's say 'too independent' and leave it at that."

"So," Corey said, "why don't we divert the plane to Cabo San Lucas? I liked it there."

Corey lay his head back; even as he missed Lexie, he also worried about what might happen to her if the campaign become as brutal as it could. "A race like this," he said at last, "will test all three of us."

"A race like this," Rustin answered, "will *define* all three of you. Right now, Christy's God's candidate and Marotta's the establishment front-runner. That makes you the insurgent.

"Your job is to create excitement, goad Marotta into mistakes, and make Christy look like the vanity candidate he is." In a tone that commingled urgency and challenge, Rustin continued: "We're throwing you into one town meeting after another, without a script, answering any fucking question the voters want to ask. It'll be political guerrilla theater—Marotta wouldn't dare do that, and the mob back there in steerage will eat it up."

Corey stood. "Speaking of the mob," he said dryly, "I'm going back to hang with them. They'll 'eat up' town meetings to a point. But they are absolutely certain that the average citizen won't ask the probing questions *they* would. So here's what we're going to do.

"Put all the reporters on the bus with me—even the Rohr News guy. No off-the-record stuff: they can ask me anything they want, anytime they want, and I'll answer."

Rustin's eyes narrowed. "Let's not get carried away."

"You want coverage, Blake? With any luck, Marotta will start looking like a hostage in Magnus Price's soundproof bubble. What's he going to do if Al Qaeda comes around again? Call Magnus?" Corey smiled. "The press hates being handled—just like I do. They'll forgive me the occasional screwup before they'll forgive Marotta if it looks like he's hiding from them. That's when the image of him peeking around the door becomes indelible."

Rustin pursed his lips. "Just win New Hampshire."

Corey grinned. "Don't worry. When I become president and they write tomes about your inspired strategy, you'll be a hero, too."

BY THE FIFTH town meeting, both the crowds and the traveling press had swollen in size, and Corey's unscripted encounters had become political events.

Microphone in hand, he stood alone on the platform of a spired church in Freedom, New Hampshire—which, Corey learned to his amusement, had acquired its name not in the Revolutionary War, but when the town had seceded from Effingham Falls in the storied conflict between partial- and total-immersion baptism. "I'm completely unprincipled," Corey told them cheerfully. "In Effingham Falls, I'm partial. But in Freedom I'm totally underwater."

The audience laughed appreciatively. Though it was a weeknight and heavy snow was falling, the pews were crowded to overflowing, and latecomers stood at the side or rear, a few sitting cross-legged in the aisles. Corey looked at the faces—older couples, teenagers, parents who'd brought their kids out to see a prospective president—and saw a bracing combination of curiosity, flinty skepticism, and simple goodwill.

A stern-faced man stood and asked, "What's your position on the war in Iraq?"

"That it was a mistake," Corey answered bluntly. "I'm sorry to say this. But we invaded the wrong country, and the results have been tragic—lost American and Iraqi lives, and the erosion of our capacity to deal with crises far more pressing.

"We need more soldiers in Afghanistan. We need to keep dealing with North Korea, which now has nuclear weapons, and to deal with Iran, which may have them very soon." Pausing, Corey added pointedly, "Senator Marotta says that it's better to be respected than loved. In too many parts of the world, we're neither."

"So you don't support the president?"

Briefly, Corey considered his response. "I support his goal of making us safer. I know he firmly believed that invading Iraq would do so.

"But a mistake made in good faith is still a mistake. One measure of leadership is the ability to acknowledge and correct mistakes. I promise you that, as president, I will learn from mine."

At the rear, reporters scribbled furiously or held out tape recorders. A young man Rustin had identified as Magnus Price's spy captured Corey's answers on a video-cam. "Reverend Christy," a plump, fortyish woman asked, "says that abstinence-only programs are the sole way to stop teen pregnancy. What do you think?"

At the corner of his eye, Corey saw Rustin frown with worry. "Abstinence is best," Corey said. "That's what we should teach our children. But if Bob Christy truly believes that abstinence alone will stop teen pregnancy and the spread of AIDS—not simply in Freedom, but all across America—then I hope he's praying overtime."

This elicited a few dry chuckles. "That brings me to abortion," Corey said briskly. "One way to lower the abortion rate is to stop unwanted pregnancies any way we can. I'm also for doing everything we can to encourage adoption—it's not enough to love children until they're born. But there aren't a lot of adoptive parents asking for drug-addicted babies born with HIV.

"That's the reality. While we work to make the world as we would like it to be, we have to deal with the world as it is."

This, to Corey's surprise, elicited brief but fervent applause. He pointed toward a somber-faced woman who had stood while others around her clapped. "Senator Marotta," she said, "is a family man who cares about family values. You're divorced. If you become president, will you marry Lexie Hart?"

Smiling, Corey shrugged and rolled his eyes, a pantomime of discomfiture that drew chuckles from those closest to the stage. "I'll have to get back to you," he said. "My people are still polling that one.

"Seriously," he said over the continued laughter, "that question's a little premature. Unless you know something I don't—that Ms. Hart would actually have me. After all, she's smart, compassionate, talented, deeply concerned for our country, and, speaking personally, not only the most beautiful woman I've ever met, but one of the best people I know. So if there's a reason not to marry her, I don't know what it is."

"Then you disagree with the Reverend Christy that your relationship sets a bad example?"

Corey saw that the audience, quite suddenly, was watching him even more closely. "Yes," he said calmly. "It's not easy finding the right person at any age. If voters want to take time out from Iraq, terrorism, the economy, global warming, and failing schools to think about Lexie and me, I hope it's to wish us well."

At the end of the evening, most people in the audience were on their feet, applauding.

After Corey and his staff boarded the bus, they and a growing pool of reporters sped down a newly plowed road. Kate McInerny of the *Washington Post,* rendered ever more cheeky by the rollicking mood of her peers, said, "Let's have it, Senator—what's your position on sex?"

Sitting beside Dana Harrison, Corey settled back in his seat. Smiling, he answered, "Missionary," and closed his eyes to sleep.

2

CAUCUS NIGHT IN IOWA BROUGHT BITTER COLD and seven inches of snow, confining the Iowa Republicans who met in their neighbors' homes to a fiercely committed cadre who, more often than not, opened their meetings with a prayer. By ten o'clock, the Reverend Bob Christy had beaten Rob Marotta so decisively that CNN had labeled it "a stunning defeat that jeopardizes Marotta's status as the front-runner."

Standing with Mary Rose before a somber crowd of supporters in the ballroom of a Des Moines hotel, Marotta struggled to conceal his humiliation, mustering a smile that, he could only hope, was less synthetic than it felt. But when he expressed confidence in ultimate victory, the applause was tepid. Marotta read the doubt seeping into the face of Donald Brandt, the county chairman who had supported him and now clapped with mechanical enthusiasm, even as the same doubt brightened the collective expression of the traveling press. This tattered evening, the ashes of his anticipated victory celebration portended both a horse race and, quite possibly, his ultimate demise. "Dead man walking," Marotta heard someone mumble as he left the podium with a last smile and wave, cringing at how artificial he must look.

He asked Price for ten minutes in his room, alone. Sitting on the end of the bed, he felt Mary Rose rest her hand on his shoulder. "How are you, Robbie?"

"Empty." Staring at a stain on the carpet, Marotta did

not look up. "Just completely hollowed out."

"It's only Iowa," Mary Rose admonished. "Not even an election, really."

"And I'm tired. I'll be better tomorrow, I know. But I'm having this premonition. Ever since I was a kid on the debate team, people told me I could realize my dreams—Father Frank, my coaches, the dean of my law school—everyone. That if I worked hard enough and never let up, I could go as far as I dared to imagine. Standing there tonight, I suddenly imagined the faces of everyone who believed in me, and what they're seeing now."

Mary Rose sat beside him. "You've never lost before. This is just a hiccup. You've overcome much worse."

"I know that. But I've started wondering if the chemistry of my life in politics changed the instant Grace decided to run across that corridor. Years of work, and"—Marotta snapped his fingers—"gone, at the moment he looked at me across that Arab's body, blood smeared on his face."

"Robbie," she interrupted with a touch of sternness. "You could have been killed. I could have been without a husband, the kids without a father. The meaning *I* take from that is that we were saved from tragedy by the grace of God.

"You're still alive. You still get to run for president. That picture of you and Corey Grace was the price you paid." Turning her face to his, she spoke more softly. "What scares *me*, sweetheart, is how you'll feel if you don't win. It's dangerous to want any one thing too much."

Marotta studied her perceptive blue eyes, the level gaze that mingled concern with a seemingly infinite patience for his ambition and his flaws. "It's hard to explain, M.R. You imagine yourself achieving something until it's the essence of who you are, more real than reality . . ."

His voice drifted off. "Is that what you believe?" she asked. "That you'll only become yourself if you're elected president?"

To hear this said aloud both haunted him and filled him with resolve. In a different voice, cooler and clearer, Marotta said, "I can't think about that now. I have to talk with Magnus."

Mary Rose appraised him, her eyes betraying worry she chose not to express. Then she kissed his forehead. "I'll call to see how the kids are doing. It's an hour later back there, and my sister's probably tired."

MAROTTA FOUND PRICE scanning a computer run with fresh polling numbers as his campaign manager, Charlie Norman, called the governor of New Hampshire. On CNN, Christy spoke with a beneficent confidence. "Tonight, the voters of Iowa have sent a powerful message: to save America, we will make God's work our own . . ."

Turning to Price, Norman said, "The governor says to turn on C-SPAN."

Clicking the remote, Price materialized Corey Grace, microphone in hand, at a town meeting in Center Ossipee, New Hampshire. "When you tackled that Arab terrorist," a Korean War veteran asked, "what went through your mind?"

Grace shook his head. "Nothing. If I'd had time to think, I probably wouldn't have done it.

"The hardest decisions are the ones where the choices aren't clear and the consequences are potentially momentous. Those are the kinds of decisions a president has to make. A split-second reaction has nothing to do with that."

"Yeah," Norman told the governor dourly, "we're watching. No one says America's hero doesn't have his role down pat."

Looking up at Marotta, Price inclined his head toward the bedroom.

Marotta followed. They stood at the end of Price's unmade bed. "I'm meeting with Christy tonight," Price said.

"To renew your old friendship?" Marotta inquired dubiously.

"To see if God's a realist." Price put a hand on Marotta's shoulder, peering into his eyes. "For that, we'll need to offer him something. More than you're going to like."

THE ONLY PRIVATE space in Christy's suite was a bathroom, last remodeled in the 1950s. Flipping down the toilet seat, Christy said in his avuncular tone, "Take a load off, Magnus. Been a long day, I know."

He was extracting his moment of retribution, Price thought; for a man of God, Christy stank of an all-too-human self-regard. Perched on the toilet lid, Price watched Christy rest his backside on the edge of the bathtub, the folds of his stomach straining his shirt, his fleshy arms exposed by rolled-up sleeves. "Grace's crowds are growing," Price said without preface. "He just might win New Hampshire."

Eyes opening in incredulity, Christy asked, "Now, why is that *my* problem, Magnus? You're the one who abandoned me to stake your reputation on Rob Marotta."

"For one simple reason," Price said flatly. "There's an absolute ceiling on a 'Christian candidate.' But not on one who makes 'Christian values' a central part of his appeal. Iowa's your apex, Bob. Sell high now, or crater down the road."

Christy chuckled without mirth. "You need me, Magnus—just like you always did, only more. The question is whether I need *you* anymore."

The overheated bathroom felt more and more stifling. "You do," Price answered. "We know each other, Bob—all too well. You want a seat at the table, and you know I'll give you one. Otherwise you'll end up as the candidate God chose to shun."

Christy received this with an air of complacence. "What seat, pray tell?"

Price felt his forehead becoming damp. "First, the conditions. Next Tuesday, you're going down in New Hampshire, which will give you an excuse to get out. You'll attack Grace from now until then, after which you'll withdraw and endorse Marotta."

"For which I get . . . ?"

"Secretary of education."

This time Christy's laugh was a bark. "So President Marotta can fire me at will? Actually, the job I have in mind is a good deal bigger."

Through the door, Price heard one of Christy's advisers leading the others in prayer. "And what might that be?" he inquired.

"You'll just have to guess, Magnus, until you get it right. In the meanwhile, I'm not running to be Marotta's lapdog—or his attack dog." Christy smiled again. "Politically and morally, Corey Grace may be the Antichrist. But I kind of like the boy's style. In fact, I've taken to watching him on C-SPAN just to get a chuckle or two. Compared to Grace, your boy has all the charm of rotting fish—tonight, I could smell the flop sweat coming off him like I can see the sweat on your forehead." Christy's voice became cold. "Get your sorry self back to Marotta, Magnus, and ask if he'd like to be *my* secretary of education. Then maybe I'll go after Grace."

This is surreal, Price thought suddenly—I'm sitting in a

hotel bathroom with mold between the tiles, talking to a megalomaniac I created while some lunatic's droning prayers outside. Standing, Price placed a hand on Christy's shoulder. "Next Tuesday, Bob, is your political sell-by date. Consider repenting before it's too late."

THAT WEEKEND, AT Price's urging, Mary Rose brought the kids to New Hampshire.

On a wintry Saturday morning, they took a ski lift to the top of a mountain—Marotta, Mary Rose, and all five children, bundled against a bone-piercing chill—followed by reporters recording the moment for the Sunday papers and the evening news, and a film crew shooting footage for a TV ad that would ask, "Can *your* family take a chance on Corey Grace?"

As Mary Rose dabbed their three-year-old's runny nose, Marotta felt the girl's misery. "Let's skip the skiing," he murmured, "and buy Jenny a hot chocolate."

Price was waiting for him inside the chalet. "A moment please, Rob."

Excusing himself with a glance at his bored fifteen-year-old son, Marotta followed Price back into the biting cold. "What is it?" he said impatiently. "Jenny's day to get pneumonia for that bedside photo op?"

"Schedule's changing. You can't go to South Carolina on Monday."

"Why not? The governor of this icebox promises that his organization will pull us through."

"That was yesterday," Price said with precarious calm. "Last night's tracking polls show the undecideds breaking three to one for Grace. Beat Grace here, and he's finished. But if you lose to him . . ."

Marotta knew the rest. Angry, he said, "So I'm staying until Election Day."

"Three more days to go." Price placed a hand on his candidate's shoulder. "For all our sakes, tell Mary Rose to keep the kids here."

ELECTION DAY DAWNED clear and bright. At three o'clock, when Corey finished his last round of radio interviews, he got back in the car to find Dana Harrison grinning.

"Why so cheerful?" Corey asked. "I thought you hated it here."

"I do—they've got more moose than black folks. But there's life after New Hampshire." Dana's thick glasses seemed to magnify the excitement in her eyes. "ABC's confidential exit poll is showing you up on Marotta by ten. You're killing him, Corey."

Elated, Corey left a message on Lexie's cell phone. "Miss you," it began. "But it's looking like I'll be on the road awhile longer."

AT NINE O'CLOCK, in Concord, Corey spoke at a meeting room crowded to overflowing. "Today," he said, "New Hampshire families decided to take a chance on Corey Grace. I guess no amount of negative advertising can substitute for fifty-three town meetings."

Across town, in another hotel room, Marotta and Price watched CNN as Mary Rose zipped their suitcases. "Before tonight," Jeff Greenfield told his viewers, "conventional wisdom held that if Grace lost New Hampshire, he was done. Now there's a new conventional wisdom: if Marotta loses South Carolina to either Grace or Christy, he's history."

"South Carolina," Price said softly. "Home sweet home."

3

"WE'RE CHANGING PLANES," PRICE TOLD MAROTTA when they reached the airport. But only when he and Mary Rose boarded, leaving the kids in the care of an older niece, did Marotta realize that the Gulfstream G5 belonged to Alex Rohr.

With cool courtesy, Rohr greeted Mary Rose, then shook Marotta's hand, a perfunctory smile briefly creasing his face. Except for Price, no one from the campaign was there. "We need to plan South Carolina," Price explained, placing a hand on Marotta's shoulder. "Without the media snooping around."

Marotta caught Mary Rose's troubled gaze. "Next time," he said coldly, "tell me before you start changing plans."

"This wasn't the plan," Rohr answered. "I didn't expect you to lose so badly."

For an instant, Marotta considered walking off the plane. "I'd better get some sleep," Mary Rose said quietly. "Why don't you three do your business."

The door of the Gulfstream closed, sealing them inside.

AS THE THREE men sat at a conference table, Mary Rose found a seat in the back. Now and then Marotta glanced at her; her eyes shut, she was attempting, or perhaps pretending, to sleep.

"South Carolina's your firewall," Price told him brusquely, "Lose, and you're dead in presidential politics. Not just this year, but forever."

Rohr, Marotta noticed, was studying him closely. "And so?"

Leaning forward, Price spoke coolly and succinctly. "We're not touching down in Plato's republic. South Carolina's my home, and things work different here.

"Before now you've skated across the surface—speaking to the right groups, visiting the right churches, meeting the right politicians. But below that placid surface is a pretty rancid pond." Price's smile was mere conversational punctuation. "A good bit of the electorate is natural selection in reverse—racists, Confederate flag nuts, gun fanatics, and fundamentalists so dumb they think Jesus spoke English. We're not going to wrest them away from Christy just by promising to abolish the federal income tax.

"Alex and I have laid the groundwork. Last year, he bought the state's biggest newspaper, and the major TV stations in Columbia and Charleston. Two weeks ago, I started telling our biggest donors where to place their money if they want to protect their investment." Price paused for emphasis. "What you need to do, Rob, is leave the details to me."

As Rohr spoke for the first time, his eyes betrayed a bleak amusement at Marotta's plight. "I assume, Senator, that you still wish to become president."

Appalled, Marotta saw his dilemma with utter clarity: for months or even years, these two men had gauged the point at which ambition would place him in their grip, and now that moment had arrived. "You forget something," he said tautly. "I'm not some disposable part in your grand design. Without me, you've got no one.

"Christy's out of control; Grace can't stand either one of you. Right at this moment, it would almost be worth losing to watch one or the other of them fuck with both your worlds."

Price's face betrayed neither worry nor surprise. Angrily, Marotta grasped his wrist. "You didn't make me majority leader, Magnus. You didn't make me anything I am today. That honor goes to my wife, my friends, my family, and, most of all, to me. Maybe I'll win; maybe I won't. But don't expect me to mortgage my balls to you and Alex in midair."

Rohr laughed softly. "Bravely spoken, Senator."

His tone hovered between admiration and derision. Price stared at Marotta's fingers until, grudgingly, Marotta released his wrist.

"All right," Price drawled. "We've all had our *West Wing* moment. If we offended you, Rob, I apologize. But would-be presidents play to win. That's what you hired me for. If you've had second thoughts about my methods, just say the word."

Turning, Marotta looked at his wife. She was curled beneath a blanket, her face placid in repose. As he gazed at her, it came to him with absolute certainty that were Price to leave him now, his campaign would collapse in disarray. He turned back to Price and said quietly but firmly, "If you choose to stay, it's on my terms."

Price merely shrugged. "As long as they include winning," he answered.

ROHR MIXED THREE bourbon and sodas, affording time for emotions to settle.

Sipping, Price raised his head, tasting the whiskey on his lips. "Before we take down Grace," he said after a time, "we gotta take down Christy."

Marotta shrugged. "That's elementary. To beat Grace, I need to own the South. Starting with South Carolina."

"But for *that*," Price said, "you have to become the Christian alternative to Reverend Bob—the believer who can win. That involves making Bob look like the candidate of folks who babble in tongues and cure deafness by snapping their fingers next to some retardate's ear. For *that*, we need the Reverend Carl Cash, and the righteous folks of Carl Cash University."

Marotta felt a fresh resistance. "From all I read," he objected, "the man is nuts. Didn't he call the Catholic Church a cult?"

"Yup," Price said serenely. "Don't find many of you papists at Carl Cash University—*or* alcohol, *or* dancing, *or* interracial dating. But as much as Cash hates Catholics, he believes to the bottom of his heart that God made blacks an evil and licentious race. That means he'll support damn near anyone to keep Corey Grace from becoming president. Even you."

Listening, Rohr raised his eyebrows, as though hearing an anthropologist's account of a primitive tribe in New Guinea. "Why not Christy?" Marotta asked.

"Christy's rich, he's arrogant, and—to a southern gentleman like Cash—he's a low-class huckster." Observing Marotta's displeasure, Price cautioned, "In South Carolina, the graduates of Carl Cash are officeholders, preachers, teachers, and businessmen. Without the Carl Cash network, you can't win.

"That's why our friend Alex here just pledged two million dollars to help fund the Carl Cash Center for the Study of Intelligent Design. That's why your first speech in my great state will be at Carl Cash University, where Carl himself will introduce you to a thousand sober, short-haired white kids aflame with the love of God."

In the dim yellow light of the cabin, Marotta stared at Price. "Have you considered what the national media will do with this?" Marotta's throat, raw from the rigors of New Hampshire, caused his voice to roughen. "You've got me sidling up in public to a bigot who's the poster boy for scientific ignorance, and who thinks my own religion relegates me to a special place in hell. I'll be a national laughingstock."

"Only if you lose," Price corrected. "Win, and most people will forget. It's the American way.

"You're not coming out for segregation, Rob. All you're doing is giving Cash what a proud man needs: tickets to the inaugural ball, dinner at the White House, the privilege of getting his calls returned. A small down payment on the Marotta administration—"

Abruptly, the plane vibrated, transforming Marotta's outrage to apprehension. "Thunderstorms," Rohr explained. "Pilot says we'll be through them in an hour."

Turning to his wife, Marotta saw her stirring, arms tightly folded as though awakening from a troubling dream. "Cash has got mailing lists," he heard Price say. "Tens of thousands of addresses, phone numbers, and e-mails, and we can use them any way we want. His lists alone could tip the election."

"Tell Rob about Dorrie Hoyle," Rohr suggested.

Price sat back, folded hands resting on his stomach. "Besides Christy," he explained, "Dorrie Hoyle's the biggest evangelist in the state. She's got a local TV program, a mailing list second only to Carl Cash's, and a creationist theme park outside Columbia—an absolute must for evangelical families. She's also fucking your most distinguished supporter, former governor Linwood Tate. Take a thrill ride through Adam and Eve's Garden, complete with serpent and the apple tree, and Dorrie will more than return the favor."

Marotta mustered a rueful laugh. "Will she bite the apple for me?"

"No. But a week of biting your tongue, Rob, is a very small price to pay."

There were so many prices, Marotta thought, some dearer than we can know. With an odd detachment, he saw himself: as a husband whose wife was beset by unspoken misgivings; as a parent who was missing his oldest daughter's middle school play; as one half of a couple who, for their children's sake, feared flying together and now were flying into a thunderstorm to further his ambitions; as a presidential contender who, newly desperate, was facing choices that might tarnish him as a candidate and as a man but might be the only way to keep his dream alive. "There's also Christy," he said to Price. "He won't be biting his tongue or turning the other cheek."

Price removed his wire-rimmed glasses, inspecting them for smudges. "Evangelists have a way of imploding," he observed. "Look at all the ones brought low by the sins of the flesh."

"Not Christy," Marotta said firmly. "He's too ambitious and too smart."

Price permitted himself an enigmatic smile. "But you never really know about people, do you? Except for Mary Rose and you."

4

"SOUTH CAROLINA," DAKIN FORD ANNOUNCED TO
Corey with a grin. "Too small for a republic, too large for
an insane asylum. You're headed for the heart of darkness,
boy."

A gifted political renegade, the junior senator from
South Carolina sprawled next to Corey in the plane, flying in the dark of night toward Ford's native state. Smiling, Corey jerked a thumb toward Rustin, sitting across
the aisle. "So I hear. Blake's just thrilled to be here."

Angling his lanky frame, Ford glanced at Rustin, a lock
of jet-black hair falling across his forehead. "Sad to say, I
hail from Jefferson's nightmare—a third-rate media and
first-rate political talent, none more unscrupulous than
Magnus Price. As Marotta's new buddy Linwood Tate
once said, 'The first rule is to get elected; the second to be
reelected. If there's a third rule, no one's written it
down.'" His smile fading, Ford added, "It's gonna be a
test of character, son. By this time next week, two of you
will have lost the primary election, and I'd guess at least
one of you will have lost his soul. But none of you will be
the same."

The comment sobered Corey. Two hours out of New
Hampshire, he felt the glow of victory fading, even as he
could read the worry in Rustin's unsmiling demeanor.
Looking up from a computer run, Rustin said across the
aisle, "These numbers from New Hampshire spell trouble.
You carried independents by forty-three percent, but

Republicans by only five. And more than half the Republicans in South Carolina self-identify as Christian conservatives.

"So let's reprise a few dos and don'ts." Rustin ticked off the points on the fingers of his left hand. "Don't tread on people's religious feelings. Don't bring up race. Respect South Carolina traditions."

"Which ones?" Corey asked, and then turned to Ford. "He doesn't mean lynchings, right?"

"Nope," Ford answered with a rueful smile. "More like deference to our state flag—the Confederate flag, regrettably, still flying on our statehouse lawn.

"Maybe in Ohio a piece of cloth wouldn't mean so much. But this one's divided our state. Most whites want to keep it; blacks are a good bit less sentimental about symbols of enslavement. The feelings on both sides run deep and bitter."

As so often now, Corey thought of Lexie. "Where do *you* come out, Dakin?"

"Oh," Ford said softly, "I defend our flag, of course. Just the sight of it brings tears to my eyes. Truth to tell, I wish the damn thing would go away."

"Price won't let it," Rustin told Corey. "Do Dakin and yourself a favor, and try to see it as a piece of southern heritage."

Corey gave him a mock-quizzical look. "I thought that's what museums are for. What else am I supposed to do?"

"Honor the Almighty. Quote a little scripture here and there—I've got a Bible in my briefcase." Rustin fixed him with a bright-eyed look. "In case you've forgotten, it was God who sustained you when that pack of Arabs hung you by your broken shoulders. That's when you first knew—absolutely and completely—that Jesus was in charge of your personal salvation."

Corey returned his gaze. "You want the absolute truth, Blake? The only thing I know for sure is that I'm lucky to be alive. I no more know whether Jesus chose to save me than if His mother was a virgin."

Covering his face, Ford groaned theatrically. Smiling at this, Corey added, "Sorry, Dakin. But anyone who claims that kind of certainty is lying to his audience or himself.

"I'm not going to *say* all that—there's such a thing as gratuitous honesty. But the last two presidential campaigns have conditioned voters to spot a phony. I'll do my damnedest not to embarrass you, Dakin. But we both agree that doesn't require me to race Marotta to the bottom."

Nodding, Ford turned to Rustin. "The state is changing, Blake. We've got transplants from the North and the Midwest; young, educated parents who want a president who's smart and honest; and a boatload of veterans who value Corey's service in Iraq. And when it comes to the war on terror," Ford added, "nobody else in this race has actually *killed* a terrorist." Placing his hand on Corey's arm, Ford said, "I agree with Blake that you've got big problems with fundamentalists around Columbia—the place where General Sherman said that the only thing between it and hell was a screen door. Even more so up around Greenville, home to Carl Cash University."

Corey laughed out loud. "What's so funny?" Ford asked.

"More like ironic. My mother wanted to send my late brother to Carl Cash, hoping to save his soul."

"What on earth did he do? Deflower the village virgins?"

Corey's smile faded. "Not exactly. Anyhow, I encouraged him to enter the Air Force Academy, where he jumped off a five-story building. Tends to put Carl Cash University in a more attractive light."

Ford propped his chin on his hand, his blue eyes fixing

Corey with a look of sympathy. "Carl Cash," he said finally, "is as rank a racist as God ever ordained."

"I know," Corey answered. "That figured into my thinking."

"Which brings me," Rustin said with obvious reluctance, "to the elephant in the room—if I can use that phrase about a beautiful woman who's also a registered Democrat. How does *she* play, Dakin?"

As Ford pursed his lips, Corey watched his friend search for a line between tact and truth. "Right into the Confederate flag issue, I'm afraid—no way Corey can duck race. We lose the bigots without picking up blacks: the voters are racially polarized, and blacks vote Democratic. But white folks of goodwill won't hold Lexie Hart against you. And people's attitudes toward race are more complex than they talk about.

"Everyone down here knew that old Strom Thurmond had a biracial daughter. But the fact that he looked after her gave him some cover with white folks who didn't want to see themselves as racists." Ford cocked his head, then asked bluntly, "Lexie gonna be coming here?"

"No. We both think it's best she steer clear of politics. At least in the near term."

Ford nodded slowly. "No matter what you do, Price will try to drag her into this. Best not to help him." He paused, then continued in an apologetic tone: "That's not just about race, Corey—it's about your sleeping arrangements. Price knows every lever you can pull down here. If he wants to invent a scandal, he can do it."

The airplane trembled, then hit a bump that drained the blood from Ford's face. "Hate flying," he admitted. "But I guess you'd fly in damned near anything."

"Only when I'm flying it," Corey answered.

*

Rohr's Gulfstream shuddered again, more violently this time. In an instant, Marotta saw lightning flash across the dense darkness of thunderclouds. At the corner of his eye, he could see Mary Rose—she was awake now, her expression queasy, and she glanced at him intermittently.

"Grace," Price said, "will get a ten percent bump out of winning in New Hampshire."

"And my stock price will drop five percent," Rohr said with a sour smile.

"You'll gain it back a week from now," Price answered calmly. "South Carolina is where we destroy him."

"Destroy?" Marotta demurred. "Corey's got more lives than Dracula."

"He's fucking a black actress, Rob. If you want to parse that sentence, the operative words are 'fucking' and 'black.'" Price cast an eye toward Mary Rose. "Just keep M.R. at your side, and bring down the kids next weekend. Compared to a childless black woman, *that* picture's worth ten thousand votes."

"You're forgetting the *other* picture I'm in," Marotta replied. "The one with Grace and two dead terrorists."

"Convenient, wasn't it?" Price sat back, eyebrows arched, his expression at once cynical and dreamy. "Ever wonder why every time Grace needs some Arabs to make him look good, he finds them?"

"What the hell does *that* mean?" Marotta snapped. "The man may have saved my life, you'll remember."

"And now he's using that to steal your nomination." Price's tone was cold and unapologetic. "You know better than anyone that politics is jujitsu. Grace looks like a film star—so paint him as an adulterous husband and lousy father who cashes in his dazzling smile for recreational sex. Grace gets adoring coverage—so cast him as a tool of the liberal media. Grace claims to be independent—so make him a man who believes in nothing, even God. Grace is running as a hero, and so—"

"Forget it. No one reputable would accuse Corey Grace in public of being an Al Qaeda plant. I sure as hell don't want *us* doing anything like that."

Price's lids lowered, veiling his eyes. "By the way," he said in a conversational tone, "did I tell you Linwood Tate wants to be ambassador to England?"

"Lots of people want lots of things. *My* question is what you told him."

"Nothing, as of yet. Deciding about Tate is your job."

Price hit a button on the speakerphone in front of him. After a moment, a man answered. Though scratchy, the southern voice announced itself with calmness and authority. "Linwood Tate here. Been waiting for your call, Magnus."

Surprised, Marotta stared at Price. "Well, here I am," Price answered. "And Alex. *And* Rob."

"Evening, Senator. Welcome to South Carolina, where a friend in need is a friend indeed."

Glancing toward Mary Rose, Price lowered the volume. "And we do need friends, Governor."

"You surely do. And with all respect to Rob's friend Alex, he can't put you across by himself—the message you need to get out here is, shall we say, not quite right for the evening news. Fortunately, there are other ways to help our fine citizens to make an informed decision." After pausing, Tate said with cool assurance, "I've worked real hard to make things in South Carolina happen how I want them. Like I already told you, Magnus, I'd be proud to be the man who made *your* man into President Marotta."

Marotta glanced sharply at Price. Calmly, Price said,

"How much you gonna need, Governor?"

"I figure the whole campaign will cost about two million, most of it offshore. A paltry price for the sovereign state of South Carolina."

When Price turned to Rohr, eyebrows raised, Rohr nodded. "We can do that, Governor," Price said smoothly. "Any questions, Rob?"

There were no questions he could ask, Marotta suddenly understood, where it was safe for him to know the answer. Staring at the speakerphone, he tried to envision himself as president—a far better president than Corey Grace, more deliberate, less impulsive, a man who accepted the world as it was. A man forced to make decisions that his rival's luck had spared him. A man who had worked too long and hard to be derailed by a terrorist's random act. A man who accepted that power had a price.

"None that won't keep," Marotta answered softly. "I won't forget this, Linwood."

Abruptly standing, Marotta went to see his wife.

Pale, Mary Rose looked up at him. "I've been watching you, Robbie. Something happened tonight."

Marotta kissed her forehead. "As soon as you feel better, I want you to go home."

Still watching his face, she shook her head. "Magnus says I can help you here. And I'm feeling like you need me now."

Mary Rose, Marotta thought, knew him all too well. He managed a smile. "I always need you, sweetheart," he said gently. "But our kids need you even more. Better that I do South Carolina on my own."

5

FLYING INTO COLUMBIA AT 1:00 A.M., COREY looked down and saw the scattered illumination of a thinly populated state and then, amid the dark rectangle of an airstrip, a field of flickering lights that resembled an array of stars. As he peered out the window, Ford smiled in delight. "Cigarette lighters," he told Corey. "We hired a band called the Blue Dogs and sent buses to damn near every college in the state, promising a concert and free beer. You're riding into South Carolina on a wave of sheer idealism."

Corey laughed. "Drunken college kids are my natural constituency."

Fifteen minutes later, when Ford and Corey jumped up on the platform to join the band, three thousand or so jacked-up college students emitted a full-throated roar, some brandishing beer or whiskey bottles. Smiling, Corey murmured to Ford, "Guess they're not from Carl Cash University."

"Doesn't matter," Ford assured him. "These young people are truly lit by a higher power." Seizing the microphone from the lead singer for the Blue Dogs, Ford proclaimed, "Guess you all saw what happened in New Hampshire . . ."

THE NEXT MORNING, on four hours sleep, Corey, Ford, Rustin, the campaign staff, and a pack of reporters sped toward Charleston in a bus dubbed the Silver Bullet.

Looking up from his BlackBerry, Rustin reported, "We're already getting a flood of Internet donations. They're calling you the new Teddy Roosevelt."

"*And* Lincoln," Ford suggested, "*and* Washington. You might even be *Franklin* fucking Roosevelt."

"Wrong party," Kate McInerny of the *Post* interjected. "What about Harding, or maybe Coolidge?"

"Or maybe," Rustin told her amiably, "the person above your head."

Looking up, Corey saw the television suspended over the aisle. On tape from C-SPAN, Bob Christy spoke at an evangelical church. "Senator Marotta," he warned, "is the face of corporate materialism, hidden behind the mask of false religiosity."

"Looks like Christy beat us here," Rustin said.

Ford shrugged. "Suits me. He's nothing but trouble for Marotta."

From behind them came the squeal of police sirens. The bus slowed, gliding to a stop on the shoulder of a four-lane highway. A burly highway patrolman appeared in Corey's window, beckoning him outside. "If I don't come back," Corey instructed Ford with a smile, "call my lawyer."

The morning air was chilly. The highway patrolman, a heavy-set man roughly Corey's age, ambled toward him.

"Going too fast?" Corey asked.

"Not for me," the patrolman said. "You can't get to the White House fast enough." Grinning, he held out his sizable hand. "I was in the Gulf War, like you. Just wanted to say 'Welcome to South Carolina' to a genuine American hero."

What, Corey wondered, would Joe Fitts think of *this*? Smiling, he shook his new friend's hand. "Want to ride with us to Charleston?" Corey asked.

*

BEHIND THE CURTAIN, Marotta sat alone with Carl Cash.

The man was near eighty, Marotta guessed, with translucent skin, a gaunt face, and the glinting, humorless eyes of a bitter saint. "A true disciple of Christ," he told Marotta in his phlegmy voice, "holds four immutable beliefs. That the Bible is inerrant. That salvation comes through Jesus Christ alone. That we must be born again. And that all Christians must spread the Word of God. Do *you* believe those things?"

What I believe, Marotta thought, is that you're out of your fucking mind. "I've never heard it summed up like that, Reverend—"

"That's because you're Catholic," Cash interrupted harshly.

"Because I'm Catholic," Marotta answered firmly, "I believe that to be fully human, man must be animated by a higher power—"

"By *Jesus Christ,* Senator." Cash's voice became sepulchral. "Moses is dead. Buddha is dead, Mohammed is dead. Confucius is dead. We alone serve a risen Christ, the son of God, who shall return to us."

This isn't a conversation, Marotta thought—it's the Spanish Inquisition in reverse. With calm persistence, Marotta said, "That's what I believe, Reverend Cash."

Cash slowly shook his head, his gelid stare riveting Marotta. "As a scholar of religion, I've dissected the Catholic apostasy. A son of Rome cannot claim, as we do, to have embraced our Lord Jesus in a single moment."

His temper fraying, Marotta fell back on the catechism that, an hour before, he had improvised with Magnus Price. "Perhaps not. But I can never recall a time I didn't believe in Jesus." Marotta hesitated, then continued quietly: "My father died six years ago, of cancer. When I said my last good-bye to him and looked into his suffering face, I felt Jesus enter my soul. That's when I knew who my father truly was."

Cash watched his eyes in silence. Gathering himself, Marotta said with quiet urgency, "I can be your messenger, Reverend, because I can win. Bob Christy can't. And can you imagine our country in the hands of Corey Grace—"

"*And* his woman," Cash chided irritably. "Don't ever forget *her*."

From the other side of the curtain came the sounds of a restive audience. "There are several reasons," Marotta temporized, "why Grace shouldn't become president."

"That colored woman's a big one," Cash snapped. "You *do* know that the godless Internal Revenue Service took away our school's tax-exempt status, solely because of our biblical opposition to the commingling of races."

This is it, Marotta thought, the core of Cash's fury at the government. Carefully, he recited the answer Price and he had crafted. "Even if—as the unbelievers say—there's a 'separation of church and state,' the state should not intrude on, let alone punish, the religious beliefs of any Christian institution.

"That will be the policy of my administration. And you, Reverend Cash, will always be welcome at the White House."

Cash regarded him with an opaque solemnity. "Let us pray together," he said at last.

As they knelt in front of the folding chairs, eyes raised to the ceiling, Marotta silently asked for John Marotta's forgiveness, both for polluting his death with a falsehood and because that decent man, unlike so many of his neighbors, had taught his oldest son that racial hatred profaned the spirit of God.

"Bless us, Lord," the Reverend Cash intoned.

*

STANDING BESIDE MAROTTA, Cash spoke to an auditorium filled with fresh-faced and attentive white kids—the boys' shirts collared and their hair uniformly short, the girls wearing skirts exposing nothing but their ankles. It was a time warp, Marotta thought, taking him back to his earliest days in a strict parochial school.

"Here at Carl Cash University," Cash proclaimed, "we live by the teaching of Proverbs: 'Train up the child in the ways to go, and when he is old, he will not depart from it.'

"From the evidence of his family, Senator Marotta has done this—at least by his best lights. Corey Grace has not." Abruptly, Cash's voice dripped with disdain. "Grace divorced his wife. Grace abandoned his child. Grace leads a personal life degrading to all *our* children. And last night, in South Carolina, he arrived amid a godless bacchanalia of whiskey, beer, and music."

Expressionless, Marotta tried to conceal his discomfort. But Cash's diatribe plainly resonated with these students. In the front row, Marotta saw, a sweet-faced blond had bowed her head in sorrow. "Corey Grace," Cash continued, his voice rising, "is the enemy of life. Corey Grace will not endorse a constitutional ban on gay marriage—that breeding ground of pederasts, that sanctuary for the most unnatural, abominable act ever conceived by man at his most evil. *Corey Grace* is an enemy of God."

Turning, Cash walked slowly behind Marotta and placed both hands on his shoulders. "*This* man," he told the students, "is a man of God."

Rapt, the students gazed up at Marotta. Experienced though he was, Marotta realized, he was not immune to the fire of this man's certitude. "Listen to his words," Cash concluded in a tone sonorous yet hushed. "Then listen to your hearts."

Applause, Marotta realized, would only tarnish such a moment. Walking to the podium in the silent spell induced by Cash, he spread his speech before him. "These are the words of the Bible," he began. " 'Being born again, not of corruptible seed, but of incorruptible, by the Word of God which lives and abides forever.' And it was Christ himself who said, 'I am not come to call the righteous, but sinners to repentance.'

"These things we all believe, and more.

"We believe the Bible is inerrant, and that homosexuality violates God's law.

"We believe that our schools should ban homosexuals as teachers; balance the teaching of Darwin with opposing theories; abolish all 'sex education' except chastity until marriage." Pausing, Marotta was grateful that the Reverend Cash had also forbidden tape recorders. "Like you, I believe that the 'separation of church and state' is the invention of modern secular humanists, not of Madison or Jefferson. Like you, I believe that churches should be free to endorse candidates for office without being punished—as was this university—for their beliefs."

Filled with pent-up emotion, the audience burst into applause. "Reverend Christy," Marotta told them, "may well believe as we do. But I alone can guarantee you a Christian presidency. I alone can keep Senator Grace from holding an office he should never, ever have."

In the first few rows, students began standing. It was too late, Marotta thought, to omit his next words. He waited for the applause to die. "I owe Senator Grace my life," he said quietly. "For that, my family and I will be forever grateful. But no amount of gratitude could justify my moral abdication.

"His beliefs and his personal conduct undermine our moral fabric. And the fibers of that fabric are the values of this university." Standing taller, Marotta said firmly, "*Not* the values of a Hollywood elite that has made drugs and violence and promiscuity our secular religion."

Suddenly they were on their feet—all of them—clapping and shouting. "*Amen,*" someone called out from the rear, and then Marotta saw the signs appear.

Across a photograph of Lexie Hart in close-up was stamped a scarlet X. "Just say no to Hollywood," the placards read—the work, Marotta knew, of a professional.

6

HEADED FOR THE COAST IN THE SILVER BULLET, Dakin Ford sat with Corey, remote control in one hand, restlessly switching channels while monitoring his cell phone. "Marotta's already been to Carl Cash," he reported. "Looks like he's letting Price put his candidacy in that old bigot's hands."

Eyeing the screen, Blake Rustin said, "Not just Cash's."

On the Rohr-owned station in Columbia, a trim brunette with an incandescent smile stood beside Rob Marotta beneath an enormous sign whose bold letters read "Creation Park." "What the hell is that?" Corey asked.

"Jurassic Park for evangelicals," Ford replied. "A thrill ride through the seven days when God created man—Adam, Eve, and the serpent, blissfully free of our simian ancestors or cesspools of primordial ooze.

"And that," Ford continued, pointing at the screen, "is Dorrie Hoyle, our leading lady evangelist and Linwood Tate's main squeeze." He feigned a wince. "Some sex acts don't bear thinking about. But Dorrie'd fuck about anyone for money, and Linwood raised the cash to help Dorrie build this Disneyland of decency."

Pointing the remote, Ford turned up the volume. "You all know I can't endorse candidates," Hoyle was telling her audience. "But I'd just love it if you'd e-mail me the names of any church where good Christians want to spread the word on behalf of a good Christian candidate."

Placing a sisterly hand on Marotta's shoulder, she finished in a mock-conspiratorial whisper: "Guess who *that* might be . . ."

Corey watched Marotta feign a smile and shrug. "Rob's feeling like a prop," he said.

"Doesn't matter," Ford rejoined. "Price is using Cash and Dorrie to cut Bob Christy's balls off. Other thing that's gonna happen is Rohr's TV stations and newspaper won't cover Bob at all. In terms of local media, the Christy crusade's gonna shrivel to a rumor."

Around them, several reporters—Kate McInerny of the *Post*, Miles Miklin of the *Times*, and Annie Stevenson of the AP—leaned forward to participate. "What's in store for Senator Grace?" Kate asked.

"Oh," Ford said lazily, "they'll dream up something different for Corey, maybe without their fingerprints on it. Once it starts, hope you bright boys and girls take the time to figure out who's behind it."

Across the aisle, Blake Rustin sat alone, consumed by his own thoughts.

THEY WERE SCHEDULED to stop in Beaufort and, later, Hilton Head—Corey's territory, filled with retirees from the North and Midwest. Driving on a two-lane road, they entered a semitropical world of palmettos, moss-draped oaks, and tidal rivers. As they passed under a bower of mossy branches, Corey saw, at the end of a tree-lined drive, a white antebellum wood home whose generous porches overlooked a rolling lawn filled with well-dressed men and women.

Their host, a trim, blond man named Henry Davis, greeted him with a firm grip and a smile. In a pleasant drawl he said, "Welcome to the New South, Senator. You got more friends here than you know, some of them even natives."

Corey returned his smile. "Thanks, Henry. I need the support of all indigenous people."

Davis's introduction was short and gracious. Standing on the porch, Corey surveyed the crowd. "If a visitor from Mars," he began, "were to drop in on us today, he or she would believe us truly blessed. And we are. But we're here because America's in trouble.

"Our country is eight trillion dollars in debt. Our political system protects those in power, and *with* power. Our political parties encourage us to distrust our fellow citizens. And all too few of us believe that we can change this.

"But we can," Corey said emphatically. "We still can build bridges to each other. We still can tackle our real problems with real ideas. Together, we still can heal our country.

"But that means starting with the truth—regardless of party, or religion, or where we live, or who we are. And the truth is this: our political leaders are weakening America by dividing us into factions.

"It's up to us to stop them."

The crowd began applauding. Only when the applause continued, growing louder, did Corey grasp how many others, even in this privileged place, were troubled by what they sensed might be an irreversible decline into dishonesty and disarray. "Our leaders," Corey said, "can prey on the worst in us or speak to the best in us. But which of these prevails is in our hands."

Afterward, the crowd pressed forward to meet him. "Maybe," Dakin Ford murmured to Corey, "this can really happen here." But it was his muted note of worry that stayed with Corey when they got back on the bus.

THAT NIGHT, AFTER a massive sunset rally on the beach at Hilton Head, Corey walked alone at the edge of the water, talking to Lexie on his cell phone.

"It went pretty well today," he told her. "So far, your native state's been okay."

"That's good, baby. I'm glad for you."

Even without seeing her, his sense of Lexie's moods had become acute. "What's wrong?" he asked. "I'm hearing a certain reserve. Maybe a woman who doesn't want to burst my bubble or worry me with troubles of her own."

After a long silence, she said, "I got a call this morning, from a friend I went to Yale with. A man came around to her apartment, asking if she knew me then. She didn't like his questions."

Corey gazed at the moon-streaked tide. "What questions, exactly?"

"Boyfriends, for one." Lexie hesitated. "He asked if she knew where Peter was. Lizzie said she had no idea, then cut the conversation short."

Corey's mouth felt dry. "Did this guy say who he worked for?"

"A tabloid. But the phone number on the card he gave her connected to a 'not in service' message." Lexie's voice seemed to fade. "Somebody's after me and has a notion of where to look. All I ever wanted was to put that in the past."

Corey imagined her face, sad and a little haunted. "I'm sorry," he told her. "I know what this dredges up for you."

"Not just me. All those years ago, trying to forget what those men did to me, I never dreamed I was ruining someone's chances of becoming president."

She sounded utterly dispirited. "I want to tell you something," Corey said. "I hope it's fair to say this to someone I haven't seen for two months.

"I'm in love with you, Lexie. I won't give up on whatever future we may have."

Lexie was silent. "I love you, too," she said at last. "So it's not only you who gets to choose. I need to sit alone with this."

Unable to be with her, or comfort her, Corey said good-bye.

HALF ASLEEP, RUSTIN sat on the edge of his bed, wearing boxer shorts and his daughter's oversized Dartmouth T-shirt. "She got a problem?" he asked wearily.

"Yeah," Corey snapped. "Someone's poking around in her life. Smells like Magnus Price to me."

Rustin blinked, his eyes still adjusting to the light. "Surprise. You knew this woman was a magnet from day one. There are no Hollywood endings in politics—especially for someone from Hollywood." Rustin drew a breath. "I want you to consider something, okay?"

"What's that?"

"Unless she's squeaky-clean, break it off with her; then put out that it was *your* decision. If she's the woman you think she is, she'll understand."

Corey placed a hand on his shoulder. "Sorry," he said and left.

IT STARTED THE next morning.

Finishing his speech at the Battery at Charleston, Corey saw the signs at the edge of the sizable crowd—Lexie with a giant X across her face. A chant rose up from those who held the signs: "Just say no! Just say no!"

Near a clump of demonstrators, a camerawoman from Rohr News recorded their shouts and placards. Determined to ignore them, Corey waded into the friendly crowd with Dana Harrison and saw Dakin Ford edging toward the back. "I just loved your speech," a plump young woman told him. "Could you please sign my T-shirt?"

"With you still in it?" he inquired with a laugh.

The woman grinned, turning her back. As he scrawled his name in felt pen, Corey saw Dakin Ford grab a bearded man by his shirt collar, barking into his face. "Go get Dakin," he murmured to Dana.

"HIRED HANDS," FORD said in disgust. "These thugs wouldn't know a legitimate issue if it bit them in the ass."

Corey and Rustin sat with him in the back of the empty bus, a swiftly improvised meeting from which they had excluded the press. Outside, reporters milled about, peering at them through the windows.

On the tray in front of Ford were his laptop and a flyer he had wrested from one of the demonstrators. "'To secure the favors of his black girlfriend,'" Ford read, "'Corey Grace has agreed to outlaw the Confederate flag.'"

"Yeah," Corey said, "right after I abolish the First Amendment."

"There's more," Ford told him. "A friend forwarded this e-mail he just got. Near as I can tell, it's viral—my friend's on an e-mail list for donors to Carl Cash University." Peering at his computer screen, Ford read aloud: "'Electing Corey Grace means mixed-race children cavorting in the Rose Garden.' And so on.

"Problem is, we can't tell where this shit comes from. Best you can do right now is ignore it. But can I give you some advice on our sacred flag?"

"Sure."

"We've come a fair distance since the whole flag ruckus started. A few years ago, we removed it from the statehouse flagpole and planted it a hundred yards away, near the monument to the Confederate dead. Not everyone was happy, but the idea was to calm things down a little."

Ford flipped his laptop closed. "Whoever put out that flyer is stirring up old trouble to put you on the spot.

"What's gonna happen, I predict, is hundreds of thousands of these flyers will start popping up in people's mail. The flyers will come from out of state; they'll have stamps so no one can track who sent them; we won't figure out who paid for them before Election Day. And as soon as that asshole from Rohr News gets back on this goddamned bus, he's gonna ask you about the flag.

"So here's what you do, Corey: embrace the compromise." Leaning back with his eyes closed, Ford intoned, " 'South Carolinians are working toward resolution without the interference of outsiders. I endorse those positive efforts and condemn the efforts of others to exploit the wounds of the past.' Or," Ford added wearily, "some other crap like that.

"The flag nuts won't like that much, and neither will black folks. But the flag nuts aren't voting for you, and blacks in South Carolina aren't ready for a Republican. At least you can come out of this with a shred or two of dignity."

Gazing at the windows, Corey saw the Rohr News reporter, wiry and bespectacled, pacing beneath a palmetto tree with a flyer in his hand. "At most a shred," he answered.

AFTER DELIVERING HIS canned response to the inevitable question from Jake Linkletter at Rohr News, Corey lapsed into silence.

On the screen above them, a washed-up country-and-western singer monopolized the afternoon talk-show broadcast on Rohr's Charleston station, expressing his indignation that Corey Grace "disrespects the precious heritage of the South."

Dakin Ford grimaced in disgust. "Dorrie Hoyle hires this turkey to warble at Creation Park," he told Corey. "Without her, he's drinking cough syrup in a gutter. Fucker can't even spell 'Confederate'—hell, he can't even spell 'flag.' " Turning to Rustin, he said, "Just got another e-mail. Last night they were passing out those flyers at high school basketball games."

Closing his eyes, Corey tried to sleep.

Marotta's voice awakened him. On the set of the same talk show, Marotta sat with the hostess, Dolly Reed, an officious brunette with tightly coiled hair. "For almost ten years," she told him, "the NAACP has persuaded out-of-state groups not to hold conventions in South Carolina—all because the Confederate flag still flies in a little corner of our statehouse lawn. Just a short while ago, our own country star Ace Harwood expressed concern that Senator Grace supports that boycott. What do *you* have to say about that?"

Frowning, Marotta straightened the crease in his suit pants, a portrait of reluctance. "As you know, Dolly, we've never raised this issue. But others have, so it seems important for the candidates not to duck it.

"Racism in any form is wrong. For too long, southerners have been the victims of racism in reverse. And it's dead wrong to make South Carolina pay in dollars and cents for honoring its history." After a pause, Marotta continued: "I support flying the Confederate flag and condemn any boycott of this state. I call on Senator Grace and Reverend Christy to join me in that stand."

Ford shook his head. "The heart of darkness just swallowed Rob Marotta. It's an awesome thing to watch."

Staring at the screen, Corey said nothing.

7

AN HOUR LATER, COREY, FORD, AND RUSTIN SAT
at a table in Corey's hotel suite in Charleston, nerves raw
with tension and fatigue. "Price is baiting you," Rustin
said. "He wants to make you lose your temper—or, better
yet, leap to Lexie's defense."

"Or," Corey snapped, "just act like a spineless robot."

"How about like a president, for Godsakes. This isn't a
school yard."

"Close enough," Ford put in. He placed a tape recorder
on the table. "Y'all better hear this. It's the tape of an
anonymous call—they're happening all over white rural
areas. A quick-thinking friend pushed the record button
on his answering machine."

The disembodied voice was itself clearly a recording.
"This is an information alert for all citizens who intend to
vote in our presidential primary.

"Would you vote for a man who gave his ex-wife AIDS,
is conducting an illicit affair with a radical black actress,
supports interracial marriage, opposes banning marriage
between men and men, supports taking away your guns,
and wants to ban the Confederate flag?

"If these values are *your* values, then Corey Grace is
your candidate."

Ford hit the pause button. "What you gonna do?" he
asked Corey wearily. "Get out a press release denying
you've had AIDS?

"You can't prove where this comes from. You sure as

hell can't blame Marotta and Price. You can't even complain—all you'd be doing is giving Price a megaphone. Only thing left, Corey, is ignore this."

Rustin looked from Corey to Ford. "Play the Al Qaeda tape," he said.

Ford inserted another cassette. "During his capture," a tinny, anonymous voice said, "Corey Grace was brainwashed by Al Qaeda. That's why two Al Qaeda terrorists raided the capital: to sacrifice their lives so Grace could be a hero. And why?" The voice finished in a conspiratorial tone: "Because Corey Grace promised to let Islamic fundamentalists plant nuclear bombs at the heart of America's cities."

The tape ended. "Sorry," Ford said softly. "Lousy payoff for surviving torture. But your connection to Al Qaeda sure puts Lexie in perspective."

Though taut with anger, Corey remained silent. "You know how it's done," Rustin said. "Phone calls come from out of state, or maybe outside the country. No caller ID shows up, and the tape's programmed to switch off if they get an answering machine. And there's no way to trace these calls, so the lazy bastards in the media just move on."

"This is the first level of attack," Ford interjected. "Next, someone starts spreading the same crap on the Internet. Then people show up in churches saying that they've heard this stuff. *Then* surrogates with no obvious connection to Marotta will start appearing on Rohr's TV stations, taking this slander all the way from anonymous phone calls to the mainstream of public conversation." Ford's brief smile was sardonic. "Last night another friend of mine went to church, and heard you're supported by an entire 'gay army.' Probably a crew of Islamic sodomites.

"That's the Carl Cash–Dorrie Hoyle connection—

e-mail lists and church phone trees being used to spread this sewage."

"While Marotta," Rustin added, "stays above the fray. When Rohr's media people ask him whether you're an Al Qaeda agent, he'll say he can't believe it—spreading the rumors while disclaiming them. Then Rohr will give a megaphone to whatever nuts and whores Price hired to slander you flat out."

Propelled by restlessness and frustration, Corey stood. "We don't have the personnel or money to pin this on Marotta, do we?"

Rustin glanced at Ford. "Not before Election Day."

"Then all we can do is keep running our campaign and encourage the press to dig." Corey turned to Ford. "You told me South Carolina would be a test of character. Let's hope, in the end, that it matters."

AT NOON, AFTER Corey's first two speeches, the passengers in the Silver Bullet watched the screen, riveted by Dolly Reed's newest guest. "Here's how I put the pieces together," the retired air force colonel told her with spiteful vehemence. "Question: Why did the Arabs kill Grace's navigator but not Grace?

"Answer: They needed to eliminate the only witness to Grace's treachery."

As Corey felt his stomach tighten, Dolly touched her throat in a gesture of alarm. "Do you truly believe *that*?"

"'Absolutely,'" Dakin Ford said for the colonel. "'Ever since Magnus Price put the computer chip in my brain . . .'"

"Question," the man continued. "Would Corey Grace have become a senator if those Arabs hadn't first made him a hero?

"Answer: No way—his candidacy would have been a joke."

"So you think this is Price's work?" Kate McInerny asked Corey.

"It's the press's job to find that out," Corey answered with some asperity. "Merely reporting crap like this is cheap and easy."

"Question," the colonel went on. "Why did Corey Grace just happen to be around when Al Qaeda tried to assassinate Senator Marotta?

"Answer: Grace knew exactly when they were coming."

"In other words," Dolly Reed gasped with apparent horror, "you're saying that Senator Grace is like the 'Manchurian candidate'—an agent of our enemies?"

The man bit his lip impatiently. "How else did one unarmed man kill two terrorists who'd already cut down an armed member of the capital police?" His tone became conspiratorial. "You know Grace's sentimental story about the Arab who kept loosening his bonds? That's his propagandistic way of insinuating that Arab terrorists really aren't so bad. So when Al Qaeda asks us to abandon our oil fields in the Middle East, 'President Grace' will have softened us up for complete capitulation."

Despite himself, Corey laughed. "That's what I get for saving Marotta's life. Next time, I'm opening the door and inviting them inside."

Above them, *The Dolly Reed Show* was interrupted by a commercial. Startled, Corey gazed at the face of his ex-wife.

The photograph had been taken during his first campaign. Standing beside him at a picnic for supporters, Janice might have looked discomfited, save that the X across her face obscured her eyes. "Do all your women wear X's?" Ford asked.

"Corey Grace," the voiceover said, "divorced his wife and abandoned his daughter. Now he's busy romancing an actress in opulent foreign love nests . . ."

As the familiar photograph appeared—Lexie in her bikini—Ford murmured, "Left out the X *this* time."

The picture changed to two men in tuxedos, holding hands next to a three-tiered wedding cake. "Maybe that's why," the narrator concluded, "Corey Grace opposes a ban on homosexual marriage. If you don't believe in marriage, why should it matter who gets married?"

The small print beneath the wedding cake read, "South Carolinians for the Defense of Marriage." "Who are they?" Kate McInerny wondered aloud.

"That was my point," Corey snapped. "Why don't you find out?"

BY THE NEXT stop, at the quadrangle of the University of South Carolina, Corey was glad to escape the bus. "Beginning to feel claustrophobic," he mumbled to Ford.

"Easy, boy," Ford said under his breath. "The press folks are watching your face."

The platform was at the center of an expanse of grass crisscrossed by brick paths and shaded by symmetrically planted trees, the dogwoods and magnolias displaying the first buds of spring. Gazing out at the lawn filled with students both black and white, Corey sensed what Lexie and he might yet come to mean.

As he ascended the platform, the campus bell tower began to sound. Lighter of spirit, he said solemnly to Ford, "A sign."

"A portent," Ford said with a smile. "Never ask for whom the bell tolls. It tolls for Rob Marotta."

RETURNING TO THE bus, Corey noted that Jake Linkletter of Rohr News had claimed a seat nearer to his own. "Can we watch my mother station?" Linkletter asked.

Shrugging, Ford changed channels.

Rohr News showed Rob Marotta and Dorrie Hoyle on the lawn of a megachurch outside Columbia, flanking the church's pastor as he addressed a noonday crowd. "In the 1960s," the minister said, "liberals with an atheistic, humanist worldview seized control of our government. Now we and they are waging the ultimate struggle over whether our country will be saved or plunged into eternal darkness.

"Today, Senator Rob Marotta has come to pray with us for America." Closing his eyes, the minister linked hands with Marotta and Hoyle. "Oh Lord," he began, "please deliver . . ."

"More ballots for Rob Marotta," Ford cut in. "May the dead arise, and vote as one."

Linkletter turned to Corey. "Senator, do you believe it's inappropriate for Senator Marotta to make appearances at evangelical churches?"

Though it took considerable self-control, Corey answered in a reasonably pleasant tone: "I'm not in the business of trying to refine Rob's sense of the appropriate."

"Are you referring to the charges that you're in contact with Al Qaeda?"

Beside him, Corey felt Dakin Ford stir in warning. He studied the reporter's face—smug, lineless, and without character. "How old are you, Jake?"

For an instant, Linkletter looked disconcerted. "Twenty-nine."

"Pretty young. Ever serve in the military?"

Of course not, the reporter's expression said. "No," he answered tersely.

Corey smiled. "Then I guess you missed your chance to be in contact with Al Qaeda. These days we reserve that opportunity for the less sophisticated segments of our populace."

As Corey turned to the screen, the crowd formed a prayer circle around Marotta.

AT THE NEXT rally, held in a high school gym, Corey took questions as a swelling phalanx of reporters watched him for signs of pressure.

A trim brunette stood with her adolescent son. "This is my son Tommy," she began. "He's always looked up to you."

"Hi, Tommy," Corey said with a smile. "Hope you're turning eighteen before next Tuesday."

Though the crowd chuckled, the woman's forehead furrowed. "Last night," she told him, "Tommy answered the phone and some man told him you cheated on your wife, just like you'd betray our country. Then he turned on the TV and heard an advertisement that said you're in favor of men marrying other men.

"He still wants to believe in you, but now he doesn't know what to think. His dad and I don't know what to tell him. Could you please help us?"

Corey took in the youthful faces of the students, the worn bleachers, the cinder-block wall on which hung banners commemorating championship teams going back for decades. "All of us," he said, "deserve better than anonymous tape recordings, or TV ads placed by groups no one's ever heard of, or postcards mailed from out of state.

"I'm running for president, Tommy, because I love our country—way too much to use tactics so dirty that I have to conceal them." Corey scanned the crowd. "Tonight, all three candidates are going to debate on television. None of us can hide. And all of us will be accountable for everything we say.

"I hope all of *you* will be watching. If you base your judgment on what we say for ourselves—in public—then you'll win, and the cowards who can't acknowledge their own lies will lose." Turning back to his questioner and her son, Corey finished: "I'd like you and Tommy to be my guests, ma'am. I'll do my best to make you proud."

Leaving the gym, Ford said to Corey, "Guess you plan on kicking Marotta's ass."

Corey's face was set. "No choice. It may be the only time he's not hiding under Price's rock."

8

"WAIT A MINUTE," RUSTIN EXPOSTULATED. "YOU'RE telling me that Corey's post-debate party is being hosted by a guy who runs a pawnshop out of his home, looks like a Hell's Angel, and flies a fucking Confederate flag on his front lawn?"

Ford glanced at Corey, eating barbecue with Dana Harrison as they honed his debate strategy. "Name's Boss Moss," Ford said with an easy grin. "Sunk about five grand into sprucing up his place for a visit from our future president.

"Okay, ever since Vietnam maybe Boss has been a little fucked up. Maybe some of his motorcycle buddies occupy the margins of the law. But he's got a network of ten thousand people in trailer parks who'd never vote for Corey unless Moss said to. Piss Boss off, and those votes evaporate."

"So we're taking the media to a pawnshop run by a wacko named Boss."

"Who's already drunk," Ford added mildly, "and just ran a brand-new Stars and Bars up the flagpole."

Rustin rubbed his eyes. "Dakin," he said, "I don't care *what* you have to do. If Corey sees that fucking flag, he'll blow."

"All I can do is try," Ford said dubiously. "Gonna tell him?"

"The mood he's in?" Rustin exhaled. "The latest poll is bad enough."

*

TEN MINUTES BEFORE the start of the debate, Rustin sat with Corey behind a partition. "This is surreal," Corey said. "We're about to debate in an abandoned shopping mall jammed with tables full of drunks. I can already hear them yelling."

"Linwood Tate is speaking," Rustin explained. "Tate bought most of the tables and packed them with Marotta people. It's like a football game out there, and you're definitely the visiting team.

"I want you to be careful, Corey. I don't like breaking this to you now, but the latest tracking polls have you sliding badly among Republicans." Frowning, Rustin put his hand on Corey's arm. "You need at least a third of them to win. The last thing you want is to make a slip Marotta can beat you up with until Tuesday."

"Then give me some time alone, Blake."

For the moments remaining, Corey thought of Joe Fitts; his brother, Clay; and the last time he had spoken to Lexie. "Whatever happens," she had told him, "just be yourself. That's the one thing they can't take from you."

Looking up, Corey saw the Reverend Bob Christy. Smiling, Christy said, "They told me I'd find you here." He placed a hand on Corey's shoulder. "We really don't know each other," he said in an avuncular tone. "And we sure don't agree about much. But I want you to know this poison isn't coming from me."

"Believe me, I know that."

"Then it seems like we've got a common enemy." Christy gave a sudden, surprising grin. "So let's have at each other. But maybe us boys can have some fun with Marotta—I'll hit him from one side, you from the other. Don't know what *your* people are saying to do, but I'm in this to save America from men like Magnus Price."

Corey smiled. "Funny, Reverend. That's how I feel, too."

*

THE RULES WERE simple and brutal: though John Coburn, a news anchor from Columbia, would moderate, the candidates would simply face off with one another. From the moment they stepped onstage, Corey sensed that Rob Marotta was tense.

The cavernous indoor mall was filled with tables whose occupants, prosperous Republican donors, cheered and applauded with the mass enthusiasm of fans at a sporting event. Shaking Corey's hand, Marotta mustered a sheepish smile that, Corey supposed, was meant to reflect their common plight. "Wild, huh?"

Corey eyed him quizzically. "I've been watching you on the tube, trying to figure out what's wrong. Now I can see what it is. You're shrinking, Rob, right before my eyes."

THEY SAT AT a table—Corey and Christy flanking Marotta—facing Coburn, a soft-chinned man with his back to the audience. From his opening statement, Christy seemed determined to make up for the attention Magnus Price had conspired to deny him.

"Americans are engaged in a second civil war," he began. "This time the prize is not land or cotton or sovereignty, but the hearts and minds of our children.

"We can lose our children to the siren song of sex education and sleazy entertainment—this whole seductive notion that sin exacts no spiritual or moral cost. Or we can point them down a righteous path and transform our entire culture in a single generation." Sternly, Christy scanned the crowd, as though searching out the inebriated, the inattentive, the cynical. "But *that* requires a leader. I *am* that leader. For me, putting faith at the heart of our public life is not a matter of convenience, a cheap maneuver taught me by political handlers." Abruptly turning on Marotta, he demanded, "Let us hear your testimony, Rob."

For an instant, Marotta looked so startled that Corey almost smiled. "Testimony?" Marotta parried. "I didn't know this was a trial."

"You just don't talk our language," Christy said with a sorrowful smile. "To born-again Christians, our testimony describes the moment we were saved. I sure remember mine." Facing Corey, Christy inquired, "What about you, Corey?"

"I have no testimony," Corey answered calmly. "Only beliefs. I believe that God endowed man with certain qualities—including the right to personal autonomy in how we worship our Creator."

Corey paused, gathering his thoughts. "I believe in the God of the New Testament—in the power of human love, and in a society that cares for the least of us." He turned to Marotta. "What *do* you believe, Rob? Seeing how you spent your first morning here pandering to a man who calls Catholicism—your faith of choice—a 'satanic cult.'

"Is Catholicism a cult? Or was your obeisance to Carl Cash, to paraphrase Bob Christy, a 'matter of convenience'?"

"Reverend Cash," Marotta responded, "endorsed *me* as the Christian candidate qualified to be president. I did not endorse, nor did he ask me to, every statement he has ever made."

"Nor did you repudiate them," Corey said sharply. "That would have shown leadership. But that would involve actually running your own campaign."

"Let's move on," the moderator hastily interjected. "Obviously, the role of religion in our civic life has become a major issue. Beginning with Reverend Christy, do you believe that Darwin should be taught in our public schools.?"

Corey scanned the crowd, made newly attentive by the edgy start of the debate. "Darwin?" Christy answered with a smile. "Utter nonsense. Using evolution to explain our world's design is like believing that a hurricane can hit a scrap heap and a 2007 Honda Civic will just pop out and drive away on its own."

Facing the audience, Christy continued in a tone that was slow, insistent, and resonant. "For me, intelligent design is the only answer. I believe that God designed us as a species, and that is what I would teach our children."

To Corey's surprise, scattered applause echoed in the cavernous mall. "Senator Marotta?" the moderator asked.

"I'm with Reverend Christy," Marotta replied smoothly. "I believe that intelligent design should be taught alongside evolution. Evolution is theory, not fact. Besides," he added with a smile, "God has been with us a lot longer than poor, dead Darwin."

The audience chuckled. "Senator Grace?" the moderator asked.

In the front row, Corey saw Blake Rustin arch his eyebrows, a warning to be cautious. "This is a tough one," Corey said. "Most people think that a candidate can't embrace Darwin and get our party's nomination.

"But as far as I can tell, Darwin was right. I can't claim to know how God set about creating man, so I don't dispute that He did so by means of evolution." Facing Marotta, he said, "In rejecting Galileo, the religious leaders of his day insisted that the earth was flat. Are *you* okay with Galileo? Or should we balance every hour of astronomy with an hour of flat-earth science?"

A ripple of nervous laughter told Corey he had struck a chord—for skeptics, Marotta's parsing of issues smelled of calculation. "I believe in freedom of inquiry," Marotta shot back. "Seems like I'm the only one up here who does."

This sound bite, showing Marotta's resilience, was greeted by applause. "In that spirit," Marotta continued, "I'd like to ask Reverend Christy if he believes in the theory of the rapture and, if so, how that relates to the Middle East."

This, Corey thought, was shrewd and even daring—by challenging Christy to defend dogma at its most apocalyptic, Marotta might paint Christy as too extreme for mainstream evangelicals. But Christy appeared unruffled. Leaning forward, he fixed Marotta with an unwavering gaze. "The nation of Israel is more than land and people. It is the place God chose for the return of our Messiah—"

"There's no greater friend of Israel than I," Marotta interrupted. "I'm asking you about the rapture."

Christy seemed undeterred. "Can you recite the first book of Thessalonians, chapter four, verses sixteen and seventeen?"

"Not by heart, no."

Eyes raised to the ceiling, Christy quoted from memory. " 'The Lord himself shall descend from Heaven with a shout. And the dead in Christ shall rise first; then we which are alive and remain shall be caught up together with them in the clouds, to greet the Lord in the air; and so shall we ever be with the Lord.' "

The audience was hushed. Corey felt a mixture of horror and fascination, as though witnessing the first moments of a terrible blunder. But Christy still seemed oblivious. "On the day of the rapture, the faithful will be 'caught away.' "

"Suppose you're on a highway?" Marotta asked.

Now Christy cocked his head. "Wherever they are," he

asserted, "those who believe will be lifted up and simply disappear."

"And then?"

"Jesus," Christy answered firmly, "will return to the biblical land of Israel at the head of an army of raptured saints, and defeat the Antichrist at Armageddon. Only then will the Lord Jesus Christ sit upon the throne of David in Jerusalem."

From somewhere in the audience came a drunken whistle of amazement. Taking the offensive, Christy asked, "Do *you* believe in God's Word, Rob?"

"Of course. But we must work in earthly ways to ensure the survival of the state of Israel."

"What does *that* mean?" Corey asked. "Does Armageddon have a place in U.S. foreign policy?"

"The Bible," Marotta temporized, "is subject to interpretation."

"You're a great interpreter," Corey said sharply. "It's your answer that's hard to interpret. Here's mine: the very idea of Armageddon breeds a scary fatalism, where an apocalypse—perhaps nuclear—becomes integral to God's design.

"I'm not prepared to consign humanity to destruction. With all respect to Bob, I have trouble imagining the smug, smiling saved being wafted from their cars or levitated from lawn chairs, while the rest of us die in highway wrecks and nuclear catastrophes. I prefer that we make the planet as it exists a safer place."

"So do I," Marotta responded. "By fighting the war on terrorism. About which you've been strangely passive."

To Corey, the oblique reference to the "Manchurian candidate" whispering campaign was deliberate and unforgivable. "'Strangely passive,'" he repeated in a low, chill tone. "As I recall, the last time you and I encountered terrorists only one of us was busy.

"But perhaps I should be charitable. Maybe you're confusing Iraq with the war on terror, and courage with sending other people to die." Catching himself, Corey continued in an even voice: "To my regret, the war in Iraq has made us far less safe. And by this time, only a fool believes that 'terror' is something you can invade."

As a smattering of applause greeted Corey's retort, he saw the first glimmer of uncertainty appear in Marotta's eyes.

"Closer to home," Coburn said, "you, Senator Marotta, have taken a strong position in support of the Confederate flag. Why should that be an issue in a presidential campaign?"

"Because I'm tired of people who divide us up by race." Turning to Corey, he said, "You've been waffling on this issue, Corey. Do you believe in punishing South Carolinians for honoring their heritage?"

At a front table, Blake Rustin shook his head, his gaze imploring Corey to deliver a politic answer. "Do you believe in slavery?" Corey asked Marotta. "To many Americans, black and white, that flag is the symbol of a cruel and degrading institution that haunts us to this day." Facing the audience, Corey said, "This is your state, not mine. But were it up to me, I'd put it in a museum with the other relics from a hundred-and-fifty-year-old war. I don't think we need to honor the dead by insulting the living."

"That's *not* what this is about," Marotta cut in. "And South Carolinians know it."

"Fine," Corey shot back. "So the next time you tell a group of African-Americans in Michigan that they should vote Republican, explain to them why black voters in South Carolina are being oversensitive. But you won't, of course. You're just trolling for votes until next Tuesday, desperate to pull out a campaign that's basically on life support. And I think South Carolinians know *that*."

A second spattering of applause made Marotta flush. "I'd like to associate myself with Senator Grace's remarks," Christy offered in an amiable tone. "I sincerely feel for those who love that flag. But I doubt you gave this five minutes thought, Rob, until someone told you there were votes in it. That's just not worthy of a president. And neither is your campaign."

Surprised, Corey repressed a smile. "That's uncalled for," Marotta shot back. "My campaign is about who's qualified to be president. You have *no* qualifications."

"Oh, I've got a couple," Christy answered, unperturbed. "One of them is that I say what I believe, and don't use other people to say what I'd be ashamed to say.

"Today—on a station owned by one of your great supporters, Alex Rohr—some former air force colonel showed up claiming that Al Qaeda sent two terrorists to your office so that Senator Grace could kill them just to make himself look good." Christy smiled. "All of us saw the picture, Rob. But do you really believe that Corey and Al Qaeda are conspiring against America, or do you agree with me that anyone who says that belongs in an insane asylum?"

A bark of nervous laughter came from a nearby table. Corey perceived anew the power of Bob Christy: neither a politician nor the product of conventional politics, he was free to do or say what he pleased, secure in the conviction that he spoke for a higher power. "That question," Marotta said with rote disdain, "doesn't deserve an answer."

Christy's eyes widened. "Are you saying," he asked in an incredulous tone, "that your campaign manager and his minions didn't put this colonel up to it? Are you telling me this lunatic got on Rohr's TV station based on the power of his own ideas?"

"That," Marotta replied with real anger, "is the kind of irresponsible invective that disqualifies you to be president."

"Senator Grace," Coburn interjected with an air of desperation, "do you have anything to say on your own behalf?"

Corey smiled. "Why spoil the moment? All I can add is that someone who'll do anything to be president shouldn't be president."

A tense silence filled the room. "I think it's your turn," Coburn told Marotta in a mollifying tone. "You've made a constitutional ban on gay marriage a centerpiece of your campaign. When all states but one ban such marriage, why is this so important?"

Seeking to recover, Marotta began speaking in a slow, insistent voice. "John, there is *nothing* more important than the moral strength of our families.

"Since before the time of Jesus Christ, marriage has been the union of a man and woman. That's the only means of raising children who are morally, spiritually, and psychologically whole." Gesturing toward Corey, he said, "Three-quarters of Americans oppose gay marriage. Yet Senator Grace does not support a constitutional ban. No one who refuses to defend the institution of marriage should be our party's nominee."

Corey turned to him. "America faces terrorism, nuclear proliferation, massive deficits, rising unemployment, and a gap between the wealthy and the rest of us in wages, education, and health care. And you're running on gay marriage and the Confederate flag." Corey made his tone both wry and weary. "I oppose gay marriage, Rob. You know that. And if you and Mary Rose need a constitutional amendment to protect your marriage, I'll vote for it. If only for the sake of the kids."

"This isn't a joke," Marotta said stonily.

"And I'm not laughing. But we both know that the greatest threat to marriage is divorce. Are you proposing a constitutional ban on *that*?"

"Of course not," Marotta said in exasperation. "But America needs a moral renewal every bit as much as economic prosperity. And it's all too obvious that you can't lead it."

They were perilously close, Corey knew, to bringing Lexie into this debate. Thinking of the unknown man delving into her past, Corey felt a retort die on his lips. Heartened, Marotta continued: "In other times, your dating life might not be an issue. But the problem with your current relationship is not that the woman involved is an entertainer, but that she personifies a Hollywood culture that glorifies drugs, violence, and illicit sexuality.

"We've all seen *those* pictures, Corey. So have many of our kids. That's the behavior of a playboy, not a president . . ."

"Enough," Christy intervened. "Let me say what *I* think.

"I disagree with Corey about gay marriage. Its fundamental ideology is 'God goofed by making men and women.' Nonsense—God made us as we are for a reason, and we ought to have the sense to put that in our Constitution." To Corey, he said evenly, "I'm also troubled by your relationship. You're not a private citizen. You're a presidential candidate involved with a woman who is at once a celebrity, a representative of Hollywood, and a liberal who embraces gay rights, abortion, and the abomination of stem-cell research. In all sincerity, I wish none of that were so."

As Corey groped for a response, Christy turned to Marotta. "But I must also say, Rob, that the aroma arising from your exploitation of Corey's involvement troubles me just as much. I don't like those signs with an X across her face—"

"I'm not responsible for those," Marotta said quickly.

"Nor for anything else, it seems. I don't agree with Ms. Hart on the issues, but I don't doubt that she's sincere. And when I see those placards, I smell racism.

"God is not a racist, Rob. His Word is meant for all of us. So tell whoever it is to take down those vicious signs."

A few women in the audience applauded. "I second that," Corey said. "But I have to say this to you both. Candidates are people, and so are actresses. Like anyone, we're entitled to choose the people we love.

"I make no apologies for that. And if you, Senator, want to exploit our relationship in whatever rancid way you will, I can't stop you. Just understand the point you're really making: that Lexie Hart is way, way out of your class."

"Don't patronize me," Marotta snapped. "Presidents should set a moral example. I'm not divorced, and I can honestly say that I've never been unfaithful to Mary Rose. Can *you* say that to this audience, and to the American public?"

Corey managed a smile. "Absolutely. I have never, ever been unfaithful to Mary Rose."

Marotta's own smile was hard. "And your ex-wife?"

To one side of the room, Corey glimpsed Tommy sitting with his mother, their expressions filled with doubt. "My divorce," Corey said softly, "was one of the saddest events of my life. That's all anyone needs to know, and more of an answer than you deserve.

"You're lucky in Mary Rose. But it must be sad for you to believe that she's your foremost qualification."

"That's no answer," Marotta said dismissively. "What about you, Bob?"

Christy looked genuinely startled. "In nearly forty years

with Martha, no one's ever asked. I find it deeply offensive that you just have."

"If I understand your answer," Marotta responded with a shrug, "you should be proud."

At this, Corey made a snap decision. He pulled out the miniature tape recorder Dakin Ford had given him, placed it in front of Marotta, and pushed the button. A disembodied voice intoned: "Would you vote for a man who gave his ex-wife AIDS, is conducting an illicit affair with a radical black actress, and supports taking away your guns? If these values are your values, then Corey Grace is your candidate."

The audience was silent, stunned. "Are you proud of *that*?" Corey asked.

Marotta shook his head. "I know nothing about this tape."

"Really? Then it's coincidence that anonymous phone calls, whispering campaigns, and sleazy mailers from out of state seem to have followed you here?" Corey leaned close to Marotta. "Why don't you start with your campaign manager? It shouldn't take long to find out who's paying for these calls."

"Look," Marotta snapped, "I can't be held responsible for people I don't control. If I find out that this involves anyone from my campaign, I'll fire them."

"They won't tell you—unless you already know. One more time: are you willing to find out if this comes from your campaign?"

The audience was hushed. "It's not enough to say you're a Christian," Christy told Marotta softly. "You actually have to be one. Why don't you just stop this stuff?"

Marotta looked from Christy to Grace. "You're both guilty of McCarthyism," he said. "The voters of South

Carolina will have no trouble seeing through this concerted effort to smear me."

Christy chuckled softly, and then the moderator came to Marotta's aid. "Time for final statements," Coburn said with evident relief. "Senator Marotta?"

When Marotta commenced, plainly off his rhythm, Corey could have sworn that Christy winked at him.

STANDING NEXT TO Boss Moss, Dakin Ford watched Corey's final statement on a giant TV screen. "I know," Corey finished, "that many of you disagree with me about one issue or another. But that's because you know what I believe.

"Americans are sick of being pandered to, condescended to, and lied to by politicians whose only principle is to say whatever they think people want to hear. These times are much too serious for that. You deserve a president who tells the truth."

Ford looked around Moss's living room—tackier than Graceland, filled with men and women wearing everything from motorcycle jackets to tuxedos, all looking to Moss for cues. Studying Moss's expressionless face, Ford imagined him contemplating the ruin of his evening with the future president of the United States. "I'll say this much," Moss said solemnly. "The man has guts. I hope y'all are still thirsty."

MAROTTA SAT WITH Price as their dark limousine sped away from the mall. "They double-teamed me," he said. "Christy played the real Christian, and Grace the plain-speaking voice of truth. He means to use South Carolina against me in Michigan, California, and wherever else there's a Catholic vote."

"Got to beat him here first," Price said calmly.

"Tonight didn't help. I told you, Magnus, that going to Cash was a mistake."

Taking out his cell phone, Price pushed the speed dial. "Carl?" he said. "Yeah, I know. But there's still time for Grace to blow a gasket—watch the morning show tomorrow on Rohr News.

"So do me a favor, will you? Invite Grace to speak at your school. By the time he gets there, he may not be able to stay cool."

As Price listened, a smile played at the corner of his mouth. "You're a blessing, Reverend."

Price put the cell phone in his pocket. "The stuff about Christy and women," Marotta asked, "you sure about that?"

Price slowly nodded. "The Reverend Bob," he said, "is headed for the Fall."

ENTERING MOSS'S LIVING room, Corey looked around himself in bemusement. "Corey," Ford called out cheerfully. "Like you to meet your host, Boss Moss."

It's Willie Nelson's cousin, Corey thought, taking in Moss's beard and ponytail. But what caught his eye was the Confederate flag folded in the grizzled veteran's hand. "Thought you might appreciate a souvenir," Moss informed him. "Tell your lady friend I mean no disrespect."

Smiling, Corey took the flag. "I'll do that, Boss. Drink some bourbon with me?"

9

"THE RULES OF THIS DEBATE," CANDY CROWLEY said on CNN the next morning, "encouraged politics waged as mortal combat. But the early consensus is that Senator Marotta lost ground to both opponents.

"Late last night, in a surprising development, the Reverend Carl Cash invited Senator Grace to speak at his university."

"No way I could have ducked this one," Corey told Rustin.

He sat on the edge of his bed in boxer shorts, briefing papers scattered around him. Dressed in the same rumpled suit he had worn yesterday, Rustin looked like a man who had not exercised in weeks, or even seen the sun. "Maybe so," he answered dubiously. "But they're counting on you to defend Lexie in a way that turns more whites against you."

Corey's cell phone rang. When he answered, Dakin Ford said, "Click on Rohr."

Rohr's leading right-wing talk-show host, Frank Flaherty, had preempted the morning news. "This relationship," he was saying in a voice etched with scorn, "involves more than extramarital sex. *She* wants a president who'll advance her radical agenda; *he* needs her to help him carpetbag for black crossover votes in South Carolina. And Lexie Hart is no amateur when it comes to playing the race card."

The clip of Lexie that Rohr used seemed several years

old. "Can Cortland Lane," the interviewer asked, "become the first African-American president?"

"Why ask me?" she answered mildly. "White people get to make that call."

"Jesus," Rustin murmured.

Shaking his head in disapproval, Flaherty declared, "By implicitly calling white voters racist, Ms. Hart introduces a divisive strain into a contest that Senator Grace insists should be more elevated. And after last night's debate, it's clear that Senator Grace has chosen to make Lexie Hart his 'running mate.'" The commentator's smile was smugly knowing. "One of the many average Americans unhappy about this is Senator Grace's own mother."

Astonished, Corey saw a clip of Nettie Grace in her living room. "If Corey wants to date a black woman," she maintained stoutly, "that's *his* affair. I'm more worried about the sex and violence in her movies."

Corey felt a jolt of shame and anger. "Mom *should* be worried," Flaherty said. "Look at this, folks."

In clips from a science-fiction movie, Lexie dispatched a creature with a laser gun and kissed her leading man, conveniently white. "Is *that*," Flaherty asked, "the role model we want for our children? In raising this question, Senator Marotta is not only speaking for America's kids but for Senator Grace's mom."

Walking to a corner of the room, Corey called her. "Corey?" she said, her voice tentative. "It's been so long since we've heard from you."

"Doesn't seem like that to me, Mom. I just heard from *you* on TV."

"Well, I'm worried about you. I thought you should hear what normal people say every time I go for groceries."

"I know what they think," Corey told her softly. "I've known since I was six."

"Corey?" It was his father, sounding blurry and hung-over, speaking on an extension phone. "You've gotta get tougher on gay marriage, son. I'm telling you, people hate that."

It was all Corey could do not to answer, *You mean like your dead son?* "Don't worry about gays," he said softly. "It's harder for them than you'll ever know."

"I'm so proud you're speaking at Carl Cash University," his mother chimed in with artificial brightness. "I so wish Clay had gone there—in a proper Christian atmosphere, he wouldn't have fallen into his depression."

Corey closed his eyes. "Yeah," he said. "I'm trying to make that up to him.

"Please do me a favor. Next time some reporter wants to talk to you, tell him to try *me*. Trust me that you've made my life much harder."

His mother fell quiet. "All right," she answered dubiously. "I'm sorry."

Hanging up, Corey felt as though he were trapped in a recurring nightmare. "Family," he said to Rustin. "The people you didn't choose, and can never escape."

A VOLUNTEER DROVE Corey to Greenville, home of Carl Cash University; he needed solitude and—at this moment—did not trust himself in a bus full of reporters. The fact that another ad had hit the airwaves, using the same clips of Lexie, had further soured his mood.

Sitting in the back seat, he took in the rolling, wooded countryside, the Smoky Mountains receding in a hazy distance. When he did not think of Lexie, he thought of Clay. He was tempted not to answer when his cell phone rang.

"Corey?" the deep voice said. "It's Cortland Lane."

This, Corey realized, was a call he welcomed more than

any. "I guess you've been watching," he said.

"Pretty rough," Lane said. "The whole tone last night was a little sharp. Before you give this speech, would you mind some advice about religion, and maybe race? Or would you rather be left alone?"

It struck Corey anew that at several turning points in his life, Cortland Lane had helped sustain him. Taking out his pen, Corey answered, "Go ahead, Cortland. If you'd left me alone, I'd have never come this far."

ENTERING THE CAMPUS, Corey saw one sterile beige building after another, as though the color was being leached out of the students' lives. The students themselves, pleasant looking and uniformly white, seemed like actors portraying some mythic time of innocence. But the school's Web site was militant in tone: "We deny the right of anyone to call himself Christian who questions the authority of the Bible. We oppose all atheistic, agnostic, liberal, modernistic, or humanistic attacks upon the Scriptures. Grounding young people in the Word before they are exposed to godless secularism inoculates them against sin, immorality, and loss of faith." In a bow toward racial amity, the Web site encouraged donors to fund scholarships for minorities, "because of the shortage of trained Christian leadership among the non-Caucasian population."

Lexie, Corey thought, would be gratified. As they approached the auditorium, he took a last look at the words that Cortland Lane and he had crafted.

AFTER THE BRIEFEST of courtesies, Carl Cash—whom Corey mentally compared to a walking cadaver—led him to the stage. As Corey had required, and unlike the rules for Marotta's appearance, the reporters at the back of the auditorium were armed with minicams and tape recorders.

The students seemed to regard him less with hostility than curiosity, as though Corey had dropped in from Zimbabwe.

Stepping to the podium, Cash told them sternly, "Listen to this man's words, and ask yourselves these questions: where does he stand on the deadly sin of homosexual congress, the degraded culture of Hollywood, and the immorality that allows so-called leaders—such as Martin Luther King himself—to preach virtue in public and practice sexual license behind closed doors?" Pointing to Corey, he concluded, "Listen, and judge."

This, Corey supposed, was calculated to unnerve him. Walking to the podium in silence, he nodded to Cash. "Thank you, Reverend, for that gracious introduction. To be compared to Martin Luther King—however obliquely— is an honor."

In contrast to the solemn students, Corey saw Kate McInerny shoot Jake Linkletter of Rohr News a wicked grin. "So here's what I believe," Corey began.

"I believe in a God of love.

"I believe that truth can be found in all religions, and that all who pray address the same God.

"I believe that how we live is a truer expression of faith than any prayer we recite in public.

"I look to God for wisdom and calm. And," he finished pointedly, "I am far more concerned with whether I'm on His side than with asserting that He is on mine."

Standing to his right, Cash eyed him with the chill sharpness of a bird studying its prey. Carey focused on two students nearest him—a pretty brunette and a boy with a crew cut—wondering who they might become if they were encouraged to open their minds. "Frankly," he told them, "I don't think God cares much about this election. The God I believe in doesn't vote, nor is He a tool of the politically ambitious. For me, there is no candidate or party of God—only *people* of God."

The brunette's mouth accented a dubious frown. "Nor does the God I believe in," Corey said, "tell us which car to buy. Instead, He gave us minds to think for ourselves, and to help improve the human condition."

Pausing, Corey reminded himself that he was speaking to two audiences: the students in this auditorium, who might be beyond his reach, and the media and voters across America, for whom this speech, given at a moment of bitter political antagonism, might define him. Kate McInerny scribbled furiously, her face as intent as her peers'. "The human condition," Corey continued, "counsels humility. For even if we deem the Bible infallible, *we* are not. And in this very dangerous world, religious absolutism—at its worst—breeds a hatred and violence that may well consume us all."

The young faces in front of him became more sober and attentive. In even tones, Corey told them, "I don't write off people who, like you, believe in the same God I do but express that belief in different ways. I believe in listening to one another. And given that it's my turn to talk, I should mention that—as one example—I can't find a single line where Jesus condemns homosexuals for being who they were born to be."

Biting his lip, the boy with the crew cut looked down, briefly shaking his head, a study of polite resistance. But Kate McInerny's head snapped up in surprise. "As *I* understand Jesus," Corey went on, "morality is about far more than sex. It is about saving people from starvation, protecting the health of the young and the dignity of the old, and giving the next generation a safer and more peaceful world. And that means the practical kind of caring exemplified by Christ himself.

"To put money in a collection plate, you need a job.

"Though you pray for the sick, you need a medical system that works.

"We may want our children to pray in school, but we also need them to *learn* in school."

Standing straighter, Corey gazed out at his audience. "Professing faith without works is empty. That's why I believe that those who invoke religion to divide us from one another serve neither God nor man." Glancing toward Cash, Corey said firmly, "The terrible tendency to cheapen our public discourse with personal attacks will, like the slow dripping of water on a stone, erode our collective sense of decency and compassion. Martin Luther King was an adulterer, and he made our country far better than it was."

The audience was still—perhaps because of Corey's challenge to Cash but also, he hoped, because he had challenged them to search their own hearts. "This school," he told the students, "condemns the religion of your recent guest, Senator Marotta, as 'a satanic cult.' As the senator chose not to challenge this, I will.

"Mother Teresa was Catholic. Pope John Paul was Catholic. Robert Kennedy was Catholic. And so are millions of your fellow Americans who try to follow Christ's teachings every day of their lives." Pausing, Corey added wryly, "Any fault I might find in Senator Marotta lies not in his religion, but in his application of it.

"Which, inevitably, brings me to another policy of Carl Cash University—its ban on interracial dating." Briefly, Corey smiled. "For those who may have missed it, I'm seeing a native of South Carolina who's a graduate of Yale, an Oscar-winning actress, and a woman of great compassion and intelligence. And whatever one thinks of *me*, I'm a United States senator and a veteran of the military, and

I've tried to make some contribution to my country. Yet if Lexie Hart and I were students here, we would not be allowed to date."

Without exception, the students in his line of sight seemed riveted. In a mild tone, Corey continued: "One can say, I suppose, that you chose to come here knowing about this ban. All I ask is that you ask yourselves whether it really represents the best in America, or whether this university should allow for the same change of heart and mind that has so enriched the South."

Someone in the audience let out a hiss of dissent. Ignoring it, Corey said calmly, "There is so much that we share. We worship God; we love our families; we cherish our friends; we are all vulnerable; and we are all mortal.

"What we need in this country is not more hatred and division. What we need is to heed the God of the New Testament, who told us to care for the weakest among us and for each other—striving always to leave our world better than we found it.

"Thank you."

After a moment, applause began—not quite enthusiastic, but more than polite. Turning to Cash, Corey smiled into his frozen face. "Thanks, Reverend. Think I'll visit with your students for a while."

Wading into the crowd, Corey saw the boy with the crew cut extend his hand. Cameras flashed and minicams whirred, capturing the moment.

ALONE IN HIS car, Corey answered his cell phone. "Tell me," Cortland Lane inquired, "where you came up with those lines about Martin Luther King."

Corey smiled. "Improvisation. The Reverend Cash inspired me."

Lane laughed softly, and then his voice became serious.

"You probably haven't seen this, but the first reaction has been extremely good. In my amateur opinion, you've just gone from 'interesting' to 'presidential.' Moments like that are rare in politics."

After the last few days, this praise warmed Corey more than he could express. "Thanks," he said. "If you and I keep talking, this may just work out."

10

On the drive back to Columbia, Corey took calls from Rustin, who was cautiously pleased, and Dakin Ford, who allowed that his political career might yet survive Corey's visit. Only then did Lexie succeed in getting through.

"The day's been interesting," Corey told her. "I just passed a billboard for a personal-injury lawyer complete with a biblical quotation."

Lexie did not respond to this. "Saw your speech, Corey." Her voice was warm. "Kind of liked it."

"Did it come across that I miss you?"

For a moment she was quiet. "I've been thinking—about all of this. It's up to you. But if you'd like me to, maybe I might fly back."

Startled, Corey tried to sort out his emotions—doubt, delight, confusion, fear. "Even before this," he said, "you've wanted to stay away. The last three days are the most vicious I've seen in politics. And somebody's rummaging through your life."

Corey waited through another silence, watching the pale winter sun slide behind a scrim of clouds. "I'm scared," she acknowledged at last. "But I'm even more angry.

"It's your call whether I'd help or hurt. But South Carolina's my state, too—not just Magnus Price's. My uncle's a congressman with his own organization. I've got a whole bunch of friends—from growing up, from church, from college." Her cool tone did not conceal her outrage. "After I won the Oscar, Governor Tate invited me down and made me Citizen of the Year. He gave a lovely speech about me as a symbol of how people's hearts had changed. If Tate's people have a right to draw an X across my face and trash you for being with me, then I've got a right to ask people—including *my* people—whether that's how our state's going to be. Seems like the least a Citizen of the Year can do."

Her last words were etched in acid. Corey tried to weigh, as a practical politician must, the risks and rewards of Lexie's offer. But two reflexes kept colliding: pride in Lexie and fear for her. "I'm afraid, too," he said softly. "We'd be putting you in the crosshairs.

"And politics is the least of it. I'm afraid for us. I'm afraid for you if they keep digging." He hesitated, then spoke aloud his deepest fear: "The reason Cortland didn't run," he told her, "is because his wife was afraid some racist would kill him. There are a lot of folks down here with guns."

"I know," she said. "Don't think I haven't thought about that. But when Mama was close to my age, she still couldn't vote. When I turned eighteen, I could. A whole lot of people sacrificed, and some died, to make that happen. I don't want to be histrionic, but they didn't do that so I could hang my head."

Watching his driver—a polite young college student who had said little in response to Corey's occasional questions—Corey wondered what the young man might have gleaned from his side of the conversation. In a lower voice, he told Lexie, "I don't have a Secret Service detail yet."

"Then maybe you should, baby. Who's to say I'd be the one they'd shoot?"

The fatalism in her tone betrayed her sense that tragedy was commonplace. Though his own life might have argued for this, Corey knew that he, as a white man, could not grasp the depths of her foreboding. "I need to think about all this," he said. "Can I call you in a couple of hours?"

"Sure. I'll be here."

This, Corey felt, was no way to end this conversation. "The most important thing, Lexie, is that I love you. Please know that."

He waited for her answer. "Yes," she replied, "I think I do." Only then did Corey realize that if his driver had had any doubt about whom Corey was speaking with, his last words had erased it.

When they reached the hotel in Columbia, Corey thanked the volunteer. "I'm usually more talkative, Jeff," he apologized with a smile. "Some days, running for president is more distracting than others."

The young man gazed at him with deep sincerity. "Sir," he said, "it's been an honor. I mean for politics to be my life."

"Leave some time for girls," Corey said, and went to find Blake Rustin.

"Jesus." In his astonishment, Rustin nearly moaned. "Please God, no."

Though startled himself, Dakin Ford said dryly, "Lighten up, Blake. It's only a liberal black lady, not a plague of locusts."

"Bring on the fucking locusts." Facing Corey, Rustin said vehemently, "You been sniffing airplane glue? The only time blacks down here even dream about voting for a Republican is when he's pitching more God, less gays, and a whole lot of prayer in school. For every black voter Lexie pulls in, you'll lose twice as many whites. Defending her is one thing—sticking her in their faces is another."

Corey stared at him. "Let me get this straight: Magnus Price can draw an X across her face, but she can't show her face in her home state? Those ads with snippets of her movies aren't in their faces—but *she* would be? Don't you think by now every racist who's not brain-dead knows to vote against me?"

"There are still people on the fence, Corey. Don't push them." Rustin picked up a sheet of paper. "Here are the latest tracking numbers: Marotta at thirty-four percent; you at twenty-nine percent; Christy at twenty-seven. That's after you got a bump for New Hampshire that put you and Marotta in a statistical tie, and after you and Christy kicked Marotta's ass around the block in that debate. And do you know why? Values. And values down here means Lexie Hart."

Standing at the bar in Corey's suite, Dakin Ford poured himself some bourbon. "Let's do the math," he told Rustin. "It's late Friday afternoon—come Tuesday morning, people vote. And even you've got Corey five points down.

"Where's he gonna make it up—Christy voters? If they go anywhere else, it's to Marotta, not Corey."

"And they *will* if she shows up," Rustin said sharply. "That's Marotta's pitch—he alone can save the believers and the bigots from Corey Grace."

"Then it seems like you're stuck." Ford took a hasty swallow of whiskey. "Want God's honest truth, Blake? I'm pretty sick of living off whites and kissing off blacks. I've been working to change that. But it's a long, hard slog, and that fucking lizard Magnus Price will set it back two decades.

"Lexie's uncle is as hard-shelled as they come—we're polite and all, but the last thing Johnny Hart wants is to be telling blacks it's okay to vote for Corey. Hell, next time they might vote for *me*." Ford took another swallow. "Race cuts both ways: Johnny remembers pissing in 'coloreds only' bathrooms, and he likes starting an election with a shitload of black voters in the Democrats' hip pocket. He doesn't trust us worth a damn—I don't know that he'd turn out votes for Corey if Lexie begged him.

"On top of that, I wish she were a missionary rather than an actress—our stay-at-home moms would swallow that better. And the country clubs are full of white people who think blacks have 'caught up' and don't cotton to hearing that it ain't so. But still . . ." Sitting down with the drink cupped in his hands, Ford said, "You got nothing much to lose, Blake. I'm the one who's got to live with this after Tuesday. If Corey wants to be the first canary in the mine shaft, I'm kind of curious to see what happens."

Corey put his hands in his pockets. "I just don't want her killed, Dakin."

Ford gazed up at him. At length, he said, "I think I can get our new governor to lend us some state police. But the pros are in the Secret Service. Might be good if you called your great pal the president."

Rustin emitted a mirthless laugh. "Can I listen in?" he inquired mordantly. "When the man said 'Wanted dead or alive,' he wasn't just talking about bin Laden."

Corey picked up his cell phone.

Within the hour, time enough for him to consume some room service soup and a sandwich, the White House switchboard called back. A few moments later, the president listened in silence to Corey's request. "I'll call the Secret Service," he said with bluff humor. "Truth is, I'd rather see Marotta kick your ass than go to your memorial service. The shape our politics is in, I couldn't afford the satisfaction."

The surprisingly amiable call ended with the president's good wishes. "I guess that's it," Corey told Rustin. "You've been wanting me to start showing up in churches. What about Lexie's?"

When he called Lexie, she had already chartered a private plane.

RETURNING FROM A church meeting where the preacher had prayed for his success, Rob Marotta watched Magnus Price in the back seat of their limousine, listening to the Allman Brothers on his headphones and tapping his feet to a beat only he could hear, eyes half shut, a dreamy look drifting across his face. "Dickey Betts," Price murmured. "Best fucking lead guitarist God ever made."

The comment, Marotta knew, was not meant to elicit a response; nor was it directed at Marotta in particular. Listening to southern bands was Price's way of letting his subconscious work for him unimpeded. When the cell phone vibrated in his pocket, Price said, "Must be the fucking Dixie Chicks, calling to spoil a good time."

Watching Price listen to his caller, Marotta saw his keen expression reappear. The moment induced an uneasy, sour feeling—too often now, Marotta felt that the forces that controlled his destiny operated beyond his reach. His cold comfort was that Mary Rose was not here to witness this.

"No shit," Price was saying into his cell phone. "I almost can't believe it—except it's Corey fucking Grace."

"What is it?" Marotta asked.

Getting off the call, Price shook his head in wonder. "One man's courage," he said, "is another man's death wish. She's coming back here to campaign."

"How do you know?"

Price laughed. "Don't think I left staffing Grace's campaign down here to Rustin, do you? There are plenty of idealistic young people just dying to work for a man like that. One or two might hear things. Anyhow," Price added, "Lexie just drove out to LAX. So now we know it's true.

"Gotta look in my iPod. Somewhere I've got a cover of 'Fool for Love.'"

DESPITE RUSTIN'S PROTESTS, Corey met her at the airport shortly after three A.M.

Alone in the car, he waited at the curb. She hurried out of the dark, threw her roller bag in the trunk, and slid inside.

"Hi," she said. "Want to go parking?"

Though her face was in the shadows, he could see her eyes and smell her hair. Seeing her after two months apart gave him a buzz of wonder and surprise. "I just want to look at you," he said.

With a swift, darting movement, she kissed him, then let her lips linger so that he felt their warmth. Pulling back, she said, "This is so dumb, Corey. It's like we're kids with a million chaperones who want to ground us."

"Fuck 'em."

"No," she corrected airily. "Not them. Wish *we* could." Her voice softened. "This is a funny time to tell you, but I miss that like I never thought I could. You, Corey Grace—of all the people in the world—seem to have made *that* a whole lot better. Sure didn't see it coming when I came to beat on you about stem cells." She gave a rueful laugh. "But then, we didn't imagine a lot of this."

"Nope. All I knew was that I liked you."

"Hmm," she said. "Guess you didn't run *that* one past Mom."

Once again, Corey contemplated his shame and

frustration. "It's been years, Lexie, since I ran anything past Mom. To me 'family values' are just a rumor." Softening his voice, he said, "Sorry about her."

"Oh, I'm about to make it up to you. Tomorrow you get to meet Uncle Johnny. He couldn't be more thrilled if I were bringing home Pat Buchanan."

The remark, though delivered lightly, carried an undertone of doubt. "I don't know how this is going to work out," she admitted. "Any of it. All I know is you were out here on your own, and I didn't want to hide. Maybe that's selfish, or maybe just stupid—whatever, it sure goes against my grain. But I wanted us to be together." Touching his face, she softly asked, "Was I wrong?"

Uncertain, Corey searched for words of reassurance. "No," she said, "don't answer. In some way or another, this is bound to go wrong. You already know that, don't you?"

Yes, Corey thought, *I know that.* "What I know for sure," he told her, "is that we had to choose. And this is our decision."

She leaned her forehead against his. "Tomorrow," he told her, "there will be Secret Service all around me. They can't be assigned to you—only me. So the safest place for you is to be wherever I am. They'll watch out for us both."

For a moment she was still, and then, very gently, she kissed him. "Curfew time," she said. "Better drive me to Uncle Johnny's."

AT FIVE A.M., bleary-eyed, Magnus Price studied the infrared photographs. "This is all you got?" he asked. "Two shadowy heads in a car, maybe kissing. For all I can tell it's a fucking sonogram."

"Look," the photographer said testily, "all I do is take the pictures. I can't tuck them into bed."

Price gazed at the useless photos. "I'd like to think they were just too tired," he said wearily. "Keep on them. Judging from those swimsuit pictures you took, that boy's an absolute fool for love."

11

At seven a.m., Corey sat at Congressman Johnny Hart's kitchen table, drinking coffee as the first morning sun lit a corner of the room. Already dressed for church in a brown suit and tie, Hart faced Corey as Lexie, to one side, looked wary but composed. To Corey, the dominant expression on the grizzled congressman's otherwise implacable face came from his large yellow-brown eyes, filled with disbelief that this upstart was proposing to reorder his corner of the world.

"So," he said to Corey, "now that they've whopped you and Lexie with the race stick, you're expecting me to turn out droves of offended blacks."

Johnny Hart, Corey saw at once, would not respect him for kowtowing. "I'm here for advice," Corey answered crisply. "No one thinks you can push a button."

"Well, I can't," Hart answered in his rumbling voice. "And won't. I love my niece dearly—if you're what she wants, so be it. But that doesn't make you black South Carolinians' new best friend."

"I've got a record," Corey said. "You can look it up—"

"I have, Senator. The chambers where we work are only a hundred yards apart. Funny we've never met, isn't it?" Hart leaned forward, elbows on the table. "Except it isn't. Your party is where southern racists stampeded to when black people got the right to vote. The only way those people try to do business in my community is by saying that Democrats aren't Christian enough."

"Funny," Corey countered, "that's what they're saying about me."

Hart shrugged his broad shoulders. "My last election, your party put up a white guy whose outreach to the black community was to call me a friend to gays and abortionists. I went right at him, reminding folks that Jesus wasn't about persecuting the weak or the despised, but ministering to them." His tone became milder. "Saw your speech at Carl Cash. You've got a good enough handle on that part."

"Johnny," Lexie intervened, "whether you help him or not, in an hour or so I'll be introducing Corey at our church. What's your advice to him?"

"Simple." Hart fixed Corey with the same impenetrable stare. "It's not enough you've been picked on—when it comes to victims of racism, you're just passing through. And don't get hung up on style: unless you're Bill Clinton, there's nothing funnier than seeing some white politician try to act all loose and comfortable in a black church. It's like watching a bear on roller skates.

"Let Lexie handle that part. When your turn comes, remember that there's no substitute for substance." Jabbing the table, Hart admonished, "Black folks can smell a phony ten miles down the road. They want to know what you'd do for their mama who's got no health care, or their kid whose textbooks are twenty years old.

"One more thing." Hart sat back, hands folded across his ample stomach, looking from Corey to Lexie. "It's all right to care for each other, but don't flaunt it. Folks aren't going to look at you and see Romeo and Juliet—let alone themselves. Let them come to the idea of you in their own way.

"God knows it's gonna take *me* a little while."

*

THE CHURCH WAS packed. But what struck Corey was the difference in atmosphere from the all-white congregation of his youth.

Even at nine or ten, Corey had intuited a joyless sense of duty among the worshippers; to him, they had seemed like bodies in life's harness, spending an hour as they would at a Kiwanis meeting, but with far less animation. Emerging into the sunlight, they engaged in desultory chitchat, then went home to mow the lawn or pay the bills or watch sports on TV, their duty to propriety discharged until next Sunday. It was little wonder, he supposed, that the parched soul of Nettie Grace had responded to Bob Christy.

Here, the pews overflowed with families dressed in their Sunday finery—from matriarchs to wriggly kids—filled with the expectation that what happened within these modest walls would help sustain them in the week ahead. The major difference for *them*, Corey was certain, were the reporters and TV cameras gathered because of his appearance with Lexie. Noticing a family in the front row—a gray-haired grandmother, a plump wife and her wiry husband, a fidgety boy and his little sister, her hair in cornrows—Corey read in their faces a deep pride in their returning daughter. As Corey sat next to the minister, Lexie stood at the pulpit and bathed in a collective embrace to which Corey was a stranger.

"I'm home," she said simply.

"I see Barbara Daniels, my first friend in kindergarten, with her handsome husband, and two beautiful babies I only wish that I could borrow. I see our neighbor, Mrs. Jones, the first to bring us a casserole the night that Daddy died. I see Mrs. Phillips, who taught the first Sunday school class I ever went to. And I see Mr. Jefferson, the first teacher—the first *person*—who ever told me that I could act."

There were murmurs of affirmation. "Without all of you, I wouldn't be who I am. You helped bury my daddy, and you loved my mama way past the day she could remember you. So now I've come back home to introduce the man I care for, and to talk about what kind of people we are, and what kind of future we're going to make for those who follow us."

Lexie's gaze swept the congregation, at one with her audience in their common memory of hardship. "All things change," she said softly. "But some things change too slowly. I remember stories Mama told me about the diners we couldn't go to, the schools we couldn't attend, the ballots we couldn't cast. I remember white boys disrespecting me when I was a little girl. And now, even though I'm three thousand miles away, I'm hearing the same old thing.

"Why?" Lexie's gaze swept the congregation, her voice firm, her carriage proud. "Because Senator Grace thinks we can be a couple, and that he can also be president. Just like he believes that hatred has no rightful place in our politics, or our lives.

"You all have heard about the phone calls, or read the flyers, or seen the ads on television." Her voice filled with quiet anger. "No one's come forward to claim them, and no one ever will. The authors of this evil mean to defeat Corey at the ballot box and just move on. But—if enough people down here are willing to stand with us—sooner or later things done in the dark will come to light, and those responsible will be exposed. And then the rest of us, black and white, will be that much closer to realizing our common humanity."

The murmurs of assent multiplied and deepened. "Will you stand with me?" Lexie asked.

"*Yes,*" a man called, and then a woman, and then the

calls of affirmation filled the church.

Lexie's eyes shone with emotion and, perhaps, tears. "Then please stand now," she called out in a husky voice, "and meet Senator Corey Grace."

When Corey stepped forward, no one was left sitting.

COREY WAITED UNTIL they sat down again and his words could be heard above the buzz. As he faced them, he was also conscious of the cameras and his own concealed nervousness.

"Thanks for making this easier," he opened with a smile. "Until a minute ago, I was feeling like the guy who found out that his new girlfriend had a five-hundred-person family—all of them ready to pass judgment."

As the congregation chuckled, Corey felt himself relax. "Actually," Corey added, "Congressman Hart feels like five hundred parents all by himself."

This got outright laughter. Standing to the side, Hart gave a small smile of self-recognition. "The congressman and I," Corey went on, "had what diplomats call a frank and candid exchange—about everything from proper dating decorum to how the Republican Party has handled race. And last but not least, his niece.

"Though I haven't known her as long as you have, I think I know how you feel about Lexie. But Americans, whether black or white, can't look at us without thinking about race. That's the reality for both of us. And it's one of the hardest things for *any* of us to talk about."

The parishioners were silent now, attentive. "As a candidate—and, frankly, as a Republican—it's my obligation to put race on the table, and talk about how it affects us all.

"All too often, some within my party—like Democrats in the past—have lived off racial hatred and distrust. That's happening in this election. And, once again, those who perpetuate racial division do so because they've got nothing else to say.

"Nothing about people without health care.

"Nothing about a minimum wage too minimal for anything but poverty.

"Nothing about schools that don't teach, and kids who can't read.

"Nothing about what separates the people who bear these burdens from those who don't: wealth and class and—all too often—race."

Pausing, Corey saw some people nodding amid a rumble of assent. "So I'm not here asking for your help just because I'm on the wrong end of a drive-by shooting where racism is the weapon. Like Johnny Hart told me, when it comes to being on the wrong end of *that* stick, I'm just passing through."

There were rising murmurs of approval, appreciation of a truth acknowledged. "So let's start with the truth about health care," Carey told them, "and go from there . . ."

COREY AND LEXIE drove away buoyed by her minister's resounding final words: "On Tuesday, help our sister help the senator."

Congressman Hart sat between them in the back seat. With the crisp pragmatism of a professional, he asked, "What's your schedule today?"

"Three more churches," Corey said. "Then Lexie's taping a radio show and a recorded message—we're phone-banking the eastern part of the state."

"That's all fine," Hart said in a neutral tone. "But you got no field operation among blacks to speak of, right?"

"Not much of one."

Johnny Hart gazed out the front window. "I'm sure as

hell not coming out for you," he finally said. "But maybe I'll do more than just stay out of your way. There are calls I can make—ministers, folks who can get people to the polls. Looks to me like if you can turn out thirty thousand extra voters, you're close to catching Marotta."

Turning to her uncle, Lexie started to speak. "Don't thank me, girl," Hart said brusquely. "Your boyfriend here's just my excuse. I'm tired of this crap, that's all—sick of it to my very bones. I don't want to die on Magnus Price's plantation."

PRICE AND MAROTTA sped through the suburbs of Greenville, heading for another church while they watched a tape of Corey and Lexie leaving hers. "It's like the battle of the bands," Price said. "The battle of the churches—or, more aptly, the races. Too bad Grace forgot which party he's in."

Marotta's discomfort deepened. "Too bad," Marotta said. "Period. Even if I win the nomination, come November I won't get one black vote in a hundred."

"'Bloc votes,'" Price amended coolly. "That's what tomorrow's ads are gonna call them. Grace is attempting a 'hostile takeover of the Republican Party' by 'outside forces.' Can't let *that* happen, can we?"

"Jesus," Marotta said in genuine disgust.

"Look, Rob, Christy beat you in Iowa, Grace creamed you in New Hampshire. You gotta take South Carolina as it is, not as Grace and his girlfriend want it to be. That means giving folks permission to be racist without saying so." Price fished out his cell phone. "We need to rally whites in defense of their party, and make sure Christy doesn't split that vote. It helps that some of the most far-out evangelicals, Christy's people, open their doors to blacks. Churches *we've* seen, you can count the blacks on your fingers and toes and still have a foot left over."

Price hit speed dial. Silently, Marotta thought of his father, who had believed in better, and then of Mary Rose. "Magnus here," he heard Price say. "Time to napalm the 'forces of darkness.'"

12

By ten o'clock, the Secret Service had caught up with the campaign, and Lexie and Corey were back on the Silver Bullet.

They careened from church to church, Lexie and Corey in a rear seat as reporters asked questions, photographers snapped photos, Dakin Ford told stories, and Blake Rustin looked quietly miserable—a man who had lost control of both campaign and candidate. But Lexie appeared serene in Corey's company: she had assessed the risks they were taking and, her decision made, seemed focused on the here and now. With quiet good humor, she answered some questions and deflected others; every so often she would take Corey's hand. When the cameraman from Rohr News seemed to zero in on their intertwined fingers, Corey gripped hers tighter.

Word spread fast. At each stop the crowds were bigger—they waited outside the churches, mostly black but some white, cheering and applauding the candidate and his lady. "Great-looking couple," he heard a reporter comment. "Who ever said politics is show business for the ugly?"

At the last appearance, the crowd waiting numbered in the thousands, and handmade "Lexie for President" signs had appeared. "What do you think of that?" Kate McInerny asked her as they clambered off the bus.

Lexie shot Corey a grin. "They've finally got it right," she answered. "But I'll give Corey's vice presidential aspirations every consideration."

When she said that to the congregation, the applause drowned out the laughter.

THEY WERE HEADED to a recording studio in Columbia when Dakin Ford, eyes glued to the TV screen, turned up the volume.

On Rohr News, a small blond woman stood behind a podium flanked by two middle-aged men in suits—one chubby, the other sleek—identified as her lawyers. Awkwardly, she shuffled the papers in front of her and began reading to a clutch of reporters in a quavering Carolina drawl.

"My name is Mary Ella Ware. I'm recently divorced, the mother of two young children, and I'm a member of a Bible-believing congregation right here in Columbia." Her throat quivered visibly. "Until yesterday, I was a volunteer in the Christy for President campaign . . ."

"Oh, no," Ford said in disbelief.

Glancing at Lexie, Corey detected a shiver of instinctive apprehension. "I am here today," Ware read in a nearly inaudible voice, "because Reverend Christy betrayed my trust."

She was dressed as if for Easter Sunday, Corey noted, and her light pink suit seemed to add to an air of girlishness. Pausing, she touched her eyes, and then continued reading. "Two days ago, worried about how my little boy was handling our divorce, I turned to Reverend Christy for pastoral counseling." She bit her lip. "When he invited me to his hotel room, I thought he was being respectful of my privacy."

Leaning toward the screen, the reporters scribbled frenzied notes. "He knelt down beside me," Ware read on. "Together, we prayed for God's guidance. Then he told me to keep kneeling with my eyes closed.

"I could feel him standing in front of me, listening to my prayers." Watching Ware dab her eyes, Corey felt a wave of horror and pity, though he was not sure for whom. "Then," Ware blurted out, "I felt his hand behind my neck, and heard him unzip his fly . . ."

Lexie turned away. From beside her came a bark of laughter, Dakin Ford's.

THEY CLUSTERED IN Corey's hotel suite—Corey, Lexie, Ford, Rustin, and Dana Harrison—watching a tape of Ware's press conference, by now the lead story on the Sunday evening newscast. "I know her," Ford said. "She was a volunteer in my last campaign, always trying to get near me. Cute little thing. But it's dumb to trust a woman so needy that she scares you."

Lexie glanced at Dana, the other woman in the room. "Doesn't mean she's lying," Dana objected. "Sometimes the fragile types are the ones that predators go for."

"She's an actress," Ford responded, darting a glance at Lexie. "No offense to the real ones, but this is right out of *Elmer Gantry*—the fallen preacher. People are conditioned to half-expect it.

"Look at the timing. It's the Sunday before Election Day, not enough time for anyone to check this out. All Christy can do is deny it, guaranteeing twenty-four more hours of lousy coverage right before the voting. He's cooked."

"And so are we," Rustin said glumly. "I can hear Price's line already: Marotta alone can protect God and the party from all the evils Corey represents."

Lexie ventured nothing. "Do you believe this woman?" Corey asked her.

Lexie looked at him, a wealth of emotions he could not assess surfacing in her eyes. "All I know for sure," she answered, "is that lives are being destroyed."

Abruptly, Corey made up his mind. "I'm calling Christy," he said.

CHRISTY'S VOICE WAS so wan that he sounded like someone else. "Somehow, I knew you'd call."

Alone in the bedroom, Corey answered, "It's just something I wanted to do."

"Good politics, too," Christy responded wearily. "But it's important to me that you know this is a total lie."

Not for the first time, Corey wished that he could separate truth from falsehood; fifteen years in politics had taught him that a gifted liar could be more persuasive than a frightened man who told the truth. "What will you do?" Corey asked.

"I helped Magnus Price get started in politics." Christy's tone combined resignation with resolve. "Remember Marotta's question about adultery? Maybe this is God's retribution for working with a man I sensed lacked any scruples. But that only deepens my obligation to keep Price's dirty hands off the White House. Marotta has become his instrument of evil."

This was what Corey wished to hear. "Guess you're holding a press conference."

"Nine A.M.," Christy said simply. "The media mortification of the flesh, complete with my beloved, shell-shocked Martha. Never thought *I'd* be the one saying I didn't have sex outside my marriage."

The futility of such a denial seemed to weigh on Christy's words. After a moment, Corey asked, "Need the advice of a good press person?"

"Couldn't hurt, Corey. Couldn't hurt."

"Then I'm sending Dana Harrison over. She won't love this, but she's a pro. And if *she* winds up believing you, maybe you've got a shot."

When Corey emerged from the bedroom, Lexie had gone to speak at another church. That night they slept apart again, Corey in a suite watched by Secret Service agents, Lexie at her uncle's house, guarded by state troopers.

THE SILVER BULLET rolled out early the next morning. An hour before Christy's press conference, the last wave of attack ads started.

Its focus was a wooden ballot box. As the voice-over urged Republicans to combat a "bloc vote by liberal Democrats" two black hands reached out to steal it.

When Corey glanced at her, Lexie had turned from the screen.

"Jesus," someone murmured, "this is getting pretty raw."

Hastily switching channels, Ford discovered a gauzy ad of Marotta with Mary Rose and the children. "A neat contrast to Christy's dilemma," Ford remarked. "Kind of makes you wonder, doesn't it?"

"About what, Senator?" Jake Linkletter prodded.

"Synchronicity," Ford answered tartly, and then Bob Christy appeared.

Flanked by his wife and grown son and daughter, Christy spoke with quiet determination. "I want all of you to know," he began, "that these charges are utterly false.

"Here's what is true. Mrs. Ware asked to speak with me in private, as she said. We prayed on our knees, as she said. Then I offered her advice—about divorce, her children, and the need for ongoing pastoral counseling to mend the bonds of her broken family. And then she left.

"That is all. My only sin was a lapse in judgment—meeting with her alone."

Martha Christy nodded, the picture of a pastor's supportive wife. "I cannot know," Christy went on, "why God has sent us this new challenge. I can only guess at why Mrs. Ware has chosen to bear false witness against me, and the emotional or economic pressures she may be feeling. And so I bear her no ill will.

"But I will not—*cannot*—allow her lies to deter our common quest." His voice became softer. "I ask you to sustain me with your prayers and with your votes. And when the reason for this trial is revealed in God's own time, His triumph—and ours—will be all the greater for it."

"Not bad," Kate McInerny opined.

Ford shrugged. "Don't matter, Katie dear. Watch what happens next."

WITHIN AN HOUR, Rob Marotta appeared on the local Rohr station. "I'm deeply sad," he said in sober tones, "for everyone involved—Reverend Christy, his family, and, of course, Mrs. Ware.

"I have nothing more to say about what is nothing less than a human tragedy."

"Not for you," Ford said. "Only question is who gets to do your dirty work."

"Simple," Corey answered. "Linwood Tate."

"You're learning, boy," Ford replied amiably. "Got real promise as an analyst of local politics." Glancing at the screen, he added, "In fact, looks to me like you just materialized old Linwood."

The former governor stood in front of his suburban McMansion, no less distinguished looking for his casual dress. "I've spent the morning," he told his interviewer, "talking to Republicans across the state, as well as some of our most prominent Christian leaders. To a man—or woman—they are saddened by these events.

"But elections wait for no man. Come tomorrow,

Republicans face a choice. Do we allow a takeover of our party by a fifth column of Democrats and liberals who reject our moral values, or do we support a candidate who stands tall in our defense?

"Right or wrong, Reverend Christy has become too great a risk. Innocent or guilty, his judgment is in question—if only because he chose to be alone with Mrs. Ware." Tate gazed into the camera with an expression of deep sincerity. "The sound choice, the right choice, is Senator Rob Marotta. He bears no taint that could prevent him from protecting America's families, and a nation under God."

"About now," Ford said, "the recorded phone calls ought to start."

He switched to Rohr News, the cable network. "How much will taxpayers pony up," Frank Flaherty inquired acidly, "so the Secret Service can babysit Grace's girlfriend? Bet *that* pillow talk don't come cheap."

Staring at the screen, Lexie still said nothing. Corey took her hand again. Though Ford turned off the television, the bus remained silent, the residue of a campaign that had turned too repugnant to be fun.

LATE THAT NIGHT, Ford and Rustin left Corey's suite, at last giving Corey and Lexie some time alone. "You were great today," he told her. "No matter how hard it got."

She leaned her back against the door. "Funny," she said softly, "on the other side of this door is a Secret Service agent. Wonder how much the next half hour is going to cost the taxpayers."

Corey managed a smile. "Is that a proposition?"

"Just keep watching." Reaching behind her back, Lexie unzipped her dress, her eyes on his face as the silk whispered to the floor.

"It's been two months," Corey murmured.

Lexie unfastened her bra. "And five hours. Seems like a long time."

With a slow undulation of her hips, half sensual and half mocking, she let her panties slip on top of her dress. But when Corey went to her, Lexie's eyes were moist.

Out of desire, and out of fear, Corey did not ask her why she was crying.

13

Tuesday morning in Columbia dawned chill and damp and gloomy.

Rustin's overnight tracking poll showed a tight but fluid race: as the bottom fell out from under Christy, Marotta surged among white Republicans, while Corey showed solid gains among blacks and independents. The result, it seemed clear, would rest on who turned out to vote. Cocooned in a studio, Lexie called black radio stations as Corey and Ford sped from mall to mall, meeting citizens and hoping that some snippet of film on the noonday news would draw more voters to the polls. But by eleven o'clock, as a volunteer drove them to yet another shopping center, Ford learned that Magnus Price was leaving nothing to chance.

Snapping his cell phone shut, he said to Corey, "They've moved the polling places—just up and moved them."

"What the hell are you talking about?"

Livid, Ford stared straight ahead. "In South Carolina, the party runs our primary. That means the party machine decides where people vote." He turned to Corey, biting off each word. "In almost all the black areas, they've moved some polling places, and flat shut others down. In some counties, blacks will have to drive fifty miles to cast a ballot."

Astonished, Corey asked, "How can they defend that?"

"History," Ford said with a bitter smile. "Historically,

blacks don't vote in Republican primaries. So our hack of a party chairman, Linwood's boy, shut the polls as a 'cost-cutting measure.' The fact that the vote counts are bound to be funky is just mustard on the hot dog. Like the flyers that have popped up in black neighborhoods, directing folks to where the polling places aren't.

"Course, we can go out right now and file a complaint about a civil rights violation and raise hell about voter suppression, making Price's point that you're the black folks' candidate. But why not?" The anger in Ford's voice was tinged with disgust. "Magnus just filed his *own* civil rights complaint—seems like we've got people out there 'coercing' blacks to vote. The bigots they're appealing to are just gonna love that—turning the civil rights law on its head."

"So how do we respond?"

Ford sat back, arms folded. "I can't live with this," he said. "If these fuckers get you, they'll come after me. It might take a while, but I'm going to figure out how they pulled off their secret campaign. Right down to arranging Christy's failed blow job.

"But that's not for today. So let's go get you on TV—some station Rohr doesn't own—so you can complain about this underhanded plot against democracy." His tone was quiet and bitter. "For all the fucking good that's gonna do."

BY FIVE P.M., Corey, Ford, Rustin, and Lexie had gathered in his suite.

The portents were troubling: though voting was heavy along the coast—favorable to Corey—Linwood Tate's apparatus was generating an even higher turnout in the white strongholds to the west. From the areas dominated by blacks came more reports of misdirection and phantom polling places. "I need some sleep," Corey told the others. "Win or lose, I've got to say something upbeat, then catch a plane to Michigan."

Rustin and Ford left—Rustin virtually silent, Ford mumbling a few halfhearted words of encouragement. As the door closed, Lexie said, "I'm staying with you, okay?"

They lay on top of the bedcover, each looking into the other's face. Her eyes, though luminous, seemed troubled. "What is it?" he asked. "Everything?"

Taking his hand, she tried to smile. "It'll keep. Right now, we need to sleep."

After a moment, Corey did. But even as he drifted off he sensed that she would not. When he awoke, Lexie was still watching his face, her expression sadder than before.

THE POLLS CLOSED at eight o'clock. Shortly before nine, CNN projected a narrow but decisive victory for Rob Marotta. "Even with all the alleged irregularities," Bill Schneider said, "Senator Grace attracted a substantial crossover vote among blacks, white Democrats, and independents. From that, one can divine a potential sea change as the race goes on, based on the breadth of Grace's appeal and the star quality Ms. Hart brings to his campaign."

Conjuring a smile, Corey squeezed Lexie's hand. Blake Rustin, he noticed, seemed to watch them closely.

"But in South Carolina," Schneider continued, "the Republican primary is still dominated by self-identified Christian conservatives. According to our exit polls, these voters give Senator Marotta a thirty-nine percent margin over Senator Grace—a mass migration to Marotta that reflects the charges against Bob Christy . . ."

"It's like watching a play," Ford said. "With Magnus as the director. Too bad the sonofabitch won't come out for bows."

As Corey scribbled his concession speech, Marotta appeared, circles of exhaustion beneath his eyes, his smile barely distinguishable from that of a loser. "Tonight," he began, "the voters of South Carolina have marked the turning point in this campaign, a victory for the values that made America, in the words of Ronald Reagan, 'a shining city on a hill.'"

"You will *never* be president," Corey promised aloud. "Not as long as I'm alive."

Silent, Rustin watched him.

AFTER COREY'S CONCESSION speech, he faced Lexie on the darkened sidewalk, watched by Secret Service agents, the state troopers who would drive her to Johnny Hart's, and, at a greater distance, the media, supporters, and the curious. Touching his arm, she said, "We tried, Corey. We really tried."

The ambiguity of her words unsettled him. "I love you, Lexie."

"I know. Me, too."

"Then maybe I rate a good-bye kiss."

She smiled a little. "In front of all these people?"

Firmly, Corey kissed her. "I'll call you tomorrow," he said.

SHORTLY BEFORE ELEVEN P.M., Corey and Rustin took a limousine to the airport.

Except for the driver, they were alone. On the radio, Bob Christy told a reporter from NPR, "I love the people of South Carolina. But this primary was less a campaign than a vision of hell. I hope this country never sees its like again."

"But you will," Rustin said. "We *all* will."

Corey turned to him. "All right, Blake. Spit it out."

Rustin grimaced, a man reluctant to deliver still more bad news. Instead of answering, he handed Corey a computer printout.

Corey stared at the numbers. "Who told you to poll this?"

Rustin inhaled. "She lost this race for you, Corey—by this morning, her image among Republicans was negative by two to one." He paused, steeling himself. "She's not Cortland Lane or Condi Rice. To our right-wing base, she's a left-wing nightmare in an Afro."

Turning to him, Corey spoke softly. "In other words, she's got to go."

Rustin looked down, eyes half shut, then slipped a second document onto Corey's lap. "What is this?" Corey asked.

"She hasn't been unfaithful to you," Rustin said bluntly. "It's worse than that. She used to be a heroin addict."

Corey felt numb, and then fury overcame him. "You prick—*you're* the one who hired some creep to crawl through Lexie's life."

"Opposition research," Rustin said tightly. "All we did is beat Price to the bitter ex-boyfriend, a failed actor who can barely afford to see her movies.

"Fame is a poison, Corey. So before you express your outrage, take a minute to imagine the day when Price hands something like this to Alex Rohr: the magazine covers, the sneers on talk shows, the reporters in her driveway. Imagine the mass shiver of delight as Price strips her bare in public. Then maybe you'll do the gallant thing and dump her before it happens.

"If not, the question is, Do you want to be president or do you want *her*? Because you sure as hell don't get both."

For a long moment, Corey stared at the darkened highway. Leaning forward, he told the driver, "Pull over."

Glancing at Corey in the mirror, the man complied. Only when they had stopped did Corey turn to Rustin. "Got a credit card?" he asked.

Rustin flinched. "Sure."

"Then you can book your own flight home." Reaching into his wallet, Corey pulled out two twenty-dollar bills. "Here's cab fare. Try to flag one down."

Stunned, Rustin reached for his briefcase. In that moment, Corey saw his campaign manager face the ruin of his own dream: he would never be the one to make Corey the next president. But this was no time for compassion. In the same cool voice, Corey said, "My statement will announce your resignation over 'tactical disagreements' with the candidate. That should absolve you of blame for my poor judgment." Folding the report, Corey slipped it into his suit coat. "Better kill this stuff, Blake, any way you can. Because if any of this gets out, I don't care *who* the source is. If I become president—and I mean to—I'll make very sure that you never work again. Now get out."

Without another word, Rustin did.

AT MIDNIGHT, COREY'S coat around her shoulders, Lexie sat with him on her uncle's porch. "I'm ashamed," he said.

Bending forward, Lexie touched her eyes. "You didn't plan it," she answered dully. "And I knew. I always knew.

"Rustin's right. Fame breeds pathology, and envy metastasizes like a cancer. What can I say? I'm not going to deny my addiction, and I'm not going on *Oprah* to weep and offer up those two rapists as my excuse."

There was nothing he could say. Silent, he tried to read her face in the shadows. "There's something else," she told him. "Remember my movie project, the story about the young black kid trying to break free?"

"Sure."

"Late last year, I sold the rights to New Line. At the time, it seemed like a good deal—if the studio made it, I got to produce and direct." Her tone flattened. "Two days ago, for more money than New Line could turn down, RohrVision bought the rights.

"Their message is clear enough. Screw with *our* world, girl, and we'll damn well screw up yours. My movie's never getting made."

Corey felt too many emotions—compassion, fury, heartache, guilt—to express any of them clearly. "It's *all* screwed up," he said helplessly. "I keep trying to say that I don't want to lose you and I don't want you hurt. And I don't even know whether that's saying the same thing, or two different things."

Lexie turned from him, staring out into the night. "This isn't meant to be," she said at length. "Not if you want to be president. Politics is consuming us, like I always knew it would."

Heartsick, Corey turned her face to his. "Can we wait until the campaign's over?"

Tears came to her eyes. "For what, Corey?"

Corey found he could not answer. She kissed him gently, a silent good-bye, and slipped back inside her uncle's house.

14

THE NEXT MORNING, COREY FLEW TO SAN FRANCISCO.

Alone, he imagined Lexie on her flight to Los Angeles—quiet, controlled, as gracious to others as Corey tried to be. And, like him, desolate. As with Corey, no one would sense the feeling of solitude that she had carried with her from childhood. For him their separation was a physical shock that left him without appetite. But he was running for president, and the survivor at his core kept pushing him forward.

He knew what awaited when he landed: news reports of Rob Marotta's resurgence; pundits dissecting the disarray in Corey's campaign; new questions about his temperament and judgment. But he could not—would not—let South Carolina doom his candidacy. Winning was all that Price had left him.

He hoped that Hollis Spencer wanted one last challenge.

ON A STRETCH of beach near Spencer's home in Seacliff, the two men trudged across the sand, unpeopled on a bright, cool weekday. Spencer stopped to admire the Golden Gate Bridge. "It's the architecture," he said. "Two spans, perfectly spaced, crossing the mouth of the bay. I never tire of studying it."

Spencer looked much older now: his hair was sparse and white, his belly sloped, his shoulders slumped, his face more deeply seamed. "I haven't run a campaign in years," he told Corey. "Like I said when you asked before, a lot's changed since I helped you get elected to the Senate."

"Yeah," Corey said. "It's gotten worse."

"Magnus Price." Spencer stopped, hands in his pockets, still gazing at the bridge. "I could see it all coming, even before he left my shop to take on Christy as a project.

"Magnus doesn't care about history, or policy, or the future. He's the epitome of the twenty-first-century man. To him, making Marotta president is a marketing exercise, where the only point is to prove that he's smarter than any strategist alive—that he can elect anyone he wants, take down anyone he decides to.

"Magnus thinks he's *much* more interesting than Marotta. That unshakable belief defines their relationship: Price's ultimate triumph is not just to elect Marotta—it's to *own* him." Spencer turned, facing Corey. "Magnus's special talent is to see other people without sentiment or illusion. He believes he knows Rob Marotta better than Mary Rose does. If he worries at all about Marotta's qualifications to be president, his consolation is the belief that Marotta can be as ruthless as a president needs to be."

"As Price is, you mean."

Spencer shrugged. "I saw Christy calling Magnus 'evil.' That's the error of a man to whom morality matters. The truth is that Price's amorality has a certain purity: the problems of race, for example, are simply logistical—inspiring racial hatred is the same to Magnus as promoting racial amity. His only bias is that the human species responds more viscerally to fear and hatred. That's the darkness he brings to American politics."

"The country can't go on like this," Corey said. "We've stopped believing in one another—more and more, people vote out of anger, or stop voting out of disgust. Price's 'marketing exercise' is remaking America in his image."

Spencer studied a starfish at his feet. "While *I'm* busy

writing books. In my day, I surely was no virgin; you can't manage two candidates who became president, as I did, without doing things you regret. But the biggest weight on my conscience is giving Magnus Price his start.

"South Carolina was vintage Price—it's like he sneaks in at night, and by sunrise the guy running against *his* guy would be dead and in a body bag. And no one can prove who it was that cut his throat."

"So will you do this?" Corey prodded.

Spencer smiled, a brief movement of his lips. "As penance?"

"I won't quibble about motives. But I hope because I'd make a decent president."

"Well," Spencer said wryly, "I'll say this much—you're a world different than the thirty-year-old hotshot I foisted on the Senate, with no qualifications beyond the fact that you'd remembered how to open your parachute."

Despite the pain associated with Joe Fitts's death, Corey could not help but laugh. "Good thing I didn't come here for flattery."

"Actually," Spencer said, "one of your finer compliments comes from Magnus.

"Two years ago or so I ran into him at Reagan National and asked how he sized up presidential possibilities. When we turned to you, he got this dreamy look. 'A natural talent,' he said. 'Charisma to burn, with the reflexes of a leader and first-rate political instincts. Love to run him. But the sonofabitch is too unpredictable.'

" 'What you mean,' I answered, 'is Grace can't be handled. Especially not by you.'

"He gave me this little smile, like I'd read him. 'Maybe so,' he answered, 'but I'll tell you something else about him. People see all that careless charm and think they know him. But they don't. No one does.' "

Except for Lexie, Corey thought. "That's a compliment?"

"Of a kind. Magnus was saying that what drives you is beyond his grasp. And, at times, mine." Spencer looked at him steadily. "But whatever it is makes you too valuable to lose. Your speech at Carl Cash was as fine a moment as I've seen in politics.

"I view this election as America's last chance. So yes," Spencer concluded with a smile. "I'm emerging from a comfortable retirement to run your damn campaign. That flattery enough?"

Corey felt a wave of relief. "It'll do," he answered.

THEY SAT ON a rock, facing the blue-gray water and, beyond that, the green rolling hills of Marin County. "First things first," Spencer said. "Let's talk about Marotta.

"Price has packaged him as a man of principle, even as Marotta tacitly consented to whatever acts of moral degradation might allow him to survive." Spencer spoke with cool determination. "We're going to tie South Carolina around his ankles like a two-ton ball and chain.

"We can't prove what Price did below the radar screen—at least not yet. But a Catholic pandering to an anti-Catholic bigot like Carl Cash should pay the price with Catholics in primaries like Michigan, Connecticut, and Rhode Island. And he will.

"That's not negative campaigning. It's evidence of what Marotta is willing to do if the alternative is losing. And it draws a stark contrast between the two of you." His tone became clipped and practical. "So let's look at the map.

"There are moments in politics when goodness triumphs. But goodness requires a helping hand; in this case, the Reverend Christy's. You need him in the race for at least the next two weeks, so he can cut into Marotta's vote in states where the Christian Right is strong: Alabama, Louisiana, Texas, Oklahoma, Georgia, and Virginia. If Marotta sweeps all those, you lose. But if he doesn't, and you survive to California—"

"We've got a deadlocked convention," Corey finished.

Spencer nodded slowly. "I've gone over this state by state, and I don't see any realistic way you clinch the nomination before our happy gathering in New York City. But if we can get you there, that's where the three governors—Blair, Costas, and Larkin—will try to auction off their delegates to the highest bidder. And, of course, Christy will do the same."

"Does God make deals?" Corey asked. "In Bob's theology, I'm pretty sure, God won't settle for anything less than President Christy."

"Maybe so. But in the back of that very shrewd mind, Christy knows that vice presidents can morph into presidents. After South Carolina, that may be God's last, best hope."

Corey watched a buoy bob in the choppy water. "In other words," he ventured, "my chances depend on whether Christy is lured into toughing out these charges by delusions of vice presidential grandeur. Maybe with a little help from me."

Spencer faced him. "What's your gut say? Did Christy come on to her?"

Corey sorted through his shifting sense of Christy's character and motives. "I don't believe Price is responsible for every bad thing in the world—or even in South Carolina. It's possible that Christy is a horndog and Magnus just got lucky. But ask me to choose, and I'd say Christy's innocent."

Spencer's eyes lit with interest. "Why?"

"Because he's not a sociopath. He may think he's

God's anointed, but I don't believe he thinks God's given him a pass. Add ambition—and the obvious price God's candidate would pay for being exposed—and I'd guess Christy's too disciplined to come on to a woman Dakin thinks has got a screw loose.

"More likely, Christy's weakness was in feeling so armored in his own integrity that he didn't worry about being alone with her." A fresh pall of gloom overcame Corey. "It's sad, but paranoia's become a requirement for running. Since the campaign started, I've never been alone with any woman but Lexie."

Spencer gave him a keen look, as though Lexie Hart was problem enough. "How much are you willing to gamble on being right?"

"I guess we're not talking about money."

"I'm talking about the presidency. And that rests on Christy staying in to the bitter end—and maybe, come the convention, on his goodwill. So what I suggest is that you give Christy a public statement of support: that in a dirty campaign like this, Christy should not be driven from the race by unsubstantiated charges."

Once more, Corey thought of Lexie. "That *is* a gamble. Women who've been abused—or sympathize with those who have—might condemn me for it. And if this woman's charges end up looking credible, I'll be damaged."

"No," Spencer corrected, "you'll be dead. Because Christy's dead. You and Reverend Bob have turned into Siamese twins."

Corey pondered this. Before he could respond, Spencer said, "Now about Ms. Hart . . ."

"Yes?"

"Personally, I'm filled with envy: not only is she beautiful, but she's plainly smart as a whip. So it's no big stretch for me to see you two together." Spencer's tone was blunt.

"But that's me. If she's why you and Rustin fell out—and I suspect it is—I have to say Blake's right."

"Blake may be right, Hollis. He's also gone."

Spencer gave a small smile of acquiescence. "I can't tell you how to live your life. In my own life, I loved only one woman, and I married her. And when she died . . ." To Corey's surprise, Spencer's eyes misted. "Whatever you decide, I'll work with it."

Corey nodded. Out of respect for Spencer's sentiment, or maybe his own unwillingness to believe that he had lost her, Corey did not say that Lexie, too, was gone.

"All right then," Spencer said. "Let's get rolling."

THOUGH HELD WITH only two hours' notice, Corey's press conference was filled with reporters either eager for a story or scenting blood in the water. But the return of Spencer to the political maelstrom clearly surprised the media.

"Hollis Spencer," Corey told them, "is the preeminent political strategist of our time, and one of the most honorable. We agree on a fundamental principle: winning the presidency should not *tarnish* the presidency.

"Which brings me to the charges against Bob Christy. Though serious, they are just that—charges. He is not accused of anything that can be proven or disproven. And so each of us must make our own judgment about his character." Corey paused, waiting for the reporters scribbling shorthand to catch up. "Here's mine: however much we disagree about issues, I believe Bob Christy. Just as I believe that, absent proof, he should not be driven from this race.

"This, as I say, is a question of character." Corey let the anger surface in his voice. "In South Carolina, as part of an avalanche of innuendo, I was accused of being an agent of Al Qaeda. Reverend Christy repudiated this charge and asked Senator Marotta to do the same. Senator Marotta declined.

"That moment said a great deal about character—Reverend Christy's and Senator Marotta's. So I'm giving the senator a second chance." Pausing, Corey spoke directly to the cameras. "I urge Bob Christy to stay in this race and to allow Americans to decide this contest on the issues. And I ask Senator Marotta to join me in that call. It's not too late for him to show some character."

And that, Corey thought with satisfaction, would lead the evening news.

IN THE CAR to the airport, Hollis Spencer said, "It'll be fun to watch Marotta deal with this one."

Corey sat back. "My favorite instructor at the Academy used to tell us that 'character is who you are in the dark.' These days I wonder what Rob would do if there was no one around to watch."

Corey's cell phone rang. When he pressed it to his ear, a deep southern-tinged voice said, "Corey? It's your semi-friend Bob Christy."

As Corey laughed, Spencer turned to him. "Come on, Bob," Corey said. "Let's go all the way."

"Not funny, these days. And I'm not sure you're my type. But here's what I wanted to say to you, as sincerely as I know how." Christy spoke each word slowly, as though hoping to establish a bond. "I'm not naive, Corey. I know you have your reasons. But you've got too much integrity to say what you don't believe.

"I don't care about Marotta. But the opinion of a hero matters to me. Whatever happens, I won't forget this day." Christy paused, then chuckled softly. "By the way, I'm staying in the race. I'd hate to leave you with only Rob for company."

15

TWO WEEKS LATER, SENATOR COREY GRACE LANDED in California for the final days of the primary campaign.

In a motorcade headed for Los Angeles, Corey and Spencer watched CNN as Dana Bash described the stakes. "The math is brutally simple," she explained. "To keep his campaign alive, Senator Grace must win in delegate-rich California.

"The California primary is 'winner take all': no matter how narrow the margin, the winner will claim all of California's one hundred and seventy-three delegates—by far the biggest prize of the primary season. And in a state where gay marriage, border security, and illegal immigration are hot-button issues, Senator Grace will face voters who are in a particularly volatile mood."

"Unlike the ones I've already met," Corey remarked. Studying new polling numbers that showed Marotta ahead in California, Spencer merely grunted.

On CNN, the picture shifted to a map of the primary states already decided. "As you can see," Jeff Greenfield told Wolf Blitzer, "Senators Marotta and Grace have played a game of electoral leapfrog, trading victories as Reverend Christy has siphoned just enough delegates to keep either senator from clinching the nomination—a task made even more difficult because favorite-son governors in New York, Illinois, and Mississippi have kept those states out of play. But the dynamics of this seesaw contest confirm that these two very different men have different weaknesses and strengths."

"Yeah," Spencer grumbled. "One tells lies."

Greenfield touched the computerized map, causing Michigan to turn blue—the color designated for a Grace victory. "In Michigan, Grace won by garnering a large crossover vote from blacks, Catholics, and independents, even while losing conservative Republican votes by thirty-five percent." Touching Virginia, Greenfield turned it to red. "Contrast this to Virginia, a more conservative state, where a similar cushion for Marotta among Republicans gave him a nine percent margin over Grace, who barely edged Christy for second place.

"So just for fun, let's look at Alabama." Once again, Greenfield tapped at the screen. "We've classified it as a purple state because no one knows *what's* going on. To everyone's surprise, Grace won the Alabama primary with a crossover vote from blacks and a whopping plurality among veterans, while social conservatives split their votes between Marotta and Christy.

"But then the party's state chairman—allegedly prodded by Magnus Price—challenged the legality of the election, and held a state convention that elected delegates pledged to Marotta. So now we have two delegations—one elected and one appointed—who will fight it out at the convention for the right to vote for their candidate of choice. In this tense and rancorous contest, such backroom maneuverings may ultimately determine the nominee and, perhaps, the next president."

In the car, Corey and Spencer were silent and intent. "That's a big part of the story," Greenfield continued. "But in terms of the candidates themselves, in many ways Senator Grace *is* the story. On the Democratic side, the contest ended swiftly, focusing national attention on the dogfight among Republicans. Based on candor, charisma, and his appeal across party lines, Senator Grace has lasted longer than most prognosticators thought he would—despite, or maybe because of, the drama surrounding his relationship with Lexie Hart."

Who rarely talks to me now, Corey thought. Since South Carolina, they had not seen each other; their conversations, while filled with affection and concern, were bereft of any plan for the future. When Corey had said, "I don't want to just be your friend," she had answered softly, "But we are friends, Corey. Friends care for each other and speak the truth. Unless the truth hurts too much to speak."

"But with or without Ms. Hart," Greenfield was saying, "Corey Grace is a political rock star, drawing young people, minorities, independents, and suburban women, all of whom have typically shunned Republicans." Smiling, Greenfield concluded, "One sentence sums up his promise and his dilemma: Corey Grace is the most popular politician in *neither* party."

Gazing out at the clogged six-lane highway, Corey took out his cell phone and called Governor Charles Blair. "It's Corey," he said. "Just calling to take your pulse."

"It's still beating," the youthful governor said, his chuckle at once practiced and evasive. "You know who I feel closest to, personally and philosophically. But Marotta has some powerful supporters out here. Best I keep the party together by keeping our delegation out of play."

"And maybe become the candidate?" Corey inquired wryly. "Or, at least, vice president?"

Blair chuckled again, the disarming laugh of a man caught out. "I'm a red-blooded American governor, Corey—I wouldn't hide if the lightning struck."

"And if it doesn't?"

"Then I promise you this much: if my choice comes down to deciding which of you becomes the nominee, you know where I stand."

And where is that? Corey wanted to ask. "Thank you," he said graciously. "Knowing that means a lot."

Corey got off. "How'd it go?" Spencer asked.

"More foreplay and polite evasion. He's waiting for the moment when I have to offer him VP. Why commit now in exchange for nothing?"

"Still," Spencer said, "it's good to remind him that you care. Among the things the so-called experts sometimes forget is that politics is about people. Who would have guessed that you and Christy would have this odd rapport?"

At once, Corey thought of Clay. "I do what I have to do," he said softly. "At least as far as conscience allows."

Spencer gave him a puzzled look, then returned to his computer run.

REPORTERS CLUSTERED IN front of the hotel in downtown Los Angeles. Looking out the window, Corey said, "What a bizarre place this is—office towers with no people in the streets. Looks like a giant Lego set someone dropped from the moon."

"Don't ever fail to not mention that," Spencer advised dryly, and both men clambered out of the limo.

Kate McInerny was in the front rank of the media, as avid as the others for an encounter with a candidate disinclined to duck their questions. "Senator?"

Corey smiled. "Loitering again, Kate? What's up?"

"This morning, Senator Marotta called for a massive effort to deport all illegal immigrants, and a thousand-mile security wall along the Mexican border. What's your reaction?"

"That Senator Marotta calls for lots of things. In the country I'm familiar with, some important segments of our economy depend on illegal immigrants. And we don't have the manpower to find ten million illegals, let alone deport them."

"And so?"

"We should tighten border security and offer illegal immigrants a carefully designed path to citizenship." Corey shrugged. "I believe that on principle. In terms of politics, Senator Marotta's trying to win a primary by pushing a volatile issue. But if he wins the nomination by offending Hispanics, come November he'll lose California by twenty points. When bad policy meets bad politics, it's an achievement of a kind."

Spencer, Corey noted, watched with resignation and veiled amusement—these unscripted encounters, for all their risk of disastrous comments, had become integral to Corey's appeal. "Senator Marotta," Jake Linkletter from Rohr called out, "has just scheduled a Senate vote Thursday to pass a constitutional amendment banning gay marriage. Clearly, this requires you to duck that vote or to cast a vote that might well influence the outcome of this primary. What is your intention?"

Corey tried to choke back his disdain. "If Rob wants to play this game," he said in a tone of resignation, "he can. All I can promise is to be there on Thursday."

"Senator Marotta," Linkletter pressed, "also repeated his charge that gay marriage is, quote, 'a second cousin to incest, polygamy, and people having sex with animals.' What is your response?"

Corey shot him an incredulous look. "What do you expect me to say? That I tremble for our nation's innocent sheep population? That I fear the day when our national anthem will become 'Embraceable Ewe'?"

Except for Linkletter, the cluster of reporters burst out laughing. "Perhaps that's not a very presidential remark," Corey told Linkletter. "But when a presidential candidate actually says things like that, all one can do is make an offering to the god of laughter.

"Listen to Senator Marotta, and you'd think America's biggest problem is gay couples burning flags to celebrate their anniversary. This strategy of turning Americans against each other is tearing us apart. That's the most unpresidential thing a candidate can do."

"What *is* America's biggest problem?" Linkletter asked in a gibing tone.

"Where do I begin—global warming, nuclear proliferation, oil gluttony, and instability in the Middle East are all contenders. But let's take another issue: fighting domestic terrorism.

"I'm grateful we've had no recent incidents of terror. But as suggested by last year's attempt to assassinate Senator Marotta, we're pressing our luck. As one example, I worry about terrorists crashing a private plane loaded with explosives into a football stadium. Our ability to prevent that is nil—"

"Senator," Linkletter interrupted, "don't you worry that simply by suggesting such things you'll give our enemies ideas?"

Corey fixed him with a cold stare. "They're not stupid. The terrorists who brought down the World Trade Center figured *this* one out a decade ago. And people who suggest that it's wrong to point that out make ostriches look like visionaries."

With that, Corey headed for the hotel entrance. "Senator," Linkletter called out, "is there a reason Lexie Hart has stopped campaigning with you?"

Bastards like you, Corey thought, *and your boss—not to*

mention your candidate and the maggot who runs him. "Lexie's easily bored," Corey said over his shoulder. "Questions about gay marriage do that to her."

ON WEDNESDAY NIGHT, Corey took a red-eye back to Washington. "This tactic stinks," Spencer had told him at the airport. "But no Republican is getting a big crossover vote from gays. And Californians overwhelmingly approved a ballot measure banning gay marriage . . ."

"So now they need a constitutional amendment," Corey had said disgustedly.

"They don't. Marotta's hijacked the Senate agenda just to fuck you. But your vote won't make a difference: a constitutional amendment needs a two-thirds majority, and the Democrats will beat this back without you. So why lose voters in California just because Magnus thinks you'll take the bait?" Spencer had unfastened his tie like a man slipping out of a noose. "Don't hand Marotta the nomination, Corey. That's too high a price for one meaningless vote."

Now, sipping Scotch, Corey consulted his conscience, suspended between memories of the past and hopes for the future. He wished that Lexie were with him.

THE GALLERIES WERE packed with spectators and reporters, anticipating what the Rohr News commentator had called "the moral watershed of this campaign."

Rob Marotta led the debate. "This," he said, "is a decisive moment in our nation's history. The future of America hangs in the balance, because the future of marriage hangs in the balance."

At that moment, Corey Grace decided to vote as, in his heart, he had always known he must.

*

WHEN COREY ROSE, a hush fell over the galleries. "The future of America," he said, "does not hang in the balance. Nor is the institution of marriage in jeopardy.

"I do not support gay marriage. But this subject is best handled by the citizens of our states. And *no* state has to recognize a marriage that violates its own laws.

"Those are the facts. Nothing is gained by holding this vote, and some piece of our humanity is lost." For an instant, he imagined Clay as he might have been had he lived. "Without our help, countless families deal with members who are gay—accepting and, eventually, embracing them. If anything, we should focus on giving gays the freedom to select stable partnerships and the responsibility to do so.

"We need not call it marriage. All we need is some small measure of decency and compassion." After pausing, Corey finished simply: "I will vote against this amendment. The consequences of that will be whatever they are."

The gallery burst into applause. But this did not alter the satisfaction Corey read on Rob Marotta's face.

AS HE DROVE back to the airport, feeling glum and resigned, Lexie called. "I'm proud of you," she said.

A burst of hope lightened Corey's mood. "Enough to see me?"

Lexie hesitated. "We should wait, Corey. After Tuesday, things could change."

She did not need to explain this. After Tuesday, Corey's race for president might be over.

"After Tuesday," he said.

BY THAT EVENING, Marotta's new television ads had hit the state's major media markets, excoriating Corey for "failing to oppose gay marriage." On Friday morning, Corey's latest overnight tracking poll showed a 4 percent slippage: Marotta 38 percent, Grace 31 percent, Christy 17 percent. Straining the campaign's finances, Hollis Spencer scheduled a final media buy: a positive ad touting Corey's expertise in military and homeland security matters, plus one showing Marotta with Carl Cash as quotes from both men scrolled across the screen. "Rob Marotta," the ad concluded. "He'll do anything to win."

Corey, Spencer judged, needed a big turnout in the less conservative areas of the state—principally in San Francisco, San Jose, and Silicon Valley—to have any hope of winning. And so on Friday afternoon, just before rush hour, Corey addressed an overflow crowd at Justin Herman Plaza in downtown San Francisco.

The area was cordoned off and surrounded by police and Secret Service agents, a reminder of the fear that permeated post-9/11 America and, in particular, the emotions that swirled around Corey himself. At his back was a thirty-story building with at least five hundred windows; the building on his right had at least a thousand more. But the Secret Service had been prudent by placing the platform at the foot of a building, which eliminated countless lines of fire.

Corey put this out of his mind. He was just beginning to speak when sirens split the air, their number increasing as their sound grew fainter. A section of the crowd seemed to stir organically, as though in response to news or rumor. The head of Corey's Secret Service detail, Peter Lake, headed swiftly to the platform with a contingent of uniformed police, his face drawn. "They've attacked the Golden Gate Bridge," he said in a choked voice. "An airplane full of explosives—they think terrorists."

Reflexively, Corey asked, "How bad is it?"

Lake shook his head. "It's not clear."

Corey hesitated, his mind reeling with disbelief. He struggled to compose himself, then turned to face the crowd, raising his hand for quiet. "Listen up," he announced in the no-nonsense tone of a military officer. "It appears that there has been an attack on the Golden Gate Bridge."

Cries issued from the crowd, drowned out by a deeper moan of shock and horror. "It's moments like this," Corey called out, "that define us for all time.

"We are all in this together. The first thing we need to do is think of those around us—to leave in an orderly manner, helping anyone who needs help. Those of you who live in Marin County should listen for instructions from civil authorities. The rest of you should go home to your family, setting an example of calm for others.

"If this is an act of terror, those who planned the attack will pay for it. Right now, let's show them the resolve and resilience that built—and rebuilt—this city." Corey searched for some final words. "Perhaps our enemies have tried to destroy a landmark. But no one can destroy your courage and compassion. Whatever people remember about this day, let them remember that."

Stirring, the crowd seemed to reach a collective decision; a few pockets of panic were overcome by a steady, orderly progress toward the exit paths. Turning to Peter Lake, Corey said tersely, "If you can, take me out there."

They got as far as the Marina District. Surrounded by Secret Service agents, Corey and Spencer walked to Crissy Field, where hundreds had gathered, their demeanor so subdued that it evoked the aftermath of 9/11.

By miscalculation or sheer luck, the plane had hit the toll plaza just short of the bridge. Corey knew at once that it had been packed with explosives. The plumes of smoke still rose above the wreckage; no doubt many commuters approaching the toll booths had died, and the approach to the span surely had become a crater. But the bridge, though eerily empty, remained intact.

At a distance of several hundred yards, Corey struggled to absorb what the attackers had attempted, an assault so brutal and yet so symbolic that it could sear the nation's soul. He imagined what could so easily have happened: the twin spires collapsing, the tide pulling a few half-submerged cars, kept afloat by air pockets, out to sea. Turning to Spencer, Corey saw tears in his eyes.

At this hour, Corey realized, close to a thousand commuters would have been on the bridge; had it toppled, no one would have survived a precipitous descent in what would have become hundreds of metal coffins. Next to him, a young girl in spandex running clothes turned to him, her lips trembling with the effort to speak. "I saw it." Her throat worked. "A small plane. It hit the top of a span, and then . . ."

She could not say more. Registering Corey's features, her eyes widened in belated recognition. As though relieved by the sight of anyone familiar, she reached out, briefly hesitant, then pressed her face against his shoulder.

A small plane, Corey thought.

AGAIN AND AGAIN in the hours that followed, America watched the same amateur video: a plane hitting the span, a spectacle made even more eerie by the silence of the film. In seeming slow motion, the plane spiraled off course, crashing into the toll booths. Obscured by thick smoke that swirled in the wind like oily fog, the spire remained standing. The later replays included a tape in Arabic, issued by the leader of Al Qaeda, proclaiming this as its latest response to America's war on Islam.

Many had died, perhaps more than one hundred. Amid national anger and revulsion, Rob Marotta's statement mixed the bellicose with the Churchillian; Bob Christy's fervent prayer for God's assistance contained the faint but ominous intimation that this was His warning that America should examine its soiled collective soul. Both men were eclipsed by the president, the governor of California, and the mayor of San Francisco, their uplifting but businesslike responses informed by the experience of 9/11. In this company, Corey alone stood out from his rivals: for his initial words of calm; for his presence at Crissy Field; and, most vividly, for his warning about private aircraft that now seemed hauntingly prophetic.

Gathered with Spencer and Dana Harrison in his suite at the St. Francis, Corey said, "Pull our ads."

Spencer rubbed his eyes. "Already have," he said in a hollow voice.

Corey excused himself to call Lexie.

"THIS TIME WE were lucky," Corey told her. "But standing with those people, it was like they were imagining the end of the world."

"Maybe the end of *their* worlds," Lexie amended gently. "In some ways, people on the West Coast never felt 9/11 as intensely as people who were closer. In *my* world, it's like we were armored by health food, exercise, hybrid cars, and plastic surgery. This feels like a second wake-up call, a reminder that we're not immune."

Curiously, this sad but sober assessment reminded Corey anew of how much he missed her. "I wish you were here."

Lexie hesitated before saying softly, "I know."

Quiet, Corey tried to decipher her meaning. "What will you do now?" she asked.

"Help wherever I can—there will be hundreds of people trying to learn about missing relatives, praying that there's some explanation better than the obvious. The election will have to take care of itself."

Lexie paused again. "I think it will," she said at last. "I think this changes everything."

AROUND THE COUNTRY, Americans gathered to mourn the victims, give thanks that the carnage was not worse, and, in several cities, protest a war in the Middle East that seemed to have made America no safer. But San Francisco was somber, its pulse stirred only by efforts to identify the dead or missing. Corey spent the weekend manning a help line and quietly attending public events organized to salve the spirits of the living. At the city's ecumenical prayer service, Corey sat beside Bob Christy, deliberately avoiding Marotta.

Christy seemed as pensive as Corey himself—burdened, Corey sensed, by the weight of believing that this was not simply the act of terrorists, but of God. Only at the end, standing on the steps of the Grace Cathedral, did Christy refer to Marotta. "This makes him look smaller, doesn't it? Like the little man on Price's wedding cake."

Corey shrugged. "Maybe to us. We've both seen him at his worst."

"Maybe so. But some men match the moment, and others don't." He shook Corey's hand. "Be well, Corey. And God bless you."

Curiously touched, Corey answered, "You too, Bob. Take care of yourself."

Leaving, he had the sense that, despite their differences, an act of terror had moved Christy to give him a kind of benediction.

*

THE IMPULSE THE attack stirred in Magnus Price was far less generous.

With grim satisfaction, Spencer and Corey imagined his dilemma: with the campaign suspended, Price had little choice but to follow Corey in pulling Marotta's ads. What remained were images of Corey perpetuated by the media—old photographs of Corey receiving his medal; the famous photograph of Corey, Marotta, and a dead terrorist; recent clips that captured Corey's warning, his presence of mind in the first moments after the attack, and his compassion to those gathered at Crissy Field. Whether intentional or not, the subliminal message was plain enough: faced with trying times, Corey Grace was a leader.

Price's only recourse was to work through surrogates, trying to break through to voters preoccupied with a trauma that made partisan politics seem trivial, even noxious. The Rohr newspapers in Los Angeles and Sacramento endorsed Marotta and attacked Corey, asserting that "Grace's criticism of the war in Iraq emboldened our enemies to bring the war to California." But this was kind compared to the remarks of Rohr News' leading commentator on a Sunday night broadcast called "The Bridge: Assault on an American Icon." With a stern expression that did not quite conceal his self-satisfaction, Frank Flaherty said, "I'm willing to take the hit for this. But someone has to ask these questions: Why did the Iraqis allow Corey Grace to survive and become a hero? Why did Grace survive the attack on Senator Marotta? Why did this attack by a private plane follow by three days Grace's prediction of such an attack? Why is it—in short—that there is such curious synchronicity between our Arab enemies and Senator Grace's rise to would-be president of the United States?" Pausing, he looked into the camera. "Those are the questions Californians must ask themselves when they go to the polls on Tuesday. The future of their fellow Americans may depend on their decision."

Furious, Corey stared at the screen. "The only Arabs that coward will ever see were in *Lawrence of Arabia*."

"No help for him," Spencer said with resignation. He set about issuing a short and dignified response, knowing, as Corey did, that slander so irresponsible was all the harder to rebut.

ON MONDAY, THE Dow lost two hundred points in the first hour after it opened; in San Francisco, absenteeism ran high, fueled by lingering apprehension and the sheer difficulty of commuting to a city with a gaping crater blocking one of its major arteries. "If our chances depend on the San Francisco area," Spencer said grimly, "God knows if these people will turn out to vote."

On Tuesday morning, the weather across California was sunny and mild. As the day proceeded, it was clear that voting could surpass the previous record: in the San Francisco Bay area, voters—as though returning to life—began to crowd the polling places. "The shocking events in San Francisco," Bill Schneider said on CNN, "seem to have awakened California's Republican voters to this simple fact: they can either hand the nomination to Senator Marotta or send Senator Grace to the convention in New York with a real shot at winning."

Corey spent the day manning the help line, trying to put aside the fact that his campaign and, perhaps, his relationship to Lexie hung in the balance. By nine o'clock, the polls were closed and Corey was back at his hotel with Spencer, Dana, and a handful of supporters, knowing only that early returns suggested that he faced a very long night.

To his surprise, he was running a close second to

Marotta in conservative southern California—Hispanics were turning out for him, and Christy was drawing evangelical voters from Marotta. In San Francisco and the rest of northern California, less populous but more moderate, Corey was running fifteen points ahead; overall, Marotta led by under forty thousand votes. At midnight, Spencer told Corey, "Get some sleep. When you wake up, it'll still be like this—a few thousand votes one way or the other."

Corey left a message for Lexie and tried to nap.

When he awoke, close to dawn, Hollis Spencer was still up, bleary-eyed and drinking his third pot of room service coffee. With a weary smile, Spencer waved at the television. "Congratulations, Mr. President. You're up by thirty thousand, with ninety-six percent of the precincts already in."

"You're kidding."

"Nope. I just finished drafting your victory statement. More than usually eloquent. Suited to the occasion, I think."

Corey felt a torrent of emotions—astonishment, exhaustion, a deep feeling of responsibility, and, quickly following, questions about Lexie. As Spencer stood, Corey gave him a bear hug. "Seems like you made a comeback, Hollis."

Once again, tears sprang to Spencer's eyes. "Getting lachrymose in my old age. Anyhow, I couldn't have done it without you."

"And Al Qaeda," Corey answered, continuing to absorb the fact that whatever Rohr and Price had attempted to imply, Californians had chosen to believe in him at a moment of trauma and challenge.

He shaved, showered, and dressed, constructing a fair facsimile of himself for his supporters and the cameras. When he picked up his cell phone to call her, he found that Lexie had already left a message. "Congratulations," she said with quiet warmth. "After all, the country needs you. Please know that I'll be thinking of you, and wishing you luck all the way."

And that, he feared, was the answer to his question.

PART III

THE KINGMAKER

1

RIDING TOWARD THE HEART OF NEW YORK CITY in his bulletproof black limousine, Senator Corey Grace watched himself on CNN as he left La Guardia a half hour before, confronted by picketers who believed that his nomination as president would ignore God's warning and violate His will.

It was the eve of the convention, a hot and muggy Sunday in July. Driven by a Secret Service agent, the limousine cruised down Fifth Avenue amid the screech of sirens, cocooned by a phalanx of black limousines and police on snarling motorcycles. Overhead, police helicopters added to the sense of a city under siege. Replacing the film of Corey, CNN's anchor materialized in front of the cordon of police officers and steel barriers that surrounded Madison Square Garden, the latest in a collage of jumpy images that, to Corey, suggested that the viewers of cable news must be afflicted by attention deficit disorder.

"Amid deep national anxiety," the anchorman began, "Senator Grace is headed for a showdown with Senator Rob Marotta of Pennsylvania that makes the most jaded political observers feel young again: the first deadlocked nominating convention in recent memory, pitting the maverick Grace against the candidate of the Republican establishment, with the Reverend Bob Christy, the choice of many conservative Christians, holding the balance of power. In the next four days, one man will lose and the other will become the nominee—perhaps our next president."

From behind the tinted glass, Corey gazed out at the pedestrians on the sidewalk in front of Central Park—old people, couples, sidewalk vendors, nannies shepherding children or pushing baby carriages—a sampling of the three hundred million often bewildered souls whom Corey proposed to govern. "This bitter contest," he heard the reporter continue, "occurs in a climate of fear that soared exponentially when terrorists linked to Al Qaeda attempted to crash a private plane into the Golden Gate Bridge during rush hour."

Corey turned to see the now-iconic amateur video: the south span of the Golden Gate Bridge in a whorl of dark smoke. The anchor continued in a swift staccato rhythm. "As the Dow fell and Americans groped for answers, the candidates have struggled to provide them. And the renewed fear of terrorism," the CNN reporter said, "has fueled calls from the Christy campaign for a 'president who deserves God's blessing.'

"For Senator Grace, this linkage of terrorism with questions regarding America's moral and religious life presents a two-pronged problem. The first is his consistent refusal to support the Reverend Christy's demand, echoed by Senator Marotta, for a constitutional ban on gay marriage. But perhaps more costly is Grace's romance with Lexie Hart, rife with both glamor and controversy . . ."

On the screen, Lexie appeared, dispatching an android with a laser gun in a science-fiction film from the beginning of her career. Even on film, Corey discovered, seeing her face intensified his sense of loss. With seeming matter-of-factness, he remarked to Spencer, "Her worst role, she once told me—shooting other minorities."

Spencer gave a shrug of resignation. "Maybe it'll help us with the gun nuts. At least it's not a love scene."

"Needless to say," CNN continued, "the personal dimensions of this campaign—reflected in the open antagonism between Senators Marotta and Grace—have escalated the bitterness and tension surrounding the convention."

Outside, a motorcycle backfired, causing Corey to flinch before he noticed that they had reached the end of Central Park. "Shit," Spencer exclaimed.

Turning, Corey saw that his manager had sat straight up, listening intently to his cell phone. "Caught in the middle of this contest," the anchorman was saying, "are the delegates controlled by four potential kingmakers: the Reverend Christy and three governors with national aspirations of their own—Charles Blair of Illinois, George Costas of New York, and Sam Larkin of Mississippi. While Larkin may lean toward Marotta, Blair and Costas are deemed more sympathetic to Senator Grace. But within the last hour speculation has intensified that Senator Marotta will choose one of these four men as his running mate in an attempt to break the deadlock—whatever the risk of alienating the remaining three . . ."

Squinting with tension, Spencer turned to Corey. "Marotta's called a press conference for six o'clock. His people won't say why."

"They don't need to," Corey answered. "Rob's picked a VP."

Nodding, Spencer spoke into the cell phone, "Start working our friends in each guy's delegation. I don't want Marotta catching us by surprise." To Corey, he said, "So which one is our Judas?"

Eyes, closed, Corey lay his head back against the seat, swiftly assessing the motives of three utterly disparate men. Then he took out his own cell phone and hit speed dial. "This is Senator Grace," Corey said. "I'd like to speak with Governor Blair."

There was a split second's hesitation. "Just a moment, Senator."

Corey waited. A half minute later, a woman said, "Hello, Corey. It's Janet Blair."

Her voice, soft but cool, told Corey that his instinct had been sound. "Having fun yet?" he asked.

"Oh, always. You can guess how much the children enjoy this little gathering, all dressed up with their hair neatly combed like they were going to church on Easter. Which seems more apt than usual."

Despite himself, the arid remark made Corey smile. "So where's Charles?"

"Meeting with his chief of staff to go over his convention speech." After the briefest of pauses, Janet Blair added, "Or so they tell me."

Or, Corey thought, so they told you to say. "How can I find him?" he asked.

"I'm not sure—it's like everyone here's on speed. You know how it is."

Discomfort, Corey thought, was making her voice more brittle. "I know how it is," he answered. "Please have Charles call me."

Getting off, Corey said simply, "It's Blair."

Spencer did not argue. "It's a risk," he said. "After all, Blair wants to be president someday, too."

"So do they all. But Blair is younger, more appealing, and absolutely squeaky clean. Even if Marotta picks Costas, he loses New York in November. And he'll win Mississippi even if he picks Al Sharpton, so he doesn't need Sam Larkin and all his baggage. In Illinois, Blair might actually make a difference.

"Then there's gay rights. Blair's been more hostile to gays than Costas, but not as nasty as Larkin—a lot of delegates feel better when we demean our scapegoats with country club politeness. Blair's the smart move—if I were Marotta, it's what I'd do."

Spencer grimaced. "Make you wish you'd gone to Blair yourself?"

Corey shook his head. "I'm not Marotta. Granted, it wouldn't be the first time this country had a vice president with the spine of a mollusk. But vice presidents have a way of becoming president, and too many people want to kill me. It's not the time to pick the wrong person. Besides," Corey added with cool practicality, "it's better if they all think I'm going to ask them to the prom. At least until I ask someone else."

Spencer emitted a perfunctory grunt. "We need to get ahead of this," he said. "If you're right, Marotta just pissed off three potential presidents—including God's anointed, the Reverend Christy. Bob doesn't take kindly to sacrilege. We need to game out how to handle him. With the media, and with the also-rans. I'll start with Costas's people."

The limousine was easing to a stop; absorbed in his dilemma, Corey had not noticed that they had reached the Essex House. As he glanced out the window, a Secret Service agent reached to open the car door, ready to shield him from danger. "Give me ten minutes alone," Corey said to Spencer. "I want to clear my head."

With this, Corey stepped out of the bubble.

Feigning unconcern, he looked around himself. The hotel was ringed with Secret Service agents, distinguished by their tensile alertness. Above, the percussive thumping of more helicopters filled the air; on the sidewalk across Central Park South, a claque of anti-gay demonstrators had gathered, some brandishing handmade placards, others praying on their knees, presumably for Corey to see the light. Surrounded by a fresh team of agents, he took an elevator to the thirty-fifth floor. Entering his suite,

Corey took a moment to gaze out at Central Park, filled with throngs protesting the war or gay marriage or immigration—their pick of the myriad controversies that roiled the country Corey so dearly loved. Now it was nearly incapacitated by a fear of terrorism that contended with more synthetic fears ginned up by the political classes—of gays, of immigrants, of a "liberal elite" so enfeebled in reality that its only power resided in the popular imagination. Perhaps Corey's deepest fear was that America would no longer face its real problems—that, despite his best efforts, Stepford candidates programmed by political hucksters had permanently reduced the campaign to lead the country to an exercise in marketing and distraction.

Corey did not much worry for himself. He worried for America's next generation, for the daughter he rarely saw, for the other children he had come to want but now might never have. And all the surface jauntiness he did muster could not dispel these fears.

As so often, he wished that Lexie were with him. Though he knew it was hopeless, Corey checked his cell phone for the voice he most wanted to hear.

Nothing.

"You know how it is," Corey mused, wondering if the presidency, like Lexie Hart, was slipping from his grasp.

As COREY'S STAFF scurried to find out whether Governor Charles Blair had pledged his delegates to Marotta, Corey and Spencer went to Madison Square Garden.

Their limousine moved slowly: the Garden was cordoned off by a two-block perimeter of metal fences manned by police and Secret Service agents, with more fences forming chutes designed to funnel delegates through magnetometers and security guards trained to check credentials. The airspace above the Garden, a no-fly zone, was filled with police helicopters whose thudding sounds penetrated Corey's windows. The oppressive sense of military occupation would, Corey thought, leach the gathering of its usual aura of a massive cocktail party, with endless liquor and catered canapés to reward loyal delegates and donors. Just as well, he decided: the fight for delegates was sucking up his campaign's last dollars.

The convention itself was a two-hundred-million-dollar rental operation, within which the principal tenants—Grace and Marotta—fought over space, amenities, and any logistical advantage the Garden offered. Convoyed by the Secret Service, Corey's limousine eased through the passageway reserved for candidates and into the bowels of the Garden. An elevator ride later, Corey and Spencer entered the main hall.

The vast indoor space, Corey saw, was on the verge of becoming a glitzy technological marvel, pulsing with more light and sound than a hundred casinos in Las Vegas. Technicians were setting up camera platforms and correspondents rendering their "eve of battle" reports, while Miss Teen New Mexico, a beautiful Hispanic girl, practiced the amped-up rendition of the national anthem with which she would open the convention. The floor space was crowded with folding chairs, above which signs demarked each delegation, including those that would decide the nomination: Illinois, New York, Mississippi—and, courtesy of Magnus Price, Alabama, with two delegations fighting to be seated. Amid each delegation were TV and computer screens on which anxious delegates could track the balloting. Walking beside Corey, Spencer stopped, listening intently on his cell phone. "All Marotta's press guy says," he told Corey, "is that he 'won't comment on rumor and speculation.'"

"Price has made his move," Corey said. "At Rob's six o'clock press conference, Blair will appear with him, the new vice president in waiting."

He resumed inspecting the premises. A red-carpeted stairway rose to the speaker's platform, behind which was an enormous TV screen and, above that, a giant American flag that glowed in violent neon. "Can't burn *that*," Corey observed. "You'd electrocute yourself."

He stopped, hands in his pockets, gazing up. Above the crawl sign on all four sides of the arena—currently flashing a fireworks display—were glass-encased luxury boxes appropriated by the networks: NBC, CBS, ABC, Fox, MSNBC, PBS, C-SPAN, and Rohr News. Hanging amid the klieg lights were nets filled with red, white, and blue balloons, waiting to be dropped the moment Corey Grace or Rob Marotta reached the magic number needed to win the nomination: 1,051 delegates.

By Spencer's current count, Marotta held 827 delegates; Corey was 2 short of that. Of the remaining 470 or so delegates, Blair of Illinois controlled 73; Larkin of Mississippi 38; Costas of New York 102; and Bob Christy 110. Tomorrow night, the convention would vote on which delegation, Corey's or Marotta's, would represent Alabama's 48 votes; roughly 80 more delegates remained uncommitted. If Blair had cut a deal, Illinois would give Marotta 900 or so—at which point, either Christy or Costas could put Marotta so close to winning that it would precipitate a stampede, particularly if Alabama went to Marotta. Corey hoped to hold New York: like Corey, Costas was a moderate, and Corey had raised money to help Costas win reelection. But then, he thought bitterly, the same was true of Blair.

As for Bob Christy, Corey thought, God only knew.

What Corey knew was that Spencer had constructed

the best delegate-hunting operation since the Ford-Reagan battle in 1976. Spencer's delegate hunters were jammed in a trailer outfitted with more communications systems than a military command post. Armed with profiles of each delegate, they would split up the undecided and favorite-son delegates and call each of them like clockwork, trolling for information and support. More delegate hunters would patrol the floor, checking the uncommitteds. High above them was Spencer's command post—a skybox positioned next to Rohr News equipped with phone banks, computers, BlackBerrys, and TV screens, from which Spencer would monitor the delegate hunters, gathering any information that might affect the outcome.

Spencer had broken the delegate hunters into six regions, each with a whip. There were separate whips for each state; a dedicated team of delegate minders; delegates assigned to police other delegates; supposedly uncommitted delegates who were acting as Spencer's spies; lawyers expert in delegate challenges and the arcane rules that governed when committed delegates could switch their votes; and star attractions—athletes, actors, congressmen, and senators—to woo delegates susceptible to celebrity. The idea was to know each uncommitted delegate on the rawest human level: strengths, weaknesses, beliefs, secrets, desires, friends, enemies, and obligations—whether moral or financial. All of this would yield a delegate count, tallied twice a day, designed to identify slippage or targets of opportunity right down to the last uncommitted delegate. As for Corey himself, he had set up camp at the Essex House, on Central Park South, and his chief role now was to keep up his profile through meetings with uncommitted governors and delegates, as well as public appearances designed for maximum impact.

Price, too, had a delegate-hunting operation. Spencer

had received reports about private investigators, paid for by Rohr but furnished through cutouts, whose business was blackmail. "Marotta needs it," Spencer had told Corey just the day before. "*Your* delegates give a damn; Marotta's are functionaries, motivated by greed or fear. More lab rats in Price's experiment.

"Our strategy is to convince the media that when we say we're gaining delegates, we actually are. Every delegate we claim will have to commit themselves in public—which has the added virtue, we hope, of creating media mini-events. All that, if we're lucky, will help push Illinois or New York our way, and get us over the top."

But now it was Sunday, and Illinois was likely gone. "Let's check out our skybox," Spencer suggested. "No one can overhear us there."

PERCHED IN THE skybox, Corey found his eyes drawn to the floor space for the Illinois delegation, ten rows of empty chairs that, tomorrow, would be occupied by seventy-three human beings with different needs and aspirations, and varying degrees of loyalty to Charles Blair. "Even if Marotta names Blair," Corey said, "I think we can split his delegation. We've got a friend there in Drew Tully."

Spencer weighed this. "Senator Tully can't stand Blair, and he sure as hell doesn't want Blair to overshadow him. But if Blair cuts a deal for vice president, he'll fight like a feral cat to hold his delegation. It would take a lot for some downstate county commissioner to cross a man who might end up one dead president away from becoming president."

"The officeholders don't want to *lose,* either," Corey replied. "In November, Marotta will lose Illinois, and some of those guys will lose with him." He took a quick sip of Diet Coke. "A deadlocked convention is a law unto itself. And in Illinois, delegates aren't bound to follow Blair. In the end, it's a matter of raw power—do you want to offend Blair or offend me and my friend Senator Tully?"

"*That*," Spencer answered bluntly, "depends on what each delegate wants or needs, and whether they think you'll lose. Part of Blair's power derives from the momentum he'll be creating for Marotta.

"So what will you offer, Corey? A judgeship? Ambassador to the Seychelles Islands?" Facing Corey, he said, "Making George Costas your vice president might be more efficient. New York's one hundred and two delegates are looking awfully good."

"And then what?" Corey asked with more calm than he felt. "With the vice presidency pledged to Costas, Larkin gives Mississippi to Marotta, and Christy follows suit. And if Blair has sold his delegation to be VP, I'm the only game in town for everyone else. Best to keep them all in play.

"There *is* one other thing, minor though it may seem. Costas is weak. To borrow a phrase from Christy, he doesn't match the temper of hard times."

"And Larkin *does*?" Spencer asked with mild scorn. "As for Christy, his selection is inconceivable. Besides Costas, those are the only guys who can sell you delegates in bulk."

"Yeah," Corey said dryly. "It's a problem, isn't it."

Spencer gave him a probing look. "Is there some thought here, Corey, that you're keeping to yourself?"

"Maybe. I need to spin it out." Corey's tone turned practical. "I'm sure I can keep Costas in play awhile longer. What's Marotta going to give him *now*—secretary of commerce?"

Spencer stared down at the convention floor. "That leaves Christy, doesn't it."

"It certainly does."

"He loathes Marotta—we know that. But in the end he can't go with you. His followers don't like you, and you've given them nothing."

"What do you suggest?"

Spencer rested his chin on folded hands. "Gay marriage," he said at last. "Civil unions, too. I know you don't like to hear this, and I don't like to say it. But if you want Christy's help, you need to throw gays overboard."

"What about Darwin?" Corey inquired softly. "You really think gays will be enough?"

"Could be," Spencer answered calmly. "If Marotta wins, he, not Christy, will be the big dog among the evangelicals, with all that patronage and power to dispense. I don't think Christy could easily abide that. But with you as a semiconvert, but not his rival, Christy is still the Christian alpha dog.

"Consider it, Corey. Sure beats making him vice president. And come Monday, you'll badly need Christy's delegates to vote in favor of seating *your* Alabama delegation. Those are forty-eight votes we can't afford to lose."

Corey regarded his manager in silence. "Tell you what," he said at last. "While you track down what's happening with Blair, I'll go to the Reverend Bob's delegate reception. Let's hope all he needs is love."

2

THE CALCULATIONS THAT HAD LED ROB MAROTTA to contemplate a decisive but dangerous move had begun that morning, with Bob Christy.

They met in a condominium, the home of a supporter, chosen by Magnus Price to avoid detection. Over coffee and Danish, Price and Marotta eyed Christy and his boyish campaign manager, Dan Hansen. But Marotta spoke to Christy as if no one else were in the room; the stakes were too high for him to fail with this man. "It's been a hard few weeks," he acknowledged. "I'm looking for a way to heal the wounds."

Christy's amiable mask did not conceal the dislike in his blue-gray eyes. "It's not for me to ask, Rob. It's for you to offer."

Price, Marotta noted, was as inscrutable as Buddha. Like his passivity, this was scripted: knowing that Christy loathed Price as a traitor, Marotta had resolved, despite their own rancor, to deal with Christy himself. "You deserve a platform," Marotta said carefully. "One that allows you to put your values into practice.

"After Iowa, Magnus offered you secretary of education. You turned him down." Smiling, Marotta continued, "I understand—you'd just beaten me silly and were hoping to get the nomination for yourself. But I sent Magnus not just out of practicality, but out of respect. The offer stands: a cabinet position that empowers you to mold the lives of America's next generation."

Even as he spoke the words, Marotta recoiled at the thought of Christy in the cabinet—too headstrong to control, too powerful to fire. Christy pursed his lips as though tasting a piece of sour fruit. "I'm flattered," he answered with a touch of irony. "But I'd feel like a man with no deed to where he slept, living at the sufferance of his landlord. I'd prefer to have some property of my own."

Marotta hoped his smile appeared less anxious than it felt. "I'm not sure I follow your analogy."

Sitting beside Christy, Dan Hansen shot Price a look of amusement. But Price seemed to have taken leave of his body, so absorbed in Christy that he noticed nothing else. "Of course you do," Christy told Marotta, as though encouraging a bashful child to speak up. "Name a constitutional office where the occupant can't be fired."

Despite his tension, Marotta joked, "Chief justice?"

"Let me make it easier for you. Confine yourself to the executive branch."

Marotta frowned. "That's a big one, Reverend."

"Not as big as president, Rob. That's what you're wanting me to deliver."

Marotta leaned forward. "You know as well as I do what happens if I pick you before I clinch the nomination. The northern moderates—Costas and Blair—will put Grace roughly fifty votes from winning."

"And Larkin would give you Mississippi," Christy rejoined. "In the end, his people won't stand for him supporting Corey. That puts *you* fifty votes from winning." He turned to Price. "Cat get your tongue, Magnus? Bet you got fifty undecided delegates in your little black book of sins and secrets. Real or imagined."

Marotta felt apprehension grip him; Christy's pointed remark brought them perilously close to the unspoken subtext of the meeting, Mary Ella Ware. Price merely sighed. "You give me too much credit, Reverend. And there's a practical problem here—come November, Rob will need at least some of the moderate voters who are so attached to Grace. That argues for Costas or Blair."

"If you help make me president," Marotta interjected firmly, "you'll have a very grateful and powerful friend. And a cabinet position to boot."

With a half smile, Christy shook his head. "We've been here already."

"Not quite." Price spoke with barely contained impatience. "Want to risk losing your delegates, Bob? Maybe they don't want to support a certain loser over a near-certain nominee.

"You're the one who's at risk. If you delay much longer, your delegates will start deserting."

Christy summoned a cold smile. "Thank you for that, Magnus. You don't usually tell me what's going to happen before it does." He stood abruptly, a worried-looking Hansen belatedly standing with him. "We've all said all we need to. At least for now."

Marotta felt a sudden connection to Christy, more intimate and real than the pretense that had gone before: Christy felt cornered, the fear of irrelevance and humiliation gnawing at his core. "Keep in touch," Marotta said.

"I will, Rob. Count on it."

Christy left, the residue of his visit a heavy silence. Marotta stared at the door. "That woman," he asked Price softly. "What do you know about her?"

"Nothing. The man's as angry at himself as he is at us. Once he cools down, he'll dread looking like a fool twice over. He's got nowhere to go but you."

Silent, Marotta tried to penetrate Price's bland expression. "No rest for the wicked," Price said calmly. "Especially *from* the wicked. Sam Larkin's on his way."

*

To MAROTTA, EVERYTHING about Larkin inspired distrust, from his background as a lobbyist who dispensed girls like party favors to his appearance: razor-cut gray hair, soft manicured hands, expensive suits, and, above the red-veined drinker's cheeks, blue eyes that could shift from candor to venality in a nanosecond. Each part of Larkin's face seemed dedicated to a separate function: the raised eyebrows signaling skepticism, the red nose a beacon of sociability, the rubbery mouth stretching to convey whatever emotion the eyes did not. Marotta found it remarkable that any man could look pious, cynical, good-humored, and corrupt all at once, when in fact he was mostly the last. But Mississippi kept electing him. And so here he was, with his hands on the levers that could make Marotta president.

"As they say in the federal government," Larkin opened with a jovial smile, " 'I'm here to help.' Bet *that* puts fear in your two dark hearts."

Smiling, Marotta awaited the latest declaration of interest in becoming vice president. "More like deep respect," he answered lightly.

Larkin put a hand to his heart. "You flatter me, Robbie—you surely do. But you can stop now. 'Cause I didn't ask to see you on my own behalf."

Marotta laughed. "That *is* refreshing."

"At least not directly," Larkin corrected himself. "Looks to me like you're needing a vice president, and the delegates that come with him. Right?"

Marotta glanced at Price, who, for once, looked as mystified as Marotta felt. "Looks like," Marotta conceded.

"Can't go to Christy—that's for sure. Too wired to his own God, and who knows *when* this woman thing will rear its ugly head again. Anyhow, you need a moderate."

Larkin paused as though imparting the answer to life's most perplexing question. "The man you want, Mr. President-to-be, is Governor Charles Blair."

Marotta did not bother to conceal his astonishment. "You surprise me, Sam."

Larkin smiled. "People don't appreciate my selfless nature. But Blair's the obvious choice, and you know it. You need a moderate, but not *too* moderate. Blair's not wildly pro-abortion, and he's good enough on gays."

"Good enough for Mississippi?" Price inquired skeptically.

"I can help you there, Magnus. I can help sell Blair to *all* the southern delegations." His tone became practical. "My people don't like Grace. And I don't want Christy poaching on my turf among the evangelicals. Looks to me like Marotta-Blair is both of our tickets out."

Once more, Marotta glanced at Price. "I don't really know Blair," Marotta told Larkin. "Seems like he's closer to Grace."

"They're not *married*, Rob. And I can vouch for Charles Blair. We've spent time together at governors' conferences. He may be a little callow, but he's bright, a quick study, and looks like the boy your mama wanted Sis to marry." Larkin nodded as though confirming his own words. "Best of all, and unlike Grace or Christy, he's squeaky-clean: pretty wife, adorable young kids, not a hint of scandal. Blair's the elixir for what ails us, and I'll help my confreres in the South to choke it down."

Finishing, Larkin looked not at Marotta, but at Price. "The thought's occurred to me," Price acknowledged. "What hadn't was that you'd help sell him."

Larkin threw his hands up in the air. "I'm the great undiscovered altruist," he said in mock dismay. "Blair can help you win over moderate delegates who would otherwise go for Grace—he might even give George Costas enough cover to be with you, at least once he recovers from his disappointment. Blair's what you need." Larkin spoke with the hush of a man imparting secrets. "But he's not what Grace needs. Grace needs someone more conservative, and Blair knows it."

"So Blair also knows you were coming," Price said flatly.

Larkin gave an exaggerated shrug. "Let's say I've come to see him as a younger brother, but with an inexplicably funny accent." With startling abruptness, Larkin's voice turned stony. "Grace won't go down easy—he's the fightingest man I've ever met, and he hates both of you worse than poison. Time for you to show some guts."

The implicit comparison to Grace stung Marotta more than he cared to reveal. "Thank you," he said evenly. "Your advice deserves my deepest thought."

"Then I'll leave you to it," Larkin said. "Not a minute to waste."

"WHAT THE HELL was *that* about?" Marotta asked.

Price's narrow gaze signaled his perturbation. "Not what Sam said it was. But if he helps sell Blair, this could be the best move for us."

"So what's Sam want?"

"I'd have sworn it was vice president—Sam's a realist about everyone but himself. Now I'm thinking he wants to go back to being a lobbyist." Price tilted his head back, contemplating the ceiling. "If *that's* what he's after, it's fucking brilliant. A man who'd made both the president and vice president would be the most powerful lobbyist in Washington. We'd owe him from here to doomsday."

"And that makes you feel better?"

"Only if I'm right. What makes me feel worse is sensing

there's an angle I don't quite understand. This is too important to get wrong."

"Sam, or Blair?"

"Both. And I'm still worried about Costas."

No longer hungry, Marotta contemplated his half-eaten Danish. "Can't we dangle VP in front of both Blair *and* Costas?"

"Yes and no." Restless, Price stood. "Tomorrow night, we win or lose the Alabama delegates. As matters stand, my sense is that Costas's and Blair's delegations would vote to seat Grace's delegates. But if we commit to Blair before then, he'll tell his people to vote with us. That gives us a chance of adding Alabama's forty-eight to Illinois's seventy-three.

"At that point, we're only a hundred delegates short. If we name Blair, sooner or later Larkin will throw Mississippi's thirty-eight delegates our way. Once Costas sees we're sixty votes from winning, he may well crack."

He finished this scenario with more conviction than he'd started with, sounding to Marotta like a man seduced. "That's a lot of ifs and angles," Marotta pointed out.

"This isn't geometry," Price rejoined. "More like an impressionist painting. So let's add another color to the palette." Price's eyes half-shut, as if seeing a vision too sensual to share. "Suppose we designate our vice president and then call for a vote of the convention, requiring Grace to name *his* vice president. At that point, *he* might crack and pick a VP. If not, the convention could force him to.

"Picking someone—*anyone*—is bad for him. He alienates the also-rans. If he picks a conservative, he alienates moderates; if he picks a moderate, he alienates conservatives—including Christy's people. That way there's no downside to us naming *our* guy, because he suffers the bigger downside of naming *his*." He began tapping his foot as though listening to the Allman Brothers. "I'm beginning to like this painting."

"A painting," Marotta said, "or a house of cards. It all rests on Blair, and what we know about him. Or *don't* know. How well have we checked him out?"

"Not as well as I'd like—we've put most of our resources into investigating delegates. But our preliminary work came up with someone more pristine than a Ken doll."

"There is no such person."

Price smiled. "There's *you*, Robbie. After all, you've never been unfaithful to Mary Rose."

"No," Marotta answered stiffly. "I haven't. But Christy came as a surprise."

Price exhaled. "Okay," he said slowly. "I'll make some further inquiries. But if for no other reason than humoring Sam, we'd better see this guy."

After a moment, Marotta nodded. Then he walked to the window, gazing out at Central Park, a gathering place for the young demonstrators who had come to protest the war, global warming, and the power of the Christian Right.

"Governor," he heard Price ask, "can you clear time for Senator Marotta?"

SITTING ACROSS FROM Charles Blair, Marotta reflected that he knew him in the way that any politician knows another—from party functions, or sharing a podium, or passing encounters at a convention. Which was to say, not well. The meeting felt like speed dating, in which Marotta was called upon to determine another man's character, and perhaps his own fate, with indecent haste.

Blair was attractive and obviously smart, a Harvard MBA who had made a fortune in the high-tech industry before venturing into politics. But, at forty, there was something unfinished about him, a boyish eagerness to please that kept piercing his veneer of self-possession. Still, the first half hour of discussion showed Blair's assets to good advantage—his answers were clear, informed, and displayed a perfect pitch for nuance. When Marotta observed that Sam Larkin seemed very fond of him, Blair answered with a smile. "Sam's the only fifty-year-old scamp I know. But that makes me like him more, even when I'm afraid that he's swiping my wallet.

"At bottom, though, Sam's a serious man with first-rate judgment and a laser eye for human weakness. I'm fortunate to have earned his respect."

It was a fair response, Marotta thought. In his laziest drawl, Price inquired, "Don't you ever curse, Governor? It's been damn near forty minutes and I haven't heard a single swearword stain your lips."

"Darn," Blair said with a self-deprecating laugh. "You nailed me, Magnus. I'm a grown-up Eagle Scout who still hears the chiding voice of his Pentecostal mother. If salty language makes the man, I'm not your man. But a lot of sincerely religious people seem to like me for it."

To Marotta, Price's half smile hovered somewhere between skepticism and satisfaction. Almost carelessly, he said, "Hear you're close to Corey Grace."

Blair nodded promptly. "I'm comfortable with Corey—personally and, in general, politically. I imagine that's part of why I'm here."

The man was facile enough, Marotta had to concede. "It is," he said bluntly. "Up to a point."

Blair regarded him with a gaze so serious that he reminded Marotta, somewhat unnervingly, of an avid first-year law student responding to a professor's barb. "I'm not a knee-jerk moderate," he answered in the same forthright tone. "Sometimes Corey's too cavalier, especially with evangelicals. I'm committed to keeping them in the fold."

"How do you propose to do that, given that you're pro-choice?"

"Pro-choice 'to a point,'" Blair responded. "I'm for the parental-consent laws and against partial-birth abortion." He paused, then added quietly, "If we're discussing the possibility I think we're discussing, I know there's only one leader. No one loves abortion, least of all me. In my *own* life, I'm pro-life."

"And stem cells?"

Briefly, Blair paused. "Again, I defer to you."

"What about gay rights?" Price interposed, slowing his speech to emphasize each word. "That's a deal breaker for Christy's people. Can you sign off on a constitutional amendment to ban gay marriage?"

Blair had already begun nodding. "In a word—yes."

"Got a position for us on civil unions?"

Blair met Price's gaze head-on. With surprising steel, he said, "Do you have a position for me, Magnus? Vice presidents don't make policy."

The glint in Price's eyes betrayed his interest. "That was admirably forthright, Governor. So let me be equally forthright. With stakes this high, only a fool tries to conceal things a normal man would conceal." He paused for emphasis. "Is there anything—anything at all—that we should know about your life before making this decision? Because if there is, and you lie to me now, I'll cut you off in politics like a dead stump."

For an instant, Blair seemed to bristle. With cool civility, he told Price, "I'll give my answer to Senator Marotta." In the silence, he turned to Marotta; then he spoke as slowly as Price had. "There is *nothing* in my life that will keep you from the presidency."

His gaze was resolute. Either this man was wholly sincere, Marotta thought, or he was a far more practiced liar than his public profile would account for. Standing, he extended his hand. "Thank you, Charles. You'll hear from us very soon."

"Well?" Price asked when Blair had left.

"He's good." Marotta tried to articulate the nagging doubt that dogged him. "But not good like Corey Grace. He's so damned good he bothers me."

3

As Corey and Dakin Ford left the hotel, demonstrators called out from across the street, "Stop gay marriage" as others formed prayer circles beneath placards reading "Stem-Cell Research=Human Cloning." Following Corey into the limousine, Ford quipped, "What about gay clones?"

Corey did not answer. Watching the faces through the glass—some mournful, some angry, some yelling—he wondered how any leader could rally a country so badly riven as this. Then his mind turned to the problem at hand. "What do you think of Blair?" he asked.

"Never liked him. He wants too much to be liked." Turning to Corey, Ford added briskly, "But all is not lost. Long time between now and Wednesday night."

"If I'm still alive by then. Every decision I face feels like a ticking bomb."

Ford stretched his arms across the back seat. "By the way, we're still working on Mary Ella Ware," he said. "The key to that particular mystery is the lawyer she hired, Dalton Frye.

"Frye's not only a protégé of Linwood Tate's, he's also a sleazebag—only time he's honest is by mistake. But his being a lawyer makes his dealings with Ware 'confidential.'" Ford shook his head. "Always said the bar exam oughta include a Rorschach test. Any fucker who looks at a bunch of flowers and sees a wolf's head ought not be armed with a law license.

"Maybe Christy wagged his weenie at her. If he didn't,

bet you a mess of barbecue that money isn't going from Ware to Frye, but from Frye to Ware."

"How do we figure *that* out?"

Ford's smile did not alter his determined air. "Devious methods, my son. Just hope they work—we got no time to waste on due process of law."

Corey decided it was better not to ask.

FIFTEEN MINUTES AFTER his own reception had begun, Christy remained huddled in his suite, strategizing with Dan Hansen. "So you think he's naming Blair," Christy said in a ruminative tone. "Ever see *Leave It to Beaver,* Dan? Boy sort of reminds me of Eddie Haskell, 'cept he makes being obsequious look like a brand-new suit."

"If it's true," Hansen answered. "That makes Grace our only hope."

Christy shook his head. "I can't abide Marotta, and I like Grace. But it's near impossible to imagine a scenario where Corey would turn to me, or I could accept."

"Then you'll wind up supporting Marotta. No gain in being a dead-ender."

Christy gave his manager a look of sheer disgust. "The man framed me. Vice president's the only thing he could give me that's big enough to provoke forgiveness.

"Making Marotta president in exchange for nothing would weigh on my conscience. Worse," Christy added, "he means to steal Christian conservatives out from under me—use them for his own cynical ends, and those of men like Price and Rohr. Politics makes it hard to separate God's purposes from my own, but I'm pretty sure that's *not* what the Almighty has in mind."

"So," Hansen proposed, "why not give Him a day or two to reveal His purpose? Maybe He'll help Grace to see the light."

Christy gave Hansen a skeptical look. "Short of vice president, Corey would have to give me something that cements my position for all the world to see. Not just some vague promise—I mean a public change of heart on an issue we deem essential. Doesn't sound like Grace to me."

Hansen shrugged. "He hates Marotta. He wants to be president. Seems like Blair's betrayed him. Things like that can work on a man—think *he* wants to say 'President Marotta'?"

"No," Christy said softly. "It would feel like a tapeworm in his very soul."

Hansen stood. "So let's go downstairs, Bob. Senator Grace is coming to pay tribute. Nice if you were there to accept it."

THE CHRISTY RECEPTION had a distinct flavor. Though its location, a hotel ballroom, was generic, the entertainment was a Christian heavy-metal group shouting dissonant praise to Jesus Christ, and the attendees, whose responses to the music ranged from ecstatic to bewildered, had a common look of determined goodwill that seemed to transcend politics. "Don't know why they all seem so damned transported," Dakin Ford groused to Corey. "Not a drop of liquor in sight."

"They're high on life," Corey answered, and made his way with Ford through Christy's friends and delegates.

Seeing him, one person after another smiled or shook hands, often with a murmured blessing or friendly word of greeting. He was not one of them, their manner said, but he had treated their leader with respect, and it was ingrained in them that no man was beyond redemption. So Corey took his time, smiling, exchanging pleasantries, making small connections. To his surprise, a round, middle-aged woman kissed him on the cheek. "Lord," she said, "you really are a cute one."

Corey laughed. "It's not too late for us," he said, and continued his progress through the delegates.

When Christy saw him, he opened his arms, causing those around him to clear a space for Corey. Amid the buzz of voices, Christy embraced Corey like a sinner redeemed. Beaming, Christy told him, "Guess you didn't come here for a drink."

Corey hooked a thumb toward Ford. "Only Dakin did. How *are* you, Bob?"

"Glad to see you." He took Corey's arm. "Let's say a few words to my folks."

The two men climbed up on a stage, the band silenced by a wave of Christy's hand. Claiming the microphone, Christy announced, "I'd like you all to meet a special guest. A man who may be my rival but is surely my friend: Senator Corey Grace."

Christy's genuine pleasure seemed to permeate the crowd: faces uplifted, they accorded Corey sustained applause. Only as it dwindled did Christy continue, his voice now solemn: "When I was at my lowest point—my honor questioned, our campaign beset—Corey Grace spoke out for me. And I saw that for all our differences, we both believe that God means for politics to ennoble us, not debase us.

"I have great hopes for Senator Grace. Among them is that God will dedicate Corey to His purposes for the betterment of us all." Grinning at this veiled challenge, Christy thrust the microphone at Corey.

For an instant, Corey was gripped by the antic impulse to announce that he had rejected cloning, fired his last gay staffer, adopted celibacy, and embraced Jesus as his personal shopper. "Thank you, Reverend," he said with a smile. "Other than the Almighty, you're the toughest act any politician ever had to follow."

This somewhat risky joke induced a chuckle of good-will. Corey gazed out at the audience, his expression serious. "Respect isn't given, it's earned. Bob earned mine one night in South Carolina, when he spoke kindly about someone I love very much—rejecting hatred based on race—and then defended me against charges that, in their own way, were as ugly as those made against him.

"For that, I will never forget Bob Christy."

Pausing, Corey thought of the other moment he would never forget—his brother listening to Christy's denunciation of the person Clay surely feared he was. "It's true we have our differences. Perhaps, over time, they will lessen. But we share the belief that brought all of you into politics: that for our children's sake, and faced with such perilous times, we must leave this country better than we found it. *And*," Corey added in an incisive tone, "that noble end cannot be advanced through sordid means."

At this—clearly a gibe at Rob Marotta—Christy's delegates burst into applause. "So I'm proud to be with you," Corey concluded. "Let us all hope, *and* pray, that we can leave this convention with something more to be proud of."

Amid rising applause, Christy leaned closer to him. "Nicely done," Christy said, one professional to another. To one side, he saw Ford grin, knowing, as Corey intended, that he had made embracing Marotta that much harder for Christy.

"Let's check out that TV," Christy said, pointing to a television in one corner of the room. "Looks like Marotta's dangerously close to a microphone."

WATCHING THE ANNOUNCEMENT, Corey judged Marotta's mood as somewhere between triumphant and anxious: he spoke each word of praise carefully, as though gauging their power to persuade. "My selection," he said, "is a man of family and faith, energy and vision, experience and idealism: Governor Charles Blair of Illinois."

Turning, Marotta embraced Blair as he stepped into the picture. Arms folded, Christy said to Ford and Corey, "They look like a couple of slick bond salesmen."

To Corey, they looked better than that. But he understood Christy's meaning: Marotta's sincerity seemed overdone, and Blair had a face on which character remained to be written. "I make this choice," Marotta continued, "with total confidence in Governor Blair's fitness, if need be, to assume the office of president."

"That's pushing it a little," Ford opined. "First Blair's gotta rise to Dan Quayle."

"And I challenge Senator Grace," Marotta said firmly, "to do what I have done—tell America who *he* wants to place one heartbeat from the Oval Office." As Christy glanced toward Corey, Marotta's tone grew sterner. "Should Senator Grace refuse, tomorrow night I will ask the convention to require him to name his running mate."

"Shit," Ford murmured. "Magnus sure knows how to spoil a party."

It was time for Corey to leave.

COREY AND FORD entered Hollis Spencer's suite and found Spencer and Dana Harrison watching Rohr News. Glancing up, Spencer reported, "They're calling it a masterstroke. Even CNN sounded kind of impressed."

Corey shrugged. "What are *we* calling it, Hollis?"

" 'A transparent maneuver.' " Looking down at his legal pad, he read, " 'This decision is too important to become another move in Senator Marotta's game of political chess. Senator Grace will make his selection based on the national interest.'"

"Good to know," Corey said. "In other words, we're not biting."

"Can't." As Corey and Ford sat, Spencer continued: "Magnus is setting up this roll-call vote as a test of strength. If the convention votes to force us to pick our VP, it means Marotta's got more delegates than we do—a signal to undecideds to hop on board. Forcing us to commit ourselves is just icing on the cake.

"We've gone over why you won't pick Costas, and can't pick Larkin or Christy."

"Why is that?" Ford asked. "They fail Blair's standard of greatness?"

"And mine," Spencer said crisply. "They don't put us over the top." To Corey he said, "I called your senatorial pal from Illinois, Drew Tully. To quote Drew, 'That little shit didn't say a fucking word to me. Marotta would get his ass kicked in Illinois, and I'll be damned if he's taking me with him.'"

Corey laughed. "Guess Blair fails Tully's standard of greatness."

"Yup. He's ready to start a rebellion in the Illinois delegation. That may slow down the stampede Magnus has in mind." Spencer's voice became more intense. "We'll do our damnedest to persuade Costas and Larkin that it's in their interest not to push you. But if we lose that vote, we're going to need a nominee."

The room fell silent. "Hate to say this," Dana Harrison ventured. "Maybe you need a southern conservative. But who?"

"Ben Carter," Ford proposed. "He's for Marotta, true. But a governor of Florida could help you in November. Plus, he's an evangelical without being absolutely rabid."

"He's another Blair," Corey objected. "Not enough gravitas to keep his loafers on the ground. We're talking about a potential president, remember?"

"So *who*?"

Corey pulled out his cell phone. "Got just the man, right here on speed-dial."

Hollis Spencer smiled a little, as though guessing where Corey was headed. "Billy Graham?" Ford asked.

"Nope. See if this profile sounds a little more presidential. Deeply religious. First one in his family to graduate from college. Two combat medals in Vietnam. Chairman of the Joint Chiefs of Staff. Secretary of State." Corey paused. "Oh, and he's black."

For once, Ford's look of astonishment was genuine. "Cortland Lane?"

Corey smiled. "Sort of puts Blair in perspective, doesn't he?"

4

At six a.m. Monday morning, Corey met with Cortland Lane in his suite.

"Sorry for the hour," Corey said. "The name of the game is 'Beat the Press.'"

With a philosophical smile, Lane shrugged his broad shoulders. Even this gesture carried a sense of power; at sixty-five, Lane remained a fit, commanding presence, and though his face was placid and imperturbable his eyes retained the keenness of a military man on alert. "I understand completely," Lane answered. "Any public disclosure of an offer—or potential offer—has consequences."

"What about 'provisional offer,'" Corey said baldly. "I'm doing my best to avoid getting cornered. But the convention may force me to decide tonight. I need to know if you're among my options."

Lane's eyes narrowed in contemplation. "Until Sally died, I wasn't. She was certain I'd be shot."

The weight of this made Corey briefly quiet. "I know," he answered. "I'm sorry I missed the service for her, Cortland."

Lane shook his head in demurral. "You were running for president. The challenges we face are far too serious for us to get that wrong."

"And so?"

Lane looked curious. "Don't you have *enough* obstacles to overcome without adding the one I'd bring you? The reason Sally feared my running for president is the same reason you wanted Secret Service protection for Lexie. Race."

Corey poured himself more coffee, considering his answer. "I can't ask you to put your life at risk. But the political risk is my concern.

"I want to choose someone fit to be president. You know your own qualities. So does the country. Can you tell me Charles Blair's your equal?"

Lane smiled a little. "If I could, I wouldn't have considered running for president myself. Deciding not to hurt some." His tone became somber. "Sally knew that. Just before she died, she told me, 'Now you can run.' As though by dying she was doing me a favor."

Corey could feel his mentor's quiet anguish. But there was nothing he could do to ease it. "Well," Lane said softly. "It's done."

"And so here we are," Corey responded. "There's a lot for you to weigh, I know. But if you had the chance to transform this country, would you?"

Standing, Lane nodded. "When I considered running, I thought perhaps I could. But I don't know that the vice presidency presents that opportunity."

"Even Vice President Lane?" Corey smiled. "I grant you that, as president, I might lack your transformative powers. But Marotta and I are the only game in town. Suppose that you're the difference in determining who wins."

To Corey's surprise, Lane chuckled. "That's a tough one, Captain. Had it been up to me, you wouldn't have made it to general in a million years. Too much of a hotshot." As though seeing the shadow of Joe Fitts cross Corey's face, Lane added quietly, "A lot's happened since then—to you, and to the country. I've known the last four presidents, and I know the qualities of heart and mind a president requires. That's why I'm here."

Even now, Corey realized, Lane's respect mattered more to him than any other man's. "And I'm grateful."

"Then let's talk about what *you* require. Seems like all the pundits think you need a southern Christian conservative."

Corey shrugged. "I'm a whole lot more concerned with picking someone who could deal with problems like Al Qaeda and the Middle East—the things you and I agree about. So in my mind, I just need a Christian. I guess we should talk about what—in terms of politics—being Christian means to you."

"The first rule is simple enough," Lane answered promptly. "Never confuse the two. Religion is a quest for spiritual betterment, not a ticket to political certainty." Lane's tone became wry. "Remember when Christy wanted to put the Ten Commandments in every public building in America? Wonder how he'd feel if somebody tried that with the Five Pillars of Islam.

"Faith is supposed to be redemptive, not coercive. That's what Christy misses. The Jesus I venerate taught humility and compassion." Lane sat back, coffee cup cradled in his hands. "As far as I'm concerned, all Americans should have equal rights and liabilities."

Corey covered his face in not-entirely-mock dismay. "You're *for* gay marriage?"

A smile touched the corners of Lane's mouth. "Given all we face, I don't much care about it. Here's the best solution I can give you: civil unions for any couple who wants one, gay or straight. Then let each religion define 'marriage' as it will.

"Separation of church and state means exactly that. If the Catholic Church wants to confine its marriage ceremonies to men and women, the state has no business interfering. Same with Christy's megachurch." Lane gave a fatalistic shrug. "Problem is, Christy wants to enshrine his distaste for gays in the Constitution. It's as misconceived as Prohibition and, in the end, as pointless. But I expect Christy's about to ratchet up the pressure. I don't see any way he can support you unless you cave."

The shrewd remark revealed that Lane was assessing the political dynamics more closely than Corey knew. "So," Corey asked, "what would *you* do?"

His expression grave, Lane put down his coffee cup. "That's a hard one. The stakes you and I worry most about—a new wave of terrorism, nuclear proliferation, oil dependence, military preparedness, and all the fissures of wealth, health, education, and religion—may well determine our future. You have the courage to deal with them; Marotta doesn't. And here we are talking about gay marriage."

"Because," Corey interjected bitterly, "that's what Marotta and Christy want to talk about. The difference is that Christy believes it."

Lane shrugged. "Given enough time, Christy will fade away. Remember what I said when Christy blamed 9/11 on gays, abortionists, and the ACLU?"

"Sure. That *you* blamed radical Islamists who fly airplanes into buildings."

"A lot of conservative Christians agreed, including younger evangelicals whose agenda—in matters like poverty, global warming, and AIDS in Africa—is much broader than Bob Christy's. For many of them, and for me, Christian values include respect for life, regard for diversity, and freedom to worship God as one sees fit. Bin Laden values none of these things. We need a president who knows the difference.

"*You* do. So what would you do about gay marriage?" Lane leaned forward, speaking intently. "Centuries ago, when Prince Henry of France converted to Catholicism in order to become king, he said, 'Paris is worth a mass.' Perhaps the principle still applies. It all depends on how you weigh kissing off the nomination—should it come to that—against your distaste for becoming a temporary homophobe."

Corey felt a stab of guilt. "I know what the answer should be. But sometimes giving it feels like a small death."

"Not such a small one," Lane said quietly. "Christy still doesn't know about your brother, does he?"

"No. Let alone about Clay's reaction to hearing, from Christy's own lips, that his gay English teacher deserved to die."

Lane watched his face. "Clay's not here to forgive you, or condemn you. It's for you to weigh how far your obligation to a dead brother goes. This much I know: were Clay alive, he'd fare no better under President Marotta."

Gazing at Lane, Corey saw the cool expression of a recording angel, free of malice or mercy—the look of a man whose decisions had required the death of others and knew that some choices must be made without sentiment. "You have a decision, too," Corey answered. "And yours won't keep."

Lane laughed sharply. "Spoken like a president." His face turned serious. "If you pass me by, I'll feel no rancor. But there's too much at stake for me to shrink from this. If you ask me to run with you, I'll accept."

Corey exhaled, relief and gratitude coursing through him. "Thank you, Cortland. If it comes to that, I'd be a better president with you beside me."

Lane shook his head in wonder. "That day at the White House, who'd have imagined *this* day?"

"That's easy. Neither of us."

Lane's eyelids lowered, as though he were pondering the improbabilities of life. "I do have another question, if you'd care to answer. What's happening with you and Lexie Hart?"

"This." Corey found that their conversation had, with respect to Lexie, only deepened his regrets. "An hour ago, I said I couldn't ask you to risk your life. Running for president means that there's pain, even danger I can't ask her to live with. If you love someone, I've learned, you care about more than what you need from them."

Lane smiled a little. "A pretty sentiment, Corey. I guess that's Lexie's gift to you."

"And Janice's—her parting gift. That's why I let her and Kara go."

Lane regarded him with a look of deepened comprehension. "Perhaps Ms. Hart needs something different."

Vainly, Corey wished this were not so. "I'll be in touch," he said. "Thank you, Cortland."

5

"We've got problems," Price told Governor Larkin. "Christy's already stirring up the southerners and evangelicals, saying that Blair's squishy soft on God and gays. Now Drew Tully's fomenting a rebellion in Blair's own delegation, arguing that only Grace can help other candidates win in Illinois."

It was eight A.M. in Marotta's suite on Monday, the first day of the convention. Marotta watched Larkin saw a corner off his eggs Benedict as he listened to Price with a slight, untroubled smile. "They're squeezing us," Marotta told him. "In return for supporting Blair, Christy's pushing for amendments to the platform calling for a ban on gay marriage and civil unions, teaching intelligent design in public schools, posting the Ten Commandments in federal courthouses, and outlawing stem-cell research.

"I can't sign off on all that stuff, Sam. I'd look like a total whore."

"And Christy knows that," Larkin responded with a soothing chuckle. "His game is to take down Blair or, failing that, to keep his name in play by asserting his leadership of evangelicals. And you boys know that all Christy gets out of it is a day or two of jerking you around."

"In other words," Price said, "Christy's got an excuse for supporting Grace in the vice presidential vote tonight. But there's no way he can support Grace for president unless Grace makes *him* VP, or at least caves on Christy's issues."

"Precisely." With surprising fastidiousness, Larkin dabbed his mouth with his cloth napkin. "All you and Blair have to do is come out foursquare against gay marriage *and* civil unions, and maybe 'overtly' gay teachers in the classroom if you're really feeling pressured. Then call on Grace to do the same.

"He won't, is my prediction—'heroes' don't cave in. What the hell will Christy do then?"

Marotta had the last spoonful of granola and skim milk, a staple in his relentless quest to remain as trim as Grace. "We need your help, Sam."

"And you'll get it," Larkin affirmed. "In one hour, I'm sitting down with the Georgia delegation, touting Charles's virtues."

"Beyond that," Price said, "we need your delegates to support us on forcing Grace to choose a VP, and on seating our version of the Alabama delegation."

"Alabama," Larkin said with a smile. "That was right out of a fucking banana republic, Magnus—coming up with an alternate delegation after Grace won the primary election. Sort of looked like your chief objection was to black folks voting in a Republican primary."

Price flashed him a sardonic look. "Hope you're not that easily embarrassed, Sam. Last time I looked, they could fit the blacks who voted for you in a phone booth and still have room for ten buckets of fried chicken."

Larkin waved his napkin in mock surrender. "You got me, Magnus. When they call our name tonight, Mississippi will stand tall and proud in defense of the purity of our primary process, untainted by the votes of strangers. Sort of like South Carolina."

The pointed remark put Marotta on edge. "There's one more thing we need you to do, Sam. Come out for my nomination."

Larkin spread his hands. "You want the sun, stars, and moon, Rob? Come judgment day, I'll be there. But I'm more credible speaking for Blair if I'm not in your back pocket. It's all a matter of timing. Like they say in those Cialis ads: when the time is right, I'll be ready."

The refusal was no less firm, Marotta knew, for being amiably delivered. Larkin stood. "Gotta go, boys. Got some missionary work to do on behalf of young Mr. Blair."

When he was gone, Price said sourly, "I feel better already. I still think Sam wants to be America's most powerful lobbyist. But I just figured out his second angle: he's also keeping alive the idea of forcing Grace to choose him as vice president.

"He's dreaming, of course. In the end, he'll be like Christy—nowhere else to go."

Price's cell phone rang. Marotta watched him listen, his concentration so total that his features became immobile. "No," he said slowly. "I'll handle this myself."

He stood abruptly. "Who was it?" Marotta asked.

"Our delegate hunter from Illinois. Seems like there's a delegate who needs my special attention." Price smiled. "I'll take care of the mechanics, Rob. Your job right now is a grip and grin with every delegate who wants photographic evidence of their close association with a future president. Better take a pocketful of moist towelettes."

Within an hour, Marotta was smiling at a car dealer from Provo, Utah, the first delegate in a line stretching to the back of the ballroom. "You feel like a president," the man assured him fervently. "Divinely inspired."

"YOU MAY NOT understand," Price told Walter Riggs, "just how important you are to us."

Riggs fidgeted. "I'm only a state senator," he answered, brushing a hand across the bristles of his graying crew cut.

"My motto's always been 'To stay in office, stay small.' No delusions of grandeur here."

"Some people," Price drawled, "have grandeur thrust upon them. This may be your time." Sitting back, he folded his hands across his belly. "Guess you know Drew Tully's making trouble for Governor Blair, trying to sell the notion that only Grace can ensure the reelection of you boys down the ticket. Word is, Walter, *you* may be one of the buyers."

Price watched Riggs hesitate, then decide on a show of candor. "You know everything there is to know, Magnus. So you know my district's becoming more suburban than rural. Those people don't care as much about gays as they do about promoting stem-cell research. And the women— well, seems like they're in love with Corey Grace." He grimaced in apology. "Last time, I only carried my district by about five hundred votes. Can't help but worry about losing the next one."

"I understand," Price said in a soothing tone. "But sometimes sacrifices simply must be made.

"We got two big votes tonight—one to seat our Alabama delegation, the other to force Grace to pick a running mate. Your delegation votes under the unit rule; if one more than half of you votes to seat Grace's delegation, the whole fucking delegation has to vote that way. So that one little vote has big-time power." Pausing, Price looked intently into Riggs's worried eyes. "Our head count suggests that you may be that vote. Maybe you can tell me, Walter, what you mean to do."

For an instant, the question seemed to rob Riggs of his power of speech. "I respect Senator Marotta," he said carefully. "But Senator Tully comes from my district, and he's the one who brings us federal money. No choice but to vote with him."

Price gazed at the ceiling, as though taking Riggs's dilemma to heart. "Suppose you didn't have to vote at all?"

Riggs gave him a queasy smile. "Don't see how that could happen."

"Maybe you'll get food poisoning," Price suggested. "I hear another member of your delegation is coming down with it, though he doesn't know that yet. I might could arrange for you two to order the same lunch."

Riggs looked at him like he was speaking in Swahili. "Food poisoning?" he repeated.

"Uh-huh. Or maybe cocaine poisoning." Price smiled. "Guess you know that enterprising college boy of yours has set himself up in business. Seems like those kids at Northwestern got money to burn, as it were."

Riggs's eyes flashed, a sudden mixture of anger, denial, and fear. Reaching into his suit coat, Price took out a cell phone. "In case you don't believe me, let's do a small experiment. I'll push 3 on this cell phone. When Walt Junior answers, I'll set up a buy at the restaurant he uses to sell cocaine. 'Cept the boy who shows up to meet him will be an undercover cop.

"Guess you know the jail time for dealing coke in Illinois. A whole lot longer since they passed that bill you sponsored."

Riggs stared at him, the color draining from his face. "Funny," Price remarked. "You're looking kind of sick already."

At ten a.m., Corey and Spencer walked through Central Park. The day was already so hot and muggy that by noon, Corey guessed, the asphalt path would shimmer. Corey's Secret Service detail surrounded them on all sides, trailed by a contingent of reporters. As they walked,

Spencer wiped his forehead. "Sorry," Corey said. "I was getting claustrophobic. So what's the schedule?"

"Three press conferences—undecided delegates declaring for you." Glancing over his shoulder, Spencer spoke softly. "But the guy in the Virgin Islands wants veto power over who you'd pick as governor."

Corey looked at him sharply. "Is he a crook?"

"No."

"Then that's little enough to pay."

In momentary silence, they walked toward the band shell. "Then there's the governor of Indiana," Spencer continued. "He's setting up his kid to run for the Senate. He'll trade his delegation's vote on Alabama if you give his son a nice-sounding job in your putative administration."

Corey gazed at the band shell. "The son's an idiot, right?"

"A glib idiot. But pliable. All he wants is a couple of years in Washington, occupying space. He won't do enough to fuck anything up."

"There's always room in Washington," Corey said dryly, "for a man like that. But first Indiana has to vote right."

"Understood. Which brings us to the governor of Utah."

Corey rolled his eyes. "Dumb as a plant, controls maybe three delegates, and got run out of office in the primary. Under any other circumstances, she'd be lucky to get a job in the post office."

"Under *these* circumstances," Spencer informed him quietly, "she wants to be ambassador to the United Kingdom. Rumor has it Marotta promised the U.K. to Linwood Tate. She couldn't be much worse than *that*."

All at once Corey was gripped by his sense of the

absurd; here they were in Central Park, bargaining for the presidency like rug merchants. "I don't care who Marotta's promised—I want a professional dealing with Great Britain. Maybe the Swiss can stand her: they're neutral about everything else. So what's left?"

"Requests for meetings." Spencer puffed his cheeks. "One's from the new leader of the Rainbow Republicans, hoping that you'll agree that gays deserve better than they're getting from Christy or Marotta. You're the gay Republicans' only hope."

Corey stopped, looking across the treetops at the gothic roofline of an apartment building on Central Park West. "What's your advice?"

"You already know what it is. There's no gain in meeting this guy—half the gay Republicans are so far in the closet that they hate the ones who aren't. And this guy seems so desperate to meet you that it scares me. If it leaks, Christy will go insane."

Corey folded his arms, no longer interested in architecture. At length, he directed, "Say I'll see him in private— no leaks, or our first meeting is our last. And not until after tonight." Noting Spencer's pained expression, Corey added, "Just do it, Hollis."

Spencer did not respond. "The other request," he told Corey pointedly, "is from Christy. He wants to discuss your position on gays."

"Christ," Corey said harshly. "Doesn't anyone think about anything else?"

"Apparently not. But meeting with Christy is as imperative as meeting Mr. Rainbow is gratuitous."

"First things first, then. When does Christy want to meet?"

"Two o'clock," Spencer said. "That gives you time for one more thing."

*

WITHIN MOMENTS OF entering Corey's suite, the delegate from Montana was slumped on the couch, tears running down her face.

Marilee Roach was a schoolteacher, with tightly curled hair and a round face that, when not contorted by anguish, was as pleasant as it was unremarkable. Miserable and embarrassed, she dabbed at her eyes. "I ran for delegate because I believe in you."

Corey glanced at Spencer. "Just tell me what happened," he requested gently.

"Brian—my husband—works for the state. If I vote for you, the governor says he'll be fired." Her voice became angry and despairing. "The only way to save his job is to vote for Senator Marotta."

"There's another way," Spencer suggested. "Go public."

She kept looking at Corey. "Hollis is right," he affirmed. "We can appear together at a press conference. Once we tell your story in public, the governor won't dare touch your husband's job."

As she closed her eyes, Corey fought back a pity he could ill afford. "There are also federal jobs in Montana," he promised her. "If I'm elected, I can put him out of the governor's reach for good."

The woman's eyes opened, windows to her hope and fear. "You want me to be president," Corey concluded firmly. "With your help, Marilee, I can be. I know we won't let each other down."

She summoned a tenuous smile, and slowly nodded.

For a moment, Corey imagined the sleepless night that would follow her moment of public courage, the slow diminution of the pride she would take in sharing the spotlight with him. But he could not let her picture that before it happened. "Until our press conference," he said, "we'll have someone with you—Dana Harrison. She'll help you write a statement."

The swiftness of events seemed to stun her. "For when?"

"Five o'clock." Standing, Corey took her hand in both of his. "I can never thank you enough," he said, and hurried off to meet with Christy.

CHRISTY MET HIM in the empty banquet room of a restaurant owned by Corey's friend Danny Meyer.

In the quiet of its off-hours, they sat across a table covered only by a white tablecloth. Even in such stark surroundings, Christy exuded strength and savvy. "Getting down to the end," he told Corey. "No time for dancing the minuet."

"No. There isn't."

"I guess you know I want to be vice president."

Corey mustered a wary smile. "I do now."

"And?"

Corey composed his thoughts. "Outside this door, Bob, is an army of Secret Service agents, a sky filled with helicopters, and a convention hall surrounded by cops and bomb-sniffing dogs. It's an age when no president can count on living out his term.

"Nonetheless, I want to be president. More than that, I think I should be. I have to choose the man or woman who can help me win, and who's prepared to serve if I die. That's the only basis I can live with."

Christy's own smile was a crinkling of the eyes. "If you don't win on Wednesday, you don't run in November. If you don't win both roll-call votes tonight, you don't win on Wednesday. All the rest of what you just said is superfluous."

Corey shrugged. "If Marotta wins on Wednesday, Bob,

you're neither vice president nor the voice for evangelicals in politics. Rob will cut you off at the knees."

Christy's smile diminished to a flicker. "And if I support you and get nothing for it, I'll be cutting off another part of my anatomy."

They shared a moment of silence. With seeming calm, Corey asked, "What do you want, Bob?"

"A change of heart and mind, publicly declared at a joint press conference—support for a constitutional ban on gay marriage *and* civil unions. Along with a condemnation of openly avowed homosexuals teaching in our public schools."

Corey cocked his head. "I've been curious for a while," he said at length. "Remember how we first met—or, more accurately, our first encounter?"

"Like yesterday," Christy said softly. "Only it was fourteen years ago. I was speaking at a band shell in a park, the first time you were running for Senate." Pausing, he quoted himself from memory: " 'Corey, my friend, come home—not just to Lake City, but to God.'

"A student had killed a teacher who'd made homosexual advances to him—a sad incident. But I thought such a man had no place among our youth. I still do." No trace of a smile remained on Christy's face. "There was another reason for that speech. I looked at you and, as young as you were, saw a threat to my own dream: to make the Republican Party the instrument of God.

"And here we both are, Corey. I've come to like you. But this was never about who you are as a man." Christy's voice was cool and level. "I could make you president. But I've got principles, same as you. Don't force me to help Marotta win because you're too deeply in love with yours."

Still Corey's gaze did not waver. "You'll have your

answer, Bob. But not before tonight's vote."

Christy looked back at Corey for a moment, then gave a mournful shake of his head. "Then we'll just have to see, won't we. We'll just have to see."

6

In Marotta's suite, Magnus Price saw with satisfaction that the first moments of the convention were unfolding as he had planned.

Outside Madison Square Garden, thousands of Christian demonstrators were protesting the candidacy of Corey Grace, their bright placards, provided by Price's field staff, showing on Rohr News. The party's recurring promotions for the opening-night theme, "Salute to the American Family," had been financed by Alex Rohr and featured photos of Marotta, Mary Rose, and their children in various happy moments. In stark counterpoint, Frank Flaherty interviewed the head of the National Rifle Association, who complained that despite the importance of an armed populace in the face of terrorist attacks, Corey Grace did not respect the Second Amendment right to bear arms. And then, at precisely the right moment, Mary Rose and the children entered the VIP box above the convention floor.

"Beautiful," Price said with a chuckle.

Marotta watched his wife kneel to comfort Jennifer, their four-year-old, confused and a little frightened by the orchestrated chant of "Mary Rose" arising from his delegates. "Yes," he answered softly. "She is."

Riding in his limousine, Hollis Spencer was jarred by the contrast between reality and the neatly packaged collage presented by Rohr News. As Mary Rose appeared on

Rohr, her round face reassuring in its serenity, the thud of helicopter blades sounded through his window and angry demonstrators pressed against the barricades. On his cell phone, the delegate hunter for Illinois reported, "Riggs and Statler called in sick. But we don't think they're in their rooms, Hollis. It's like they've disappeared."

A creeping dread fogged Spencer's thoughts. "What's the count in Illinois?"

"Senator Tully thinks we're one vote short."

"Call their wives," Spencer snapped. "People don't just disappear."

WATCHING MARY ROSE Marotta, Corey thought of Lexie.

He longed to call her. But there was little he could say, and nothing he could fairly ask of her. And so he watched as the camera panned the delegates: a couple of Jews in yarmulkes; a few well-dressed blacks nearly lost amid the affluent whites; senators and congressmen basking in their own prominence, grandees among their subjects. But he could already feel the sweat and tension emanating from the delegates, beset by so many vote counters that their nerves must feel raw. Side by side, the Ohio and Pennsylvania delegations—the former Corey's, the latter Marotta's—brandished their signs like primitive weapons. The sound system blared R&B and soul music chosen ostensibly to demonstrate the Republican Party's funky and festive heart, but more likely to agitate delegates already wound too tight. Then the speaker's podium caught Corey's eye: by some visual wizardry, the klieg lights angling toward it materialized a faint but discernable cross.

Corey felt a shiver pass through him: in an instant, the convention morphed from the Las Vegas Strip to a megachurch. He called Spencer in his skybox. "I'm not hallucinating, am I?"

"Nope. This is Magnus's symbolic gift to evangelicals. The party of Rob Marotta is their spiritual home."

On the giant screen behind the podium, a cartoon elephant appeared, emitting a screech so frightening that one of Marotta's kids shrank back. "Sounds like its testicles are in a vise," Corey told Spencer.

"Ours, too," Spencer said. "Gotta find those missing delegates."

Corey had never felt more useless.

SUSPENDED BETWEEN PAST and future, he watched an American Legionnaire recite the Pledge of Allegiance, stressing the words "under God" so vehemently that some delegates burst into applause. Then the Garden went dark and silent.

On the giant screen behind the podium appeared the Golden Gate Bridge. Beside the podium itself, a young violinist, caught in a single spotlight that again materialized the cross, began her haunting rendition of "Amazing Grace." In the darkness, delegates held lighters aloft; across the screen a sequence of photos showed San Franciscans with tear-streaked faces, a mother and child at a funeral, a young woman holding a picture of her father. The last photograph, taken at the memorial service, was of Marotta embracing a woman who had lost her husband.

"A touching tableau," Frank Flaherty intoned.

Corey switched the channel.

WHEN THE LIGHTS came on, CNN's camera scanned delegates in dueling caps, red for Marotta, blue for Grace; Texans in cowboy hats and denim shirts; well-groomed young women who looked like former sorority girls or debutantes; middle-aged whites who conformed to the rules as they understood them, proudly and, on occasion, bitterly; a smattering of blacks, Hispanics, Asians. And all of them would determine, perhaps as early as tonight, whether Corey Grace would become their nominee.

His cell phone rang. Certain it was Spencer, Corey anxiously pushed the talk button. "Hey," she said. "What are you up to?"

Despite his anxiety, Corey laughed with pleasure and surprise. "Channel surfing," he answered. "Life's pretty dull without you."

She was briefly silent. "I know this must be hard."

"Yeah. It is."

He imagined Lexie with him, her discerning look as she assessed his moods, at once affectionate and astute. "Would you have done anything differently?" she asked.

It was the right question. "There are things I wish I'd done better. But differently? I don't think so."

"Not even us?"

"Especially not us." He searched for the words to tell her. "How many chances do we get to love a person who's so right that she feels like home? In my life, I count just one."

"And where is she now?" Lexie asked. "Watching Mary Rose Marotta practice her First Lady smile."

"For Godsakes, Lexie—you were never meant to be like her. You can't be, and I don't want you to be." Corey spoke more softly. "You and I came to each other as adults. I fell in love with the woman you'd fought damn hard to be—with experiences very different from my own, a life of meaning that is your own. Politics is parasitic; it sucks the life out of everyone but the candidate. I don't want that for you, any more than I wanted to drag you through the past.

"South Carolina was a wake-up call for us both. I chose to run for president—not you. The price for that is mine to pay."

"Ours," she answered. "Don't you know I miss you? *And* worry for you."

"I'm not Marotta," Corey insisted. "Losing won't destroy me."

She was silent again. "I hope not, Corey. But I want you to win."

His cell phone buzzed, indicating another call coming in. Looking at the caller ID, Corey said, "I need to take this. Can I call you later?"

"My life will keep," she said with a rueful laugh. "No one's voting on it."

"I miss you, too," Corey told her, and pressed the flash button.

"We've lost Illinois," Spencer reported bluntly.

AS THE ROLL-CALL vote on Alabama began, Dana Harrison and Jack Walters showed up to watch with him.

On CNN, the party's schism was on display, the anger and distrust palpable among delegates too closely packed together or trapped in aisles jammed with security guards, police, reporters, big donors with VIP passes, and delegate hunters barking into cell phones. Answering a question, a frazzled Grace delegate snapped at Candy Crowley, "The Alabama vote is about racism. Marotta's showing America who he really is."

Jack Walters emitted a soft whistle. "Amid the pandemonium," Jeff Greenfield said on CNN, "the convention must decide which set of delegates will cast Alabama's critical forty-eight votes. And even that is complicated. Within some delegations, individual delegates are free to vote as they wish; others—such as Illinois—follow the unit rule, under which every delegate must vote with the majority regardless of his preference. So what we're seeing in many delegations are contentious mini–roll calls.

"The bitterness this generates is as obvious as the results are unpredictable. But an early clue to the outcome will be the pivotal vote from Iowa, the first delegates among Christy's disciplined cadre to tip the reverend's hand."

Walters turned to Corey. "Hollis still doesn't know which way they're going?"

"Nope. But neither do the delegates from Iowa. They're awaiting a cell-phone call from on high."

On the screen, the roll call began. *"Alaska,"* the chair of the convention called out in her rough-edged voice.

Corey's antagonist Carl Halprin, Alex Rohr's chief supporter in the Senate, proclaimed loudly, "The great state of Alaska casts its twenty-nine votes to seat Senator Marotta's delegation."

On the right corner of the screen, the number 29 appeared beneath the name Marotta. Through to Idaho, the vote proceeded as expected, with California's 173 delegates accounting for Corey's margin of sixty votes.

"Illinois."

A raddled-looking Charles Blair, shaken by the near loss of his delegation, summoned a reasonably strong voice to answer, "Illinois casts seventy-three votes to seat the Marotta delegation." At his shoulder, Senator Tully shook his head in disgust.

The tally showed Marotta thirteen votes ahead. *"Indiana."*

The head of the delegation, an NRA loyalist, said tersely, "Thirty-two votes for the Marotta delegation."

Marotta, Corey saw, was now ahead by forty-five. "It all comes down to Christy," Corey said. "If he votes with us, maybe New York will. If not, Hollis thinks Costas may cave in to Marotta."

"Iowa."

Waiting, Corey felt his fists clench. The head of the Christy delegation, a minister who looked dazed by his sudden prominence in politics, said in a shaky voice, "Iowa casts all thirty-two votes to seat Senator Grace's delegation."

Corey released a breath. "Thank God," Dana whispered without irony.

Corey's cell phone rang. "That's it," Spencer reported. "Costas just told me New York's going with us. That means we'll win with fifty votes to spare."

"What about the vote on forcing me to name a vice president?"

"Costas will support us there too, hoping for your goodwill. That leaves it up to Christy." Spencer lowered his voice. "Is Cortland Lane ready to go?"

"If need be."

Spencer was briefly silent. "If anyone can talk to Christy, Corey, it's you."

"Not now. It's his moment of maximum leverage—he'll push me again on the anti-gay stuff. I'm going to play out our game of chicken all the way to tomorrow."

"New York."

"New York," Governor Costas proclaimed on CNN, "casts its one hundred and two votes in favor of Senator Grace's delegation."

Corey's cell phone buzzed, clicked, another call coming in. "Hello," he answered.

Christy chuckled quietly. "Sweat a little?" he asked.

Corey fought back his surprise. "A little. Thanks for Alabama, by the way."

"No thanks needed. Truth is, a preacher who wants

blacks to join his flock ought not reject them at the polls. I told my people this vote was a matter of principle, and it was."

"Principles," said Corey. "Everybody ought to have some."

Dana and Jack Walters had turned from the screen, gauging Corey's expression. "Half-expected you to call me," Christy told him in a disappointed tone. "You gonna ask how I'm voting on vice president tonight?"

"I want to, Bob. But why spoil the surprise?"

Briefly, Christy laughed. "You're a hard one, Corey. I've decided to cast another vote of principle. Only this time the principle is to keep Marotta dangling.

"Your new delegates from Alabama almost offset Illinois. Tomorrow morning, having lost two roll-call votes, Marotta will need me all the more. And so will you. Do us both a favor and think on that a little."

"I'll do that," Corey promised, and Christy said good night.

THE LAST CALL, after Corey had defeated Marotta's vice presidential ploy, came from Lexie. "Congratulations again," she said. "Seems like you keep on winning."

Corey tried to decipher whether, beneath the warmth, he detected a faint note of regret. "How about you?" he asked. "Are you okay?"

"As okay as I need to be. You should know that about me by now." She hesitated, then said simply, "Sleep well, Corey. You've got another long day tomorrow."

IN SEMIDARKNESS, ROB Marotta sat on the side of the bed, Mary Rose behind him. "You should sleep," she told him.

Marotta could not respond to advice so well intended

and yet so pointless. "To have done so much," he murmured.

Mary Rose kneaded his shoulders. "You're still the favorite, Robbie."

But Marotta could not tell her what he meant. She had not, by his own wish, been with him in South Carolina.

7

THE NEXT MORNING, AFTER LABORING ON A TREADMILL at the hotel gym, Marotta went to Price's suite for breakfast.

"How are the kids?" Price asked.

"Still sleeping, most of them. Jenny had a nightmare about that goddamned elephant. Mary Rose had to get in bed with her."

"A pachyderm on steroids," Price mused. "Whose bad idea was *that*?" Picking up the remote, he said, "Word is Christy's making an announcement."

"What about?"

"Not a clue."

Coupled with a new tension around his eyes, the bald admission suggested that the strain of last night's failure was wearing on Price as well: there were too many moving parts—men with motives and ambitions of their own—for Price to feign omniscience. As though to underscore this, Christy's head and shoulders filled the screen, his pipe-organ voice betraying pleasure in his ability to command the stage.

"Our delegates have caucused," he announced. "To help us discharge our awesome task, we are inviting Senators Grace and Marotta to pray with us on bended knee for the guidance of Almighty God in selecting our nominee.

"Regardless of their answer, we will do so at noon today. We invite all Americans to watch us and, we hope, to join us in our prayers."

"No fucking way," Marotta snapped at Price. "He's pulling this stunt to seize center stage. I'll look like *his* supplicant, not God's. Next he'll want me to condemn the Teletubbies because Tinky Winky carries a purse."

Price snatched up his cell phone. "I'll call Dan Hansen," he said.

Marotta watched him listen anxiously for an answer. "Dan? Magnus here. Let me suggest that the candidates pray together in private. We'll bring Blair along, if you want."

Price listened intently. "All right," he answered coolly. "We'll wait for his call." Hanging up, he murmured, "Fucker."

"What is it?"

"Christy's gonna talk to you directly." A flush crept across his forehead. "Dan's instructions were to tell me that prayer's too grave a matter to be negotiated by functionaries."

Despite his worries, Marotta laughed.

"I DON'T GET it, Rob," Christy said over the telephone. "Seeing their leaders humble themselves before God can only be good for America's children."

"I'd be humbling myself before you, Bob."

"That part's good for my delegates," Christy responded calmly. "They want it. *I* want it. Seems like you need to do it." His voice dropped a register. "Remember South Carolina, Rob? I remember it like yesterday."

A fresh stab of fear pierced Marotta's soul. Not for the first time, he wondered whether Christy had been falsely accused and, if so, what part Price might have played. Glancing at Price, he said, "What South Carolina has to do with this escapes me."

Price's face was devoid of all expression. "Does it now?" Christy said.

Marotta's sense of foreboding deepened. "About the prayer, I'll let you know."

"IF MAROTTA DOES this," Spencer told Corey, "and you don't, Christy loses control of events. Marotta knows that. He also knows you. That's why he'll show up."

Corey shook his head. "A public prayer circle. Who'd have thought the nomination could turn on *that*?"

He drifted to the window overlooking Central Park. Condensation was forming on the glass, the thin barrier between his air-conditioning and the already searing heat of a summer morning. "I'll call Bob myself," he said.

"WELL?" CHRISTY ASKED.

"Remember my speech at Carl Cash? I said I didn't believe that God much cared about this election, and that how we live is a truer expression of faith than any prayer we can recite in public. So that's the answer I'm stuck with." Though filled with trepidation, Corey spoke evenly. "In the end, Bob, this isn't about God. It's about you and Marotta. Even if he shows up, whatever prayer Marotta recites is only as good as the man himself.

"You know the man. In exchange for an act devoid of spiritual meaning, he expects you to make him president. I don't blame you for extracting your pound of flesh. But your moment of satisfaction ends at around twelve-thirty. Marotta's begins at twelve thirty-one, and it could last a whole lot longer. "

Christy was silent. "It's not just about me," he said frankly. "It's about my people. I need to hold them. A lot of them are wondering what influence I have here on earth, and what possible good—by our lights—would come from your nomination." Christy's voice held a note of mournful resignation. "This is my way of keeping them, Corey, and you're not helping me. The time for maneuver is running out."

IN HIS SUITE at the Michelangelo, Sean Gilligan perfected the Windsor knot in his Hermès tie, thinking, as he often did, that he had exceeded the most hopeful imaginings of a Catholic boy from upstate New York whose dad worked on the ore boats that plied the Great Lakes. But then luck was a talent—as a sophomore in college, he had realized that the Republican Party could not merely become his passion, but a lucrative career. And so years of assiduous labor as a congressional staffer and party functionary—planning fund-raisers, dispensing favors, helping in campaigns, and, eventually, devising tactics—had led him to an office on K Street and, at last, to become lead partner in his own consulting firm, with friends in every nook and cranny of Washington. Gilligan had become more than a lobbyist: he was a strategic adviser.

But there were still a few powerful men, to Gilligan's regret, to whom he owed more favors than he had been able to dispense. Turning from the mirror, he glanced at the manila envelope in his open briefcase, then tried to listen to Frank Flaherty pontificating on Rohr News. "According to our sources," Flaherty said in a disparaging voice rich with satisfaction, "Senator Grace informed the reverend that he says his prayers in private, and that he would not presume on God to pick a favorite." Flaherty's mouth twitched. "Little wonder, some would say."

When the telephone rang, Sean knew who it was. "I know," he said. "Grace is fucking up."

"Man can't help it," his patron said. "Time to save him from himself."

*

SITTING AT THE round table in Hollis Spencer's suite, Gilligan slid the envelope across its lacquered surface. "What's this?" Spencer asked.

Gilligan hesitated, unhappy in a role he thought he had transcended. "Something you didn't get from me."

Spencer opened the envelope. Clipped together were photographs, credit card receipts, and, knitting them into a damning narrative, a report with no attribution of authorship. Staring at a photograph, Spencer murmured, "Blair."

"Queer as a three-dollar bill." Gilligan put his finger on the edge of a particularly telling photograph. "This guy met Blair on nearly every trip he took out of state. A couple of us wondered why his wife never came to governors' conferences. This one picture clears that up all by itself."

"Who is he?"

"His name's Steven Steyer. Used to be a fitness trainer at the gym in Chicago where Blair worked out." Gilligan spoke with mild distaste. "Two years ago, Blair gave him a cushy job in Springfield—'adviser to the Governor's Council on Physical Fitness.' Looks like he gave his best advice at night."

Impassively, Spencer perused the pictures and then scanned the report. "This trick is so seamy," he remarked, "that it's almost quaint. Whose idea was this?"

"A secret admirer of Senator Grace's. That's all I'm at liberty to say."

Spencer looked up from the photographs, his eyes cold with contempt. "*You're* no admirer of Corey's, Sean. And neither are your pals. Corey's everything you can't stand, a senator who deplores the world you operate in." Spencer's voice hardened. "This is about knifing Blair. Whoever sent you wants Corey's fingerprints on the knife.

Risky for us, *and* for you. Just who do you owe that much to?"

Though stung, Gilligan merely shrugged. "Not your concern, Hollis. Your mission is to beat Marotta. And if you don't use this and Marotta wins the nomination, the Democrats will use it to defeat him. You owe it to your candidate—not to mention your party—to burst Blair's bubble now."

Head raised, Spencer regarded him over his reading glasses. Gilligan imagined the progression of his thoughts, including one that said silence was best. "You've done your job," Spencer told him. "Why don't you just run along."

SPENCER FOUND COREY in his suite, studying his notes for an informal talk to undecided delegates. CNN droned in the background. "What's up?" Corey said with mild irritation. "I'm running late."

"This won't keep." Tossing the envelope in front of Corey, he said, "I don't want you to open this. I'll tell you what's inside—proof that Charles Blair has a gay lover on his payroll."

Corey felt the color drain from his face. "Where'd this come from?"

"Sean Gilligan gave it to me. He's running this nasty errand for someone else."

Corey tried to sort out his emotions, ranging from pragmatism to wariness to a deep sadness, despite everything, for Blair and his family, the victims of his weakness and folly. "It's not the Democrats," he said at length. "They'd save this for October. And it's sure as hell not Marotta."

"Hardly. Used right, this could blow him out of the water—the anti-gay crusader who picked a pansy for his running mate. The evangelicals would explode."

Hearing a familiar voice, Corey glanced at CNN and saw Marotta standing in front of Christy's delegates. "Please tell us, Senator," a delegate implored him, "what reason you'd give our Lord for admitting you to heaven."

Marotta lowered his eyes. "I wouldn't give Him a reason," he answered. "I'd simply ask for mercy, because of what our Lord Jesus Christ did for all of us at Calvary."

His questioner nodded vigorously. In that instant, Corey wanted to take Marotta down by any means at hand. "I can't let him become president, Hollis."

"Blair's fucked," Spencer said matter-of-factly. "If we don't leak this, someone else will. What bothers me is that whoever went to all this trouble has an agenda that predates Blair's selection. And we don't know what it is." Spencer's expression clouded. "If we were to leak this, and it was traced to us, you could be as tarnished as Marotta."

On CNN, Marotta stood beside Christy, brandishing a Bible. "I believe as Bob does," he said emphatically. "The only rules you need to build a decent society are right here in this book. That's how I know that homosexuality is a sin; that gay marriage and its surrogates violate God's law and send the wrong message to our young people."

Corey watched Christy summon a halfhearted smile, then turned from the screen. "How long do I have to decide?" he asked.

"Hours, at most. If Christy goes over to Marotta, *you* may be over. After the undecideds, your next meeting is with Mr. Rainbow. I'll call him up to cancel."

Corey headed for the door, then turned. "No," he said. "I'll see him, however briefly."

"*Why*, for Godsakes?"

"It's a debt I have. To someone I used to know."

On CNN, Marotta knelt with Christy in a prayer circle, beseeching God for help.

8

EVEN AS HE GREETED THE NEW LEADER OF THE
Rainbow Republicans, Corey was impatient for the meeting to be over. He had made little headway with the undecided delegates, and his decision about Blair's secret
life—perhaps a poisoned chalice but also, quite possibly,
his only hope—could not wait. When his new supplicant
introduced himself, Corey waved him to a chair with
minimal warmth.

Jay Cantrell was a handsome man, surprisingly young,
with jet-black hair, an athletic bearing, and dark, perceptive eyes that signaled his awareness of Corey's mood. "I
won't waste your time, Senator. But at least you've been
decent on our issues. Christy and Marotta are scapegoating us—Christy because he believes in it, Marotta because
he'll do whatever he needs to.

"I know you're under pressure to join the club. I
implore you—please don't."

Beneath Cantrell's poise and discipline, Corey sensed
his desperation to be heard. Bluntly, Corey asked, "Why
do you perform this thankless task? You're dealing with
people who hate you not for who you are, but *what* you
are. Why bother being a Republican at all?"

"Because I am," Cantrell answered promptly. "There
are millions of gays who, as people, are deeply conservative. Why should we have to be Democrats?" His tone,
though urgent, was even. "A lot of this issue is personal.
Once a person learns that someone they care about is gay,

their prejudice begins to soften. And every significant movement for human progress in our history—women's suffrage, civil rights, interracial marriage—needed supporters in both parties. If we can make our party more accepting, even at the margins, then all the pain involved will be worthwhile.

"That brings us back to you, Senator. The Christian conservatives want you to embrace their homophobia. But your instincts are inclusive—you've shown that in your political *and* personal lives. The choice you make now is as defining for you as it is critical for us. I pray that you don't throw us overboard."

Listening, Corey felt conflicting emotions—guilt about his brother, sympathy for Cantrell's argument, annoyance at the young man's unsubtle reference to Lexie, and ambivalence about Blair. With as much dispassion as he could muster, Corey asked, "What do you propose I do about reality?"

"What you have been doing. You don't have to be a crusader for gay rights. Pick a Christian conservative for vice president if you have to." Cantrell leaned forward, his eyes locking Corey's. "That would give you leeway to gradually change the tone. All we need is for you to allow Americans to let us join their family. Besides, I think this issue is as important to you as it is to me. Or should be, at least."

Discomfited and annoyed, Corey decided to conclude the meeting at once. "Thank you," he said coolly, and stood to signal the man's dismissal. "To my regret, we're out of time."

Cantrell made no move to leave. He inhaled, as if preparing himself for a difficult moment, and then removed a letter from the pocket of his suit coat. "Until now," he said, "I wasn't sure I'd ever do this."

Reaching up, he placed the envelope in Corey's hand.

The only words on it were "For Corey Grace." But even after thirteen years, Corey knew the handwriting at once. With clumsy fingers, he took the letter from the envelope and read its first line.

By the time you read this, I'll be dead.

Corey sat, briefly closing his eyes, then read on. *Something happened between me and my roommate. I can't face Mom and Dad. But especially I can't face you. I can't let myself embarrass you, or be used against you by people like that Reverend Christy.*

This is my way out. I found out I don't belong here. I don't know where I belong—nowhere, I guess. I'm disgusted at myself, and too confused to go on. I just can't live like this.

I love you. You've always been a good big brother to me. It's not your fault I could never be like you.

At the bottom, in handwriting so shaky that the name was barely legible, his brother had scrawled *Clay.*

When Corey looked up, Cantrell's face was drawn. "Where did you get this?" Corey asked.

Cantrell held his gaze. "He left it in his bag."

"You're 'Jay,'" Corey said slowly. "The cadet he wrote me about."

"His roommate," Cantrell corrected. "The cadet who chose to live."

The last phrase, Corey perceived, explained much about who Cantrell had become. With unspoken dread, Corey held up the letter and asked, "How did it even come to this?"

"From my first day at the Academy," Cantrell answered in a bitter tone, "this senior made me his special project."

"Cagle," Corey said.

For an instant, Cantrell looked startled; then he slowly nodded. "Once you show weakness, some people enjoy finding out how much you can take. But Cagle was different.

"Most seniors have gotten over the fun of hazing—even the sadists who like singling out the weakest link. But Cagle had 'gaydar.' He hated me for being what he knew I was, and Clay for sticking by me." Briefly, Cantrell touched his eyes. "I warned Clay to keep his distance, not to befriend me. He wouldn't listen. Maybe he knew I didn't want him to.

"We became Cagle's only targets. He'd come to our room at three A.M., wake us up for inspection. One night he tore our room up, supposedly searching for alcohol, and then kept us awake to clean up after him. At mealtime he made us stand at attention, answering question after question so we didn't have time to eat. He forced us to clean the latrines with toothbrushes, scrubbing on our hands and knees while he stood over us screaming that we'd missed a spot. Day after day, our only question was *what* he'd do to torture us, not whether." Cantrell stared at the carpet. "It was sick, and I think most people sensed it. It was like Cagle put all his fear and hatred into forcing us to leave. But none of his classmates wanted to be a rat. So it just went on and on and on."

Corey shook his head. "Then why on earth did you let him catch you having sex?"

"I didn't know," Cantrell answered miserably. "I mean, I knew about myself. But not Clay.

"That night Cagle woke us up after midnight, once again peppering us with questions and complaints until we were exhausted. I was ready to break. When he finally left, I started crying." Cantrell paused, then continued in a monotone: "Clay put his arms around me. He was afraid, too, he said—afraid of failing, of what his parents would say, of letting you down. 'If it weren't for Corey,' he told me, 'I wouldn't be here. I'm only here because he helped me.'"

"So he knew?" Corey said quietly.

Cantrell did not seem to hear. "Pressed against him, I felt myself get aroused, and then I realized he felt it, too. 'It's all right,' he told me. 'It's all right.'" Cantrell's eyes shut. "For that one moment, Clay made it all right.

"I forgot about everything but that. And then Cagle threw the door open and caught us in the beam of his flashlight. It was as though he knew that it would happen," Cantrell finished softly. "They called Clay's death a suicide. I still think of it as murder."

"Murder?" Corey said with equal quiet. "If so, there's blame to go around."

Cantrell still stared at the carpet. "Cagle shouldn't be an air force officer," he said.

"He's not. He hasn't been for thirteen years." When Cantrell looked up at him, Corey said, "Once I became a senator, I got a seat on the Armed Services Committee. I took an interest in Cagle's career. So did a powerful friend of mine. Cagle found it convenient to leave."

Cantrell's face registered surprise, then satisfaction. "Good."

"Maybe for the air force," Corey answered. "I found it did very little good for me. The person I was angriest at wasn't so easy to get rid of."

Cantrell studied him in silence. They were no longer senator and supplicant, Corey felt, but two strangers uncomfortably bound by guilt and sorrow, and its claim on their very different lives. "Would you have accepted him, Senator?"

"When he was alive? I guess so. I certainly accepted him once he was safely in death's closet."

The comment, no less corrosive for Corey's flatness of

tone, caused Cantrell to stare at the letter. "What will you do with this?" he asked.

Corey thought first of his brother and then, unavoidably, of Rob Marotta, Bob Christy, Charles Blair, and, last of all, his parents. "Other than wish you'd never given it to me?" he answered. "At this particular moment, I honestly don't know."

"How was Mr. Rainbow?" Spencer asked Corey.

Corey sat at the table in Spencer's suite, the manila envelope so damning to Blair between them. "Let's talk about Blair."

"Let's talk about the nomination. As I see it, your choices come down to this: out Blair or accept Christy's demands about gays—or both. Unless you want to take this to Blair and warn him to withdraw."

"I can't do that," Corey said flatly. "It'll look like *we're* the ones who had him followed. I've got no debt to Blair that justifies that risk."

Spencer paused, looking at Corey more closely. "Are you okay?"

"I'm just tired. So let's get this done. I can't see outing Blair ourselves—as you point out, we don't know where this came from. I don't want our fingerprints on it."

"I've thought about that. Why not give it to Mr. Rainbow? He'll know what to do, and he's got to be sick of closeted gays who play the homophobe card."

"No," Corey said softly.

Spencer eyed him across the table, as though waiting for an explanation. "Think about it," Spencer urged. "Now or later, Blair's toast. Why give this switch-hitting Judas a temporary reprieve at the risk of making Rob Marotta—a morally challenged opportunist who trashed both you and Lexie—president of the United States?

"Sometimes the things we don't want to do are necessary. Do you want to be president or a fucking plaster saint?"

Corey thought of the letter in his pocket. "I'm not going to play someone else's game, Hollis. Give Gilligan back his file, with instructions to tell whoever sent him we're not interested."

"So you're not doing *anything*," Spencer burst out in frustration.

Corey felt a genuine sympathy: Spencer did not know, and Corey would not tell him, the reasons he was acting as he must. "Oh, I'm doing something. If you're right, someone whose motives are obscure is desperate to take down Blair—now, not later.

"If we don't bite, they'll do something else. The balloting starts in about twenty-eight hours; by that time, we'll know what it is."

"By that time," Spencer responded, "Christy may have put Marotta over the top. What do you mean to do for *him*?"

"Nothing," Corey said. "Except to tell him that myself."

COREY AND CHRISTY sat facing each other, three feet apart. "This *is* a surprise," Christy told him. "Is there reason to hope you've seen the light?"

"This is about something else, Bob." Corey took the letter from his coat pocket. "I want you to read this."

Christy looked at Corey more closely. Raising his eyebrows, he fished the reading glasses out of his shirt. "What is it?"

"My brother's suicide note."

Christy's expression froze, as though perceiving something in Corey that was alien and new. With obvious reluctance, he began to read. In the time it took for him to finish, Christy's features sagged. For the first time, he looked old.

"That day in the park," Corey told him, "my brother was there, too."

Christy shook his head, the movement slow and heavy. "How you must hate me," he said after a time. "And how you must have hated pretending otherwise."

"I did hate you," Corey said simply. "But not as much as I despised myself. He was my brother, and I missed the most important thing about him. If I hadn't, nothing you said or did would have wound up in a suicide note."

Gingerly, as though passing a fragile china cup, Christy put the letter back in Corey's hands. "What do you want from me, Corey?"

"Nothing."

Christy shook his head, his expression bleak. "No, you want something. Unless this moment is pleasure enough."

Corey shrugged. "It'll have to do. I'm not going to use this against you. There won't be a bathetic press conference where I exploit my brother's death to 'humanize' my position on gay rights. I don't even expect you to soften; the respect I've conceived for you stems from the fact that you believe in what you say." Corey paused, his voice quiet but firm. "All you need to know is that I can't go with you on this—now, or ever. If there *is* a God, which I sincerely wonder about, I think He judges both of us more harshly than He judges Clay. Or maybe we just judge ourselves. Whatever the case, for me to scapegoat people like my brother because of your beliefs would only make things worse."

Christy gazed at him without speaking, as though the finality of Corey's words made any response superfluous. "So do whatever you need to do," Corey told him, and let himself out.

9

By five o'clock, two hours before the Tuesday night session was to open, Corey and Senator Drew Tully were plotting how to crack Blair's hold on the Illinois delegation.

His broad face resembling slabs of granite, Tully took a swift gulp of Scotch. "With Riggs and Statler I could have done it. But now they're supposedly so sick from 'food poisoning' that they've scurried home, replaced by a couple of Blair's toadies.

"No question that Blair has leapfrogged me in clout—I may be on the Appropriations Committee, but now my delegation is imagining *him* as president, for chrissakes. The idea of Blair making life-and-death decisions makes me want to puke—if I could break that twit, I would. He's just so fucking 'perfect.' "

"Keep trying," Corey urged. "And if you think I can make a difference by talking to a delegate, just call." He placed a hand on Tully's shoulder. "This much I'm sure of, Drew—I'm a hell of a lot more likely to be president than Charles Blair ever will be."

Looking doubtful, Tully nodded, then tossed back his remaining Scotch.

The next two hours passed in skirmishes. At the risk of becoming a party pariah, an aging delegate from Missouri—pledged to Marotta but not bound by state law—announced that she would vote for Corey because of his stand on stem-cell research. "My husband has Alzheimer's," she said at a press conference. "God doesn't mean real people to suffer for the sake of a speck in a petri dish." But a few minutes later, one of Corey's delegate hunters, desperately seeking votes, was booed at a meeting of the Idaho delegation. Then Rohr News reported rumors that Bob Christy would pledge his delegates to Marotta.

About Blair, Spencer reported to Corey, he heard no rumors at all.

And so the delegate hunters, in Spencer's account, were hunkered down in trench warfare, inveigling undecided delegates who wanted favors both trivial and profound: Super Bowl tickets, dinner with Lexie, a joint appearance with Corey on *Larry King Live,* a round of golf with a former president too old to walk. Then there was Harold Simpson, the pompous and venal congressman from Oklahoma, who, though leaning toward Marotta, proposed to barter his vote for a vacancy on the Supreme Court.

"Try the court of appeals," Corey instructed Spencer. "No way I could put him on the big Court."

A few minutes later, Spencer called back. "Simpson's not biting," he told Corey. "He insists on calling you directly."

His temper fraying, Corey glanced at his watch. "Does he now," Corey said. "Then I hope he enjoys our talk."

When Corey's cell phone rang, Simpson said bluntly, "You need me, and so does the Supreme Court. I can bring a lot of real-world experience."

"I'm sure you can," Corey said. "So let's review what the real world looks like.

"In the real world, you've got cash and favors from military contractors spilling out of your pockets. If I decide to make a lousy nomination, I'll at least want it to stick. Yours won't—the Democrats would sink you like a bagful of dead cats.

"If Marotta told you anything different, he's lying. But he hasn't—or else you wouldn't be coming to me. So take the court of appeals or the hell with you."

"Are you trying to piss me off?" the congressman said loudly.

"I don't care enough to try. If I become president, you won't have to like *me*. But I damn well better like *you*." Corey lowered his voice. "Don't waste my time with hurt feelings, Harold. Just give Hollis your answer."

Hanging up, Corey realized there was sweat on his forehead.

He inhaled, still for a moment, the nearest thing to meditation he could manage.

The convention had started. On CNN, a convention film on volunteerism—entitled *People Who Care* and featuring Mary Rose Marotta reading to preschoolers—was followed by Mary Rose's well-timed nightly entrance. *This is a parody,* Corey thought to himself. *It simply can't be real.* Then the orchestrated chants began: "Mary Rose, Mary Rose, Mary Rose . . ."

Outside the convention, demonstrators had gathered to protest the war and the power of the Christian Right, while at the podium Senator Lynn Whiteside, one of Corey's supporters, tried to pick her way through the minefield of stem-cell research. "Though we may disagree about issues," she ventured gamely, "we are united in our love of God."

On the convention floor, the members of several delegations—some pledged to Christy, others to Marotta—stood up, turning their backs on her. One, an elderly man in a red hat that sported an elephant trunk, fell to his knees to pray, tears streaming down his cheeks.

Corey took out his cell phone and called the head of his Secret Service detail. "I need some fresh air," he said.

DRESSED IN JEANS and a polo shirt and shepherded by Secret Service agents wearing casual clothes, Corey edged into the crowd of demonstrators pressing against the barricades surrounding Madison Square Garden.

These particular demonstrators were young and disaffected—angry at Corey's party over the war, the environment, and its opposition to abortion and gay rights. But what unsettled Corey most was the sheer irrelevance of the rhetoric inside the Garden to anything that addressed the quality of these young people's futures. He looked around him at the placards—"End Ecoterrorism, Defeat the GOP" and "Iraq—25,000 Americans Dead or Maimed, 600,000 Iraqis Dead" and "Protect Our Fighting Men—Uphold the Geneva Convention" and "Jesus Supports Universal Health Care, Not Tax Cuts for the Wealthy" and "Human Rights Means Gay Rights." Two thoughts struck him: that the world of politics was far more complex than those protestors could ever imagine, and that politics as currently practiced richly deserved their hatred and contempt. Though the press of bodies was so close that his shoulders touched theirs, no one seemed to notice him.

Reaching the metal barricades, Corey faced a line of police officers in gas masks. Two Secret Service men were at his back; on one side a tall, awkward-looking young woman held a sign reading "Let Us In"; on the other, a skinny kid with intense dark eyes shouted, "Fuck God, fuck God, fuck God" so loudly that the muscles of his throat strained and his voice nearly drowned out the throb of chopper blades. The target of his catcalls, Corey saw, was a line of delegates, their faces stony and their eyes focused straight ahead, being channeled through an entrance by security guards. Once inside, they would add this experience to their list of grievances against the philistines who opposed the Republican Party, redoubling their efforts to purge America of influences so alien. The barricades, Corey decided, were a metaphor.

Trapped amid the angry, thwarted, and intemperate, Corey waited until the boy next to him had fucked God so many times that he had shouted himself hoarse. "Think they heard you?" Corey asked.

The boy turned to Corey with a look of tension and residual hostility. "They don't see us, they don't hear us—they only hate us. They're no different than Al Qaeda."

This would not be a Hollywood moment, Corey thought, where the candidate circulated among a restive crowd, spreading hope and understanding. That process, were it possible, would take years—and a president far different from what Magnus Price meant to give them. "They don't know you," Corey answered. "You don't know them. And tomorrow it'll be a little worse."

The boy stared at him in sudden recognition. "What the hell are *you* doing here?" he asked.

"Escaping the bubble. It's as insane in there as it is out here."

The boy shook his head. "*You* have all the power. No one listens to us."

The reasons for that, Corey knew, were too complex to convey with a facile answer. "*I* would," he answered. "But you'll have to devise a better slogan."

Torn between hostility and confusion, the boy did not answer. "Good luck," Corey said. Turning, he left behind the heat and sweat and press of bodies, the shouts of demonstrators, the thump of chopper blades.

*

OVER THE PAST hour, Corey discovered, nothing had changed. Blair's secret remained a secret; the rumors about Christy supporting Marotta remained rumors. The convention speaker appearing on Corey's television, a black fundamentalist minister, had been selected by Magnus Price to fuse symbolic diversity—the better to expunge Marotta's racist smears against Lexie in South Carolina— with a denunciation of gay marriage fiery enough to please evangelicals. On Rohr News, the cameras panned frequently to Mary Rose Marotta and her children, the human faces of the party's "Salute to the American Family." Added to the tumult outside the convention, Blair's potential ruin, and his brother's thirteen-year-old suicide note, this choreographed display of hucksterism and hypocrisy deepened Corey's despair. With a resolve no less emotional for its suddenness, he called Lexie.

"You watching?" he asked.

"On and off. There's a limit to what I can stand."

"I don't know how to express this, Lexie, except to simply say it. I want you here with me."

For a moment, Lexie was quiet. "What is it? Are you so convinced you'll lose that whatever you do no longer matters? Or are all those shots of Mary Rose getting to you?"

There was just enough truth in this to give him pause. "I may well lose," he admitted. "And looking at Mary Rose makes me want to scream. But there's more to it than that.

"A lot's happened to me today, more than I have time to tell you. So this may sound selfish. But I'm so much better *with* you that it hurts—I think more clearly, perceive more, face the facts more honestly. I miss that, just like I miss that jolt that comes from looking at you. You've screwed up being alone for me." He paused, then let the rest spill out. "For me, there's never been anyone like you. I don't think there ever will be. I want a life with you."

For a time, Corey's answer was more silence. "I can't be a guest star," she said evenly, "coming in and out of your life, depending on your needs and your ambitions. It's just too hard for me." Repressed feeling broke through her efforts to speak with self-control. "You still want to be president. I'm still black, and I still used to be a heroin addict. Nothing's changed except that you need me."

Glancing at CNN, Corey saw Mary Rose whispering in her daughter's ear. "What if I want to marry you," he said abruptly.

Lexie's laugh was soft, yet astonished. "You *have* had a bad day. By tomorrow, you'll want a child with me."

"Or two," Corey answered. "I admit it's been a difficult day. But one thing's blindingly clear: I don't want to be president without you, and I don't want a life without you . . ."

"You're in the middle of a crisis," she protested, "and suddenly you're talking about marriage, even a family, when we haven't seen each other for months. What am I supposed to think?" Emotion made her speak more quickly. "I still love you, all right? No matter what happens, I believe I always will. But it's one thing to marry a senator, another to marry a president. A call like this isn't fair to me."

Corey felt his frustration rise. "You don't want to be just a guest star in my life. You can't deal with the idea of marriage. Where does that leave you?"

"Waiting out the convention." Lexie's voice softened. "Which, after all, is one of the most important events in your life."

Suddenly, Corey sensed that she was arguing with herself, and that it was best that he stay silent. After a long pause, she asked, "You *really* want me there?"

"Yes."

More silence. "This is crazy," she said. "But if you can find me a hotel room, I can find myself an airplane. I'll have time to regret it later."

"SHE'S COMING?" SPENCER asked.

Corey pictured Spencer in his skybox, fretfully distracted from the madness unfolding below. "She's coming," Corey affirmed.

"Then you know what I'm obliged to say. If Lexie shows up, it's another signal to social conservatives that you're not really one of them."

"Look, I've just refused to sign off on Christy's anti-gay agenda. After *that*, Lexie's arrival won't matter all that much. Except to me."

"Except to Christy," Spencer said tiredly. "I just heard that he's planning to hold out through tomorrow night's first ballot. If Lexie appears, loaded down with all that stem-cell baggage, Christy may lose control of his delegates. This impulse of yours could cost you the nomination."

For an instant, Corey wondered what he might have done had he known of Christy's decision. But this was the first down payment on his plea to Lexie, and he could not, would not, turn back. "I want her at the Garden," Corey answered, "in time for the first ballot. Tell Jack to find her a room."

10

"ROHR'S THE ONE," HIS PATRON HAD INSTRUCTED Gilligan. "He's got too much invested in Marotta to let him go down the drain. Besides, the story's even more fatal to Blair if it comes from the right-wing media."

Over breakfast, Gilligan pondered this. His patron was a shrewd man, but as Grace's reaction had proved, politics practiced under such excruciating pressure was far more art than science, governed by motives too complex to predict—especially those of Marotta and Price. Nevertheless, there was one thing he felt certain of: before tonight's balloting, the destinies of several men would be altered by what he was about to do.

With deep misgivings, he picked up the phone and called Alex Rohr.

TOO MUCH BUSINESS, Price thought, was coming to him directly. It was Wednesday: with so little time until the balloting began, those delegates in a position to bargain insisted on leaving nothing to chance. In the last hour he'd promised to construct a dam; threatened to unleash an IRS audit; promised an ex-officeholder a plum job lobbying for auto manufacturers; given away his own Super Bowl tickets; and confronted a state senator with political ruin. And now Congressman Harold Simpson of Oklahoma, unctuous and borderline corrupt, was back, pimping his endorsement in exchange for a seat on the United States Supreme Court. "Grace has promised me the court of appeals," Simpson said without discernible shame. "That's where I'm perched unless Rob does better."

Nine o'clock in the morning, Price noticed, and the armpits of his dress shirt were already soaked through. "Harold," he promised, "you'll have the second vacancy."

Price's cell phone clicked; a quick look at caller ID showed Alex Rohr's phone number. "Not the first?" Simpson was asking testily.

"Those justices are fucking *old*," Price snapped. "One of them's eighty-six; another's failing mentally; another's had a bout with cancer. Just keep yourself out of trouble long enough for two of them to retire or expire."

Hitting the flash button, he answered Rohr's call. "What is it, Alex?"

"More trouble than you know. You fucked up big-time, Magnus."

ROB MAROTTA HAD promised Mary Rose that they could take the kids on a Circle Line boat around Manhattan. Though planned as a photo op—partly to display Marotta's confidence, partly to depict his familial devotion on the defining day of his candidacy—it was important to Mary Rose, a reward to the kids for playing their stressful role in a pageant the youngest boy and girl barely understood. And so Price's summons for a private meeting provoked in Marotta both exasperation and anxiety. When Price opened the door to his suite, Marotta shut the door behind him and asked, "What the hell is wrong?"

Sitting down, Price looked shaken. "Blair."

In an instant, Marotta felt anxiety become dread. "What about him?"

"Sit down," Price demanded. "Then call Mary Rose."

Marotta knew better than to quarrel. Phoning his wife,

he said, "There's no time to explain, but you'll have to go alone. Tell the kids I'll make it up to them."

Even as he spoke, he knew that Mary Rose shared his thought: the kids were too accustomed to such promises. "There's a problem," he added hastily. "I don't know how bad yet."

"I'm sorry," she answered in an even tone that did not conceal her disappointment. "Is there anything I can do?"

"Just give them a nice morning." Marotta paused, acutely aware of Price's presence, then finished: "I love you, M.R."

Getting off, Marotta stared at Price so fixedly that, for once, Price looked daunted. "Blair's gay," he said in a monotone. "He's been sucking or fucking some fitness trainer he sequestered on his payroll. Alex has got documentation, pictures, credit card receipts—everything the media needs to put this out today."

Marotta felt a sudden wave of nausea, leaving him cold and clammy. With the discipline of a lifetime in politics, he tried to break this disaster into its component parts. "Where did Alex get it?" he asked.

"From Sean Gilligan. But Sean claims it came to him anonymously."

"Do you believe that?"

"No. But that's not the immediate problem." Price's speech was jittery. "Rohr's not even telling his own newspeople—as far as he's concerned, Blair's safely in the closet. But whoever gave this stuff to Gilligan has twelve hours left to fuck us. Once he realizes Rohr's covering up Blair's not so little secret . . ."

Price's voice trailed off, as though the potential consequences were too ruinous to articulate. "He just sat here and *lied* to us," Marotta said angrily. "If the Christian conservatives find out, they'll pull the rug out from under

Blair *and* me. I'd be the guy who gave them a gay candidate for vice president."

"Blair has to go," Price said flatly. "The only question is how we do that without giving Grace the nomination."

"Blair goes *now,* dammit. We'll say his family had a change of heart."

"Then you can kiss off Illinois," Price countered. "If Blair withdraws today, Drew Tully will take the entire delegation over to Grace."

Marotta felt their careful calculus spinning out of control. Every decision they made had consequences no one could anticipate; every decision seemed to pose a choice between victory and integrity. "Maybe we make a deal with Costas," Marotta said at last, "and roll him out at a press conference. That'll distract the media. If someone outs Blair after that, he's already off the ticket."

"You'd only be trading Illinois for New York," Price responded. "The Bible-thumpers don't trust Costas at all, and even if Blair's gone, finding out your first choice was a screaming fag will rile them up still more—especially Christy's people. Then there's Larkin. If we drop Blair now, *he'll* press his case to be your VP."

"Fuck Larkin," Marotta said with quiet vehemence. "The oily bastard owes us—*he's* the one who sold us Blair in the first place."

For a moment, Price's expression became enigmatic. "Yeah," he said. "I remember. But Sam may not see it that way. He may even try to cut a deal with Grace."

Marotta stood. "So we're screwed no matter what we do—is *that* what you're saying?"

"Maybe." Price's voice was tight, its register higher than normal. "Suppose we prop up Blair for another eleven hours or so, try and keep this together long enough to win on the first ballot. *Then* we'll cut Blair's balls off."

"How does *that* work?"

"It's a risk." Price dabbed at his forehead, seeming to think as he spoke. "We go to Costas in confidence, tell him Blair's got problems, and promise him vice president if he helps deliver his folks. The one condition is that he tells absolutely no one until we've sewed up the nomination. Costas will take that deal, I'm sure of it. That way you've held Illinois *and* added New York."

"And suffer through the next twelve hours with two vice presidents?" Marotta sat down again. "The other problem is sitting on Blair's secret. Whoever's after him has got twelve hours to go public."

For a moment Price propped his chin on his clasped hands, eyes half shut. "Suppose Alex tells Gilligan that Rohr News is outing Blair tonight—and then doesn't. When the balloting begins, Blair's still in the closet."

Marotta sat down heavily, tempted, yet troubled by the risks inherent in such duplicity. "Let's call Costas," he said. "Then we'll go from there."

DESPITE GOVERNOR COSTAS'S patrician features, the look of perplexity in his large brown eyes put Marotta in mind of a handsome but bewildered frog. "You're dumping Blair?" he said in wonder.

"It's confidential," Price said coolly. "This is so closely held Blair doesn't know yet. But I guarantee he'll step aside."

Pensive, Costas looked from Price to Marotta, as though his antennae had picked up something feral. "You're not telling him," he said flatly.

"He doesn't deserve the courtesy. He lied to us, and we need his delegates. The question is whether you can bring us *yours*."

Marotta watched several emotions play across Costas's

features—caution, interest, doubt, and, regarding Blair's secret, a mixture of curiosity and dread. "I feel like I'm walking across someone's grave," he said.

Marotta leaned forward. "It can't be helped, George. Magnus's question stands: can you deliver your delegates?"

Costas blinked. "I think so. But Grace has a lot of supporters, some of whom don't like you much. It would help to tell my delegates I'll be your nominee—"

"You won't be if we throw away Illinois," Price cut in. "This is a test of your leadership, George. Convince your people that endorsing Senator Marotta is the best thing for New York."

A frown drew down a corner of Costas's expressive mouth. "The only way they'd believe me is if they knew what I can't tell them. Come November Rob won't carry New York. Grace at least has a chance, and my delegates know that. You're putting me in a catch-22."

"Look—" Marotta began.

Holding up a hand, Price signaled for his candidate's silence. Softly, he asked Costas, "Do you want to be vice president?"

Costas nodded. "Yes."

"Then listen well, Governor. You look at yourself and imagine a vice president, even a president. The party's leaders look at you and see a pussy. This is the only chance you'll ever have."

Inwardly, Marotta flinched, not only at hearing the truth so brutally delivered, but from imagining Price's private estimate of Marotta himself. And yet he himself held Costas's eyes, then nodded.

The governor's gaze broke. "Give me an hour," he said. "I need to talk with Louise."

*

WITHOUT PREFACE, PRICE removed the contents of the manila envelope and spread the photographs in front of Charles Blair. For an instant, Blair stared at them and then, though it made no sound, his mouth began working. "You're dead," Price told him. "The only question is whether you're roadkill or we arrange a decent embalming."

A wet sheen moistened Blair's eyes, as though he'd been stung by a blow across the face. "What do you want?" he managed.

"You as my love slave, Charles. You'll withdraw whenever I tell you. If that's two hours from now, it is. But my current preference is to sit on this for a day, so that you can hold your delegates." Price's voice dripped with loathing and disgust. "You'll have to act your little heart out, Charlie. But God knows you're good at *that*."

Blair closed his eyes. "I'm sorry . . ."

"'I'm sorry,'" Price mimicked. "'Sorry I lied to you, Magnus.' 'Sorry I may have cost Rob the nomination.' 'Sorry I gulled my wife into thinking I was straight.' 'Sorry I put some dimwit body builder on the public dime so I could fuck him in the ass.' You're the sorriest piece of shit I've ever seen in politics. But not as sorry as you will be unless you deliver your delegation to my candidate.

"If you don't, Alex Rohr will publish this file in every media outlet he owns. You're not just fighting for my candidate. You're fighting for your marriage, your family, and whatever scraps of dignity you can pretend to deserve. *Do you understand me?*"

Blair nodded mutely, paler than before. "I need to go to the bathroom," he began to say, then hurried from the room.

Gazing out the window, Price could hear Blair vomiting through the bathroom door.

11

AT TWO O'CLOCK—FIVE HOURS BEFORE THE CONVENTION would reconvene—Spencer and Corey watched CNN as Governor Costas appeared at a hastily called press conference, Rob Marotta at his side.

Though tall, Costas was stoop-shouldered, and he read his statement in a halting manner that detracted from its force. "This has been a bitter contest," he recited. "But after days of soul-searching, I have concluded that Senator Marotta is the candidate who can best unite the disparate elements of our party—including those who support Senator Grace and Reverend Christy."

Corey began counting Marotta's delegates. "If Costas holds New York," he said, "Marotta is only twenty votes shy of winning on the first ballot."

Eyes glued to his text, Costas droned on. "Senator Marotta's openness to the center of our party is exemplified by his selection of Governor Blair."

"They *know*," Spencer murmured. Turning to Corey, he said more decisively, "Marotta and Price know about Blair, and they've promised Costas VP."

"I can't believe that."

"Believe it—it's exactly what Magnus would do if he were desperate enough." Observing Corey's expression, Spencer grabbed his cell phone. "I'll prove it to you."

"Who are you calling?"

"Blair."

Spencer waited impatiently, a portrait of silent fury,

then said, "Hollis Spencer here. Get me Governor Blair."
His eyes narrowed. "I don't care if he's meeting with Jesus
and John Lennon—if Blair doesn't take this call, he'll wish
he were as dead as they are."

On the television, Costas clasped Marotta's hand.
"Hello, Governor," Spencer said. "I guess you know
you're being dumped. For sure Marotta does." He listened
briefly, then spoke again in a lower voice: "Quit vamping.
We *know*, you pathetic bastard. I'll leave it to Corey to
decide what we do about that. But if I were you, I'd withdraw before the balloting starts."

Spencer hung up. "So you were right," Corey said.

"Yeah. The poor sonofabitch is scared witless."

"What happens if he doesn't withdraw?"

"We out him ourselves—no other choice."

Slowly, Corey shook his head. "With what? We gave
the evidence back to Gilligan, and just as well. Even now,
I don't know if I could do this to his wife and kids."

"*Magnus* could—he's blackmailing Blair to hold on to
Illinois. That's why we're so damn close to losing."
Spencer's cheeks flushed, the look of an older man dangerously overexerted. "For Godsakes, Corey, wake up. Do
you really want to hand this thing to Rob Marotta?"

Sitting back in his chair, Corey watched Marotta on
CNN managing a smile of spurious triumph as he stepped
up to the microphone. "Find Drew Tully," he instructed
Spencer. "Tell him we think Marotta's dumping Blair for
Costas.

"He can call a meeting of the delegation and ask Blair
to deny it. If Blair cracks at all—if even two delegates flip
from Marotta to me—under the unit rule Drew controls
the entire delegation, and Illinois goes with me.

"Blair *will* crack, I'm guessing. He'll think that Tully
knows what *we* know."

Spencer gave him a dubious look, then reached for his ringing cell phone. "Sure," he told his caller, and covered the cell phone. "Sam Larkin wants to meet with us."

Corey glanced at his watch. "Tell him five o'clock."

"Why so late?"

"There's someone I need to see." Heading for the door, Corey said, "Call Tully."

WITH TWO SECRET Service agents watching from a decorous distance, Corey knocked on the door of her suite.

After a moment it opened slightly, revealing Lexie's face. "It's only me," he said.

"Only you." She smiled a little. "And only a few months late."

"Not my fault," he said with mock exasperation. "Are we going to debate this through a crack in the door, or do I get to come in?"

She opened the door. Corey stepped through, and pushed it closed behind him. Then he brought her close to him, feeling her body against his, smelling her skin and hair. "I haven't changed my mind," he murmured. "Marry me."

Drawing back, she placed a finger to his lips, and then her own lips replaced it. For a time their kiss was soft, lingering; then it went deep.

Corey reached for the zipper of her dress. "Now?" she asked.

"It's just that it's been so long . . ."

Her head against his shoulder, Lexie gave a shaky laugh. "Forgotten what it's like?"

Looking into her face, Corey slipped the dress from her shoulders. Her skin, a sepia brown, drew his lips again. As they brushed her nipples, he felt her quiver. Her dress slid to the floor, then the flimsy silk that covered the soft tangle of hair below her waist.

"Follow me," she whispered.

Breaking away, she went to the bedroom and stretched out on the bed. He stood at its end, undressing, caught in the beauty of her nakedness.

Even when he entered her, Corey still looked into her face. "I love you," he told her softly, and then neither of them spoke at all.

AFTERWARD, THEY LAY close to each other, their faces inches apart. Smiling again, she said, "Too bad nothing else is as simple as this."

Corey did not smile. "You don't know the half of it."

"Tell me."

Swiftly, Corey told her about Clay's letter, Blair's secret, and all the permutations that followed. When he was through, her eyes were grave, even sad. "All these broken lives."

Corey could say nothing to this. She took both of his hands in hers. "I love you, too," she said. "That's why I'm here. I even think that, as a couple, we have something unique to offer the country. But if you become president, I don't think we can survive."

"And if I'm not president?"

"I still *want* you to be," she answered. "So I can't see beyond tonight. But if you want me at the convention, I'll be there. That may be all I have left to give you."

Filled with worry and regret, Corey glanced at his watch. "I have to go," he said reluctantly, and kissed her one last time.

FROM THE SUBLIME to the treacherous, Corey thought, and focused his full attention on Sam Larkin.

Sitting comfortably in Corey's suite, Larkin glanced at Spencer, then trained his solemn gaze on Corey. "You got a problem," he said bluntly. "Your so-called moderate friends, Blair and Costas, are jumping ship like rats. And now, rumor has it, your lady friend is back."

Corey shrugged. "Lose some, win some."

Larkin's eyes widened slightly. "What you're about to lose is the nomination. Time to cut to the chase, son.

"You need my delegates. You need my explicit support to keep Christy and his delegates from jumping on Marotta's bandwagon. And what with your choice of romantic entanglements—which I envy you, by the way—you need a southern running mate to appeal to whites with, shall we say, a more traditional outlook."

Corey smiled. "Why so decorous, Sam? Why not just say 'racists'?"

"Racists vote," Larkin said coolly. "Some even get to be delegates. You're way past being choosy. In less than two hours the nominating speeches begin, then the voting. Sometime between then and now you'll either get me or lose everything."

Corey glanced at Spencer. "Help me here, Sam. Last time I looked you were touting Blair's virtues to southern delegates. Now you want the job yourself. What's changed?"

"The delegate count." Larkin gave him a slow smile. "It never eluded me that I don't exemplify your notions of good governance, what with all the lobbying I did on behalf of America's embattled corporations. But now I'm thinking that maybe a man who's wanting to be president needs to overlook such things. Unless the man's a fool."

Corey found himself staring into Larkin's cynical blue eyes, even as he tried to calculate the odds that Blair would fold, or be outed, between now and the first roll call. He steeled himself for one final bluff. "I'd like your support," he told Larkin. "Maybe I need it. But I have reason to think my situation isn't as dire as you suggest.

"If you hold out tonight, I'll give your offer every consideration." His voice softened. "Marotta's got problems. Maybe you've heard that, Sam."

For an instant, Larkin hesitated. Then, cool again, he said, "I'll give your nonoffer 'every consideration,' Corey. I surely will. Unless I get a better one, of course."

With little ceremony but a handshake, Larkin left. As Spencer closed the door behind him, Corey said, "That bastard. He's the one who dropped the dime on Blair."

Spencer paused, hand still on the doorknob. "Think so?"

"Sure. When he sold Blair to Marotta—which I'm certain he did—he hoped to pressure me into picking him. But if Marotta actually wins, Sam loses. So he slipped the dirt he'd collected on Blair to Gilligan, then told Sean to give it to me."

Spencer smiled a little. "But you didn't play. So Larkin's started improvising."

"I think so. Somehow or other Larkin fed the evidence to Marotta. But Price and Marotta decided to tough out the first ballot. Then Sam doubled back to me, hoping to exploit my hour of weakness." Corey glanced at his watch. "If I'm right, Larkin won't let Blair survive past nine o'clock. He can't."

"And if you're wrong?" Spencer asked pointedly. "Unless Blair snaps under the pressure, your only choice is to out him or lose. But you can't bring yourself to do that, and you won't make Larkin VP. Your virtue comes at a cost, and its name is Rob Marotta."

Corey fell quiet as, one after another, a gallery of faces filled his thoughts: Clay, Lexie, Larkin, Marotta, and, finally, Joe Fitts. Then his cell phone rang and, as he answered, Spencer's.

"Hey." It was Dakin Ford. "No time to explain, but I've made headway with Mary Ella Ware—most particularly, her lawyer.

"Boy's begun to worry about his law license, maybe spending time in a prison cell with a 'special friend' named Bubba." Ford gave a sardonic laugh. "Busy night for me—in a few minutes, I've gotta second your nomination with a deeply moving speech. But I'm meeting this shyster right after. Whatever you can do to survive the first ballot, do it."

When Corey looked up, Spencer was holding out his cell phone, his expression grim. "It's Marotta."

Corey took the phone, "Hello, Rob. Looking for Super Bowl tickets?"

Marotta did not laugh. "It's time to talk," he said. "Just the two of us, in person."

12

When Marotta opened the door of their meeting place, the television was tuned to the convention.

The two men did not shake hands. Waving Corey to a leather couch, Marotta sat on the edge of a wing chair, his posture alert, his face composed but expressionless. Corey decided to wait him out; the course of the conversation, he guessed, would be dictated by whether Blair had warned Marotta that Corey knew his secret.

"This has been hard," Marotta began. "Politics for stakes like this are brutal."

Corey shook his head. "Not everything is politics, Rob. Nor is politics an excuse for doing anything to win."

As Marotta considered him, Dakin Ford's voice issued from the television. "In a time of war," Ford told the convention, "there is no substitute for character, and no surrogate for courage."

Angling his head toward the television, Marotta said softly, "No one can take those from you."

"Perhaps not. But people can try. You certainly tried in South Carolina."

Marotta frowned. "You don't mean to make this easy, do you?"

Corey shrugged. "What reason would I have?"

A cacophony of shouts and cheers caused Marotta to glance toward the television. When his gaze remained there, Corey followed it.

Grinning, Ford waved to someone in the convention hall, and then the camera panned to a smiling Lexie Hart waving back from the VIP box. More delegates turned to watch as cameramen scrambled toward her—all at once, the business of the convention simply stopped, given over to the full-throated roar of excitement from Corey's delegates after suffering through three nights of choreographed adoration for Mary Rose Marotta. In that electric moment, Lexie, appearing entirely at ease in this new role, looked transcendently like the First Lady of a country filled with promise.

The applause kindled a demonstration, Corey's supporters filling the aisles. From the Ohio delegation, and then from the delegates around them, a chant rose amid the outcries. "*Lexie*, Lexie, Lexie . . ."

Ford propped his arms on the podium, still grinning, a spectator deeply enjoying the scene before him. Then Lexie sat, breaking her connection with the crowd, allowing the convention to refocus on the daunting task before it.

"A nice moment," Marotta commented matter-of-factly. "But you're about to lose."

Edgy, Corey turned to him. "You still think that?"

"I *know* that. The only question is what you gain by playing this out." Leaning forward, Marotta spoke over the ebbing tumult broadcast from the convention floor. "If you withdraw tonight and give me your support, you'll gain the party's gratitude, and perhaps a great deal more."

Corey hesitated, left to guess at Marotta's motives; if Marotta knew that Corey had learned about Blair, his air of calm bespoke an iron nerve. "And what might that be?" Corey asked.

"Your choice of cabinet positions," Marotta said evenly. "State or Defense."

He doesn't know. Corey was suddenly sure. Several realizations flowed from this: that Blair was more afraid of Marotta and Price than of Corey; that Blair meant to gut out the first ballot as Marotta had demanded; and that his own chances of surviving to a second ballot rested on whether the anonymous leaker—Sam Larkin, in Corey's guess—exposed Blair within the hour. As if Marotta's offer was of little moment, Corey turned to the television.

For a moment, the two men watched a conservative black congressman—a former football star chosen to nominate Marotta—succeed Ford at the podium. Casually, Corey asked Marotta, "You really think Blair can hold Illinois?"

Though he repressed the temptation to study Marotta's expression, Corey could feel a new tautness in the room. In a dismissive tone, Marotta said, "Why wouldn't he?"

Corey shrugged again, still watching as Marotta's advocate warmed to his task. "We cannot," the man proclaimed, "and *will not* turn this party over to those who would protect neither innocent life nor the sanctity of marriage."

"Forget the party," Corey said conversationally. "How could any president turn the Defense Department over to a guy like that?"

Marotta did not answer. "*Who,*" the congressman cried out, "will stop the gay agenda from unraveling the moral fabric of America?"

With fleeting and bitter amusement, Corey tried to imagine Marotta's discomfiture, trapped with a rival he was trying to co-opt as his surrogate denounced him. "*Who,*" the congressman demanded, "will speak out against those who personify the degraded Hollywood culture that schools our young in promiscuity and violence?"

As a guttural outcry came from Marotta's delegates,

some turned to stare up at Lexie. His voice level, Corey said, "You could have stopped this in South Carolina, Rob. You could have stopped it anytime you wanted to."

He heard Marotta stir, and then the congressman's lips began silently moving above the word "mute." Only then did Corey turn to Marotta, remarking, "Beginning to wish that hatred made no sound?"

Marotta's expression evinced sincerity, even regret. "I wish a lot of things, Corey. But whoever you blame for whatever's happened, it'll take both of us to stop this now. If we don't, the party may be torn apart, the nomination not worth having. Then both of us will bear the blame."

Not for the first time, Corey marveled at the complexity of humans, and of *this* human, the beloved son of a hardworking family, by all accounts as good a husband and father as his ambition allowed, and yet so ambitious that, in the end, his strivings to achieve his most cherished goal robbed him of the decency that would give this achievement meaning. "We both are who we are," Corey told him. "The race has taken us too far."

Marotta shook his head, offering a small smile of demurral. "Even for the sake of the country? Who we both *are*, I hope, is men who believe that some things are bigger than ourselves."

Watching Marotta, Corey felt goose bumps on his skin. "What are you suggesting, Rob?"

"That you hear me out." Marotta seemed to will his body into stillness, his expression into a semblance of calm. "I'm offering you the vice presidency. Not just the nomination—the office. If we run as a ticket, no one can beat us."

For all his readiness, hearing this from Marotta stunned Corey. "After all that's happened," he said softly.

"Yes." Marotta leaned forward. "Is it really so astounding? We both want to be president. After eight years as my vice president, it'll be your turn."

Caught between ambition and revulsion, Corey saw them as two men about to define themselves forever. "So Blair is willing to step aside."

Slowly Marotta nodded, his eyes still fixed on Corey. "For the good of the party, yes. But only for you, Corey."

Corey felt a quiet laugh escape him. "After the Gulf War," he said, "I never thought another man could make my skin crawl. But I should never underestimate you, Rob."

Anger and confusion surfaced in Marotta's eyes. "I *know* Blair's gay," Corey told him. "I know you're blackmailing him to hold his delegates. I know you've offered his spot to Costas. And now you've offered it to me.

"If you were me, Rob, and knew all *that*, what would you do?"

In the silence that followed, Marotta's face turned ashen. "But then we both know the answer," Corey said. "You'd take me down by destroying Blair. That gives you the next hour or so to wonder whether I've become like you."

Marotta stood. "What do you want, dammit?"

Corey rose to face him. "We'll both have to see. But there's one thing you shouldn't worry about. I won't ask you to be vice president."

Turning, Corey left the room.

RIDING BACK TO the Essex House, Corey watched CNN and talked to Spencer. "Tully can't crack Illinois," Spencer reported.

"Hear any rumors about Blair?"

"Not yet—he's still holding the delegation by a single vote. What the hell did Marotta want?"

"Me for a running mate."

"You're joking."

"No. By the end I could almost smell his desperation. He's like us—worried about Illinois. Except that he doesn't know what we're going to do."

Spencer was silent for a moment, and then said sourly, "Or not do. If Blair holds on, I think we'll lose on the first ballot."

On CNN, Jeff Greenfield told Wolf Blitzer, "To clinch the nomination, Senator Marotta needs the votes of one thousand and fifty-one delegates. According to our count, Senator Marotta is within five or six delegates of that. Even should Governor Larkin hew to his favorite-son status, if Christy breaks for Marotta, the game's over."

"What about Christy?" Corey asked Spencer.

"He's still holding out. But he's under pressure to pledge his delegates to Marotta. Why be on the sidelines when Marotta hits a thousand fifty-one?"

Corey thanked him, and called Drew Tully.

WHEN COREY PHONED, Tully was in the middle of the Illinois delegation, his forehead covered with sweat, watching Blair give a hasty pep talk to a cluster of delegates Tully was pursuing. Blair's frenetic attentiveness suggested desperation, and his gaze darted from one face to another as though he were a playground monitor among a gaggle of fractious children. The atmosphere of antagonism within the delegation was exacerbated by the heat and the claustrophobic anger of rival delegates packed too close together. As he answered, Tully scrolled his Black-Berry for fresh intelligence. "Anything new?" Corey asked.

"Nothing," Tully said, and then a text message from his friend Sean Gilligan appeared: "Urgent—check out the Gage Report ASAP."

"Call you back," he told Corey.

*

BY THE TIME Corey reached his suite Dana Harrison and Jack Walters had gathered to watch the balloting, and Spencer was calling on his cell phone. "Tell Dana to get the Gage Report on her laptop," Spencer said hurriedly.

For an instant, Corey wondered why Spencer was bothering with that rabid right-wing blog and then, as swiftly, understood. "Someone fed Blair to David Gage."

"Everything but the pictures," Spencer replied.

ON THE FLOOR, Drew Tully grabbed Blair by the arm, wresting him from a huddle with two supporters. In a shrill voice, Blair snapped at Tully, "I've got no time for you."

The delegates—a paunchy state senator and a well-coifed teacher, the substitute for Walter Riggs—gaped in astonishment as Tully clapped his hand behind Blair's neck and pressed his face inches from his own. "Make time," Tully whispered roughly. "I just opened your closet door."

He watched Blair's eyes turn glassy. From the podium, the chair of the convention proclaimed, "The roll call of the states will begin . . ."

"You're all over the Gage Report," Tully told Blair under his breath. "So here's what you're going to do. We're having our own caucus, right here on the floor, and you're going to enlighten us as to your 'status.' It's not kosher to make people vote without them knowing that you're finished."

IN THE SKYBOX, Spencer called Christy's manager, Dan Hansen. "Crunch time, Dan. What you boys gonna do?"

"Hold out, if we can. But Louisiana's crumbling—we may have an uprising on our hands."

Spencer gazed down at the Louisiana delegation and saw two delegates face-to-face, their posture and gesticulations betraying bitter conflict. "They got a laptop over there?"

"Sure."

"Then tell them to check out the Gage Report. That may be all you'll need."

AT THE ESSEX House, Corey and Jack Walters watched the balloting begin as Dana Harrison scanned the screen of her laptop. Turning, she looked at Corey in wonder. "Blair's gay. The Gage Report just outed him."

Torn between pity and relief, Corey imagined the scene in the Illinois delegation and then, in the hours to follow, the swift and terrible unraveling of Blair's entire life. "I know," he said softly. "Blair's done."

"But that's *good* for us. The man sold you down the river."

"Alabama," the chair called out on CNN.

The head of the delegation, a silver-haired ex-congressman, proclaimed, "It is with much pride that, on behalf of the great state of Alabama, I cast all forty-eight votes for the next president of the United States, Senator Corey Grace."

As the crowd erupted, the camera panned to Lexie Hart, smiling as Dakin Ford's wife, Christie, whispered in her ear. But amid the Alaska delegation, the next to vote, a tall man in an Uncle Sam costume screamed, "Traitors!" at the delegates from Alabama.

"Alaska," the chair called out.

THE ROLL CALL proceeded, with each delegation hewing to its expected vote.

"Idaho."

Impatient, Corey waited for Idaho to follow the script. "The great state of Idaho," its governor shouted back, "home of Boise State, the new football power of America, proudly casts all thirty-two votes for Senator Rob Marotta."

"*Illinois.*"

As the camera panned to Illinois, Corey saw that the delegation had pressed around Blair and Tully in a disorderly scrum, straining to see and hear. No one acknowledged the call of the roll.

"*Illinois,*" the chair repeated shrilly.

Sitting beside Corey, Jack Walters mumbled, "Come on, Drew." On the screen, Tully spoke rapidly to Blair, his expression venomous, as a rumble of confusion spread across the convention floor. Then Tully thrust a microphone in Blair's face.

Taking it, Blair turned toward the podium, his face slack. In a strained voice, he responded, "Illinois passes."

"*That,*" Jeff Greenfield said on CNN, "is a shocker. What's going on, Candy?"

Standing in the aisle beside the Illinois delegation, Candy Crowley looked stunned herself. "At this moment," she answered, "I can't answer you precisely. But rumors have begun to circulate that Governor Blair will withdraw as Senator Marotta's choice."

"*Indiana.*"

"Indiana," its chairman responded in a subdued and bewildered tone, "casts its fifty-five votes for Senator Marotta."

WATCHING FROM ABOVE, Hollis Spencer could see it happening: like a large and clumsy organism—Spencer thought of a dinosaur sending a message from its small brain to its tail—the convention was responding to a stimulus it did not fully comprehend. "The next harbinger," Jeff Greenfield said, "is Louisiana."

On his cell phone, Spencer asked his chief delegate handler, "What's the count?"

"Depends on Christy. If he goes to Marotta, it's over; if he holds on, looks like it's down to Illinois."

"What the hell are *they* doing?"

"Trying to take a head count. It's way fucked up down here."

"*LOUISIANA,*" THE CHAIR called out.

"Here it comes," Dana said to Corey.

The head of the delegation, a minister himself, announced firmly, "The Louisiana delegation—committed to a nation under God, which respects the sanctity of marriage and human life in all its forms—proudly casts all forty-five votes for the personification of those values, Reverend Bob Christy."

Corey slumped in his chair. In a tone that hovered between wan and wry, he said, "Thank God."

"With this vote from Louisiana," Jeff Greenfield reported, "the sole remaining shoe to drop belongs to Governor Larkin."

The next states fell into line: first Maine, then Maryland, Massachusetts, Michigan, and Minnesota.

"*Mississippi.*"

The state chair, Larkin's ally, crooned smoothly, "Mississippi votes for its favorite son, Governor Sam Larkin."

He still wants a job, Corey thought.

TWENTY-ONE MINUTES LATER, Corey watched as the chair called out the final state.

"*Wy-o-ming.*"

On the corner of the screen, CNN's running total

showed Marotta with 1,015 votes, Grace with 837, Christy with 109, and Larkin with 38.

"Wyoming," the chair of her delegation answered with a sense of moment, "casts all twenty-eight votes for the next president of the United States, Senator Rob Marotta."

"With that," Wolf Blitzer said excitedly, "Senator Marotta is within eight votes of winning the Republican nomination. And so this ballot comes down to Illinois, the home state of the senator's putative running mate, Governor Charles Blair. Under the unit rule, a single delegate can determine the vote of the entire delegation, and thus decide whether Senator Marotta will win on this initial ballot."

Agitated, Corey pushed the speed dial on his cell phone. "What's happening?" he asked Spencer.

"They're still voting, we think."

The camera closed in on the Illinois delegation. In its midst, Senator Drew Tully thrust a scrap of paper in Blair's face and wrested the microphone from his grasp. Swiftly, the picture switched to Lexie, impassive but for the slight parting of her lips; then to Mary Rose Marotta, fingering the cross dangling from her neck as her other hand clutched her oldest daughter's; then back to Illinois. In close-up, tears surfaced in Blair's eyes.

Corey's hand tightened around his cell phone. With his back turned to the governor, Drew Tully announced with evident satisfaction, "Illinois casts all seventy-three ballots for the candidate who will lead us to victory in November, Senator Corey Grace."

As the convention erupted in cheers and bitter catcalls, Corey bent forward. "*Yes,*" Dana shouted as Walters placed a hand on Corey's shoulder. "We're still alive."

"This," Wolf Blitzer said, "is one of the most dramatic,

not to say unexpected, political moments in this reporter's memory. And it comes amid fresh reports—neither confirmed nor denied by Senator Marotta's communications director—that Governor Blair will be replaced."

"To say the delegates are confused," Jeff Greenfield added dryly, "fails to do justice to those who are catatonic."

On the podium, the chair of the convention huddled with the chairman of the Republican Party, an ally of Marotta's, as Blitzer continued: "The next development, it would seem, will be to call the roll for a second ballot. Candy?"

Reporting from the Illinois delegation, Candy Crowley looked somber. "The turnabout in this delegation, we now know, resulted from an Internet report detailing Governor Blair's alleged involvement in a homosexual affair."

"There won't be a second ballot," Corey said quietly. "Not tonight. Marotta's friends will pull the plug."

"Because of Blair?" Dana asked.

"Yup. They need time to roll out Costas and try to repair the damage while they work on Christy and Larkin. Either one will do—all Marotta needs is eight more votes."

Appearing flustered, the chair of the convention returned to the podium. "The convention is adjourned," she hastily announced, "until one P.M. tomorrow."

Reaching for his cell phone, Corey called Lexie Hart.

IN A DARKENED limousine, Corey rode with Lexie to a post-balloting party being held in a hotel ballroom. "Sure you want to do this?" she asked.

At the hotel, Corey saw, several stretch limousines were already massed in front, with others ringing the block. "I'd rather be alone with you," he answered. "But after tonight's near-death experience, I'm required to make a ritual show of confidence."

Lexie smiled. "Some would call that acting," she said, and kissed him.

SPONSORED BY A lobbying firm with close ties to the party chair, the event had been intended to serve as Marotta's victory celebration. It remained the hottest ticket in town, with numerous bars, tables of hot food, uniformed waiters passing drinks and hors d'oeuvres on silver trays, and an R&B band serving as the warm-up act for a famous comedian. Standing with Lexie at the entrance, Corey murmured, "Here we go."

Within seconds, their appearance sent a current through the revelers. A crush began to form around them, the crowd as avid to touch Lexie as Corey and overcome by the excitement of the moment. Looking as fresh and cool as though it were morning, Lexie touched hands and smiled into faces, making the small connections that those she met were craving. And then Sam Larkin stood in her path, grinning broadly.

Taking Lexie's hand, Sam held it longer than necessary. "A pleasure," he purred. "You leave me breathless."

Lexie laughed. "First you inhale," she advised him, "then you exhale. Pretty soon you'll be breathing just fine."

Larkin's eyes glinted with lascivious amusement; then he turned to Corey. "Damn near got voted off the island, boy. But for poor old Charles, you would've been. Looks like you'll be needing an ally."

With this, Corey felt any doubt about Larkin's role evaporate. "I certainly will," Corey said easily. "Or two."

A chill entered Larkin's eyes. Placing a hand on Corey's shoulder, he leaned forward for an intimate word. "Not much time left, Corey. I hear Rob's scheduled a press conference for ten o'clock tomorrow. That gives us about ten hours, mostly at night. One good thing is that I don't need much sleep."

Corey gazed into Larkin's shrewd face, wondering how it would feel to be at this man's mercy. "I need *some* sleep, Sam. Let's meet for breakfast."

As Larkin stared at him, slowly nodding, Corey's cell phone rang. Without taking his eyes off Larkin, he answered.

"Party's over," Dakin Ford told him. "I just met Mary Ella Ware."

13

AT FOUR O'CLOCK IN THE MORNING, ROB MAROTTA found himself staring at the red illuminated numbers of a hotel alarm clock—unable to sleep, he was so weary that it felt like a fever coming on.

Mary Rose lay close to him, crowded by their daughter Jenny, who had once again commuted from another bedroom to theirs. But the presence of his wife and daughter did not make him feel less alone. On the eve of achieving his life's ambition, to be secured by the anointing of George Costas, Blair's public meltdown had filled him with a foreboding he could not name. The dynamics of this convention had too many moving parts—important things he did not know, human motivations he could not control, enemies he could not identify. Even the nearness of victory haunted him.

Eight votes, and he had not been able to get them—despite all he had done, for good or ill.

Larkin, who could have made him the nominee, was still holding out. Christy, who by now should have capitulated, had chosen to taunt him for a few more hours. And Corey Grace was still alive.

Grace. Always Grace.

Some men were lucky. Some, without deserving it, seemed to be God's favorites. Some, apparently defeated, seemed always to rise from the dead. Grace's navigator had died, but Grace had returned from Iraq. Had Grace come to Marotta's office a minute earlier, the terrorists would have killed him with the others; had he come a minute later . . .

Marotta cringed at his own thoughts.

Looking across the body of a terrorist into Grace's blood-spattered face, Marotta had felt the wrenching certainty that he owed his life to a reflexive act of courage that he, in Grace's place, never would have performed. And so he had looked away as Magnus Price and nameless others worked to transform Grace from a hero to a traitor, all to make Marotta president. In this moment of searing honesty, Marotta understood why he despised Corey Grace so thoroughly—not just because he was arrogant, or handsome, or fortunate beyond any man's deserving, but because Grace's contempt for Marotta, his utter refusal to ally with him, surfaced Marotta's repressed contempt for himself. To wish Grace dead was insufficient; with a visceral longing more painful for its impossibility, he wished to banish Grace from his psyche. But Rob Marotta, the striver, would always feel inferior, forced by fate to do things that Corey Grace would never do, to know things about himself that no one else could know.

Are you awake? he wanted to whisper to Mary Rose.

But what would he tell her? His opportunity to change the course of events was gone. It had been lost when he sent her home from South Carolina, knowing that things would happen that he did not wish her to see. Perhaps Mary Rose could love him because he hid the reasons she should not.

Rob Marotta, the striver, was alone.

So be it, then. In the morning, he would banish all doubts and fears, go forward with the relentless ambition that had brought him to this moment. The picture of confidence, he would appear with Costas, and then defeat Grace once and for all. He would finish what he had started.

In the silence, he listened to his wife's quiet breathing, envying her repose.

"YOU'RE REALLY GOING to do all that," Lexie said.

She sat up in bed, the sheets gathered around her to ward off the chill of the air-conditioning. His tie unknotted, Corey sat in a nearby chair. "If I can," he answered.

Her smile, the smallest movement of her lips, did not change her questioning expression. "That's a lot to pull off. Even if it's possible, how will you feel?"

Gazing into her face, Corey realized how precious, and perhaps how fleeting, it was not to feel alone. "I guess we'll find out, won't we?"

She let his tacit question, expressed by the use of "we," pass without comment. "I just want you to be okay," she said. "How much sleep have you gotten, baby?"

"None."

"There's room in here," she said, and pulled down the bedcovers beside her.

Undressing, Corey slid in next to her, holding her as he had that first night on Martha's Vineyard. "Remember this?" he asked.

"Of course I do," she answered. "Now go to sleep."

AT EIGHT FORTY-FIVE on Thursday morning, Rob Marotta was in Price's suite, preparing to meet George Costas in half an hour. On Rohr News, the videocams outside Charles Blair's hotel captured his departure. Blair tried to smile, a ghastly reflex; walking stiffly beside him, his wife looked drawn and mortified, already separate from him. Their two young children, a boy and a girl, appeared mystified, and the way Janet Blair grasped their hands seemed proprietary, an attempt to exclude her husband. Watching, Marotta felt a brief frisson. Blair's ruin was complete.

"I told him to leave," Price said. "Better for us that he's gone."

As Charles Blair slipped into the limousine, vanishing from view, Price's cell phone rang.

He listened intently, his body so still that it put Marotta on edge. Softly, he asked, "How could that happen?"

As Marotta studied his face, Price squinted as if emerging from darkness into glaring sunlight. "Don't talk to anyone," he ordered, and snapped his phone shut.

"Who was that?" Marotta demanded.

"Alex," Price answered hurriedly, and switched the channel to CNN.

It took a moment for Marotta to recognize the woman at the podium. "I'm Mary Ella Ware," she said, and Marotta felt himself go numb.

Standing beside Ware were Dakin Ford and a man Marotta did not recognize. "I came here this morning," Ware said in a halting voice, "to seek forgiveness from Reverend Christy.

"Early this year I was approached by a local lawyer, Stephen Hansberger, who asked me to volunteer in Reverend Christy's campaign. He said he knew I needed money, and that someone could provide me two thousand dollars a week. All I had to do was keep my eyes and ears open, and call a certain cell phone with any information that might help people who thought the reverend shouldn't be in politics."

When Marotta turned to him, Price's expression was less surprised than watchful. "I never knew who I was calling," Ware read on. "But each week two thousand dollars in cash came in the mail."

Good, Marotta thought reflexively—no meetings, no checks for anyone to track. "One day . . ." Ware began, and then her voice failed, forcing her to start again. "One day, this man told me I could make enough money to buy a house. When I asked him how, he said by putting Reverend Christy in a 'compromising position.'"

Feeling clammy, Marotta looked at Price and saw that his expression remained opaque. With a burst of indignation, Ware said, "I told him I couldn't do that. Don't worry, he told me, I didn't have to 'do' anything. All I needed was to get Reverend Christy alone.'"

Seeing Ford gaze off in the distance with the fleeting trace of a smile, Marotta felt his mouth go dry. "I told this person," Ware said, "that I couldn't discuss this with someone who was only a voice on a cell phone. He said he'd call me back.

"Two days later, he called me to say I should meet with a lawyer who could counsel me about my financial problems, Dalton Frye."

When the other man beside her seemed to examine his shoes, Marotta knew the worst was yet to come. Then it struck him that Price had still not spoken a word.

TOGETHER, COREY AND Spencer watched CNN. "Hard to believe," Spencer told Corey, "that this guy's going to admit all that."

As Ware stepped aside, the man beside her bent to the microphone.

"You heard Dakin," Corey answered. "He's already got the canceled checks."

"My name," the man began, "is Dalton Frye."

WATCHING, MAROTTA FELT his apprehension turn to dread.

Frye appeared paunchy and chinless, a man whose native shrewdness was unleavened by much character. "In

February," Frye began, "I received a call from an old friend, Governor Linwood Tate. He asked if I could undertake a 'special project' for someone who might become my most important client.

"When I asked him who the client was, he swore me to secrecy." Frye took a hasty sip of water. "Then he told me it was Alex Rohr."

Ashen, Marotta glanced at Price, who remained impassive. "According to the governor," Frye went on, "I was to receive a check from the Netherlands Antilles Corporation, an offshore subsidiary of RohrVision. My initial role was to convert this check to cash, then await instructions on who to give the money to, and exactly what to say . . ."

In his mind, Marotta was back on the flight to South Carolina. *What you need to do,* Price told him, *is leave the details to me.* And then Rohr said, *I assume, Senator, that you still wish to become president . . .*

"I wasn't comfortable," Frye continued, "doing what seemed like laundering money. When I asked what the money was for, the governor told me, 'Politics.' If I went along, he promised, my fee would be another check for two hundred thousand dollars."

Frye stopped abruptly, as though he was losing his resolve. Ford fixed him with a gelid stare until Frye continued in a halting voice: "I asked Governor Tate to at least tell me who'd be giving me my instructions and whether he could be trusted. As if it were enough, all he said was 'Magnus Price.'"

"He's lying, of course," Price interposed calmly.

Marotta stood and jerked Price upright by his shirt collar. "You sonofabitch," Marotta said tightly. "You set this up and now you're going to walk away."

His eyes hard, Price placed both hands on Marotta's wrists. "Yes. *I* am."

Sickened, Marotta stared at his manager, seeing the contempt Price no longer bothered to conceal. The cell phone in Marotta's pocket had begun to vibrate.

Releasing Price's collar, Marotta jerked his right hand free and snatched out the phone to read its caller ID.

Corey Grace.

Marotta's hand shook as he hit the talk button. "Corey?"

"You're done, Rob—Costas is backing out. Price finished you off in South Carolina. But it took this long for that to become obvious." Grace's voice was implacable. "You could try to survive, but that would only make things worse. I'm having my own press conference at ten o'clock. If you want to come out of this marginally better than Blair did, I suggest you watch for cues."

Grace got off without waiting for an answer, leaving Marotta alone with Price.

PUTTING AWAY HIS cell phone, Corey turned to Christy. "Well, Bob?"

His expression somber, Christy shook his head. "Imagine being Marotta."

"You can't. That's among your saving graces." Glancing at Spencer and Dan Hansen, Corey said, "Mind if we talk alone?"

"No problem," Hansen said. "We'll see you two downstairs."

When they had left, Christy said, "I guess you know how grateful I am—makes me wish I could support you."

Corey shrugged. "If you were a politician, you could. Politics is compromise, a search for common ground. But religion as you define it is a matter of absolute belief. We've been fated to disagree since that first day in Lake City."

Christy shook his head, his expression rueful. "Sad, isn't it? We respect each other, and we love our country. But our idea of what that means is different."

"As I said," Corey answered with a smile, "politics is compromise. For the moment, at least, you *are* a politician. So let's go downstairs and see what we can do."

14

THE SCENE IN THE BALLROOM WAS CHAOTIC BUT electric: reporters overflowed the folding chairs and crowded two deep along the walls, while cameramen elbowed for position, their competitive instincts ratcheted to a fever pitch by Blair's humiliation, the charges against Rohr and Price, and the abrupt cancellation of Marotta's press conference with George Costas. When Corey Grace and Bob Christy entered, followed by Governors Costas and Larkin and former secretary of state Cortland Lane, the forward surge of the media was so disorderly that Corey was forced to stand silently at the podium, the others seated behind him, waiting for the tumult to subside.

These few minutes gave him time to experience all of his conflicting emotions: hope, regret, apprehension, and a profound weariness from making so many decisions with so little time to reflect. But as quiet descended, what he felt most deeply was a certain peace, and his voice was calm and firm.

"In the last twelve hours," he began, "much has happened, much of it troubling: the withdrawal of Governor Blair; the accusations against Alex Rohr and Senator Marotta's campaign; the intensification of the already bitter divisions within the convention itself. But this moment of crisis has impelled Reverend Christy and me to put aside our differences in an effort to find a new beginning for our party and our country."

Corey paused, poised on the brink of a life-changing

moment. And then, believing that this was best, he continued in the same steady voice: "Reverend Christy cannot support my candidacy, nor can I support his. But we agree that there is one man we *can* support: a man of unquestioned patriotism, deep religious faith, unparalleled experience, and the capacity of mind and spirit to make America a place that all Americans—of every race and circumstance—can believe in.

"The best evidence of this," he added with a smile, "is that Governors Costas and Larkin also agree." At once, Corey saw, Kate McInerny of the *Post* grasped where he was going and turned to Jake Linkletter with a grin of surprise and satisfaction. "This afternoon," Corey continued, "we will ask the chair to reopen the nominations, so that we can place before the convention the name of Secretary Cortland Lane."

The room erupted. Amid the deafening noise, Corey turned to Lane and said, "Seems like they're excited, Cortland."

Lane smiled, his eyes keen—the look of a man resolved within himself to answer a challenge that he thought had passed him by. Seeing this, Corey knew with certainty that what he had done was right. Facing the media again, he held up his hand for silence. "This is the secretary's moment," he told them, "and, the Reverend Christy and I agree, the final and finest moment of our campaigns. And so we have also pledged that neither of us will seek, or accept, an offer to become the vice presidential nominee. From now until November, our sole ambition is to help this good and gifted man become president of the United States." Corey paused, then added with irony so faint it was almost undetectable, "We have every reason to believe that Senator Marotta, once he reflects on this opportunity to renew our party and our politics, will join us in this effort."

He turned again as Cortland Lane, his mentor and old friend, stood. As they shook hands, embracing briefly, Corey recalled that long-ago day at the White House and his impulsive confession about Joe Fitts. "Who knew?" Corey said into Lane's ear.

"Who indeed," Lane answered with the briefest of smiles, and then stepped forward to face the media, a commanding yet calming presence.

WHEN THE PRESS conference was over, Corey shook hands with Sam Larkin, who looked sourly amused; George Costas, plainly hopeful that he might become Lane's running mate; and then Bob Christy. "As we say in the South," Christy told him, "you done good."

Corey smiled. "We both did."

"Well," Christy said with a trace of humor, "we put off Armageddon for a while. At least until next time."

"I think the country can afford to wait," Corey answered. "By that time, I'm hoping to be raptured."

Christy had the grace to laugh.

BACK IN HIS suite, Corey and Hollis Spencer busied themselves with details, postponing the inevitable letdown.

In the next few hours, there was much to accomplish, and neither would leave anything to chance. On CNN, Wolf Blitzer said, "As of this hour, the Grace and Christy delegates are falling into place for General Lane, as are the New York and Mississippi delegations. It now seems certain that sometime this afternoon, Cortland Lane will become the Republican nominee for president of the United States."

Listening, Corey felt both satisfaction and a certain residual sadness. After a time, he tried to acknowledge all that Spencer had done to deliver him the prize that he had given away.

"I owe you a lot," Corey told him. "I'm sorry if I was a difficult client."

"You always were," Spencer acknowledged with a rueful laugh. "But that also made you my best one. And this morning was one for the books. How long did you have this trick in mind?"

"A few days. The first glimmer was on Sunday, when Blair went over to Marotta."

Spencer's eyes lit with interest. "I thought as much. So when you interviewed Lane for vice president, you were also figuring out whether he'd run for president?"

"I was," Corey conceded. "But a lot of things had to fall into place, some of which I couldn't anticipate. The one that surprised me most was Sam Larkin's historic role as a catalyst for social progress—making Cortland Lane the first African-American nominated by a major political party. But not as much as it wound up surprising Sam."

Spencer laughed. "Karmic justice."

"To a point. But I think he'll get away with screwing Blair."

"*That* poor bastard. What made him think he wouldn't get caught out?"

Once again, Corey thought of his brother. "Denial is a complicated thing," he answered. "Too bad we seem to require it."

THOUGH THERE WAS scant time before the convention reopened, Corey needed to see Lexie.

They stood at the large picture window of her suite, looking out at Central Park on another hot summer day. Deprived of purpose, the assembled demonstrators milled about, their numbers slowly dissipating.

"So," she asked, "are you okay?"

Corey still gazed out the window. "Pretty fair, all in all. I've settled my accounts. Marotta's done, as he should be. Price may be done, and Rohr's tainted if not indictable.

"On the more positive side of the ledger—no small thing—my friend Bob Christy and I may have helped change our country for the better, and given it a candidate who can meet all the challenges we have to face. Cortland Lane is a good man, and for reasons both philosophical and personal, his nomination means a great deal to me. Now we'll see if he can win."

Lexie turned to him. "And you?"

"I'm still a senator. I'm just not a would-be president— certainly not in the present, and maybe ever. That means I'm free to define my future for myself." Smiling, he added, "Starting with a week or so in Cabo San Lucas, hopefully with some company."

The implications of this, he saw, were too serious to prompt a smile of her own. Gazing up at him, she inquired softly, "Does that mean I'm still free to consider your proposal?"

He *was* lucky, Corey realized. Fate had given him a life beyond his youthful imaginings and now, if he was wise enough to deserve it, a new beginning. Quiet, he looked into her face. *I'll be a good husband,* he silently promised, *a good father to our children. Whatever else we decide will be right for us.*

"Of course," Corey answered with a smile far more careless than he felt. "Why do you think I did all this?"

AUTHOR'S NOTE AND ACKNOWLEDGMENTS

I began researching *The Race* in early 2004. Late that same year, I put the project aside in favor of writing *Exile*, my Palestinian-Israeli novel, reasoning that a novel of American politics would be more pertinent closer to 2008.

In the intervening years, some of the principal themes of *The Race* have become more widely perceived: the uneasiness of the alliance between business interests and religious conservatives; the politicization of science; the adverse impact of political polarization on governance and public policy; the corruption of our system of campaign finance; the erosion of America's social compact by a politics of self-concern; and the domination of our political dialogue by a marketing mentality so cynical it invites contempt and disbelief. Other themes, including the consolidation of the media and our continuing difficulties in honestly confronting race, are becoming more salient by the day.

In the end, I wrote *The Race* because, like so many of us, I think contemporary politics as practiced are accelerating America's decline. The 2006 election made one thing clear: millions of Americans want common sense solutions to our common problems, not more division, distrust, and disdain. Even clearer is the central theme of *The Race*—our craving for authentic leaders who tell the truth as they perceive it, and care more about the country than themselves.

Hence Corey Grace, a politician as we wish politicians to be.

One of the pitfalls of creating a fictional politician is that observers start casting real politicians as his prototype. Given that, my debts to two friends in public life include absolving them of any blame for what Corey Grace believes about politics or religion. Specifically, Corey's debt to John McCain ends with his military biography and his penchant for candor; his debt to Bill Cohen ends with Bill's political and personal integrity and his marriage to an exceptional African-American woman, Janet Langhart Cohen. Most important, Corey's views diverge so markedly from John's and Bill's that he can only be blamed on me. Facing the partisan primary process uncomfortably perched in the political center, Corey Grace is sui generis.

Similarly, I would like to thank, and absolve, everyone who was so generous in helping me. As always, the viewpoints—and the errors—are mine alone.

MY STARTING POINT was to assess the current political dynamic of the Republican Party, including where a candidate like Corey Grace might fit—if anywhere—and how a deadlocked convention might actually occur. I'm grateful for the time and patience of political scientist Michael Barone; Republican strategists Rich Bond, Rick Davis, Ron Kaufman, Scott Reed, Mark Salter, and John Weaver; and public opinion experts Bill McInturff and John Zogby. Special thanks to Speaker Newt Gingrich, Senator John McCain, and Governor Mark Sanford for helping me consider certain aspects of Corey Grace's personality, and how events might affect his behavior. Others who helped me flesh out the political context include strategists Peter Fenn, Chris Lehane, Ace Smith, and Marshall

Whitman; Patrick Guerrero of the Log Cabin Republicans; Cheryl Mills; and Rob Stein, who traced the roots of conservative dominance in the last quarter century or so. I'm also indebted to my old friend Terry Samway, who refreshed my knowledge of the Secret Service, and to Congresswoman Stephanie Tubbs Jones for helping me imagine the behavior of Corey Grace and Lexie Hart in the crucible of South Carolina.

The recent history of South Carolina politics caused me to focus the primary season there. I'm grateful to the wonderful South Carolinians who, while in no way responsible for my grim portrayal of the imaginary primary, helped me on my way: journalist Lee Bandy; Congressman James Clyburn; radio host and former consultant Michael Graham; and strategists Rod Shealy and Trey Walker.

The last hard-fought Republican convention was the Ford-Reagan battle of 1976. I was lucky to have the advice of some key survivors: Secretary James Baker, David Keene, John Sears, and, memorably, the late Lyn Nofziger. And Ben Ginsberg was indispensable in helping me imagine the Byzantine dynamics of such a contest in the present day.

The role of religious belief in politics is a matter of considerable controversy. I was fortunate to interview experts with many points of view: Michael Bowman, Dr. Harvey Cox and Jason Springs of the Harvard Divinity School, Morris Dees, Carol Keys, Elliot Minceberg, Reverend Barry Lynn, Dr. Alfred Mohler, Jay Sekulow, Phyllis Schlafly, Reverend Lou Sheldon, and Doug Wead. And Dr. Tom Murray gave me a short course in the science and ethics of stem-cell research.

Pivotal to constructing Corey's character were his military experiences, from his own career to the suicide of his brother. Deepest thanks to Lieutenant Colonel Phil Kaufman, my cousin Bill Patterson, General Jack Rives, General Joe Ralston, and Bob Tyrer. Thanks also to Celia Viggo Wexler of Common Cause, who gave me a thorough grounding in the issues surrounding the consolidation of our media and threats to Internet neutrality.

Obviously, the relationship between Corey and Lexie Hart is central to my narrative. I'm grateful to my friend the Oscar-winning actress Mary Steenburgen for helping me imagine Lexie's relationship to her craft, and, especially, to my dear friends Secretary Bill Cohen and Janet Langhart Cohen, who shared their thoughts on how politics and race would bear on the romance between Corey and Lexie.

Finally, I had wonderful support from my partner, Dr. Nancy Clair; my always perceptive assistant, Alison Thomas; and my terrific agent, Fred Hill—all of whom commented on the manuscript. John Sterling, publisher of Henry Holt, helped sustain me throughout my last two novels—from believing in them to discussing every aspect of their substance and their style to editing me with a clarity and discernment that has supposedly vanished from modern publishing. For all of that, this book is dedicated to John.

Visit **www.panmacmillan.com** to read more about all our books and to buy them. You will also find features, author interviews and news of any author events, and you can sign up for e-newsletters so that you're always first to hear about our new releases.